Susan Mallery

"Susan Mallery is warmth and wit personified.
Always a fabulous read."
—*New York Times* bestselling author Christina Dodd

Susan Mallery is the bestselling author of over forty books for
Harlequin and Silhouette. She makes her home in the Pacific
Northwest with her handsome prince of a husband and her two
adorable-but-not-bright cats.

Bronwyn Williams

"Bronwyn Williams has an earthy, rare
and glorious understanding of romance."
—*New York Times* bestselling author Elizabeth Lowell

Bronwyn Williams is the pseudonym for the sister writing team of
Dixie Browning and Mary Williams, who have published a dozen
titles with NAL/Topaz and now write for Harlequin Historicals. As
with many of Dixie Browning's nearly seventy contemporaries for
Silhouette, most of Bronwyn Williams' stories have been set in
northeastern North Carolina. Montana was a refreshing change!

Carolyn Davidson

"Davidson wonderfully captures gentleness in the midst
of heart-wrenching challenges, portraying the extraordinary
possibilities that exist within ordinary marital love."
— *Publishers Weekly*

Reading, writing and research: Carolyn Davidson's life in
three simple words. At least that area of her life having to do
with her career as an author. The rest of her time is divided
among husband, family and travel—her husband, of course,
holding top priority in her busy schedule. Carolyn welcomes
mail at P.O. Box 2757, Goose Creek, SC 29445.

Dear Reader,

Who can resist three strong and proud Montana men *(the forefathers of the Kincaid clan!)* who haven't a clue that they're about to fall head over heels in love and say "I do?" That's only the beginning of what will be unveiled in our very special anthology, MONTANA MAVERICKS: *Big Sky Grooms,* by reader favorites Susan Mallery, Bronwyn Williams and Carolyn Davidson.

In these brand-new short stories, you'll discover how it all began...and learn of the secrets that have fueled Kincaid family legends over the years! Even better, MONTANA MAVERICKS: *Big Sky Grooms* is just the first of many new MONTANA MAVERICKS stories we have in store for you in the coming months. In September, October and November of 2001, Harlequin Historicals will bring you three full-length historicals about Montana's beloved family. And in December 2001 through February 2002, the series moves back into the contemporary realm with three new Silhouette Special Edition titles.

We hope you enjoy this anthology, as well as the upcoming MONTANA MAVERICKS books. This is truly a series where legends and love live on beneath the Big Sky....

Happy Reading!

The Editors

MONTANA

BIG SKY COUNTRY—WHERE LEGENDS AND LOVE LIVE ON...

MAVERICKS

BIG SKY
Grooms

Susan Mallery

Bronwyn Williams

Carolyn Davidson

HARLEQUIN®

TORONTO • NEW YORK • LONDON
AMSTERDAM • PARIS • SYDNEY • HAMBURG
STOCKHOLM • ATHENS • TOKYO • MILAN • MADRID
PRAGUE • WARSAW • BUDAPEST • AUCKLAND

ISBN 0-373-83491-8

MONTANA MAVERICKS: BIG SKY GROOMS

Copyright © 2001 by Harlequin Books S.A.

Special thanks and acknowledgment are given to Susan Mallery,
Bronwyn Williams and Carolyn Davidson for their contribution to the
MONTANA MAVERICKS series.

SPIRIT OF THE WOLF
Copyright © 2001 by Harlequin Books S.A.

AS GOOD AS GOLD
Copyright © 2001 by Harlequin Books S.A.

THE GAMBLE
Copyright © 2001 by Harlequin Books S.A.

Visit us at www.eHarlequin.com

Printed in U.S.A.

CONTENTS

KINCAID FAMILY TREE

Leo Kincaid (d.) m. Melissa Taylor (d.)

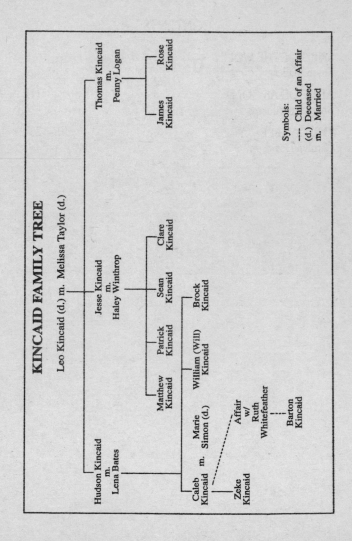

Symbols:

---- Child of an Affair
(d.) Deceased
m. Married

Spirit of the Wolf

Susan Mallery

CHAPTER ONE

Whitehorn, Montana
April, 1896

"I WANT to be an Indian."

Ruth Whitefeather glanced up from the herbs she'd been examining. A boy of about seven or eight stood beside her garden. He wore worn Levi's and scuffed boots, and held the reins of a bay gelding in his right hand.

Ruth took in the firm set of the boy's mouth, the defiance in his blue eyes, not to mention the too long blond hair brushing the bottom of his frayed collar.

A runaway, she thought, trying not to smile. How often did the children from the nearby ranches, or the town of Whitehorn itself find their way to the Indian village? Those children, mostly boys, had great plans for running away. They imagined a life of endless bare-back riding across wide plains, hunting game, not going to school, never having a bedtime. Life with the Cheyenne was not so undisciplined, but the runaways never wanted to hear that.

The job of the tribe was to convince these children that life at home was not so very horrible. Usually the visitors could be convinced to return before their parents had much time to worry.

Ruth allowed her mouth to soften slightly. "I believe you would make a fine Indian," she said softly. "You look strong." She nodded at the horse. "Obviously you can ride."

"Yup. And rope. I help my pa with the cattle all the time." He glanced toward the wooden structures that made up the main section of the Indian village. "You got cattle? I could help with them."

"We have a few dozen head. We raise them for food, not to sell. And there are already several men to tend them. If you wish to stay, we need to find you other work."

The boy nodded. At least he understood that he couldn't stay without giving back to the community. That was something. Ruth rose to her feet and wiped the damp earth from her skirt.

"What is your name?" she asked.

"Zeke." He squinted up at her. "Who are you?"

"Ruth. Ruth Whitefeather."

His nose wrinkled as he frowned. "Ruth's not an Indian name. My friend Billy has a grandma named Ruth and she's from Boston."

"My mother wasn't an Indian. She named me."

Zeke accepted her explanation without asking any more questions. She picked up the basket of herbs she'd already gathered and led the way toward the Indian lands.

Spring had come early to Montana, giving the residents a longer growing season. Ruth had been busy planning her herb garden, and thinking about the different plants and roots she would harvest for her healing tonics and potions. Spring was always her favorite time of year, when the earth renewed itself and all of life was given a second chance.

"Why did you leave your home?" she asked as they walked down the main path of the village. "Do your parents beat you?"

"Nah. My ma died just after Christmas and my pa..." His voice trailed off. "He's not mean, but there's gonna be a new school teacher and he says I gotta go to school." He turned toward Ruth, his expression earnest. "I don't need to read. I can ride and rope and when I turn ten, Pa said he would teach me to shoot so when I grow up I'll be the best cowboy ever."

"An admirable goal," Ruth said, no longer paying attention to all of Zeke's words. His mother had died? She tried to remember hearing about the death of a rancher's wife in the past few months. There hadn't been any except—

She stopped in the middle of the path and stared at the child. The sound of her heart was suddenly loud in her ears. "What is your last name, Zeke? Tell me."

"Kincaid."

She tried to speak but could not. Zeke Kincaid. Caleb's son. She forced herself to start walking again, wondering why she hadn't noticed the similarities in the eye color, the smile. Even the attitude of defiance was the same.

She told herself it didn't matter where the boy came from. His parents—his father especially—were not her concern. She told herself that it had been nearly nine years and that she could barely remember what Caleb looked like. They had been friends for a brief time. Nothing more.

Then she tried not to think about any of it because what was the point of lying to herself?

She saw someone walking toward them. Relief filled her when she recognized her brother, John, and she nearly broke into a run. John would take care of Zeke, finding him work, then escorting him home when he was ready to return to his father.

"This is Zeke," she said by way of introduction and quickly explained how the boy wanted to join the tribe.

John listened solemnly, then offered to take Zeke so they could find some work for the boy. Ruth waved as they walked toward the barn. She remembered the recently slaughtered steer and thought that her brother might set Zeke to work scraping the hide. A smelly, difficult task guaranteed to convince any seven-year-old boy that he did *not* want to be an Indian after all.

Ruth returned to her small house. The herbs she'd collected required preparation before they could be dried. She would have to...

She sighed when she realized she didn't remember what she had to do. It was as if everything she'd ever known had been thrust from her head, leaving her empty except for her memories of Caleb Kincaid.

"Foolish dreamer," she murmured as she stepped into the workroom at the rear of her house and closed the door behind her. She set her basket on the floor. "That time is long finished. My future is here."

She clutched the familiar, wooden table that stretched the length of the room. The wood had been rubbed smooth. A shelf held her bowls and grinder. Dozens of glass jars and bottles sat on the far wall, each filled with different leaves or roots, extracts or combination of plants.

It was here she blended the teas and poultices that healed those in need. Long ago she had made the decision to dedicate herself to her people. Upon her birth she had been granted a gift, and using that gift was her destiny. There could be no other.

For much of her life she was content with the solitude that healing demanded. But sometimes, when she heard the laugh of a child or the soft conversation of a couple in love, she longed for something different. To have had the life offered to everyone else. Sometimes, like today, she remembered a man's passionate kisses.

Without meaning to, she became lost in the memory of the strength of Caleb Kincaid when he'd taken her in his arms. He'd been tender. So very understanding. His large hands had slid around her body, drawing her close, yet allowing her the freedom to escape if she needed to. She'd thought she would be afraid, but instead she'd welcomed him. Even now her body heated as she recalled their passionate kisses.

He'd claimed to love her and had asked her to be his wife. When she'd refused, he'd married someone else within a few months. As if she, Ruth, hadn't mattered at all.

"It doesn't hurt anymore," she said aloud, as if speaking the words forcefully would make them true. "He doesn't matter."

She had never loved Caleb, would never have married him. She was content with her place in the world. Healing others was a great gift and she was grateful to have been honored by the sacred trust. Her life here was what mattered—not the past.

THREE HOURS LATER, Ruth had nearly forgotten Zeke Kincaid was still in the village. At least that's what she told herself as she hung tender roots to dry. She wasn't listening for his voice, nor that of his father. For Caleb would know where his son had run to.

It was late in the afternoon when someone knocked at her back door. Her heart jumped into her throat and she had to take a steadying breath before she could cross the scarred wooden floor to let in her visitor.

Her brother stood on the rear step, a dirty and obviously tired Zeke behind him.

"Our young friend has decided he wishes to return home," John told her.

"I see."

She noticed dried blood staining the boy's fingers and knew that John had set Zeke to work on the hide. She couldn't blame the child for giving up. If she had to spend her day on that particular chore, she would take off for parts unknown as well.

"You might like to take him home," John said. "Zeke has told me there has not been a woman in the house since the passing of his mother. Caleb and Zeke are in need of a temporary housekeeper. It would just be for a short time. I knew you would welcome the opportunity to repay the family for its kindness to you."

Ruth opened her mouth to protest, then pressed her lips together. Not only couldn't she think of a single thing to say, but she had no breath with which to speak. John's words hovered in the afternoon, echoing like the call of the wolf.

She wanted to tell him no, that she would not, *could* not go to the Kincaid ranch. It was sad that Zeke had lost his mother and Caleb had lost his wife, but they weren't her family. As for her debt—she didn't want to think about that.

The thought of seeing Caleb again, *speaking* with him, made her light-headed. She felt as if the world had started to spin and she was afraid she would lose her balance and fall.

"I would not have suggested this if I thought you were disturbed by going back to the ranch," John said, his dark eyes seeing far more than they should.

Pride came to her rescue, stiffening her spine and making her straighten. "I'm not afraid." She gestured to her workroom. "But it's spring and there are many plants for me to gather. I'm very busy."

John kept his attention on her face. "The boy has no one but his father. Caleb has only the boy. Caleb's brothers are gone."

She wanted to scream her protest. John might be wise and a good leader of their people, but sometimes he was nothing more than her annoying brother.

She knew that if she told him she couldn't face the ghosts from her past that he would insist she stay here. John would never do anything to hurt her. But she couldn't bring herself to admit that truth—not even to herself. It had been nearly nine years, she reminded herself. Why would she think that seeing Caleb again would bother her?

Zeke stepped around John and stared at her. "Can you make biscuits? Pa makes stew and he can fix eggs, but his biscuits are hard enough to be horseshoes." He grinned. "At least that's what my ma used to say."

His humor lasted for a heartbeat, then faded as if he'd just remembered his mother was gone forever.

Ruth could have stood against anything except the sadness in the young boy's eyes. John was right—Zeke was now alone in the world. How long had it been since he'd seen a woman smile at him? When was the last time he'd heard a soft voice speaking words of comfort?

"Zeke tells me that his father has hired a new housekeeper. She's due to arrive at the end of the month. That's only two weeks away. Surely your plants can spare you that long."

She bowed her head to the inevitable. "I'll go with him. Please ready my horse while I pack my bag."

In less time than she would have liked, she and Zeke were on their way. He rode his horse, while she sat in her small cart pulled by a single black gelding. She had brought her healing herbs along with clothing and personal items. Zeke chattered about the ranch and all the things he would like her to cook but she found it difficult to concentrate. Her mind wandered to the past and what it had been like when she'd stayed with Caleb and his family before.

It had been so many years, yet she could recall certain details as if they'd just occurred the previous week. As they approached the ranch, her stomach tightened and her fingers twisted around the reins. She and Zeke crested a low rise and suddenly she could see the ranch house, the barns and stables. Everything was different, yet nothing had changed. Nearly nine years after Caleb had promised to love her forever, she had returned.

"STORM COMING in tonight, boss," Hank said as he reached the barn. He turned and squinted at the setting sun, studying the dark bank of clouds heading their way.

"It won't snow," Caleb Kincaid replied, not even bothering to look at the potential threat. He was too tired to raise his head that far.

He hadn't slept in three nights and he didn't doubt he'd be forced up sometime before dawn this morning. Spring was always a busy time at the ranch.

"I swear those damn cows are deliberately stupid," he muttered as he swung down from his saddle. "The way I see it, they know when they're gonna have trouble giving birth and they find the most difficult place to hide, then dare me to find them."

Hank lifted his hat and scratched his nearly bald head. "I don't think they're out to get you, boss. It just happens."

Caleb grimaced. "You're wrong. They talk about it. One of them finds a new canyon or gully and spreads the word."

Hank's dark eyes narrowed in concern. "You need some rest."

"I know. But until they're done dropping their calves, none of us is going to get it." He led his horse into the barn, handing him over to Tully. "Everyone in?" he asked the fifteen-year-old boy who had started work at the ranch the previous fall.

Tully had hair the color of fire and enough freckles to share with every person in the state of Montana. He was short, had a stammer and looked skinny enough to blow away in a good wind. But there was magic in his touch. In all his thirty-one years, Caleb had never seen anyone so good with horses.

"All the m-men are b-back," he said. "Zeke brought back c-company."

Caleb scowled. "Who? A boy from town?"

Just what he needed right now. Some stray kid for him to look after. Dammit, they were in the middle of calving. Zeke knew better than to—

"No. A w-woman."

Caleb stared in surprise. Hank raised his bushy eyebrows. "Looks like your boy done found you a new wife."

Caleb didn't even bother responding to that outrageous statement. Instead he glanced in the direction Tully pointed and saw a small black gelding with a white star between its eyes. The creature looked dainty, but Caleb knew it was a strong, sturdy horse. Dependable. Familiar.

He'd sold that horse to John Whitefeather nearly five years before. John had wanted the animal for his sister to use when she visited sick folks in the area.

Caleb felt as if he'd been poleaxed. The pain inside was white-hot and unrelenting.

"Ruth," he said, barely able to speak her name.

"Yes, s-sir," Tully stuttered. "S-she's up at the h-house."

Ruth. Here. He didn't know what to think. It had been long enough that her being here shouldn't matter. But it did. Because once, she'd been all he'd wanted. Once he'd thought they would get married and have half a dozen children together. He'd imagined the Kincaid ranch becoming a dynasty—something he could be proud of.

But as much as he'd wanted her, she hadn't wanted

him. Instead she'd walked away. And he'd married Marie.

He cursed his own rule of not keeping liquor in the barn, then turned his back on Tully and Hank and headed for the house. He was halfway there when he realized his foreman hadn't said a word about Ruth being here. Hank had been around for nearly fifteen years. He knew what had happened the last time she'd visited. He'd been the one who'd suggested Caleb needed to get away when he'd lost the only woman he'd ever loved.

The house loomed in front of him. Bright lights spilled out the kitchen windows, but the pulled curtains kept him from seeing more than shadows. He felt weary beyond feeling, yet oddly alert. Why was she here?

It couldn't be because of Marie's death. His wife had been gone nearly five months, so it was a little late for condolences. No one was sick. Tully would have mentioned Zeke being injured. So why now?

He climbed the single step that led to the mud room and quietly opened the door. Voices came from the kitchen. Voices and a sound Caleb hadn't heard in too long. Zeke's laughter. Caleb stepped through the doorway and stared into the kitchen.

In the second it took him to find Ruth, he saw the mess he hadn't had time to notice before now. Once sparkling floors were scratched and dirty. Filthy dishes had been stacked on counters and in the sink. Once white curtains had turned gray with grime. If he wasn't careful, the mail-order housekeeper he'd sent for would turn tail and run as soon as she saw the place.

When he could no longer avoid the inevitable, he

turned his attention on the woman and the boy. They sat together at the big kitchen table. Ruth sat with her back to him. He saw her crisp white blouse tucked into a dark skirt. Her long hair had been pulled back in a thick braid. Something hot coiled in his belly as he recalled what it had felt like to unfasten that braid and run his hands through her silky hair.

She sat straight and proud—still slender. She hadn't turned to face him, but he knew she was beautiful. Eyes the color of chocolate. Honey-colored skin. A full mouth so tempting it had taken every bit of willpower not to kiss her the first time he'd seen her.

Zeke knelt on the chair next to hers, watching intently as she spooned biscuits onto a pan. There was trust in the way the boy leaned close. Trust and an ease he'd never had around Marie.

This is what he'd wanted, Caleb thought as pain filled his chest. This is what he could never have.

Suddenly there was anger. Anger that she'd left and anger that she'd dared to return. He didn't need her pity or her gentle ways. She'd said she didn't want to live in his world. So what the hell was she doing here now?

CHAPTER TWO

ZEKE SHIFTED in his seat, then grinned and jumped to his feet. "Pa!"

Ruth felt herself stiffen as once again she found it impossible to breathe. Caleb. She started to turn in her chair, then stopped—frozen by fear. What would she see on his face and in his eyes? How could she have simply shown up in his house after all this time?

"This is Ruth," Zeke was saying. "She's a Cheyenne, at least half Cheyenne. I was there today and she's real nice. She came back with me when I told her that you didn't make very good biscuits and John—that's her brother—said she would stay until the new housekeeper arrived."

As the boy spoke, she gathered together her shreds of courage. She had survived much in her twenty-eight years of life...surely she could survive seeing Caleb again.

She rose and turned to face father and son. Even as Zeke continued to chatter, Caleb's steady gaze settled on her. His gray-blue eyes were still the color of a winter storm. The lines around his mouth had deepened. He was a tall, strong man—honed by the hard land and the difficult task of raising cattle. She saw the changes in him. The wariness in his expression, the ease with which he drew his son to him. She saw the things that were the same. The hint of a dimple, even though he wasn't smiling and the heat of desire long denied but still alive within him.

She'd thought he might yell, telling her that she had no right to be here. Not after she'd refused him all those years ago. Instead, he simply spoke her name.

"Hello, Ruth."

"Caleb."

Her lips barely formed the words. There were only a few feet between them, yet she felt as if they were on opposite ends of the world. For reasons she couldn't explain, she found herself wishing he would open his arms to her and draw her close. She needed the comfort that only he could give. Yet he didn't offer and, of course, she didn't ask.

He glanced around the kitchen. "You shouldn't have to see the ranch house like this. You remember it being nicer."

She nodded. "But I know you haven't had a house-keeper out here in several months."

"Sarah left when her sister was widowed. I've sent for someone. She should arrive by the end of the week, this one or next."

"Zeke told me. I thought I could help out until then." She paused and bit her lower lip. "I'm sorry about Marie."

At her words, his expression closed. He rested his hand on his son's slender shoulder. "Tully's finishing up with the horses for the day. Aren't you supposed to help him?"

Zeke looked as if he were going to protest, but then he nodded and headed for the mud room. "When is dinner going to be ready?" he asked her.

"Not for another half hour. You have time to complete your chores."

He shot his father a grin. "Ruth made cobbler with the last of the dried fruit."

"Then bring in some cream when you come back to the house."

"Yes, sir!"

The back door slammed as the boy ran toward the barn. Ruth smoothed her hands on her skirt.

"Caleb, I know this is a surprise for you," she said quickly, needing to make him understand what had happened. "Zeke came to the village today. He was running away. Something about a new schoolteacher."

"He's not too fond of the idea of learning to read and do his numbers."

"So I gathered." She stared at the center of his broad chest, not able to look him in the eye. "John set him to work scraping a hide, which is a difficult enough task to make anyone want to return home. When Zeke finally admitted school might not be so horrible, he also mentioned that you and he had been without a housekeeper for some time. John suggested I fill in until your new one arrives. He thought it would be a way for me to thank you...for what you did." She cleared her throat. "Back all those years ago."

"What did *you* think?"

She didn't know what *to* think. Standing here in the Kincaid family kitchen, she felt as if nothing had changed. It was once again nine years ago and her foolish young woman's heart had fallen in love. She'd allowed herself to dream about what might have been, until she'd remembered her responsibility to her people. Her destiny was to heal those in need. Being a wife and mother was someone else's destiny.

"I'm pleased to have the opportunity to repay my debt," she said formally.

"Is that what I am? A debt?"

She forced herself to look into his face. "That's not what I meant, Caleb."

"Then why are you here?"

At least she had an honest answer for that question. "I don't know. If you want me to leave, I will. Otherwise, I'll stay until the new housekeeper arrives."

Emotions flashed through his eyes, but she couldn't read them. Instead of responding, he simply shrugged as if her decision didn't matter to him one way or the other. Then he turned on his heel and walked out of the room, leaving her standing in a place of both past and present, wondering how she'd ever thought she had forgotten what it was like to love Caleb Kincaid.

"PA, RUTH SAYS she can teach me my letters," Zeke said as he stuffed half a biscuit in his mouth. He chewed it and swallowed before continuing the familiar argument. "And if you teach me my numbers, then I don't need to go to school. Right?"

Caleb tried to concentrate on his son's words, when every part of his being was intensely aware of the woman sitting across from him at the freshly scrubbed kitchen table.

Instead of chili from the bunkhouse, they were dining on stew and fresh biscuits. The sugary smell of the baking cobbler filled the kitchen. The counters were clean, the dishes washed and put away. But even those unusual circumstances weren't enough to keep him from thinking of Ruth.

She was so damn beautiful. He found himself wishing she'd grown ugly in their time apart. But he had a bad feeling that all the ugly in the world wouldn't take away his wanting. She had always been able to ignite the fire within him with just a look or the sway of her hips. Now she had returned, and breathing in her sweet scent made him ache with longing.

Nearly as powerful as the need was the anger. He resented being reminded of how he'd once cared for her. How he'd been a fool, offering marriage. She refused him and had left the same day. Left him wondering what he'd done wrong.

"School is important," Ruth said in her quiet voice. "A measure of a man is more than strength and experience. The measure of a man is taken by what he knows of his people and his world."

"I know most everything 'bout the ranch," Zeke announced before gathering up another spoonful of the stew. "Hank's teaching me 'bout putting the right bull with the heifers and Tully's teaching me how to repair tack. We're working on a saddle right now."

"There's more to the world than the ranch," she pointed out. "You need to know about other places and times."

"Why?"

"It's important to use your mind," Caleb told his son. "When you grow up and inherit the ranch, you'll probably head East to buy breeding stock. You don't want those fancy East Coast breeders to think you're stupid."

"They won't. I'm real smart."

Before he could stop himself, Caleb exchanged a look of affection and exasperation with Ruth. She smiled as if to say Zeke was a handful, but worth the effort. The shared moment cut through him like a freshly honed blade, leaving him to bleed to death from the inside. He didn't want to share anything with Ruth. Not now. Not ever. He should tell her to get the hell out of his house.

Yet he didn't speak the words. And when his son finished his supper and carried the plate over to the sink, then announced he had to head out to the barn to help Tully with the saddle, Caleb didn't stop him. The back door slammed again and he and Ruth were alone.

Silence stretched between them. He found himself staring at the way the lantern light gleamed on her dark hair. She kept her gaze on her plate, allowing him to study her smooth skin and the fullness of her mouth.

She looked older than she had the last time she'd been in this house. Mature. "It's been nine years and you never married."

He spoke the words he'd only meant to think. She glanced up. Color stained her honey-colored cheeks.

"I couldn't. I'm a healer."

"There's nothing in the history of the Cheyenne that makes marriage forbidden."

"I can't explain it more than saying I believe deep in my soul that my duty is to be a healer. For me that means staying there—I can't divide my heart by marrying. That's why I couldn't marry you."

She'd said the same thing when he'd proposed. He hadn't believed her back then, either. "I thought you were just afraid. Not that I blamed you. After what happened."

Something dark and ugly flared in her eyes. She ducked her head. "It wasn't that."

"But you *were* afraid. If not of me, then of my world."

She shrugged. "Your world is not a place I feel comfortable. I prefer living with my people."

"You're only half Cheyenne."

She looked at him. "I have embraced their ways and their traditions. In all that matters, I am only Cheyenne. You never saw that because you wanted me to be like you."

"No. I simply wanted you."

He hated the remembering. He knew exactly how she kissed. So tentative at first, then with a growing passion. He knew the feel of her lips on his, the taste of her, the small sounds she made when passion threatened to overwhelm her.

She sat across from him—where his wife had sat, and his mother before her. He had imagined Ruth in that chair so many times. Now that she was here, it was too late. He was old enough to know there were no second chances, and dreams about them were only for fools.

RUTH PUT the last of the dishes away in the cupboard. She could hear voices coming from Caleb's study. The sound of his low voice followed by his son's laughter. Their obvious love and affection made her feel out of place in the ranch house. She had no place here; Caleb had made it clear he didn't want her help or her company. So why was she staying? Shouldn't she simply leave in the morning? The new housekeeper would arrive soon. If Caleb and Zeke had survived this long on their own, what was a few more days?

She closed the cupboard door, then made her way to the kitchen table. She sat down and wrapped her hands around a mug of fresh coffee. Why was she surprised that Caleb wasn't happy to see her? Had she secretly expected him to welcome her with open arms?

She searched her heart looking for truth and found only confusion. Perhaps she had been hoping he would be happy to see her. Now that he wasn't, she didn't know what to do. He was a different man than the one she remembered. There was an air of sadness about him. Was that because of the loss of his wife? Marie had only been gone a few months. If theirs had been a love match...

She sipped her coffee and tried not to think about the fact that Caleb had married and fathered a child within a few months of his proposing to her. At the time she'd wondered if he'd ever cared about her at all, or had simply decided it was time to marry and start a family. Maybe he'd never loved her. She hated thinking that could be true, but she had to consider the proof in front of her. Zeke was a charming child who was impossible to ignore. Maybe—

"I'll show you to your room."

She glanced up and saw Caleb standing in the doorway. "Where's Zeke?"

"I put him to bed. He always complains that he's not tired, but then he's snoring before I get the door closed." Pride filled his blue-gray eyes and a smile tugged at the corners of his mouth.

"He's a fine boy," Ruth told him. "He spoke very highly of you."

Caleb crossed his arms over his chest. "Even when he was running away?"

"You have to know that was about his unwillingness to go to school."

He nodded. "I guess every boy would rather be out riding horses than in a schoolroom learning lessons. I don't doubt I complained when I had to attend."

"And your son is very much like you."

"I hope so."

His statement surprised her, but before she could question him or figure out what he'd meant, he repeated what he'd said before.

"I'll show you to your room."

She rose and walked toward him. When they were close enough for her to feel the heat of him, she drew in a deep breath.

"It was a mistake for me to come," she told him. "I see that now. John's suggestion that I repay my debt to your family by offering help surprised me so much that I didn't consider what it might mean. I know you want me to leave, and I will do so in the morning."

He gazed down at her. He was strong and powerful. Perhaps she should have been afraid, but she couldn't be. Not of Caleb. He'd always been so kind to her. Gentle. Understanding. She wondered if time had destroyed that part of him.

His gaze darkened, and for the first time she saw the wounds within him. Deep, unrelenting pain filled his being and she nearly cried out as she felt its coldness touch the edge of her soul. Mortal wounds, she thought, shivering slightly. What was their cause? The death of his wife?

"Stay or not," he said, turning away. "It doesn't matter to me."

Without thinking, she touched his shoulder to stop him. "How can you say that? You're obviously uncomfortable having me around."

He spun back to face her, breaking the physical contact between them. "Can you blame me? Nine years ago, I asked you to marry me. Not only did you refuse me with a ridiculous story about staying pure for your healing, you left that same day. As if you couldn't stand the sight of me. In all this time you've never once come to the ranch or spoken with me. When I've had business with your brother, you've always managed to be gone. So what the hell are you doing here now?"

His raw anger washed over her like lye, burning her, making her wish she'd stayed quiet. Why had she come? Was it about her debt or something else?

"I can't answer that." She forced herself to look into his blazing eyes. "I don't know why. But now that I'm here—" she paused and drew in a breath "—perhaps I *should* stay." She could see that there was healing to be done between them. This might be her only opportunity to right the wrong she'd created by her impulsive behavior when she'd left the last time.

He shrugged and started walking. She followed him up the stairs, confused by her own indecision and his fury. So many emotions still boiling between them. So many questions.

They moved down a hallway. There were three open doors, one on the left and two on the right. He entered the former, pushing the door wider. She hesitated until he'd lit a lantern sitting on a small table, then she stepped into the room.

She'd expected him to show her to the small guest room she'd occupied during her last stay. She remembered the pretty floral wallpaper and the four-poster bed that had been so cozy. Instead she stepped into a large room filled with expensive carved furniture, including a dressing table with an oval mirror. Dozens of pillows covered the oversize bed. Lace flounces decorated the window coverings. There were bottles of perfumes and other cosmetics, paintings of horses and portraits of people she'd never seen before.

Ruth could not imagine Caleb living in such feminine splendor, and Caleb didn't have any sisters. Which meant...

"This was Marie's room." He spoke the words without giving away what he was thinking. "I cleaned out most of her things a few weeks ago and aired everything. It's the only room ready for company. The guest room hasn't been touched in a couple of years, and I didn't think you'd be comfortable in my bed."

She knew he meant that she would be in his bed without him. But his words painted a picture of them together, under the blankets. She could almost feel him touching her, kissing her, taking her and making her his own. She should have been frightened or appalled by the thought, yet she was not. If anything, the sudden trembling of her thighs came from anticipation not disgust.

"Your wife had her own room?"

He glanced around and nodded. "Marie never adjusted to living in Montana. Having this helped her deal with her change in circumstances. Will you mind sleeping here?"

Ruth was not afraid of Marie's ghost. She had always found the spirits of the recently departed to be kindly, lost souls eager to be on their way.

"The room is very elegant," she told him. "Thank you for allowing me to stay here."

He hesitated, but all he said was, "Good night."

He stepped out of the room and closed the door behind him. Ruth crossed the floor to press her fingers against the wood. She listened to his footsteps in the hall, then the sound of his own door closing.

She sighed. Nothing was as she'd thought it would be. Why had Caleb's wife slept in this beautiful room? There were no signs of a man's presence. Had he moved out after her death?

Ruth turned to face the lace and frills. No. Caleb would not have slept in a space such as this. So he must have had his own room. Why? If she, Ruth, had married him, she would have wanted to spend every night at his side. She couldn't imagine another woman feeling differently. Of course she'd never met Marie Kincaid.

"Who were you?" she whispered into the darkness. "And why did he marry you?"

CHAPTER THREE

CALEB DIDN'T SAY much the next morning when he and Hank headed out to check on the herd. Despite his prediction, no one had awakened him in the night, so he'd had the opportunity to get some sleep. Unfortunately, it hadn't happened. He'd been too aware of Ruth across the hall. She hadn't made any sound, but he'd known she was there. He would have sworn that the sweet scent of her body had drifted to him, calling to him. He'd been on fire for her, longing to go to her. But he hadn't. Because she'd made her feelings damn clear.

So why was she back? Why after all this time? Was it only about repaying a debt? Did he care? The best thing for both of them was for her to leave, yet he knew he wasn't going to tell her to go. He couldn't. Because having her here, wanting her and knowing he could never have her was better than never seeing her at all. Which made him worse than a fool.

"You're mighty quiet," Hank announced when they'd ridden for about an hour.

"What do you want to talk about?"

"Me? I've got nothing to say. I thought you might have, what with Ruth being back on the ranch and all."

"She's staying until the new housekeeper arrives."

Hank pushed back his worn hat and frowned. "Why?"

"I have no idea. She said something about repaying old debts."

Hank snorted. "After all this time? You think she's sweet on you?"

He wasn't that lucky. "No."

"Then it don't make sense."

"I'm not going to make trouble. If you'd tasted her cooking, you wouldn't, either."

Hank licked his lips. "I thought I smelled something good this morning."

"Flapjacks, eggs and sausage."

"Maybe I could stop by tomorrow and have a little taste."

"You do that."

If there was another person at the table, the tension might not be so thick. This morning Zeke had been the only one talking. Caleb and Ruth had been polite, careful to avoid each other's gaze.

Up ahead one of the cowboys crouched next to a cow and called to them. Caleb squinted, then groaned when he saw a half-born calf coming out the wrong way. It was going to be a hell of day.

Six hours later, his prediction had proved true. Calves were falling like apples, most doing fine without help, but enough were in trouble to keep the men jumping. They'd only lost one cow. Fortunately her calf had been born healthy and was being nursed by another cow.

He headed for the wagon Tully had driven out. He needed coffee and something to eat. But as he rode toward the group of men, he found his thoughts once again drawn to Ruth and her reappearance in his life. She'd been avoiding him for so long, he figured he would never see her again.

He still recalled exactly how they'd met. He'd been in town for the day, picking up supplies and she'd been in Whitehorn buying medicine. It had been a cold, rainy afternoon, with not many folks about. If he'd been just a few minutes later or earlier, he wouldn't have seen four men dragging a woman behind the saloon.

Caleb reined in his horse as the old, familiar rage filled him. They'd been drunk and too long on the trail. She'd just been some Indian to them. That's what they'd told him when he'd grabbed the first man and began punching with all his might. He hadn't had time to even glance at the woman. Fury at the injustice had given him strength and he'd beaten them all. One man had nearly died, and Caleb hadn't found it in himself to care that he'd almost ended a life.

When the drunks were broken and bleeding in the mud, he'd turned to the woman. Only she wasn't really that grown-up. Barely nineteen he'd learned, which made her plenty old enough, except for the innocence he'd seen in her eyes. She'd been shaking with fear and cold, hardly able to speak as she'd sobbed out that it was her fault. She should have dropped her precious bundle and run, but she hadn't wanted to lose the medicines she'd ordered from back East.

Caleb urged his horse forward. He remembered that Ruth's dress had been torn, ripped down to her waist. He'd seen the side of one breast and a tight nipple. She'd been pushed down into the mud, her skirt pulled to her thighs, her chemise reduced to ragged bits of cloth. He'd looked away, then offered her his coat. She'd been unable to take it, so he'd knelt over her, pulling down her skirt and covering her with his coat.

Before she could protest, he'd lifted her onto his wagon and had brought her back to the ranch where she'd stayed for nearly a month. He'd even thought to rescue her medicines and the whispered thanks she'd given him when he'd handed them to her had been worth the scraped knuckles, black eye and broken nose.

The first two days, she'd done nothing but shake and cry. The housekeeper had tried to shoo him away, but Ruth couldn't sleep if he wasn't with her. She'd clung to him, sometimes speaking, mostly not. So *he'd* talked. About the ranch and his brothers. About breeding cattle and the price of beef. How the railroad could make or break a rancher by raising or lowering prices to market. Her brother had visited, and had been content to let her stay and heal in the solitude of the ranch.

Caleb had tried not to want her or to remember how he'd seen that curve of her breast and the honeyed skin of her thighs. He'd ached for her and had made sure she'd never known. Because he'd wanted her whole more than he'd ever wanted anything in his life.

He still remembered the first time he'd seen her smile. He'd taken her out to the corral to watch the new foals playing in the summer afternoon. She'd smiled and then laughed. When she'd reached for his hand and squeezed it, he'd known that he had lost himself to her.

He reined in as he approached Tully's wagon. After dismounting, he took a mug of coffee and a couple of the biscuits the boy had brought with him. One bite told him Ruth had made them and not the bunkhouse cook.

Even as he chewed he thought of Ruth standing in his kitchen, working the dough, setting the pans to bake. How it all should have been…if she'd agreed to marry him. But she hadn't, claiming some female nonsense about having to be true to her healing arts. He'd recognized the excuse for what it was. A cover for her fear. He'd vowed to forget her.

Instead he'd married Marie.

Now Ruth was back. How was he going to survive being with her—if only for a few days—and how was he going to recover from losing her a second time?

A SOFT KNOCK on her bedroom room awakened Ruth sometime after midnight. She was used to being awakened, for the sick often worsened in the hours of darkness. Instinctively she reached for the heavy cloak she always kept by her bed, along with the valise of her medicines. But when she opened the door, she saw only Caleb in the hall.

It took her a moment to speak. At first she wanted to get lost in the male beauty of his face. The way the shadows turned his blue-gray eyes to black. The contour of his jaw, the slight bump in his nose from when it had been broken. He'd been hurt because of her. How many times had she tenderly touched his healing bruises, apologizing for her part in his injuries? How many times had he told her he would do it a hundred times again just to protect her?

She blinked and reminded herself that someone needed her. "Who is it?" she asked. "Did they bring the person here, or am I leaving?"

He frowned slightly. "No one's sick. That's not why I awakened you."

"Then what?"

Instead of answering, he took her valise and set it on the floor. Then he reached for her hand and drew her along with him. They walked down the hall and into the kitchen. In the mud room he paused while she stepped into her boots.

"Where are we going?" she asked.

Instead of answering, he smiled. The first smile she'd seen in nearly nine years. Her heart jumped in her chest. The sensation was both painful and exciting.

As they stepped into the darkness outside, he again took her hand. She liked the feel of his strong fingers curling around her own. Perhaps it was wrong, but she was content to be in this moment, enjoying being close to Caleb.

The sky was thick with stars and a sliver of moon drifted across the crisp, clear blackness. She inhaled the scents of spring—plants budding and turning bright green—the turned earth. Even the smell of the horses and cattle was pleasant in the spring.

"This way," he said quietly, leading her into the second barn. He released her hand to open the door.

There were several lanterns hanging on hooks, illuminating oversize stalls. Three mares stood in the three front stalls. Their wide bellies explained the purpose of the building—it was for foaling. Her heart quickened.

"Is one being born tonight?"

"Yes. Right now."

They walked down the second row of stalls. Sounds came from behind a low door. Grunts and whinnies.

Not from uncontrolled pain, but from the hard work of bringing forth life.

"This is Ellie's fifth foal," he said as they stopped in front of the stall door. "She's never had any trouble, but I like to check on her, just to be sure."

Ruth turned to watch the birth in progress. She gasped softly as she saw two small front legs appear. They were covered by a transparent skin that protected the foal while it developed in its mother. Patches of Ellie's coat darkened with sweat as she grunted and pushed, thrusting her foal into the world.

A small head appeared next, then the shoulders. The transparent skin broke and the small, damp foal drew in a shaky breath.

Ruth pressed her hands together in delight as the foal was delivered safely. The small animal was the same rich brown as its mother, with a white blaze on its face. After a few minutes of trembling, the foal made its first attempt to stand. It teetered for a second, then tumbled back into the straw. Ellie reached around and began licking her baby.

"He'll be up and around shortly," Caleb told her. "If the weather stays good, Tully will turn them out into one of the corrals the day after tomorrow."

"He's beautiful," she murmured as the long-legged foal staggered to his feet. He managed a couple of steps which took him closer to his mother. The mare rose and turned, making it easier for him to nurse.

"Zeke will be pleased," she said, leaning against the outside of the stall. "He's been waiting for this little one to be born."

"He names the foals." Caleb smiled slightly. "Or at least he gets to make suggestions. Sometimes his ideas about good names for horses don't agree with mine.''

She glanced at him out of the corner of her eye. He was still dressed in his Levi's jeans and a woolen shirt. Had he even been to bed? But then she remembered all the long hours he'd always put into the ranch and she knew that he had not. He'd been up with Ellie, making sure everything went well with the mare. He could have told Tully to stay with the horse, but that wasn't Caleb's way.

''You're good with horses and with little boys,'' she said, turning her attention back to the nursing foal. ''Zeke loves you very much. As important, he respects you.''

Caleb didn't disagree. ''We've always been special to each other. I've been taking him out with me since he was old enough to sit on a horse.''

Ruth frowned. Wouldn't Zeke have stayed home with his mother? She started to ask, then pressed her lips together. Marie's relationship with her child and Caleb wasn't a subject Ruth wanted to explore. At least not tonight.

''It's obvious he adores the ranch,'' she told him. ''He constantly speaks about growing up to be the best cowboy in Montana.''

''As long as he learns reading and his numbers along the way.'' Caleb jerked his head toward the stall. ''We should probably leave them alone now. I'll walk you back to the house.''

She nodded and fell into step next to him.

''You've made a lot of improvements on the ranch,'' she said. ''This special birthing barn is new.''

''It's easier to keep the foaling mares together. And

yes, there have been some changes. More stock. More men working the stock. I've been breeding horses, as well.''

Anything that kept him away from the house, he thought grimly. Marriage to Marie had been hell on earth. The only decent thing to come of it had been Zeke. He'd seen the questions in Ruth's eyes when he'd talked about taking his son with him out onto the ranch, but he hadn't answered them. He wasn't ready to explain that Zeke's mother hadn't given a damn about him. She'd seen the boy as a noisy inconvenience and had often told him so. Caleb had done his best to spare his child the hurt of knowing his mother not only didn't love him, but didn't like him at all.

''So many changes.'' Ruth stepped out into the night and breathed in the cool air. ''While there are more animals, there are less people.'' She glanced at him. ''Will and Brock are also gone. Do you miss them?''

''Brock always wandered away. He'll be back.''

''And William?''

He didn't want to think about his brother. Too many angry words had been spoken between them. ''I don't hear much from him.''

Caleb didn't like that his once large, happy family had been reduced to himself and Zeke. He had the gnawing sense that somehow it was all his fault, but he didn't know how. His parents' deaths hadn't happened because of him. As for Will and Brock being gone... He shook his head. No point in chewing over the past. It was finished.

They reached the rear porch of the main house, but instead of going inside, Ruth dropped gracefully onto the top step. She pulled her thick cloak around her and stared at the sky.

"Why do the stars seem different here than they do at my house?" she asked. "I always thought the sky was bigger on your ranch."

"It's not. Maybe the land is more open."

He told himself to get back to the barn, or at the very least, head up to his room. But he couldn't seem to stop himself from sitting next to her. He made sure they weren't touching in any way. He'd already made the mistake of taking her hand in his. He'd done it without thinking...or maybe because he'd wanted to. Regardless, he'd closed his fingers over hers and had been caught up in a wanting so intense, he'd found it hard not to take her right up against the wall. His skin still burned from her delicate touch. It had been so long. Why couldn't he have forgotten what it was like to be near her? Why did she still have to matter?

"I know you don't want me to say this," Ruth said softly, "but I have to." She turned to look at him. "Thank you for rescuing me."

"Ruth—"

She cut him off with a quick shake of her head. Her hair was still back in a thick braid. He ached to loosen the gleaming black strands and run his fingers through the heavy silk of her hair. He'd had more than one fantasy about her on top of him, loving him, her long tresses tumbling over his shoulders, his belly, his thighs.

"Caleb, you saved me from those men, and that deserves thanks enough. But it's more than that. You brought me here and gave me time to heal. You never left my side."

Her dark eyes stared at his face. "You were kind and gentle. Then you reminded me that it was safe to be a woman—at least with you."

He didn't want her gratitude. "I didn't do anything special."

"Yes, you did. I'll be grateful all the days of my life."

He swore silently. "Then you be what you need to be. It doesn't matter to me."

She smiled. "How can you be so tender and so gruff at the same time? You took me to see the foal being born because you remembered that I have a soft place for all kinds of babies. Yet you won't let me thank you."

He wasn't about to explain that thanks weren't what he was interested in. He didn't know what he wanted from Ruth, but he would rather have nothing than this.

"If babies are so important, why don't you have a half dozen of your own?"

She stiffened as if he'd slapped her. He saw her swallow. The pleasure faded from her eyes, leaving her looking alone and vulnerable.

"You know why," she said, staring at her clasped hands resting on her lap.

"I didn't believe your talk about staying pure for your healing before and I still don't believe it."

"I know." She shrugged. "Maybe it's an excuse, but it feels real to me. I keep thinking that if I don't honor my gift, it will all be gone."

"That's crazy. You know things. Loving a man and having children isn't going to take away your knowledge."

"I don't always know what I'm doing." She looked

at him and some of the darkness left her eyes. "Sometimes I have to guess the right thing to do. I have a feeling inside, almost as if someone else is telling me what to do. What if that voice goes away?"

"It won't."

"You can't be sure."

He was damn sure, but she wasn't about to listen. Just like she hadn't listened all those years ago. Ruth was afraid. Whether she was afraid of him, or living in the white world, or of being married, he didn't know. But her fear had kept her from marrying him back then and it was still keeping her from living the life she should.

"You need to be married," he told her flatly. "You need a husband to take care of you and give you babies."

"I can take care of myself."

"Your life is proof of that, but so what? At the end of the day you go back to your house and there's no one waiting for you. No one to worry about you or talk to you. No one who thinks you're the most special person ever. All you've got is that ache in your gut that tells you there should be more."

He wasn't sure where the words had come from, and as soon as he spoke them, he wanted to call them back. He sounded like an idiot, or some shyster selling snake tonic.

Ruth's eyes widened. "How do you know?"

Because he'd lived that private hell every day of his marriage to Marie. She'd made it clear she would never forgive him for loving someone else. He would admit to his part in destroying their marriage, but he'd always been willing to make things better. She hadn't agreed.

She'd set her course on punishing him every day that they were together and she'd been successful more often than not.

"I do get lonely," she admitted, and crossed her arms over her chest. "I think about what it would have been like if things had been different. But then I know I made the right decision."

He wished he could say the same thing about himself. "Are you happy?"

"Sometimes. I'm at peace and that's usually enough."

He nodded. He was at peace, as well. At least he had been before Ruth had shown up at the ranch house, turning his world over and leaving him wondering what it would be like when she left him again.

"I'm sorry about Marie," she told him.

Ruth was a kind woman, so he knew she spoke the truth. He nodded his thanks, because he wasn't going to tell her he wasn't sorry at all that his wife was gone.

CHAPTER FOUR

RUTH BENT DOWN to remove the warm bread from the oven. The yeasty smell made her mouth water. It was well after noon and she'd only had coffee that morning. She smiled as she glanced at the clock and knew that Zeke would come tearing into the house shortly. The boy would skitter to a stop in front of her and demand to know what was to eat.

It had been nearly a week since she'd first arrived at the Kincaid ranch. A week of cooking and cleaning and trying not to mind that Caleb didn't go out of his way to spend time with her. A week of trying not to think about the fact that his new housekeeper was due any day now.

Ruth set the bread on the counter to cool, then stirred the soup she'd prepared. When she set the spoon down, she glanced around at the now clean kitchen. She'd had a chance to scrub down the walls and the floor. Everything gleamed like new. In the rest of the house, she'd oiled the wood, beaten the rugs and washed the linens. Even now sheets flapped in the warm breeze. She knew she was being foolish but sometimes, like now, she allowed herself to pretend this was real. That she belonged here. If she'd accepted Caleb's proposal back then, the ranch house *would* be hers. She would have a child like Zeke, perhaps more than one. She closed her eyes against the vision of a toddling little girl with dark hair and blue-gray eyes like Caleb's, but that didn't take away the empty feeling in her heart.

Three nights before he'd taken her out to watch the birth of a foal. Later they'd sat together in the dark and talked about their lives. He'd accused her of refusing him because she'd been afraid. Ruth didn't believe that was true. She had a duty to her gift. Fear of the white world might haunt her but it didn't influence her decisions.

The back door burst open, then slammed into the wall. Zeke raced into the room, heading directly for her. He didn't stop until he ran into her, flinging his arms around her waist and holding her close. She hugged him back.

"How was your morning?" she asked.

"Good. What's to eat?"

She laughed as she stroked his smooth blond hair. "Soup and fresh bread. Did you wash your hands?"

He held up damp fingers for her inspection. "Outside. And I used soap!"

"Good for you. Now set the table."

Zeke collected linen napkins and lined them up with the concentration of a general ordering troops into formation. Bowls and side plates were put out next, then the butter crock.

"Is Pa gonna eat with us?" he asked.

"I don't think so. He didn't say anything to me."

Caleb never joined them for their noon meal, but Zeke asked about him every day. Ruth wondered if the boy craved more time with his father, or if he sensed that there was a distance between Caleb and herself.

She knew Zeke had grown fond of her, as she had

begun to care about him. Perhaps she should remind him that her stay was just temporary, but she hated to say anything that would take the sparkle out of his eyes.

"How's Jake?" she asked, mentioning the newborn foal. Zeke had named him the previous day and Caleb had accepted the suggestion, writing the foal's name and date of birth down in the ranch's account books.

"Great! He's running around with his ma." Zeke slipped into his seat. "He's kinda skinny, but he's fast. Pa said I could help Tully train him. And Tully says that we have to start handlin' him real soon. He's got to get used to being around people."

"Tully knows a lot about horses," Ruth said.

"Yeah. He's the best. And he's not that old. Pa says—"

Zeke chattered about his father and the ranch, the men who worked as cowboys, his horse, the new litter of barn kittens and how many days until the new schoolteacher arrived. Ruth listened attentively, soaking up the boy's conversation, allowing him to paint word pictures so she would have more memories to carry with her when she left.

She'd always wanted to have children, but never more so than these past few days. Her heart ached to love a child, while her body felt empty. As if it had never fulfilled its greatest purpose. She wished she could believe that she was allowed to have the simple pleasures most women took for granted. A husband and a family. But she couldn't take the chance.

Zeke finished his bowl of soup and held it out for a second serving.

"I like what you cook," he said as she ladled him

more of the steaming liquid. "Ma never cooked. She said it wasn't her place. That she'd been raised for better things." He wrinkled his nose. "I asked her what things once, but she got real mad, so I didn't ask again. Pa said she was raised on a ranch like this, but it was in Texas and life is different there. He said Ma's family was real rich and they had lots of servants. We always had housekeepers, but Ma never liked 'em. I did. They would make cakes and pies, but not as good as yours."

The artless compliment made her smile. "I'm glad. As long as you keep bringing me fresh berries, I'll keep making pies."

Zeke grinned. "Yes, ma'am." His smile faded. "Do you like this house?"

Ruth wasn't sure what he was asking. "It's lovely."

His mouth twisted. "Ma hated it. She said she didn't like one thing about it. That's why she was gone all the time. She went riding a lot—all day. Mostly by herself, but sometimes with one of the cowboys. One of them—I can't 'member his name—went with her a lot. Then he had to leave. Pa was real mad. Even though he was quiet, I could tell. And Ma cried. I didn't like it then. I spent a lot of time in the barn. Then it was better and then she died."

Ruth set down her spoon. She didn't know what to say to the boy. Had Marie had an affair with one of the cowboys? She couldn't imagine a woman wanting to be with anyone else when she could be with Caleb. Of course Marie sounded like a very unhappy woman.

"How did she die?" she asked at last.

"She was thrown from her horse. A wildcat spooked him. Pa and Hank found her when she was late gettin' home. It was a bad winter, so I guess the cat was hungry. Pa brought Ma home, but Hank stayed behind to find her horse and he's the one who saw the tracks of the cat. Some of the cowboys went out and found it later. It had gotten Ma's horse."

"I'm sorry," Ruth said and touched his arm.

He looked at her, then returned his attention to his soup. "I miss her sometimes. But I don't think she liked me very much."

Ruth felt her heart tighten in her chest. She longed to know what to say to comfort this wonderful child, but words failed her. There was a noise in the mud room and they both turned. Caleb stood in the doorway to the kitchen. He held his left arm cradled in his right. Blood seeped through his shirt.

"Pa!" Zeke pushed back his chair and raced to his father. "What happened?"

"I was moving wire for fencing and wasn't paying attention. I caught myself."

Ruth rose as well, but instead of going to Caleb, she headed for the stairs. "I'll get my supplies," she said.

"No need. It's just a scratch."

Typical man, she thought as she hurried. "Don't go anywhere. And try not to drip on my clean floor," she called over her shoulder.

She returned quickly. Caleb stood by the sink. Zeke had already cleared the table.

"I'm gonna help Tully," he said when he was finished and headed for the door.

"Stay away from the wire," Caleb yelled after him. "Yes, Pa."

Ruth opened her valise and pulled out a jar of her special soap. It cleaned wounds without stinging too much. Some of the herbs she used helped prevent infection.

"Let's see how bad this is," she said as she moved close and began to roll up his left sleeve.

"It's nothing," Caleb said, but he didn't shift away.

She folded material toward his elbow until she'd uncovered an ugly gash nearly six inches long. Blood had already begun to clot.

"It's not deep," she said, trying not to notice the heat of him. They were standing so close; she felt herself start to tremble.

"I should have washed it in the barn and been done with it." His voice sounded gruff.

"You're here now. Let me earn my keep."

He sighed. "You're already doing that and more. Any debt you had to this family was paid a long time ago, Ruth." He leaned toward the sink and allowed her to pump water over the cut. "You don't have to stay if you don't want to."

"I know. I like being at the ranch. It's a nice change from what I usually do."

She rubbed her soft soap into the wound, then rinsed. Caleb had to be in pain, but he didn't even catch his breath when she applied the soap a second time.

He was strong to her touch, she thought as she felt his muscles bunch when she moved him closer to the flow of water. After rinsing his skin again, she wrapped his forearm in a clean towel. They were still standing close enough that it was difficult for her to think. She told herself to walk away, or at least say something to distract herself. But she couldn't seem to make her feet obey her thoughts, nor did her mouth want to work.

Caleb was the one who seemed unaffected as he

stepped back and leaned against the counter. "I'm sorry you had to hear that."

She blinked. "What?"

He shrugged. "What Zeke said about his mother."

"Oh."

She didn't know how to respond. Instead of saying anything, she reached for her bandages. After removing the towel, she smoothed an ointment on the gash, then wrapped it, careful to hold the edges of skin together.

Caleb flexed his arm when she was finished, then nodded his thanks. "I guess what I'm really sorry about is that Zeke figured out that Marie never wanted to be his mother."

His matter-of-fact statement made her catch her breath. "What are you talking about? How could any woman—especially his mother—not love that boy?"

"I don't know but it's true. Marie didn't want children." His expression hardened. "Of course she didn't tell me that until after Zeke was born."

"Oh, Caleb." She sighed. "I didn't realize. I wish—" She broke off. What exactly did she wish for?

"It doesn't matter. Not anymore."

"Of course it matters, to both you and Zeke. How can you say it doesn't?"

He shook his head. "This was a mistake. You shouldn't have come here."

"What are you talking about?"

He moved toward her, looming. She had the oddest feeling he was trying to frighten her, yet she wasn't the least bit worried that he would try to hurt her. Not Caleb. That wasn't his way.

He put his hands on her upper arms. "You don't belong on this ranch. You should go home."

His words stung. "I'll leave if you want me to," she said stiffly.

"That's not what I'm saying."

"Yes, it is. You're—"

But she never got to finish her sentence. Instead of listening and responding, Caleb bent down and brushed his mouth against hers. The kiss was so warm, so tender and unexpected, for a heartbeat she couldn't do anything but stand there and feel it all.

His mouth—his hot, sensual mouth—molded itself to hers. She found herself swept up in instant passion, and instant memories. Past and present blurred as she raised her arms and wrapped them around him. He put his arms around her waist and drew her against him. They were touching and pressing and his mouth was on hers and she never, ever wanted him to stop.

His kiss was everything she remembered. As he brushed back and forth against her, heat filled her body, starting in the center of her being and radiating out. She could inhale the scent of his body. The fragrance of man and horse and the spring combined into a perfume that stole her will. Not that she *wanted* to protest or even pull away.

His hands were firm, yet gentle as he held her. She could feel his individual fingers pressing into her skin. Her breasts flattened against his chest and the pressure made her want to squirm. She rubbed her palms against the hard strength of his shoulders, then moved one hand lower and the other higher so that she could caress both his back and his neck. The silky ends of his hair tickled her skin.

He tilted his head slightly, angling his mouth so they fit perfectly. He parted his lips and licked her bottom lip. A shiver rippled through her. He'd kissed her like this before, she recalled. He'd put his tongue in her mouth and had stroked her. Long after she'd left the ranch and returned to her life among the Cheyenne, she'd relived the heated kisses she'd shared with Caleb. During the day she told herself that she had forgotten that brief month with him, but at night, she remembered.

So now she responded to his gentle urging and parted her lips. She welcomed him as he slipped inside her. Such hot sweetness, she thought hazily. Another shiver shot through her, then another, until it was nearly impossible to stay standing. She clung to him as her knees nearly gave way. Every part of her body seemed hotter and more sensitive. The pressure of his chest against her suddenly swollen breasts was both intense pleasure and pain. She wanted so much more.

The ache between her thighs caught her attention. She squeezed her legs together in an effort to relieve it, but the movement didn't help. Instead she had a nearly uncontrollable urge to rub against him. She had a sudden vision of his thigh between hers. The ache intensified until she wanted to sob. Frustration made her close her lips around his tongue and suck on him.

Caleb broke the kiss and stepped back as if she'd slapped him. Ruth felt as if she'd been plunged in cold water, except for her face, which burned with embarrassment. Obviously she'd done something horribly wrong.

She could barely bring herself to meet his gaze. Once she did, she was confused. Where she would have expected some kind of passionate fire, she found only stark anger. He glared at her as if she'd betrayed his trust.

"Caleb?"

Her voice came out soft and trembling. It was difficult to speak, difficult to concentrate, for despite her embarrassment and inability to understand what was wrong, her body remained on fire for him. Ruth knew that she wanted to be with Caleb in the most intimate way possible. His empty eyes told her that he didn't share her passionate desire.

Shame joined embarrassment.

"I won't be fooled by a woman again," he said, then turned and stalked out of the room.

Ruth stared after him. "Fooled by a woman?" she repeated. What on earth was he talking about?

"YOU GET ANY MORE bad tempered, I'm gonna start hoping you get kicked in the head by a steer," Hank said forcefully as he rode next to Caleb that afternoon. "Dang it, boy, what's gotten into you?"

"Nothing."

Caleb grimaced. He didn't think he'd been taking out his anger on anyone else, but Hank didn't share that opinion. And there was no way he was going to explain to his foreman that he was having trouble concentrating on the cattle because all he could think about was Ruth and the way they'd kissed that morning.

"It's more than something," Hank grumbled. He jerked his head toward Caleb's arm. "Is that bothering you? Did you let Ruth see it?"

"Yes. She took care of it. I didn't need stitches."

Hank drew his bushy brows together. "We've only lost a couple of cows and one calf. The weather's fine, cattle prices are up. You've got no call to be as ill-tempered as a—''

He broke off in midsentence, as his gaze turned knowing. "Maybe you do at that."

Caleb felt his temper flare. "Mind your business, old man. I don't have time for this."

"Yes, boss."

Hank didn't say another word, but then he didn't have to. He and Caleb had been working together for so long that they often knew what each other was thinking. No doubt the old coot had figured out that Ruth was the reason for Caleb's unusual shortness.

Caleb wanted to claim it wasn't that at all. That he didn't feel like putting his fist through the side of the barn—except the image of the act almost made him feel better. What the hell was wrong with him?

A stupid question, he told himself. He knew exactly what was wrong. It came in the form of a beautiful woman who still made his blood boil the way it had all those years ago.

One kiss. One damn kiss and he'd nearly lost control. Caleb had never forced himself on a woman. He'd never had the desire, nor the need. But the moment his mouth had touched Ruth's he'd wanted her with a passion he'd barely been able to keep in check. For the first time in his life, he'd been afraid of his need. He'd had to use every ounce of self-control to keep from touching her all over. Her softness, the scent of her, the way she'd kissed him back—they'd about done him in.

He shifted on his horse and tried to concentrate on the beauty of the land stretching out in front of him. For as far as the eye could see, Kincaid property reached out and touched the sky. His family had worked hard to claim this land and now it was his legacy to pass along to his son. He was no longer married to Marie, whose sole purpose in life had been to make his days a living hell. Wasn't that enough? Was he really going to start thinking about Ruth now?

Except he didn't know how to forget her. He didn't know how to erase the feel of her body pressed against his, or her soft cries of passion when he'd slipped his tongue in her mouth. She'd responded with a combination of innocence and desire that had about sucked the life out of him. Was she still a virgin or had she given herself to someone else?

The question plagued him because there wasn't a good answer. If she wasn't a virgin, then he could more easily take her to his bed and ease the ache inside him. But he hated the thought of her having been with someone else. He reminded himself it had been nearly nine years and that Ruth was a beautiful woman. She would have had many offers. Had she turned them all down?

"You're lookin' fierce enough to scare the cattle," Hank commented. "Come to think of it, you've been fit to be tied since Ruth showed up at the house nearly a week ago. Maybe she's got something to do with all this."

Caleb grunted, because he wasn't going to outright lie to Hank.

His foreman sighed heavily. "Seems to me that some folks would be pleased to be gettin' a second chance with a woman like her, but then you've never been like some folks."

"This isn't a second chance. She's helping out is all. Don't make it more than that."

"Helping out is sending over a couple of dinners. Maybe baking a pie or two. She's moved right into your house and is tending you and Zeke like she's part of the family." He stuck a wad of tobacco into his left cheek. "Of course I could be wrong about all of this."

"You are."

Hank ignored him. "Not that it matters. You're gonna scare her off the way you've scared off everyone else who matters."

Caleb turned to stare at the old man. "What are you saying?"

Hank spit. "Seems to me that everyone important to you is gone. Your folks died, though that's not your fault. Will and Brock took off for faraway places. It's just you and the boy. Seems like a lonely way to live."

"You don't know what you're talking about."

"Probably not," Hank agreed cheerfully.

Up ahead they saw a cow on her side in the mud. Her half-born calf struggled to get free of its mother's tightening muscles.

Caleb urged his horse forward, then slid off when he was close enough. He waded through the mud and reached the panting mother's side.

"Give me a hand," he called to Hank.

Between them they managed to pull the calf free, saving the mother as well. There were two more births that needed assistance and it was after dark by the time Caleb finally turned his horse toward the house.

Despite his bone-deep exhaustion, he couldn't get Hank's words out of his head. The ones that said he'd run off everyone he'd ever cared about. Caleb knew he hadn't run off his brothers. At least he didn't think he had. As for Ruth—he'd wanted to marry her. She'd been the one to turn *him* down. He couldn't have forced her to accept him. He'd had no choice but to let her go.

He could have gone after her.

The thought came out of the darkness, and once it appeared, he couldn't push it away. Is that what had gone wrong? Should he have pursued her? Had his pride gotten in the way of his happiness? He'd never considered going after her. She'd made her decision and he'd respected that. Had he made a mistake?

He still hadn't decided when he reached the back door of the ranch house. All he knew for sure was that he had to apologize for what had happened that morning. Not the kissing, but how he'd stalked out. He'd seen the hurt in Ruth's eyes, but he hadn't been able to stop himself.

He told himself that life would be a whole lot easier when Ruth left and his mail-order housekeeper arrived, but deep down Caleb doubted it would be any happier.

He sucked in a deep breath, then stepped into the house. Zeke and Ruth were sitting at the table. It was too late for them to be eating. Still it took him a moment to realize that instead of food, several books and sheets of paper were spread out in front of them. Zeke glanced up, his expression an odd combination of pride and embarrassment.

"Good evening, Caleb," Ruth said, her voice cool.

He drank in her beauty—the sleek, darkness of her hair, her large eyes and the way her mouth moved as she spoke. He was aching and hard in less than a heartbeat.

"Ruth." He forced himself to turn his attention to his son. "Zeke, what are you doing?"

Zeke sprang to his feet and ran over to him. Caleb caught the boy in his arms and pulled him close.

"Ruth is learnin' me my letters. I can almost read."

He glanced at her over Zeke's slender shoulder. "I didn't realize you had taken on the chore of school-teacher."

She busied herself with collecting the books into a neat pile. "It's not a chore. I enjoy reading. Zeke started asking me questions about my book. One thing led to another and now he knows his letters. He's very smart. I suspect he'll be reading in a few days."

Zeke grinned with pride. "See, Pa. I'm real smart. Ruth says so."

"I heard. However you still have to go to school when the new teacher arrives." He set the boy on the floor.

Zeke put his hands on his hips. "Aw, Pa. Why?"

Caleb ruffled the boy's hair. "It's time for you to get ready for bed. Change your clothes. I'll be right up to say good-night."

Zeke started to argue, then turned and gave Ruth a brief hug. He ran out of the room, then thundered up the stairs. For the thousandth time, Caleb found himself wondering how his parents had survived having three boys instead of just one.

Ruth picked up the books and carried them over to a shelf by the window. "He's learning very quickly. If there's time before the housekeeper arrives, I might start him on his numbers, as well."

She was careful to keep her back to him. Her body was stiff, her voice clipped. Caleb wished there was a way to go back to that morning and change what had happened between them. Or if he wasn't willing to give up the kiss, perhaps he could simply act differently when it was over.

"I'm sorry," he said simply. "About this morning."

Her spine straightened even more. "There's nothing to apologize for."

"Yes, there is. I shouldn't have..." He hesitated. "When we were kissing and you—"

She turned to face him. Color flared on her cheeks. "I'm aware that I acted in an unladylike manner and shocked you. I'm the one who should apologize for my unnatural behavior."

She sounded formal and very cold. He noticed that her hands were tightly clasped together. Without thinking, he crossed to her and took those two small fists in his hands.

"No," he said quietly as he slipped his thumb under her curled fingers. "You didn't do anything wrong. You shouldn't apologize. It's not that you shocked me or—" What was it she'd said? "—acted in an unnatural way. I very much enjoyed what we were doing. Too much."

A frown pulled her delicate brows together. "I don't understand. When I—well, while we were kissing and I responded in that way, you got angry."

That way. He knew she was talking about how she'd sucked on his tongue. He'd nearly lost control right then. He'd felt as randy as a sixteen-year-old boy, and about as practiced.

He released one of her hands to touch her face. "No. I wasn't angry." He hesitated. "All right. I *was* angry, but not at you. Never you, Ruth. I was aroused by what we were doing. I wanted to do more. I wanted to be with you, make love with you. I was afraid I was going to lose control. That's why I pulled back."

Some of the stiffness left her body. Questions filled her eyes, followed by a vulnerability he wouldn't have thought possible. Ruth always seemed so strong.

"You weren't shocked or offended?"

"Never. It was me, not you."

Her lips curved in a gentle smile. "Thank you for telling me."

"You're welcome."

He had a strong urge to kiss her again, to pull her close and claim her. But he didn't. For one thing, his son was waiting for him upstairs. For another, he'd learned his lesson where Ruth was concerned. For whatever reasons, she hadn't wanted him before and he wasn't about to make the mistake of asking her again.

CHAPTER FIVE

THE FOLLOWING MORNING, John appeared at the ranch house. Ruth opened the front door and smiled at her brother. "I hope you're here because you miss me and not because someone is sick."

He bent down and kissed her cheek, then stepped into the house. "I do miss you. I had business in town, so I stopped by to check on you before heading back to the village."

When he straightened, the bright sunlight illuminated him, reflecting off his dark hair and highlighting his strong cheekbones.

While Ruth and her brother shared the shape of their mouth and eyes, John had more sculpted features, and was several inches taller. He moved with the easy grace of a man at one with his world. She envied that—she had often been uncomfortable in both the white and Indian world, while John moved effortlessly between them. For her, being half white had made her feel different, and she'd been aware of a sense of being an outsider. It was only after several years of living among the Cheyenne that she'd finally felt as if she belonged.

He sniffed the air, then turned toward the kitchen. "You've been baking," he said, following the scent of cinnamon.

She laughed. "Yes. I made cinnamon rolls for breakfast. There are even a few left over. Have a seat. I'll pour you some coffee.''

She prepared them each a plate of the sticky treat and poured two mugs of coffee. As she slid into a seat across from her brother, she asked him to tell her about life in the village.

''We're well,'' he said, then told her all that had happened in the week she'd been gone. ''Your herbs and plants are growing well. You need not worry.''

She avoided his gaze as she realized she hadn't been worried. If she were honest with herself she would have to admit that she hadn't given her Indian life more than a passing thought since she'd arrived at Caleb's ranch. That was because she had so much to do, she told herself, refusing to feel guilty, yet still feeling strange. How could something so important be so easily dismissed?

''Are you happy here?'' her brother asked.

''I'm busy,'' she said, hoping he wouldn't notice she hadn't answered the question. ''Between caring for the house and cooking, I can fill nearly all the hours of the day. I'm also teaching Zeke his letters. He's going to be reading soon.'' She sighed happily. ''He's such a good boy. Smart and eager. I predict great things for him.''

John's dark gaze never strayed from her face. ''And Caleb?''

Her brother knew too much about her past, she thought. He knew about her month on the ranch nine years before and even that Caleb had proposed.

''He has changed some,'' she said. ''I find him a good father.''

''Nothing more?''

She forced herself to smile slightly, showing no extraordinary interest—as if they were discussing the weather. She would *not* allow herself to remember the kiss they'd shared the previous day, or the tingle that filled her when she recalled Caleb's confession of how he'd nearly been swept away by passion.

"We're friends," she said firmly.

"I'm pleased. Then you won't be upset to hear he has a telegram." John drew a piece of paper from his jacket pocket and pushed it across the table.

Ruth stared at the printed words, but couldn't seem to make herself read them. Was it bad news? Had one of Caleb's brother's been killed? When she didn't move to pick up the sheet, he leaned toward her.

"Martin, in the telegraph office, gave it to me when he saw me in town. He knew that I would be coming here to see you. Caleb has hired a housekeeper. She was due to arrive any day, however she has been delayed. An illness in the family. She won't be here for at least three weeks."

Ruth touched the paper, but still didn't try to read it. Three weeks? She hadn't allowed herself to think about the arrival of Caleb's new housekeeper because that would mean it was time for her to leave. But in the back of her mind, she'd known the day was coming when she must return to her own world. Now there had been a reprieve...or had there?

"What will you do?" John asked.

"I don't know." She drew in a breath and let it out slowly. She had come to the ranch because she'd been unwilling to admit that seeing Caleb again after their many years apart might disturb her. Now that she'd spent nearly a week here, she found she was enjoying herself.

She felt strange stirrings when Caleb was around. She looked forward to seeing him and speaking with him. Their kiss had been everything she'd remembered and quite a few wonderful things she had not. While she'd spent the previous day convinced that she'd behaved like a loose woman and had disgusted him, he'd carefully explained that wasn't true at all. He'd liked her attentions.

Last night she'd found herself wanting more. She'd lain awake wondering what it would be like to be with Caleb in the most intimate way possible. Making love. He'd said that to her. While she didn't have any first-hand knowledge, she knew what went on between a man and a woman. She'd never imagined herself wanting such a thing—until now.

And yet this wasn't her world. She didn't belong here, and if she stayed too long she would be forcibly reminded.

"I suppose I should return to the village," she said slowly.

"Why?"

"It's where I belong."

John shook his head. "I think you belong here. I think you're afraid."

Caleb had also accused her of acting out of fear.

"I had good reason to worry," she reminded him. "Had I stayed here, I could have been murdered in my bed."

"Caleb would never have permitted that to happen. He would have died first." John spoke with great certainty, as if the two men had discussed the possibility.

Ruth stirred restlessly, placing her hands in her lap and twisting her fingers together. "That's easy to say, after the fact."

"Fear steals the warrior's strength, making him vulnerable to his enemies."

"I'm not a warrior."

"In battles of the heart, we must all fight for that which we desire. Are you so sure that leaving nine years ago was the right thing to do?"

She started to answer, then pressed her lips together. Was this a battle of the heart? Had it been so back then?

"I have a healing talent," she reminded him. "I have to respect that, or it will be taken from me."

Her brother's expression turned impatient. "Why do you persist in thinking that your gifts are only temporary? The spirits do not give to you only to take it back if you love a man and have his children. The spirits celebrate life. Which of your words are truth and which are an excuse?"

She had never really been angry at her brother, but at that moment Ruth was ready to start throwing things. She glared at John. "You come in here and eat my food, only to criticize me."

"Never. You are my sister by blood and the sister of my heart. I only want your happiness. I've watched you struggle all your life. When our parents were alive and you left to travel with them each spring, I saw how you weren't sure you wanted to go. You were confused by the marriage of an Indian man to a white woman. When you returned each fall, you had to relearn our ways. Not the actions, for those you remembered, but the soul of the Cheyenne. I held you as you suffered after the loss of our parents.''

She set her hands on the table and he reached across to place his fingers on hers.

''I have seen you grow from a girl to a beautiful woman,'' he continued. ''I ached when I heard what those men had tried to do to you and I rejoiced when I learned of the Kincaid family's kindness. Caleb wanted to marry you and you refused him, which was your right. But I have always wondered why. I heard the words you spoke, but I didn't believe them. I don't believe them today. But what I believe isn't important. All I ask is that you search your heart and soul so that you can believe yourself.''

With that, he rose and walked around the table. After kissing her cheek, he moved toward the back door and was gone.

Ruth stared after him. She wanted to dismiss his words, but she couldn't. There was a small chance that he was right. What was truth and what was just an excuse?

She spent the rest of the morning trying not to think about John's visit, or the fact that there was no house-keeper arriving anytime soon to make the decision for her.

Shortly after noon, a woman drove into the yard. She was small and pale, with wisps of lank blond hair fluttering around her face. Ruth noticed her as she hurried toward the rear of the house. She recognized the worry in the woman's face and the urgency in her step. Ruth already had her medicine bag in her hand when she answered the door.

''I'm Mary Jefferson,'' the woman said quickly. She

couldn't have been more than twenty-five, yet there were lines of weariness around her mouth. Her dress was threadbare and patched, hanging loosely on her too thin frame. "My baby has a fever. I can't make it go away. It's been two days." Tears filled her pale-green eyes and trickled down her cheeks. "Please. You must help me."

"Of course," Ruth said. She paused long enough to set the soup on a back burner of the stove and write a note for Caleb, then she collected her cloak, left the house and the two women ran toward the waiting wagon.

"I think she caught a chill," Mary explained as she urged her horse forward. "She'd been coughing for a few days, but there wasn't any fever. I made a poultice for her chest and that seemed to help."

The woman looked at Ruth anxiously, as if expecting criticism.

"I'm sure I would have done the same," Ruth said calmly, knowing there was no reason to discuss what should have been done until she had seen the baby.

"My Ronald spoke to your brother when he was in town this morning," Mary told her. "We're saving to buy some horses and Ronald says your brother is the best judge of horseflesh in the county. When Ronald mentioned that our little one was running a fever, John—Mr. Whitefeather—mentioned you were staying at the Kincaid ranch. It was so close. That's why I came to get you. I hope you don't mind."

More tears filled Mary's eyes. Ruth put a reassuring hand on her arm. "I understand, and I'm happy to help."

"I don't know if we can pay you. At least not right

now. Maybe when some of the crops come in. Would that be all right?''

The shame and worry in Mary's voice cut through to Ruth's heart. "Please don't worry about payment. I'll do what I can to save your daughter regardless of your circumstances."

Mary nodded gratefully, then concentrated on the rutted road.

The journey to the Johnson ranch took nearly two hours. It was early afternoon by the time they arrived. The house was small, but well built. Only two or three rooms from the looks of it. Four children spilled out the front door, the youngest barely able to walk on his own. A thin teenage girl followed them. Despite the cool, damp earth and the slight chill in the air, all the children were barefoot.

"How is she?" Mary called to the teenager.

"About the same."

Mary murmured something that sounded like a prayer before setting the brake on the wagon. After securing the horse to a post, she hurried toward the house. She scooped up the two youngest as she walked, smiled at the rest and bent to kiss the teenager's cheek. "You're a blessing to me, Alice."

The teenager blushed slightly. She was dark haired, while the rest of the children were fair, and looked nothing like Mary or her children. Plus Mary wasn't old enough to be mother to Alice. A child of Ronald's from a previous marriage? Ruth wondered as she stepped into the tiny house. Or perhaps an orphan Mary and her husband had taken in.

The kitchen was small but clean. Open shelves held bits of crockery, while a pot simmered on the stove.

There were books on the scrubbed table, the pages tattered, but still readable.

"In here," Mary said, holding open a narrow door.

A bed took up most of the floor in the small room. A crib had been wedged between the bed and the wall and a child's labored breathing could be heard.

Ruth shrugged out of her cloak. As she bent over the child, she could feel the waves of heat radiating out from her too warm skin. "I'll need two bowls of cool water and a bottle," she said as she touched the soft skin of the baby girl. Small eyes opened to reveal dark pupils.

She unwrapped the cloths from around the child, then looked in her mouth and her ears. There wasn't a rash, but the fever was high—too high. Ruth deliberately pressed a fingernail into the bottom of the baby's foot. To her relief, the child murmured in protest and pulled her chubby leg toward her chest. At least the little girl wasn't too far gone.

"What's her name?" she asked when Mary returned with the requested supplies.

"Lily, after Ronald's mother."

"A pretty name for a pretty girl," Ruth said with a slight smile.

She reached in her bag for several herbs and poured them into one of the bowls. The children crowded around the door until Alice led them away. Mary might be too thin, but her children weren't starving, which meant she gave them the best of what she had. The patched clothes were clean, the house tidy. Ruth wished she'd thought to bring food along with medicine. Mary and Ronald were obviously doing their best for their children. They simply needed a helping hand.

When the herbal mixture was ready, she carefully poured it into a bottle. She picked up Lily and handed the baby to her mother.

"Feed her this. She doesn't have to drink all of it. I'll be giving it to her throughout the day. But get her to take as much as you can."

Mary's eyes widened, but she did as Ruth requested. While the baby fussed and drank a little, then fussed more, Ruth prepared the medicines she would use to draw out the fever.

Over the next few hours, the two women worked together. Ruth and Mary took turns bathing the baby with tepid water. Ruth rubbed a special paste over her back and arms, then laid damp cloths over the medicine. Little Lily didn't cry, although she made tiny, sad noises and occasionally had trouble breathing.

Time passed slowly, but Ruth didn't mind. She understood about healing. She put treated wood into the small fireplace and filled the room with a scented smoke that eased Lily's restlessness.

"Do you mind if I pray?" Mary asked late that afternoon.

Ruth looked up from her task of running a cooling rag along Lily's legs. "I think we should pray together," she said quietly, then joined Mary at the foot of the bed where they knelt.

Ronald appeared as the sun set. He was a slight man, nearly as thin as his wife and pale with worry. Ruth urged him to help Alice with the children, then told Mary it was all right to leave the sick room long enough to eat with her family. Ruth sat alone in the small bedroom, her hand on Lily's bare back, her body beginning to tire. She kept all her attention on the small life. She had prayed with Mary and now she began her own words of request to the great spirits. That this life would be allowed to continue. Not for Lily's sake, but for the family's. Death was always harder on those left behind.

Sometime later, the baby's skin temperature seemed to rise. Ruth remained calm, even as she knew the tiny body couldn't hold on much longer. Then a sharp cry pierced the night. Lily opened her eyes and screamed out her displeasure as she suddenly began to sweat.

Mary rushed into the room. Ruth rose and smiled. "The fever's broken."

Mary wrapped her daughter in a length of cloth and held her close. The rest of the family spilled into the room. Ronald reached her first and gravely shook her hand.

"I'm beholden to you," he said.

"I'm happy I could help." She touched the baby's forehead. Already her skin had cooled to nearly normal. "She'll be hungry. Don't give her too much over the next two days. And keep feeding her the herb broth. I'll fix up another batch for you. In three or four days, she'll be just like she was before. Babies always recover so quickly."

Or they don't recover at all, she thought, but didn't speak the words. The Jeffersons were happy with their blessing and she was content as well.

Alice took her into the kitchen and offered her a bowl of thin soup. When she'd eaten, Ruth prepared a sleeping potion for Mary, then told Ronald he was to let his wife rest through the night. She had just begun to wonder how she was supposed to make her way back to the Kincaid ranch when there was the sound of a wagon outside.

She had no way of knowing who had arrived this late in the evening, but that didn't stop her foolish heart from beating faster. Gladness lightened her step as she hurried toward the kitchen. As she flung open the door, she saw Caleb stepping down from a large wagon. He held a lantern in his hand, and another sat on the seat.

Their gazes locked in the still night air. In a flash, she remembered what it had been like to be in his arms and it took all her strength to keep from running into them now. She wanted to touch him and be held close. She wanted him to kiss her fiercely and tell her that he'd missed her. Instead he gave her a slow smile that made her stomach clench and her toes curl.

"I was worried about you," he said simply.

"I left a note."

He nodded. "Thank you for taking the time to do that."

Ronald stepped out of the house and walked toward Caleb. "I'm sorry you had to make the trip out here. I would have brought Miss Ruth home."

Several thoughts filled Ruth's head. First that Ronald assumed the ranch was her home. It wasn't, of course. She belonged with the Cheyenne. Yet she knew she wasn't ready to return to her people. She also realized that Ronald had been calling her "Miss Ruth" ever since he'd arrived at the house. In fact both he and his wife, along with their children, had been respectful and grateful for her assistance. No one had said anything about her being half Indian.

The two men shook hands. "I knew she'd be safe with you," Caleb told the much smaller man. "But I thought I'd save you the trip." He glanced back at her. "How's the baby?"

"Doing well. The fever broke. I think she'll be fine."

"Good." He walked toward the rear of the wagon. "Ronald, would you help me unload these?"

It was only then that Ruth noticed the supplies loaded into the back of the wagon. There were barrels of flour and sugar, sides of beef, great hams and bags of dried fruit.

Ronald hesitated as Caleb rolled a barrel of flour toward himself. He drew back his shoulders and stood a little taller. It might be dark out, but Ruth could easily imagine his expression of pride.

"We don't need your charity," he said simply.

Caleb put his hands on his hips. "It's not charity. It's the way things are. The first four or five years of starting a ranch are hell. Half the settlers don't make it through the first winter. My own parents nearly starved to death three or four times. If the Cheyenne hadn't brought them fresh game, they would have."

He hoisted the barrel onto his shoulder and started for the rear of the house. "This is the way we do things out here, Ronald. I'm only sorry that I've been so busy. I should have been by sooner."

"But we can't accept this."

"You can and you will. But don't think you get it for free. In a year or two, when you're settled and comfortable, then you have the responsibility of looking around the community and finding out who's in need. Then you do the same for them. This is Whitehorn. We take care of our own."

Ronald glanced at the house. Ruth could practically

feel the struggle taking place inside him. She wasn't sure what finally won him over, Caleb's words or the hunger in his children's eyes. Either way, he nodded and grabbed a large ham, then showed Caleb into the house.

Less than an hour later, Ruth and Caleb were on their way back to the Kincaid ranch. She pulled the extra blanket he'd brought with him around her shoulders and allowed her weariness to flow out of her.

"Cold?" Caleb asked as he urged the horse forward.

"Not really. Just tired. It was a long day."

A bright moon illuminated the rutted track and the horses easily picked their way.

"Thank you for helping them," he said.

"You don't have to thank me. It's what I do." She paused for a moment. "No one in the ranching community has come to me for help since I've been at your ranch. At first I thought it was because they didn't know I was here. Then I thought maybe it was because they didn't want my help."

He turned his head and glanced at her. "Did you ever consider that it's only been about a week? Maybe no one's been sick. Why do you have to assume that your being half Cheyenne makes people not trust you?"

"Because some don't. I know you think I've made a fuss about things that don't matter, but you haven't been around when people have stared and ignored me, or been rude."

There were also those men in town who had tried to rape her, but she wasn't going to talk about that. Not tonight.

"You can't know what it's like not to fit in either

place," she continued. "I've worked hard to make my peace with the Cheyenne. That's where I belong now."

"Seems to me Mary and Ronald would disagree."

"They're the exception."

"I disagree."

It wasn't a declaration of any kind. He was simply saying that she shouldn't shut herself away from the white world. She knew that and yet a part of her wanted to believe he was speaking about something more. Something special. She wanted to think that he'd been caught up in the past as much as she had, and that he liked her now as much as he had then...perhaps more.

"Thank you for bringing food to them," she said, knowing she was a coward for changing the subject.

"I meant to do it before. Ronald Jefferson has a lot of heart and is willing to work hard, but he didn't have much before he started his ranch, and he has even less now. Every penny is turned back into the ranch. From what I can tell, the children don't go hungry, but the same couldn't be said for him and Mary."

"I agree. And you knew just what to say to convince him to accept your gift."

"I was telling the truth. In a few years, he'll be a wealthy rancher. Then it will be his turn to help out his neighbors."

Caleb was describing a close-knit community. Was it one she could be a part of? Did she want to be? Were the two of them being given a second chance?

Hope and fear battled in her stomach, making her press her hands to her midsection.

"Is Zeke alone in the house?" she asked, in an effort to distract herself.

"No. When I read your note, I sent him to spend the night in the bunkhouse. The men will spoil him. I told Hank I didn't want them teaching him how to play poker, but it's just a matter of time until he learns."

"Maybe they could play a card game that involves counting," she said. "At least then he would be learning something."

Caleb flashed her a grin. "Ever practical, aren't you?"

She nodded, then relaxed against the seat. They settled into a companionable silence. There were occasional night sounds around them. Eventually the terrain became familiar and she knew they were back on Kincaid land.

How would her life have been different if she'd accepted Caleb's proposal? Would she, as she'd feared, have lost her healing gift? Or would she now be a wife and a mother, going out to help others whenever she was needed? She tried to imagine what her children would have looked like. Her own mother had been fair, with light eyes. She looked more like her father. Yet what about their children? She imagined a boy not too different from Zeke, and maybe a little girl with dark curls. Then she remembered the men who had attacked her and realized that instead of happily married, she could easily be dead—killed by strangers who didn't like half-breed Indian women.

When they arrived at the house, Ruth was no closer to an answer about the past, or her future. Had she, as her brother had claimed, acted out of fear instead of respect for her gift? And if it had been fear, what would happen if she allowed herself to let it go? Would she want another chance with Caleb? Would he be interested in her?

The barn door opened, and a yawning Tully appeared. "I'll t-take care of the horses, b-boss," he said sleepily.

"Thanks."

Caleb stepped down, then came around the wagon to help her to her feet. His hands were strong and sure on her waist. She found herself leaning into him when she should have been steady.

"Are you all right?" he asked.

She nodded, even though she wasn't.

"Are you hungry?" he asked as he led her into the house. "Do you want me to fix you something?"

That made her laugh. "You know how to cook?"

"No, but the soup you left is still warm."

They walked into the kitchen. Ruth breathed in the scent of her cooking and the polish she'd used on the furniture the previous day. Although she'd only been at the ranch a week, it had already become a welcoming place. Did she want it for her home?

Caleb touched her arm. "Ruth, what are you thinking? You have the strangest expression."

What was she supposed to say? That she was rethinking her past? That maybe he and John had been right and nine years ago she'd acted out of fear?

She remembered how all those years ago, he'd been so gentle with her. He'd kissed her, but had never tried to dishonor her. She'd felt so safe in his arms. Safe, but very alive. Their last kiss had made her feel a passion she'd never experienced before.

He startled her by swearing loudly. "Stop it," he insisted. "I know you don't mean it."

"I have no idea what you're talking about."

"Your eyes. They're saying things."

"What things?"

He shrugged. "Things a woman says when she—" He broke off.

Then she knew. Her eyes were speaking the truth of her woman's heart. She took a step toward him and placed her hand on his arm. "Are they saying that I'm remembering what it was like to kiss you and that I want to do it again?"

"Yes." The word came out on a growl.

"Perhaps you should listen."

CHAPTER SIX

Ruth held her breath. Was Caleb going to turn from her, as he had before? Fear threatened, but she pushed it away. She had a feeling that fear had ruled her for too long. This time she was going to make the decision that was right because it was what she wanted, and not because she was afraid.

But instead of rejecting her, Caleb swept her up in his arms. Even as his arms came around her, his mouth dropped to hers. They were kissing wildly, passionately. This was no tentative brush of lips—instead they plundered each other, tasting, circling, nibbling, wanting. She wrapped her arms around his neck as he started to carry her up the stairs of the ranch house. They moved into darkness and still she clung to him because he was all that she'd ever needed.

His footsteps on the wooden floor sounded nearly as loud as the thundering of her heart. He didn't even break the kiss as he carried her through a door into his bedroom. They clung together until he set her on her feet.

He left her alone long enough to light a single lantern, then he returned to stand in front of her.

"I want you," he breathed, cupping her face in his hands. "I want you."

Kisses rained on her face, soft, tender touches that made her shiver and long for even more intimacy.

"Ruth," he breathed. "Tell me you want to make love with me as well."

"Yes," she told him. "I want to be with you. I want to know everything about you."

Fire danced in his eyes. The bright passion convinced her as no words could have done. His fingers trembled slightly where they traced her features.

"Take down your hair," he said hoarsely, as he reached for the buttons on the front of her blouse.

That morning she'd put her hair up, just for a change. Now she reached for the pins holding it in place. As she loosened the knot at the base of her neck, he unfastened the front of her blouse, then pulled the fabric aside. His gaze settled on her breasts pressing against the thin fabric of her chemise.

A trickle of uncertainty made her freeze in place. No man had seen her this way. She wasn't worried that their joining was wrong—just that she was unsure of the details of what would occur.

Caleb caught her hesitation. He dropped his hands to his side and swore under his breath. "You're a virgin," he said flatly.

In that moment, she knew the honor of the man before her. His arousal pressed against the front of his trousers. She could see the need in the harsh lines of his face. He wanted her. She didn't doubt that he hadn't been with a woman in a long time and that his desire was nearly uncontrollable. And yet he would walk away because it was the right thing to do.

Warmth filled her heart. It surrounded the old pain and fear, heating it until it melted away, leaving her feeling light and nearly giddy with happiness. Why hadn't she seen the inherent goodness of him before? He was as much a part of her as the color of her eyes. He had always been a part of her. She'd simply been unwilling to see the truth of it.

"Love me," she said simply, and took his hand in hers. She pressed his palm flat against her breast, then gasped aloud at the intense pleasure that shot through her.

He closed his hand around her curve, moving against her tight nipple and making her cry out. Then she was in his arms, his mouth on hers. She clung to him, wanting him as she'd never wanted anything in her life.

Still kissing her deeply, he held her against him even as he carefully finished unfastening her hair. Then he slowly removed her clothing until she was in only her chemise and pantaloons. He shrugged out of his own clothing, leaving on drawers that did little to conceal his arousal.

"I'm a healer," she said with a smile as he drew back the covers on the large bed and urged her to slip onto the mattress. "I've seen naked men before."

"Good."

He accepted her challenge and responded with one of his own. With a quick, fluid movement, he shoved his drawers to the ground and stepped out of them.

Ruth had one knee on the bed. She froze in place, her gaze fixed on that most male part of him. Seeing naked men who were ill and seeing *this* particular naked man were two very different things. He was powerful and sleek, a thick crown of blond hair adorning his male glory.

As she continued to look her fill, she felt herself

ready and swell. An ache settled deep in her belly and radiated to that place between her thighs, then higher to her breasts. It was as if she'd waited for this all her life. She felt only rightness, and a sense of fulfilling her destiny.

She slipped onto the mattress and held out her arms. Caleb joined her. He touched every part of her, stroking her bare arms, then cupping her breasts in his palms. Strong fingers teased her tight nipples, making her arch against him. They kissed again, and as his tongue stroked against hers, she felt his fingers slip down her belly toward her rising heat.

Instinctively, she parted her legs, welcoming him. She knew he was going to touch her and that she was probably going to like it. In the village, women talked freely among themselves. Ruth knew about the physical pleasure available to a woman when a man took the time to please her. She responded eagerly when he pushed against the thin layer of her pantaloons and touched her dampness.

She felt as if she'd been bathed in warm pleasure. Delicious sensation filled her as he rubbed and circled one incredibly sensitive spot. He dipped his head and, at the same time, took a nipple in his mouth.

The combination of sucking and touching made her call out his name. Suddenly her clothes were too much. She pushed at her pantaloons. Caleb helped her drag them off. She opened her legs for him, practically begging him to touch her again in that way. To make her feel the things she hadn't known she could.

He didn't disappoint her. Instead he slipped a finger deep inside her and used his thumb to rub that magical pressure point. She found herself tensing and squirm-

ing, grasping for him and then crying out his name as
her world came apart. It was perfect, she thought hazily, lost in the sensation. Perfect and better than she'd
imagined.

When the last ripple faded, she reached for him,
drawing him over her, urging him to enter her.

"Make me yours," she breathed, then pressed her
mouth to his.

His maleness probed her virgin center. When he
reached a hand between them to guide himself inside,
she stroked the length of his back and thought how she
would like to lie like this every night, knowing that he
wanted her and that together they would teach each
other to soar and touch the heavens.

He eased into her slowly. The sensation of something too large stretching her faded into a heaviness
that promised another release. A sharp pain made her
stiffen, but she didn't tell him to stop.

"Ruth," he murmured, staring deeply into her eyes.

She gazed back at him, feeling her love grow. He
thrust into her fully, then groaned.

"More," she told him. "I want to know everything."

He drew back and filled her again. The pain disappeared, leaving only a tingling. Next time, she thought
contentedly as he moved faster, then stiffened. Next
time they would find their release together.

She held him as he stilled and cried out, then he held
her as they curled up together, and slept into the night.

"IT'S MY FAULT Will left," Caleb said into the darkness.

Ruth rested her head on her pillow. They had slept

for a few hours, then had awakened to make love again. This time they had moved together, both of them soaring at the same moment. In the tender quiet that followed, Caleb had begun to speak of his brother.

"Why would you say that?" she asked.

"Because I'm the one who drove him away. I never understood how he hated being second born. Our father insisted on leaving everything to me. As the oldest, I knew of my inheritance practically from the time I could walk. I never thought that Will would resent getting nothing. He lashed out in anger."

"What did he do?"

She heard a rustling sound and knew that Caleb had sat up. A match scratched, then flared. She watched as he lit the lantern on the bedside table. Then he leaned against the headboard and rubbed his temples.

"I never told anyone," he said quietly. "At first because I couldn't believe he'd done it and later because I was ashamed of him. Or maybe I was ashamed of myself." He looked at her. "Will stole a lot of money before he left."

She sat up and drew the sheet to her breasts. Her long hair tumbled over her shoulders. "Do you think he wanted to go somewhere else and start over?"

Caleb nodded. "At the time I'd been furious, but now I understand. I want—" He hesitated.

She touched his cheek, rubbing the back of her hand against his blond stubble. "You want him to come back."

He nodded. "I don't know where to find him. I've thought of hiring a detective, but I couldn't even tell him where to start." He grabbed her hand and kissed her palm. "Brock's gone, too."

"He was always a wanderer."

"I know, but this is the longest he's been gone. I worry that something's happened to him."

He spoke of his brothers and the ranch, his hopes for Zeke. Ruth realized Caleb was a man who held himself apart. He didn't trust many people with his secrets and she was honored that he was willing to share them with her now.

"What do you want for yourself?" she asked.

He looked at her, but didn't answer the question. She told herself not to be disappointed. She and Caleb were just beginning their journey. She didn't know where it was going to end, but this time she wasn't going to let fear drive her away.

"I always wanted a wife and a family," he said at last.

"You have had both."

"No. I have a son, but I never had a wife."

He took her hand in his, then gave her a slight smile. "I want you to know the truth, Ruth. But I don't want to tell you what it is. I'm afraid of what you'll think of me."

She leaned toward him and pressed her mouth to his. While she wasn't ready to tell him that she loved him, she was more than prepared to offer reassurance. "I know the truth about you. I know you are a good man. You can't say anything to make me change my opinion."

"I hope that's true." He squeezed her fingers. "After you went back to the Cheyenne all those years ago, I couldn't stay on the ranch. There were too many memories."

She winced slightly. "I never meant to hurt you."

"I know. I even understand why you made the choice you did." He drew in a deep breath. "To distract myself, I headed to Texas to buy a couple of bulls. The owner of the ranch had a daughter—Marie."

Ruth tried not to let the truth hurt her. She forced her voice to stay steady as she said, "You fell instantly in love with her."

With his free hand he tucked her hair behind her ears, then smiled. "Not even close. She was a viper-tongued, selfish, spoiled woman who only cared about riding and buying expensive clothes. What I didn't know was that she'd chased off all the local men and was in danger of being an old maid. She had vowed to marry the next suitable man she met. Who turned out to be me."

"I don't understand."

His blue-gray gaze settled on her face. "I missed you," he said simply. "One night I got drunk and Marie came into my room. I'll admit I could have turned her down, but I was tired of being alone. So I let her crawl into my bed." His mouth twisted. "She wasn't a virgin, but the next morning she told her father that she had been and I found myself facing the business end of a shotgun. The marriage went downhill from there."

"I'm sorry," she said, and meant the words, although she couldn't help feeling a little happy that he hadn't dismissed her so quickly by falling in love with someone else.

"Weren't there a few pleasant times?" she asked.

"Some. They're hard to remember. Marie hated everything about being a mother and she hated Montana even more. The winters were too long and too cold.

She wanted me to sell everything and head to Texas. When I refused to do it, she set out to make my life hell. She did a fine job. The only decent think to come out of her was Zeke.''

He squeezed her hand, then released it. ''I want you to know how it was between us. I don't want you wondering.''

''I understand.''

He rubbed his thumb against her skin. ''Do you know why I didn't send for you when Marie died?''

''No. I thought she'd gone quickly.''

He shook his head. ''She lingered for days, but she wouldn't let me bring you to help her. It wasn't because you're half Cheyenne,'' he added quickly. ''It was something else entirely.''

Suddenly she wasn't sure she wanted to know the rest of the story. But when she didn't speak, Caleb continued.

''On our wedding night, when I was inside her, I called out your name,'' he said flatly, staring at the far wall. ''She never forgave me. When we arrived here, she managed to find out about your stay and how I'd wanted to marry you. She made sure I paid for having loved you.''

Ruth leaned toward him and rested her head on his shoulder. ''I'm sorry.''

''Don't be. I got over you, in a manner of speaking.''

''But I'm back now.''

''For how long? I saw the telegram. My housekeeper won't be here for a while. Are you staying or leaving?''

She kissed his neck. ''After last night, how can you ask?''

"After last night the question matters more than ever."

"I'm staying."

Caleb wanted to ask for how long. Was it just until the housekeeper arrived, or could he convince her to stay forever? Because that was still what he wanted. The same thing he'd wanted all those years ago. He'd realized it the moment he'd arrived at the house that evening and had found her gone.

The silence of the kitchen, the darkness spilling into every room had nearly destroyed him. Even finding her note and knowing that she hadn't left but was instead helping a neighbor hadn't made him feel any better. Because he'd realized then that her stay was only temporary. And when she left, she would be taking the rest of his soul with her.

He supposed that a sensible man would want her to go now, rather than endure the uncertainty. But he didn't, because he would rather have these few weeks with her than nothing at all. She'd always been the best part of him. He was a better man when she was around. Talking about his brothers and all he'd done to run them off had reminded him that he needed to be at his best. Not just for them if they returned, but for his son. And possibly even for himself.

THE DAYS slipped by quickly. At times Caleb knew that he needed to tell Ruth that he wanted her to remain on the ranch. He had to confess his feelings and give her the chance to make a decision. However, he never found the right time, or even the right words.

He walked toward the house one evening, nearly three weeks after she'd first made love with him. He could hear the sound of her conversation with Zeke and their laughter. The happiness in his son's voice tugged at his heart. Ruth had done so much. She'd brought joy into his child's life and had shown Zeke that not all women were like his mother.

"I'm back," Caleb called after he'd wiped his feet. He stepped into the kitchen and Zeke bounded from his chair to greet him.

"Pa! You're early!"

Zeke threw himself at his father. Caleb caught him in midjump. "I know. What have you been doing with yourself?"

Zeke hugged him hard, then grinned. "Ruth was reading me a story about a boy and his dog. They're from England, but they went on a big ship and ended up in Spain. Then we looked at a different book and she showed me where Spain was." He paused and his expression turned serious. "It's very far."

"I know."

Caleb glanced at Ruth. She was busy rolling a pie crust, but she paused long enough to give him a slow smile of welcome that made his blood run hot and had him picturing exactly what he would do with her later that evening when she slipped from her bedroom into his.

Zeke drew in a deep breath. "Then we went back to the story. It was very good. The boy and his dog made it home and everyone had missed them and he had lots of great stories to tell."

He squirmed slightly, so Caleb put him down. Zeke shoved his hands in his pockets. "But Ruth had to start dinner and we were almost finished with the book, so she said I could read it aloud to her and we'd finish it together and I did!"

Caleb stared at his son. "You read the story by yourself?"

Zeke nodded vigorously, his too long hair flopping into his eyes. "The end part. So could we order some more books? Ruth says she knows the names of lots of stories about boys and dogs and even horses. And then we can read them together."

Caleb looked at the woman who had haunted him for so long. Her dark hair hung down her back in a thick braid, but he knew exactly how it felt when it was loose and spilling over her shoulders, onto his body as she leaned over him, teasing him in the delicious ways he'd taught her. He knew the sound of her voice in delight and in compassion. He knew she would be quick to put everything aside, if someone came needing help, which happened a couple of times a week.

He knew his footsteps were lighter because of her, and the days easier. What he didn't know was if she would stay.

Zeke tugged on his sleeve. "Can we, Pa? Can we buy some books?"

"Of course."

Zeke yelled with pleasure, and ran out of the room. He was back in a heartbeat, holding out a tattered envelope. "Tully went to town and brought this back. It's for you."

He glanced at the handwriting. It was nearly as familiar as his own. "It's from Will."

Zeke wrinkled his brow. "My uncle Will? Do I know him?"

"No, Zeke, he moved east before you were born."

Ruth abandoned her pie crust to come stand next to him. "Maybe it's good news."

"I hope so."

He took a seat at the table. Zeke slid onto his lap while Ruth put her hand on his shoulder. She squeezed gently.

"Do you want to read your letter in private?" she asked.

"No."

He opened the envelope and pulled out a single sheet, then read the letter aloud.

"Dear Caleb,

"I left the ranch and Whitehorn a long time ago, for reasons that don't seem so important now. I've traveled a long way and seen my share of the world. But no matter how far I go, I can't forget home. Now I think it's time for me to return. If you'll have me.

"I hope this letter finds you well. I'll wait to hear from you.

Will."

Caleb had to clear his throat. Will coming back? Was it possible?

Ruth leaned down and pressed her mouth to his cheek. "Are you going to answer him right away? So much has changed, and he doesn't even know it."

He nodded, not bothering to ask how she'd known that he would indeed welcome his brother home after all this time. Because Will was as much a part of the Kincaid ranch as himself. Will belonged here.

Ruth belonged here, too. Soon, he promised himself. Soon he would figure out how to ask her to stay.

CHAPTER SEVEN

Two weeks later

RUTH PUT OFF her trip into town for as long as she could. She knew if she'd mentioned her nervousness to Caleb, he would have accompanied her into White-horn, but that wouldn't force her to face her fears, which was what she wanted to do. So she waited until he had a full day planned out with the cattle, left Zeke in Tully's excellent care and headed her horse and wagon south.

As she traveled along the rutted road, she tried to remember if she'd been back in Whitehorn on her own even once in the past few years. But she didn't think she had. At first, after the attack, she'd sent others in with her medical supply list. Then she'd started going in with her brother, or others from the village. She'd never considered giving up the use of the medicines she could buy because they were too good for certain ailments. Patients came first regardless of her personal fears.

Yet she'd managed to avoid making this journey on her own since she'd been attacked. Ruth tried not to think about that horrible afternoon so long ago, then realized there was no point in continuing to hide from the past. It had happened, it had been ugly and she'd survived. In many ways, she'd been lucky. The men had bruised her and terrified her, but they hadn't physically hurt her. Only her spirit had been battered.

Even as the beauty of the land around her eased her soul, she tensed slightly as she remembered the horror of those men surrounding her and grabbing at her. They'd torn her dress, touched her, then tripped her so she'd fallen in the cold mud. Suddenly an avenging angel had appeared. Caleb had fought them off and rescued her.

She recalled him gently covering her with his coat and pulling her to her feet. He'd wrapped an arm around her to support her as he'd helped her to his wagon. Looking back, she supposed she should have been frightened of him as well, but she hadn't been. She'd taken one look into his eyes and had known she would be safe with him.

Safe. Comforted. Loved. She sighed with contentment as she reveled in the warmth filling her. She felt adored by both Caleb and Zeke. In a very short time, barely a month, the ranch had become her home. She knew now that her claims to have to stay unmarried to honor her gift had been what both John and Caleb had claimed—an excuse to hide. Now she was finished with excuses and turning her back on what was important. As soon as she faced the demons from her past and got through her trip to town unscathed, she would confess her feelings to Caleb. Last time he'd been the one to come to her with his heart in his hands. Now it was her turn.

When Whitehorn was in view, she sat straighter and squared her shoulders. She would go to the general store, pick up her supplies and leave. Simple enough.

Being afraid might make it difficult for her to breathe, but she would not give in to the fear. Not again. It had already cost her nine years of being with Caleb. They had much to make up for.

It was midweek and there was the usual crowd of shoppers walking along the wood plank sidewalks. A woman in a large pink bonnet decorated with unattractively large feathers called out a greeting.

Ruth waved in response, recognizing the mother of a teenage girl with terrible skin. Ruth had given the girl a special cream that had helped with her blemishes. Several other people spoke with Ruth, including the father of a young boy who had broken his arm the previous week. Ruth had set the bone and wrapped it tightly to heal.

"He hardly complains about the pain," the father, Harry Talbert, was saying as she drew her horse to a stop in front of the general store. "Runs around like it doesn't bother him at all. You said it would be about six weeks for the bone to knit back. Is that right?"

"Yes, Mr. Talbert." He was a tall man with bright-red hair and an easy smile. "Make sure the wrapping stays tight so the bone can't move."

"My wife checks it several times a day, but keeping young Peter quiet is nearly impossible. No doubt we'll need your services again."

He tied her horse to the hitching post, then held out his hand to help her down. Ruth hesitated, a little surprised by his politeness. It wasn't that Mr. Talbert had ever been rude, it was just that she wasn't used to being treated like everyone else.

Perhaps she'd never given people the opportunity.

She had no idea where the thought had come from

but once it arrived, she couldn't dismiss it. Not completely. Her disastrous trip into town nearly nine years before had been her first and only trip into Whitehorn by herself. Otherwise she'd always come with several other Cheyenne. She'd avoided the residents and ranchers, barely speaking, even when former patients stopped to chat. She'd expected to be slighted, so had seen disrespect in every glance, each tilt of the head or awkward word.

But what if they'd only been saying hello? What if they'd felt awkward too—grateful for her services and not sure how to thank her? Perhaps she had been the one to be rude, not them. Perhaps the slights had all been on her side.

The idea was so extraordinary, she wasn't completely able to believe it. Yet it rang with a truth that left her giddy. She tested her theory when Mr. Talbert returned to his barbershop. Instead of ducking her head, she nodded at people she knew. Amazingly, they all smiled at her. Most stopped to speak. The conversations were so friendly and long that it took her nearly an hour to walk the few feet to the front of the store.

Ruth entered the Mercantile with a lightness of heart she hadn't felt for a very long time. Perhaps everything was going to work out after all.

IT WAS NEARLY three by the time Ruth headed for her wagon. Her arms were full of packages and her face ached pleasantly from smiling so much. Several women she knew had been talking in the general store and they'd insisted Ruth join them for a meal at the restaurant across the street. There they'd all laughed and talked about their husbands and children, teasing

Ruth about Caleb. When Ruth had blushed, their looks had turned knowing and they'd asked about any special announcements.

Now, as she moved toward her horse, Ruth found herself smiling again. There was going to be an announcement—of that she was sure. She didn't know what Caleb would say when she told him, and she wasn't going to say anything until they'd had a chance to talk about their future, but come winter there would be another Kincaid in the world.

She'd only missed her monthly once, but the other signs were very clear. A baby, she thought happily. Having Caleb's child felt so very right. She had no concerns that loving him and having his baby would affect her healing gift. If anything, she felt more connected with her Cheyenne ancestors than before. She had stepped into the circle of birth, life and death with a contribution of her own.

"Get out of my way."

The loud voice startled Ruth. She jerked to a stop and stared at the tall, bearded man stopped in front of her. His thick coat hung open, exposing dirty clothes and a lean, strong body. Hatred spilled out of his small eyes.

"You heard me," he grumbled, and shoved her roughly to the side. "Damn Indian bitch."

Ruth was so stunned by his violent hatred that she couldn't do anything but stare at him. He shoved her again. This time she had trouble staying standing and several of her packages went flying. The man deliberately stepped on a small glass bottle containing laudanum, crushing it beneath his boot.

"What gives you the right?" he growled. "Showing

your face, same as white women. Only you're not like them, are you? Not good enough. Not good for anything.''

He advanced on her and grabbed the front of her dress. Somewhere in the scuffle, she'd lost her cloak.

'''cept maybe one thing.''

He shook her like a dog, then pushed her between two buildings. Even before his hand reached for the buttons on the front of his trousers, she knew what he was going to do.

She told herself to fight, to scream, to run, but she couldn't move. The world had tilted until everything had slowed and it was impossible for her to breathe. There would be no rescue this day. Caleb was out with the cattle and she hadn't even told him she was planning to come to town.

The man's lips continued to move, but she didn't hear him. She didn't hear anything until a rifle shot cut through the deathly silence.

''Take your hands off her or I'll shoot you where you stand.''

Ruth found the strength to turn and saw Ronald Jefferson pointing a rifle at her attacker. Several more men joined him. Two of the largest ones grabbed the man and threw him to the ground. Harry Talbert stepped on the back of his neck.

''I don't know who you are, but you're about to learn that no one attacks one of our women. This here is Whitehorn, mister, and we take care of our own.''

Ruth started to shake. The women who had invited her to lunch were suddenly at her side. They wrapped their arms around her and drew her to safety. When she started to cry, they held her and promised her vengeance.

"I'LL BE FINE," Ruth told the painfully young deputy who had escorted her back to the ranch. It was nearly dark and she knew she had to get dinner started right away.

"Are you sure, ma'am?" he asked, starting to dismount from his horse. "I could stay with you until Mr. Kincaid returns for the day."

"There are more than enough protectors on the ranch. Besides, I doubt that man will be bothering anyone for a while."

The deputy grinned. "Yes, ma'am!"

Ruth collected her packages from her wagon. She still felt shaken, but no longer afraid. The people in town had come to her rescue. The big bear of a man who had attacked her had been thrown in jail, but not before several of the men had taken a few hits, leaving him battered and repentant. Her packages had been collected, the broken ones replaced and there had been several offers to escort her home. Eventually the sheriff had sent a deputy, who now lingered despite backward glances toward them.

"Go!" she said, smiling for the first time since the attack. "If you hurry, you'll still be able to get a meal at the restaurant."

"Yes, ma'am." The deputy touched his hat and turned his horse back in the direction they'd come.

Ruth watched him go, then walked toward the house. While her lovely day had taken a turn for the worse, she'd managed to survive the experience. The assistance of the townspeople made her feel less frightened about what could happen. The worst had occurred and she'd survived.

"Ruth?"

She glanced up and saw a young woman hovering by the rear door of the house. "Nalla?" she asked, peering through the growing darkness.

The fourteen-year-old Cheyenne teenager ran toward her. "You must come," she said quickly. "My aunt has been delivering her baby these past two days. Her strength is gone and we fear for both her life and the unborn child. Please, you must come now."

Ruth didn't stop to think. Instead she simply dropped her packages where she stood, ran into the house and grabbed her bag. "Come on," she yelled at Nalla as she raced toward her wagon.

Tully stepped out of the barn. "M-Miss Ruth. You h-have a visitor."

"I know. Tell Caleb I had to go back to the Indian village," she called as she urged her horse north. "They need me. I'll be back as soon as I can."

Next to her, Nalla began to cry. "You must save her," the girl said. "I was waiting so long for you. I feared you would never come. My mother and father are gone and she is all the family I have left. Please, Ruth."

"We are all your family," Ruth said, sparing the teenager a quick smile. "I will do my best."

But was her best good enough? If only she hadn't gone into town. She would have been at the house when Nalla arrived. Two days in labor. Nalla's aunt already had three children. She would have known what to do when her time came, so there must be something very wrong. Ruth urged the horses to go faster and sent out a prayer that she could save both mother and child.

THE HOUSE WAS DARK when Caleb and Zeke stepped out of the barn. Tully had given them Ruth's message, so Caleb wasn't worried, even when he nearly tripped over the packages Ruth had dropped. He and Zeke picked them up and carried them inside, where they heated a stew she'd made the previous day.

"You think she'll be back in time to listen to me read tonight?" Zeke asked hopefully.

"I doubt it, son. Delivering babies can be a slow business."

Tully had told him about the pretty young Indian woman who had waited for Ruth most of the day. Caleb wondered briefly where she'd gone. Had there been another emergency? Had she—

The sound of a wagon made him frown. She couldn't be back already. But when he stepped outside, he found Ronald Jefferson stepping out of his rickety wagon.

The younger man nodded respectfully. "Evening, Caleb. I came by to check on Ruth. Is she all right?"

A dark, ugly cold filled Caleb's chest and sank into his belly. "Ruth isn't here. She had to go to the Indian village to help one of the women. Why did you want to make sure she was all right?"

Ronald shifted uncomfortably. "I'm sorry, Caleb. I thought you would already know." He cleared his throat. "She was in town today. When she was ready to leave, a man attacked her." He held up his hands. "Don't worry. He didn't do anything. Just scared her a little. I saw him grab her and found them standing in the alley. The other men in town helped me capture the man. He's in jail, although a little worse for wear. The sheriff sent a deputy to escort Ruth home.''

Ronald shrugged. ''I told Mary what happened and she wanted me to come see that Ruth was fine. After what she did for us, we're beholden to her.''

''I see.''

Caleb wasn't sure how he'd spoken the words. He felt as if he'd fallen into an icy lake and couldn't move or breathe. Nothing was as it should have been. Nothing was right. He'd lost everything.

Sharp pain cut through him, slicing his heart into tiny pieces then setting them on fire. His hopes and dreams—the ones he'd barely allowed himself to acknowledge—turned to dust and disappeared on the wind.

She was gone. A medical emergency had called her back to the tribe, but this time she wouldn't return. Her worst fears had been realized. She wasn't safe in his world.

Caleb closed his hands into fists. ''I'll kill him,'' he growled.

''You'd have to stand in line,'' Ronald told him. ''Ruth has helped most of the folks around here. To tell you the truth, we damn near killed that man already. The sheriff is going to send him to see the traveling judge when he arrives. Then he'll serve his time elsewhere. We don't want a man like that around our womenfolk.''

''Thanks for coming by,'' Caleb forced himself to say. He didn't bother to explain that it was unlikely Ruth would be worried about the man. After what had happened today, she would never go to town again.

Instead she would return to the Cheyenne to live her life in safety.

Ronald waved, then left. Caleb continued to stand in the yard, trying to tell himself that it wasn't as bad as he thought. That maybe Ruth would come back to him. But he knew the truth, just as he knew he couldn't survive without her. He'd loved her back then and he still loved her. He didn't want anyone else and if he couldn't have her, he would rather live alone.

He turned back to the house, then stopped. Nine years ago he'd allowed her to make the decision. She'd refused him and had returned to her people. He'd let her go without trying to stop her. Was he going to do that again? Or was he willing to fight for what he needed?

"Tully," he yelled, walking toward the barn.

"Yes, s-sir?"

"I'm heading out. Stay with Zeke until I get back. There's stew heating on the stove. Feed him and eat some yourself."

Tully nodded and jogged toward the house. Caleb saddled a fresh horse and headed out into the night. However long it took, whatever he had to do, this time he wasn't going to let her go.

IT WAS NEARLY DAWN when the soft cries of a newborn baby filled the warm house. Ruth placed the small female infant on her mother's stomach. Nalla's aunt tried to speak, but Ruth pressed her fingers against her dry lips.

"Don't," she whispered. "You are granted a healthy child. You must rest to regain your own strength. After you've nursed her, I'll prepare an herbal tea to ease you into sleep for an hour or two.''

The weak, weary woman nodded gratefully, then pulled her daughter close and smiled. Nalla brushed aside her tears as she stepped close to the bed.

"She's beautiful, like you," the teenager told her aunt.

Ruth rubbed the small of her back, trying to ease the ache there. She'd almost lost them both, but somehow a miracle had occurred. It was as if she'd been given new knowledge.

"Was that your doing?" she asked quietly, placing her hand on her belly. Had the spirits gifted her in more ways than one?

Seeing that all was well with the happy family, Ruth stepped into the predawn grayness. She shivered slightly, but didn't bother to go back for her cloak. She would sleep for the morning, she thought wearily, then pack a few things and—

"Ruth?"

She turned toward the sound of a familiar, beloved voice. "Caleb!"

He appeared out of the darkness. She could see the lines of weariness and pain around his eyes. Something was very wrong. "What is it?" she demanded. "Is Zeke—"

"He's fine. We're all fine." Cautiously, he touched her arm. "Except you."

He slipped out of his coat and wrapped it around her shoulders. She hugged the warm sheepskin to her while she mulled over his words. Then she understood.

"You found out."

"Ronald Jefferson came by to make sure you were all right."

She sighed. "Caleb, I'm fine. I'll admit I was terrified at the time and I don't want that to ever happen again, but you didn't have to come here to check on me."

"Yes, I did." He squeezed her upper arms. "Ruth. Don't do this. You mean everything to me. Please don't run away again. Don't turn your back on the life we could have."

She leaned forward and pressed her forehead against his chest. "Is that what you think? That I'll stay here and never come back to the ranch?"

"Won't you?"

She inhaled the familiar scent of the man she loved with all her heart, then thought of her life here, where she'd grown up. Then she straightened and looked Caleb in the eye.

"I will always be more Cheyenne than white. I had thought that meant I couldn't fit in. But I'm starting to see I may be more concerned about my differences than most other people."

When Caleb started to speak, she cut him off with a sharp shake of her head. "I'm not a fool. There will always be those who hate what they cannot understand. There will always be men like those from before, or the one today. But I can't continue to hide from my fear."

She took both his hands in hers. "I love you, Caleb. I loved you before and I love you still. My greatest regret in life is the time we have wasted. I want to be with you always. I want to be your wife and bear your children."

Happiness flooded his face. "You'll marry me?"

"If you ask me to."

"Please. Now. Say yes." He pulled her close and kissed her. "I love you," he mumbled against her mouth. "Only you. For always."

She gave herself up to him, savoring the warmth of his body and the passion flaring between them.

"When?" he asked, breaking the kiss and cupping her face in his hands. "When will you marry me?"

"Today," she said with a smile. "But I would prefer to be married in a Cheyenne ceremony."

"Zeke will love it." He kissed her again. "And he'll love having you for a mother. He needs someone to care for him. You're very good at loving people, Ruth."

He gazed into her eyes. "I wish I'd come after you all those years ago."

"I doubt I would have listened," she said honestly. "Perhaps we needed those years apart to become the people we are today. Besides, I wouldn't give up Zeke."

"Nor would I."

The sun suddenly crested the horizon, bathing them in a soft light. Around them, people awoke and the village stirred to life. Ruth felt a sense of contentment she had never experienced before. In time she would tell Caleb about the child growing within her. A child of both their worlds. Together with Zeke, they would create a future as big and untamed as the Montana sky.

As Good as Gold

Bronwyn Williams

To my beloved granddaughter, Cherylyn Ruth,
whose image is reflected in Kate, the heroine of this story.
Strong, and blessed with a beauty that glows from within,
she makes her grandma proud.

And to Mr. Ed, who loves me.

CHAPTER ONE

June, 1896

EVEN BEFORE the train pulled out of the station, Will Kincaid was entertaining serious second thoughts. The night before, with the fragrant smoke of an expensive cigar swirling around his head, a shot of the finest whiskey in a fancy, imported glass, with a lovely and obviously willing woman silently offering to serve his every need, he had suffered a few more twinges of uneasiness. Not enough to make him change his mind, but the doubts had already begun to filter in. He'd held on to his glass until his palms had grown damp, then downed his drink in a single gulp.

The woman, a well-endowed redhead who went by the unlikely name of Delilah DeLyte, had loosened his black silk four-in-hand with skilled fingers. Close up, he could see that the paint on her eyelashes had smeared onto her cheek, lending her a slightly owlish look.

"Thank you kindly for sharing dinner with me, my dear, but I'm afraid I've an early train to catch." Gently, Will Kincaid had set his glass on the table, risen to his well-shod feet and extracted a large bill from his money clip. Her smile had been quick, her fingers even quicker.

Nine years, he reminded himself now as the train

left the yards and began to gather speed. Nine years and roughly fifteen hundred miles. For the first time it occurred to Will that his own brother might not recognize him as the same reckless young hellion who had robbed his safe and fled town in a fit of righteous anger.

Two months ago he had written to tell Caleb he'd like to mend the rift. There'd been no response. Now that Will was actually westward bound, the uneasiness that had been creeping up on him for weeks could no longer be denied. Could something have happened to Brock, the baby brother both men had done their best to raise?

Caleb had been left with the sole responsibility. Through his own reckless action, Will had missed seeing the boy grow to manhood. Caleb would have done a good job of raising him, for his sternness had never extended to the youngest Kincaid.

Could something have happened to Caleb, himself?

Quickly, Will shut off the chilling thought. Things would have changed, but if anything like that had happened, surely someone would have responded to his letter.

There'd once been a time when the three Kincaid brothers had been a solid unit—two rangy young hell-rakers and a tagalong kid who thought his older brothers had hung the moon. Then the old man had suffered a stroke and Caleb had been forced to grow up overnight and take over the entire operation. That's when things had begun to change. Will had stepped into Caleb's boots and taken on the task of herd manager, a vast responsibility on a spread as large as the Kincaids' ranch. He'd done well enough until Caleb had taken to questioning every move he made, every sale, every purchase, every hire and dismissal. It got to the point that the two brothers couldn't spend five minutes together without butting heads.

At barely twenty years old, Will had still had a lot of wild oats to sow, a lot of hell to raise, but he'd kept it to a minimum. He might have occasionally had a few drinks too many, might have ridden into town a time or two for a few hours of late-night carousing, but he'd never once shirked his duty. No matter how big a head he had the next morning, or how sour his belly, he'd been on the job come daybreak.

And then, just when he'd thought they might eventually works things out, the old man had died and left the entire Kincaid ranch to Caleb. Will couldn't have been more stunned if someone had knocked him in the head with a cross-tie. After that, Caleb had completed the transition from being a tough but fair big brother to a hard, cold stranger. It was as if they were no longer related. As if Will had no more rights than the newest stable hand.

For weeks tension had simmered just beneath the surface. The flash point had been reached after a minor disagreement about whether to mend the south fence or start moving the herd down to the east pasture. Straining with pent-up fury, the two brothers had launched at each other. Neither of them had pulled any punches. After the first roundhouse swing, Will had paused to rub his bleeding knuckles. Caleb had made some biting remark and Will had lit into him again, catching him off guard. Recovering quickly, Caleb had decked him, turned on his heel and stalked off without another word.

Will had stormed out the door on Caleb's heels and

headed for the Double Deuce Saloon. It had been after midnight when he'd returned to the ranch. Resentment fueled by drink, he had let himself into the office and helped himself to a third of the cash in the Kincaid safe, justifying the act by telling himself that the ranch should have been divided equally among the three Kincaid brothers. Brock was too young to play an active role yet, but he was still a Kincaid. As for Will, he had worked his butt off since he was old enough to saddle his own horse, but he flat out refused to put in another day's work for the coldhearted bastard who now owned every stick, stone and head of cattle.

So he had taken a third of the money in the office safe and fled.

For the first few years he'd blamed Caleb. Resentment had festered like a bad tooth. Gradually, he had shifted the blame to the old man for favoring one son above the others, pitting them against one another. The result in Caleb's case had been guilt for being chosen; in Will's case it had been jealousy at being left out.

Eventually he had matured enough to shift the blame to his own shoulders, where it rightfully belonged. The old man had built the Kincaid spread up from the ground. He had a right to leave it to the man he considered best suited to run it. By nature, Will was a tad hotheaded, inclined to act on impulse. Given the advantage of hindsight, he eventually realized that Caleb had been forced to move in the other direction to counterbalance what he called Will's gut-for-brains recklessness.

In some ways, Will Kincaid thought as the train gathered speed, he had changed. The touch of gray at his temples was new, as was the habit of wearing custom-tailored suits, handmade shirts and oxfords instead of Levi's, flannel shirts and battered stock boots. Yet somewhere underneath all the dandified barbering and citified clothes, vestiges of the same reckless brawler remained. Good thing he had learned in the early days after leaving home to tamp down his recklessness and rely more on his brains than his fists, otherwise he might not have survived.

Instead, he'd not only survived, he had thrived. In the nine years since he'd left Montana with a horse, a single change of clothing and two thousand dollars in cash, he had managed to get himself an education, spotty, but sufficient for his needs. He had acquired enough polish to see him through most social occasions. Eventually, building on a combination of instinct, luck and perseverance, he'd gone on to pile up a fortune in gold, hard cash and solid investments. What's more, he had done it honestly, although he'd be the first to admit he could as easily have swindled his way into a fortune. From somewhere among his ancestors he seemed to have inherited two distinct traits: rectitude and recklessness. It was a damned uncomfortable combination, but thank God he had finally learned to make it work for him.

LEAVING THE TRAIN at Butte, Will took the stagecoach from there to Whitehorn, exhausted, but savoring the familiar countryside. The hit-and-miss village he remembered had grown into a small but thriving town. Which made his plan of opening a bank all the more feasible.

But first he had a few fences to mend. That is, if there were any fences still standing.

He was standing outside the stage stop, flexing a few tired muscles, when he heard a familiar voice. "Will? Will Kincaid? Well, damn my bones, it *is* you!"

"James? Good God, man, are you still on the loose?"

James Kincaid, first cousin and once favorite drinking and gambling companion, hadn't changed. Pure black Irish, he'd always had the kind of good looks that attracted women of all ages between cradle and grave. The signs of dissipation might be a bit more pronounced now, his gait a bit too careful as he sauntered across to the stagecoach stop, but the smile was the same.

"Have you seen Caleb lately?" Will was almost afraid to ask.

"Not since the wedding."

"The what? Caleb's married?"

"You didn't know? Yep, she made him wait a respectable time after Marie died, but—"

"Marie?"

"Oh, hell, you didn't know about Marie?" Reaching for one of Will's two bags, James took his arm and steered him toward the nearby saloon. "Come on, cousin, you can buy me a drink while I fill you in on what's been going on around here."

It was early for drinks, but Will needed some answers. Who better than his cousin to provide them? "Don't tell me the old Double Deuce is still in business."

"New owner, but still in business and getting ready to expand. I like to think my support over the years is in some small way responsible for the old Deuce's success," James said with patently false modesty.

"You haven't changed," Will observed dryly.

"You have."

The Double Deuce was neither the oldest nor the newest saloon in Whitehorn; neither the fanciest nor the shabbiest. It happened to be the one favored by his generation, however. That much, Will was pleased to note, had not changed. He recognized several faces from the past.

James led the way to a table and signaled one of the saloon girls. There'd been a time, Will remembered with a twinge of something akin to nostalgia, when he had done his share of hell-raising in this same noisy, cheerful, dimly lit establishment. James had usually been a part of whatever carousing he'd done.

"So who is this Marie you mentioned?" Will prompted after both men had been served.

"Your late sister-in-law, may she rest in peace." The expression in James's startlingly blue eyes belied the pious sentiment. "I'm sure she had some wonderful qualities, only I never could figure out what they were. The only good thing to come out of that marriage is little Zeke. Hey—I reckon you don't know you're an uncle, either, do you?"

It was a lot to take in all at once. Will finished off his drink and signaled for another. For the past few years he had limited himself to a couple of drinks after hours, a single cigar and an occasional woman. Moderation in all things, that was his new motto. For the most part, he'd managed to stick to it pretty well.

James finished his own drink. "Don't mind if I do," he said, and ordered another. "Now, Ruth, she's different. You remember Ruth, right? Her brother, John, is now one of the top dogs out at the Laughing Horse

Reservation. She and Caleb met again this spring when Zeke ran away to the reservation. Ruth's now married to Caleb.''

Will took a moment to digest the news. "Just tell me this much—is Caleb all right? Is the ranch still a going concern? Am I going to have any more surprises if I show up there unannounced?"

"He doesn't know you're coming?"

"I wrote a couple of months ago, but I hadn't heard back by the time I decided to just up and return." He wondered if James knew about the money he'd stolen. Pride alone would probably have kept Caleb from reporting it. At least, Will thought wryly, there'd been no wanted posters with his picture on them, so far as he knew. "Is there a decent hotel in town?"

Since his brother now had a wife and a child, Will was even less certain of his welcome.

"Old lady Harroun's boardinghouse or Amos Carlton's hotel, take your choice. She sets a good table, but Amos's beds are better." He grinned the same old infectious grin that had won him forgiveness for many a transgression. "'Course, if you're hard up, there's still the old Tanner mansion."

"God, is that thing still standing?"

"Been on the market as long as I can remember. With things building up in town the way they are, wouldn't surprise me if it got snapped up by some poor jerk with more money than brains and turned into another boardinghouse."

Will shook his head and chuckled. "That reminds me, I'd better secure a room and clean up before I head out to the ranch. Livery still got a few decent horses for hire?"

"Ask for Mose. Tell him I sent you."

IT WAS EARLY evening when Will, having rented a room at the hotel, bathed and changed into a suit that wasn't speckled with fly ash from the long train ride, finally headed out of town. The high granite ridges of the Crazy Mountains were awash in a clear golden light, the lower reaches shaded with blue. Before him rolled vast acres of grain, ready for harvest, while overhead the sky was a deep cobalt bowl. Had he even noticed such things as a young man?

Probably not. Once he'd left home he'd been too caught up in the rush of freedom, the excitement of being out from under his brother's watchful eye. Then, too, even before he'd left Montana, the guilt had begun to fester. Not only had he stolen money, but he'd left the ranch shorthanded. To this day he wasn't sure if it had been pride, shame or curiosity about what lay just over the horizon that had kept him from turning back. Maybe he'd known even then that some vital element was missing from his life. Trusting his instincts, he had kept on moving, staying a few weeks here, a few months there, learning as he worked his way eastward. Thank God he had hung on to his stolen nest egg until he'd reached Chicago.

For the first few days the noise of a bustling city had nearly driven him away, but before he could make up his mind where to go next, he'd been trapped by a sense of raw energy unlike anything he had ever experienced. It was the kind of energy that made a man want to do big things, to be a part of it—to set his own wheels to turning.

Determined to double Caleb's money to prove—well, to prove something or other to them both—it was almost by chance that he'd discovered a talent that had lain dormant for the first twenty years of his life.

Money. High finance. Wheeling and dealing, speculating, recognizing investment opportunities before they were even a speck on the horizon. It was not unlike the days when old man Gibson had taught him how to read the forest—how to study the lay of the land until he knew precisely where to set his traps.

The irony of it had not escaped him as he'd found himself turning into even more of a dedicated businessman than his brother.

Pausing now beneath the familiar circular gate, Will took stock of the changes. New fences. A fresh coat of paint. Someone had planted flowering bushes around the house, the scent layering with the rich smell of ripe grain and cattle on the warm evening air. Breathing deeply, he swung down from his rented gelding and braced himself to face the music.

For better or worse, he was home. If he ended up getting himself kicked out on his backside, so be it. He had survived the big city. If he could get through the first few minutes, he could probably survive his homecoming.

Tugging at his necktie with one hand, he rapped sharply on the door with the other. Before he could knock a second time, the door swung open.

Silence. And then, "Will? Jesus, is it *you?*"

"You gonna send for the sheriff or invite me inside?"

TIME FLEW as both men talked at once, then both fell silent for long moments. Hungry eyes devoured the tracks of time on two faces that bore a striking similarity. Will said, "I ran into James in town. He told me about Marie and Zeke. And, uh—Ruth?" He'd caught sight of a small boy that reminded him of a much younger Brock.

Caleb, never a garrulous man at the best of times, nodded. And then a stunning, solemn-looking woman came in with a tray of coffee and fry bread dusted with sugar and cinnamon. Immediately, Will recognized her.

Ruth, his brother's Cheyenne wife, smiled, and any question of why Caleb had married her disappeared. She exhibited the same blend of dignity and shyness he'd seen in so many of the women from Laughing Horse Reservation.

As for the small boy clinging to her skirt, playing hide and seek with him, Will nodded, smiled and said, "Zeke, pleased to meet you." He didn't push it. Time was on his side.

Caleb scooped the boy up onto his lap. "How about you, are you married yet?"

"Lord, no, I don't have time for a wife. I plan to start a bank. Not just savings and loan, but investments, as well. Learning the business didn't leave a whole lot of time for courting."

"In some ways, little brother, you haven't learned anything." The blue-eyed little boy scrambled down, grabbed up the last of the fry bread and darted away, drawing a fond swat from his father.

Will leaned back in his chair and grinned. "I learned how to make money. Learned how to make it work for me, too. Hey, I did it honestly," he added when Caleb's eyebrows rose to majestic heights. Deciding that the moment had come, he stood, excused himself and went outside to retrieve his saddlebags. Filled with gold—a rather theatrical gesture, he thought now that it was too late—he staggered under the weight as he returned to drop a small fortune at his brother's feet.

"Two thousand in gold coin, plus interest compounded over ten years. If you want to count it, I've got nowhere to go for the next few hours."

Caleb slowly lost all the color in his face until his eyes looked like twin bruises. He swore softly. "Count it, hell. Take it back, William. I don't want it."

"It's yours. Fair and square. I hadn't even got as far as town before I regretted taking it, but I was too big a coward to go back and face the music."

Caleb swore some more. Once he'd inherited the ranch he'd all but stopped swearing. Turned into a stranger almost overnight. Stopped damn near everything that came as second nature to most men in their early twenties. "Do anything you want to with it, Will, but I'm not taking it."

"Dammit, Caleb, I need to do this!"

"All right, then how about if we park it somewhere safe until you climb down off your high horse."

"You and your damned stiff-necked pride, you've always got to call the shots. How about—"

"How about if we bury it for now. First one that needs it can dig it up."

Grumbling a bit, Will gave in. Knowing his brother, it was the best he could do for the moment. The last thing he wanted was to come to blows and have to leave town again. He didn't have another ten years to spare.

Predictably, they argued over where to bury it. Will suggested someplace on the ranch. "You can leave a letter in the safe so that Ruth or the boy, or maybe Brock will know where to find it if they ever need it. By the way, where is our baby brother?''

Caleb looked away and frowned. ''Your guess is as good as mine. I mentioned sending him east to school, and he took off. He's been doing that lately. Last time he was working on a spread down in Wyoming. Got busted up doing a little rodeoing and came home to mend.''

''Is he—?'' Will didn't know how to frame the question, but Caleb answered it anyway.

''Yeah, he's a good kid. Rock-headed, but sound as a double eagle.''

''Speaking of double eagles—''

''Forget it. All of them, Brock, Ruth and Zeke, are taken care of in my will. Besides, burying it on my property would give me the advantage. How about we wait and put it in this bank you're talking about building?''

''That would give me the advantage. So far I don't own a square foot of Montana, much less a bank. At least the ranch is Kincaid property.''

''We'll cut cards then. High card gets to call the shots.''

''No thanks, big brother. I learned two things the night I left here. One of 'em is not to get in the way of your right cross, the other is never to argue over money. I guess we'll just have to dump the gold in the river and make some poor miner downstream happy.''

Settling back in his chair, Caleb steepled his hands, studying his younger brother. ''You've changed.''

Warily, Will nodded. ''So has the rest of the world. Ten years is a long time.''

"Yeah. I notice you've got a few gray hairs now."

"I see you've got a few more frown lines."

"Looked in a mirror recently?"

Both men grinned as the tension that had threatened momentarily seeped away. "Remember how we used to settle our disagreements?"

Will rubbed his jaw, and Caleb chuckled. "Not that way. I'm getting too old for fistfights, but the old Double Deuce is still standing."

"I noticed. James says they're getting ready to expand."

Caleb shrugged. "Town's growing. What d'you say we ride into town and have a drink to celebrate. Maybe on the way we can come up with some way to settle this business with the gold. I'll have Ruth make up a bed while we're gone."

"I'll take you up on the drinks, but I've already got a room in town. If I'm lucky, my trunk will have been delivered by now."

Caleb hesitated, nodded, then went to say good-night to his son. Will sought out his sister-in-law and thanked her for her hospitality, then went outside to wait.

God, it was good to be back. The smells, the sight—the freedom...

Will mounted up and waited until Caleb had saddled his own horse, then the two brothers headed toward town to celebrate the long overdue reconciliation. There'd been a time in their carefree days when they had needed no excuse to repair to the Double Deuce. Whisky and women served the purpose, whether a man was celebrating a win, consoling himself for a loss or just passing time with friends. Even after all this time, there was still a certain feeling of rightness in riding into town together.

"Place has changed a lot in ten years," Will observed as they passed a new construction site just north of town.

"New school going up. I doubt if we'll rival Bozeman or Helena anytime soon, but yeah, it's growing," Caleb said laconically. "New people moving in. New businesses. I'll say this for you, baby brother—your sense of timing's still as sharp as ever. If you're serious about this bank business, I can introduce you to a couple of men who might be able to help you find a suitable property. Fellow named McCutcheon moved to town a few years ago. Bought up a few places on speculation."

"Hmm?" Will's attention had strayed to the sagging balcony outside the back of the saloon, where a few of the "girls" with their low-cut, wasp-waisted bodices and their short, knee-baring skirts, were leaning over the railing, calling down to the cowboys below.

The town might have changed almost beyond recognition, he mused, but some things never changed.

CHAPTER TWO

LAUGHING OVER the remembrance of games they had once played—hunting for lost gold mines, discovering bank robbers' loot and rescuing fair maidens whose grateful fathers' paid huge rewards, the two men bickered lightheartedly over whether to bury the gold on the Kincaid ranch, thus giving the advantage to Caleb, or save it and deposit it in Will's bank.

In the end, on the farthest corner, hidden by a shed, they buried the treasure under a cornerstone of the expansion that was already underway. Each man dropped in a personal token. "Proof of ownership," Caleb said, "In case it's ever needed"

Will wiped his brow and grabbed his shovel. Digging was damned hard work. Thirsty work. A few minutes later, still grinning, they shoved open the double swinging doors and went inside to celebrate a long overdue reunion.

There was a new mirror above the bar and a new man behind it, but other than that, little had changed. The table over in the corner where five men shoved piles of chips back and forth and scowled over their cards could be the very same one Will had carved his initials in when he was fourteen and used to sneak inside to ogle the women.

Caleb held up two fingers. A few minutes later, one

of the girls headed toward them with a carefully balanced tray. "It would have to be the homeliest one in the house," Will muttered as he reached inside his coat for his wallet.

He was still struggling to extract a bill when all hell broke loose. Someone near the bar drew a pistol and fired a shot. Half a dozen women screamed in shrill unison as the mirror shattered noisily. Before Will could react, something hard whacked him across the nose. Sticky liquid splashed all over the front of his shirt and leaked down into his trousers.

He stared down at his lap in disgust. "Dammit, lady, watch where you're going!"

Caleb covered a snort of laughter with a cough while Will dragged out his handkerchief and began mopping the whiskey off his chin. The handkerchief came away bloody. His nose was bleeding!

The woman was on her knees, babbling apologies and trying to mop his pants off with the tail of her gauzy skirt. Glaring down at the back of her skinny neck, Will scowled at the pale silken valley of her nape and growled, "Dammit, quit that, haven't you done enough damage?" He grabbed a wrist that was scarcely bigger around than a child's and yanked it away from his privates. He didn't *think* she was trying to drum up business, but if she was, he could tell her flat out she was doomed to failure.

"Lizzy, get the hell off your knees and go fetch a bucket and a clean rag!"

"It wasn't her fault, Cam," Caleb said quietly. "Fellow at the next table dropped onto all fours when the shooting started and she tripped over his boots."

Will looked pointedly at the next table, which was

a good four feet away. "Nice try, brother," he muttered. The woman was trying to drum up business, that was the long and short of it. Judging from her looks, she probably had to run a man down, knock him out and drag him upstairs. No wonder she looked as if she hadn't had a decent meal in days."

"I'm really dreadfully sorry, sir, I'll pay for—for everything." Juliet Elizabeth Price-Hawthorne forced herself to speak calmly. Pay with what, she hadn't a clue. She already owed a small fortune—at least her brother did, which was why she was here, calling herself Lizzy Price and trying her best to earn her keep as a serving girl.

Just moments before Cam had sent her over to the table with two doubles and two cigars, he had informed her that as payment was overdue, starting tonight she was going to have to earn her keep upstairs, same as the other girls. "'Cause you sure as shootin' ain't any good to me as a waitress."

She could have argued that if he'd allow her to wear her own shoes, she might do better, but she'd been too paralyzed to speak a word. Besides, it was true. No matter how the other girls tried to coach her, she constantly mixed up orders because she couldn't bring herself to look at the faces of the men she served. She jumped whenever anyone pinched her, backing into other girls and causing them to spill their trays.

Cam was right. She was a failure. But she couldn't do the other, she really couldn't. She would die first. Thankfully, no one wanted her, anyway. Tonight she'd been on her best behavior, trying doubly hard not to spill anything and to keep her orders separate. She'd been doing really well until that drunken fool at the bar had started shooting. When the gun had gone off, she'd panicked, tried to turn too quickly, and in the wobbly red satin high heels shoes that didn't fit her because they had belonged to another girl, she had tripped over her own feet.

Cam's hard fingers grabbed her by the arm and jerked her to her feet. ''Gol-dammit, girl, I warned you!''

She clutched the nearest thing she could find for support. It happened to be a hard, wet thigh. Slowly, the man she had drenched rose to his feet. Reeking of whiskey, he stared down at her until she wanted to crawl under the table and hide. Ignoring her, he spoke to the proprietor. ''I believe the situation is under control.''

The bartender, still gripping the frail arm, shook his head. ''This wench here, she ain't worth what it takes to feed her. I'm real sorry about that, Kincaid.'' He addressed his remarks to Caleb, who was barely managing to repress his laughter. ''Next round's on the house.''

''No problem, Cam, the poor girl really couldn't help it.''

''Can't earn her keep downstairs, too damned snooty to earn it upstairs—I don't run no charity operation here, y'know.''

Will knew how these places operated, knew the kind of women who worked in saloons. For the most part, the ones he'd known had enjoyed their work, using it as a stepping stone to something better, more often than not. Some married, some went into business for themselves.

So it didn't make sense that he should feel sorry for

the clumsy girl who had just broken his nose and ruined a perfectly good outfit, even though she was shaking like an aspen, obviously scared out of her wits.

He scowled at his monogrammed Irish linen handkerchief. It was ruined, too, but at least his nose had
stopped bleeding. His gaze fell on the thick fingers that
were still biting into the poor girl's wrist. With skin
like hers, so delicate it looked almost translucent, she
would bear the marks of that grip for days to come. "I
think you can unhand her now," he said quietly.

"Go get a rag and bucket and scrub this mess up,
and be quick about it, girlie. You still got to turn a
trick or two before the night's over."

Even Will had the grace to blush at the crudeness of
the remark. He'd long since lost count of all the women
he had taken upstairs in one saloon or another. He did
know he'd never once been ashamed of buying what
they were selling. With this one, he would. That is, he
would if he were to do it. Not that he would, because
as women went, she didn't have much to offer. A
skinny body with no curves to speak of, red hair that
was badly dyed and tangled into an impossible nest.
Paint had been layered onto her small face with a
trowel, probably in an effort to disguise her youth.

Will couldn't have said which of them was more
surprised—Cam, Caleb, the girl or himself, when he
stepped forward and removed the proprietor's hamlike
hand from her arm. Crooking his elbow, he said politely, "Miss, er—Lizzy, if you would be so kind as to
accompany me upstairs, we might see what we can do
about repairing the damage." His nose was beginning
to swell shut.

Cam grunted something about drunks and whores

and stalked off to deal with the mess behind the bar. Caleb was grinning like a possum while Lizzy, her eyes round as saucers, continued to tremble. Looking from one to the other, Caleb slowly shook his head. "You been hitting the locoweed, William?"

"That might explain it," he replied ruefully, holding the wet handkerchief to his nose. Nothing else could. He'd had a single drink back at the ranch. Hadn't even got around to having another when disaster had struck in the form of a clumsy lady of the evening.

"I'll ride out to the ranch tomorrow," Will said, resigned to spending the next few minutes getting himself cleaned up. Damned if he was going to walk through Amos Carlton's lobby smelling like a distillery.

Taking the poor girl by the arm, he led her toward the stairs, miserably aware of the eyes that followed their progress. There were a few hoots and catcalls. Someone called out a ribald comment. Squaring his shoulders, Will ignored them. He tried and failed to ignore the trembling hand tucked under his arm.

Dammit, it didn't make sense. After nearly a week of traveling he was exhausted, mentally and physically. He wasn't drunk, unless the fumes were more potent than he thought, but how else could he explain going upstairs in sodden clothing on his first night home, with the woman who had busted him on the nose? A woman who had all the attractions of a starving cat?

Surely she wasn't expecting him to...

There was no way in hell he was going to— Besides, even if he wasn't too tired, he wouldn't have been interested. He felt sorry for her, but that was all. It wasn't the expression in her eyes. It wasn't the shape of her mouth under all that paint. It sure as the devil wasn't her figure.

He'd always been a sucker for strays, human and otherwise. It was one of his few weaknesses. If he could get the poor creature past an uncomfortable moment with her boss, then why not? He'd been on the receiving end of a few favors in his young and reckless days.

She led him to a closet-size room at the end of the hall. "It's not much," she said apologetically. "I haven't been here all that long, and the best rooms were already taken."

"If there's a basin and a pitcher of water, that's all I'm interested in."

Her look of relief was almost comical. Evidently, he appealed to her no more than she did to him. Wordlessly, she poured tepid water into the heavy bowl and set a towel and a sliver of soap beside it. Will unbuttoned his shirt.

"You want to make yourself useful? How about finding me a mirror so I can see how much damage you did to my nose." He peeled off his shirt and reached for his belt.

Lizzy widened her eyes, then turned away. The mirror she produced was purse-size, the back sterling silver. It was so obviously out of keeping with the room's cheap furnishing that he stared at the fleur-de-lis design and then glanced up and the woman hovering beside the door.

"Pretty," he said. "A gift?"

"No, I—yes. Sir, do you think—that is, could you possibly...?"

"Probably not," he admitted truthfully, his eyes

meeting hers. Her eyes were startlingly beautiful, even surrounded by a heavy layer of paint. "You don't have to worry, though, I'll pay for your time."

Then he looked in the mirror and winced. His nose looked even worse than it felt. He was probably going to be breathing through his mouth for the foreseeable future. Good thing he wasn't out to impress anyone with his looks.

"Oh, no, you don't have to pay me. But if you stay here, Cam might think—" And then, struck by the alternative, she blurted, "But if you leave too soon, he'll think—"

Will knew precisely what the manager would think if he left now. That Lizzy had failed one more trial. Although why he should care if her boss kicked her out on her bony little backside was beyond him.

Still, he couldn't help but wonder if she had a place to go.

Easy question. If she had another place to go, she wouldn't be here trying to hustle a paying customer when it was plain as day she hadn't a clue about how to go about it. The wonder was why she'd been hired in the first place.

"Listen, I'd like to help you, but—"

"I know. Please, you don't have to explain. Let me sponge off your trousers and I can rinse out your shirt. Of course, they'll still be wet…unless you'd care to wait until they dry? But then, Cam…"

She looked ready to burst into tears. God help him if that happened. He was exhausted, but diplomacy didn't require much energy. "I'm tempted, Lizzy, I surely am, but I've been traveling all week. I arrived in town this afternoon, so you see, I wouldn't be very good company, even if I were—'' He almost said, even if he were interested, but stopped just in time. The poor girl couldn't help her looks.

Well, actually, he thought as he pressed the wet towel against his swollen nose, she could. Someone should tell her that whatever her natural hair color was, it had to be prettier than bright orange. And her face didn't need all that paint. Didn't need any at all, now that he'd taken time to look more closely. She had a small nose, a high forehead, pretty teeth—a rarity in itself—and a jaw that might even be called elegant if it weren't for the stubborn tilt of her chin.

Interesting face, Will mused as he wet the towel again and used it to blot the front of his pants. ''Are we spending enough time up here to satisfy your boss?''

Lizzy forced herself to look away from the big, bare-chested stranger who was using her soap, her water, her towel. In her bedroom. ''I'm afraid he'll expect money. How long does it usually take?''

''How long does what take?''

She looked at him suspiciously. Surely that wasn't laughter she saw in his eyes…was it? There was nothing even faintly humorous in the situation. ''You know. *It.*''

''*It?*''

Impatience overrode embarrassment. ''Oh, for heaven's sake, you know what I mean! How long would it take for Cam to think that you—that I—that we—''

''Engaged in a bit of commerce?''

She could feel herself flushing. If her face got any hotter, her face paint would probably melt and drip down on her bosom. The bosom she'd been advised to pad, as nature hadn't endowed her with enough to fill out the bodice that was part of her working costume.

A large man, with a square, clefted chin and square, capable hands, he lifted a questioning brow. "How much do you charge?"

"Charge?"

"How much would it cost me if I decided to take advantage of your...offer?" He picked up his shirt, sniffed, scowled, and gingerly slid his arms into the sleeves.

"Oh. You mean if I—"

"Right. If we, meaning you and I, climbed into the bed and did what Cam thinks we're supposed to be doing."

Will didn't think her face could get much hotter without bursting into flames. "Two dollars," she whispered. "I get to keep fifty cents. Some girls charge more because they're—well, I guess you could say they're experts. I'm only a beginner."

Only a beginner. If she had to live on what she earned on her back, no wonder the poor girl was so skinny. Abruptly, he pulled off his soggy shirt, slid the only chair in the room over to the small window and draped it over the back. He hated wet clothes. Being caught in the rain up in the high meadows on a hot day was one thing—getting doused with whiskey was another.

"We've been up here just about long enough to have earned your commission." He doubted if any of her paying customers lingered too long—unless they were drunk enough to pass out. But then, she'd said she was a beginner. Probably didn't know enough to keep a man entertained for more than a few minutes.

Funny thing, though...he couldn't quite make up his mind about the look in her eyes. Was it hope? Fear? Desperation? He was pretty sure it wasn't greed. A greedy woman would have tried harder. No matter what a woman looked like, if she really knew her business, there were ways of seducing a man, regardless of how tired he was.

This one admittedly didn't know her business. She dropped onto the edge of the bed, removed her left shoe and began rubbing her foot. It was then that he noticed that the foot was considerably smaller than the shoe. No wonder she'd stumbled. "You need a smaller size."

"A what?"

He nodded to the red satin pump she had tossed onto the bed. "Next time, get the right size and look for a pair with lower heels and maybe ribbon ties."

"These aren't my own."

"Then why the devil are you wearing them?"

"Cam makes all of us wear the same costumes. These belonged to one of the girls who quit to get married. Cam buys all our things and takes it out of our pay, so mostly he gets to keep everything whenever someone leaves, because who would want to wear things like this if they didn't have to?" Studiously avoiding looking at his bare chest, she plucked at the ill-fitting corselet.

That answered one question, although why he should be interested, Will couldn't have said. He wasn't—not really. An inquiring mind was a tremendous asset when it came to business. When it came to women...

Well, hell. A man had to do something to pass the time. He wasn't interested in passing it in the usual manner, but if he left too soon she'd be in trouble with her boss. For some reason, the thought of her trooping up and down the stairs with a string of paying customers didn't set right on his conscience.

"So...tell me about yourself, Lizzy. Is that your real name?" He thought about the woman he had shared dinner with the night before he'd left Chicago. Delilah DeLyte.

"Hmm—almost."

"Almost. Let me guess. Dizzy? Tizzy?"

She blinked several times in rapid succession, causing flecks of black mascara to break off. If she burst into tears, Will told himself, he was out of here. One thing he'd never been good at was dealing with a woman's tears. Not even a woman like Dizzy Lizzy.

Instead she laughed. Dimples appeared in her cheeks and two tiny wrinkles marred the bridge of her small nose.

Delighted in spite of himself, he said encouragingly, "So, you're Lizzy...?"

"Price," she admitted after only the briefest of hesitations.

"I'm Will, Miss Price. Now that we've been properly introduced, tell me about yourself. Where you came from, how you came to be here." His wide gesture included the Double Deuce, Whitehorn and all of Montana. Her accent said South, but south covered a lot of territory.

And what the hell—he had nothing better for the next few minutes. Caleb had probably already gone back out to the ranch.

She turned the tables on him. "Was that your brother downstairs with you? You look alike. Cam called him, um—Kincaid?"

Clever lady. The Kincaid name was still the most prominent name in the territory, although it was no longer a territory now. A few years ago congress had conferred statehood on the vast, untamed reaches of God's most beautiful creation. Didn't change much, so far as Will could tell. The skies were still as vast, the waters as clear, the mountains as high and the prairies still rolled on forever, statehood or not.

Waiting for him to answer, Lizzy flexed her shoulders and sighed. Will touched his swollen nose and sighed. When the silence grew uncomfortable, he wondered why the devil he didn't simply get up, sling his wet shirt over his shoulders and leave. It wouldn't be the first time a man had come downstairs with his shirttail out. The new management, if anything, was rougher than the old.

And besides, he was under no obligation here. Actually, the lady owed him. She'd cracked him in the nose with the edge of her tray, causing his nose to bleed all over his front, doused him with two doubles, and then made matters worse by trying to wash his clothes while they were still on his body.

Not that he was about to take off his pants. No sir, when it came to women, his survival instincts were sharp as a mule deer's hooves. And big blue eyes notwithstanding, this one was not his problem. Warily, he glanced across the small room, wondering how soon he could walk away with her safety and his own dignity more or less intact.

Blue tears, peppered with tiny black chips of mascara, zigzagged down her cheeks. "I'b sorry," she sobbed. "I dever cry. Dow't look at be, please."

Oh, shoot, her nose was in as bad shape as his own. He'd have handed her his handkerchief, but between them, they'd already ruined it. "Dry your tears," he said, and handed her the towel. It was wet, but she took it and held it against her face for several moments.

Mopped and blotted, her face was a clown's nightmare. Will rose and went to stand over her. Removing the towel from her hand, he dipped it into the basin again, wrung it out and picked up the sliver of soap. "Here, hold your face up," he growled.

And then she growled. At least her belly did. "You hungry?" he asked before he could stop himself. There was no way he was going to take her out to dinner. Just no way. In the first place, he had a reputation to establish if he wanted to be taken seriously as a banker. In the second place, neither one of them was fit to be seen in public.

She shook her head, then nodded. "I couldn't eat after Cam told me I had to—that is, I can never eat when I'm worried."

No wonder she reminded him of a starving cat. He'd seen more curves on the trunk of a cottonwood tree. "Does this place run to room service?"

She shook her head. "Cheese and pickled eggs at the bar."

"A man used to be able to order a decent sandwich here. Downstairs, I mean," he added, lest she think he was too familiar with the second floor. "Come to think of it, I haven't had dinner, either. Why don't I see what I can do about it?"

"Cam doesn't like for us to have food in our rooms on account of mice."

Why am I doing this? Will wondered a few minutes later as he loped halfway down the stairs and signaled to the new owner, who served as his own bartender. "What does it take to get a meal around here these days? Does Mrs. Harroun still send over a tray?"

"Working up an appetite, are ye? Glad to hear it, son. Tell the truth, I didn't hold out much hope for that one. If the gent that left her here didn't owe me more than I can afford to lose, she'd not've lasted out the first day."

Will didn't know what he was talking about, nor did he have any intention of getting involved. He ordered two beefsteak dinners and a pot of coffee sent up to the room, handed over the stated price, which was considerably more than the same would have cost in the finest restaurant in Chicago. A few minutes later, he climbed the stairs again, his feet dragging. Just down the street in Amos Carlton's hotel, his own bed was waiting. There wasn't a single reason why he had to hang around a noisy saloon, playing nursemaid to an inept lady of the evening.

"Dinner's on the way," he announced, letting himself back inside the ugly little room. For some reason it struck him that the room was all wrong for the woman—hardly more than a girl—who managed to look both tawdry and oddly dignified. This whole damned setup was out of kilter. But that was her problem, he told himself—not his.

Lizzy hadn't moved except to unpin her awful hair. "If it'll make you feel any more secure, Cam is happy to see you're settling into your job."

Without the paint, there was no mistaking her sudden pallor. "Lizzy? Are you all right? Supper'll be here as soon as the boy can fetch it from across the road."

She nodded, a mop of stiff orange curls bobbing with every motion. "Thank you. I don't know why you're being so kind."

Damned if he knew, either. He'd heard any number of fanciful tales from various saloon girls. At least half of them were royal princesses, to hear them tell it. Oddly enough, with her face scrubbed clean, this one just might have had a shot at convincing him. There was something almost regal about the way she held her head when she got all defensive.

Only she hadn't tried to convince him of anything.

"By the time supper gets here, my shirt'll be dry enough. We'll eat, then I'll pay for all night and slip out the back way. You should be able to get a good night's sleep."

He waited for a response. If she burst into tears again, he was walking out, supper or no supper. And he was hungry, not having taken time to eat since breakfast. Ruth's fry bread and coffee wasn't enough for a man with healthy appetites.

She didn't cry. Back as stiff as a board, she stared at him with that wary look in her eyes and said softly, "I appreciate it more than I can say. If ever I'm in a position to return the favor—" Her words trailed off.

Will could have made the obvious remark, but he didn't. He'd known a lot of women in his life, respectable and otherwise. He still didn't know what to make of this one, and for the life of him, he couldn't figure out why he was even here. He sure as hell wasn't interested in what she was selling.

An hour later he paid Cam the going rate for an all-night stay, headed upstairs again and then crept along the balcony and down the back stairs, confident that he'd done everything in his power to see that Miss Lizzy Price would have at least one undisturbed night.

Back at the hotel he asked to be awakened at noon, then collapsed in his bed, taking time only to remove his shoes and his necktie.

CHAPTER THREE

BY THE TIME Will had bathed, dressed and gobbled down three eggs, a stack of flapjacks, half a dozen slices of bacon and a couple of pints of coffee the next morning, he felt considerably more optimistic. It didn't take long to locate the lot he wanted for his bank and to track down the owner. It turned out to be the gentleman Caleb had mentioned, one Maximillian McCutcheon, rumored to have made his money in several highly suspect ventures.

Presenting himself at the man's home, Will stated his interest and then braced himself for some serious dickering. He declined a drink, knowing a clear mind would be to his advantage. Evidently, McCutcheon knew it, too, for he waved toward a chair and proceeded to examine everything from the cut of Will's suit to the high gleam on his fashionable oxfords.

"Well now, I'll tell you the honest truth, Mr. Kincaid," the older man declared, which in Will's experience was a warning that what he was about to hear was a mixture of lies and truth, at best. "I hadn't figured on letting that piece go for a few years. Bought it on speculation, and judging from the way the town's growing, it'll double in value every year I hold on to it. So you see, I'd be losing money if I was to let you have it now."

The door opened and a woman poked her head into the office. Will judged her to be in her middle twenties. Neither plain nor pretty, she was overdressed for a Thursday morning in a small Montana town. "Papa, I told you yesterday I need you to wire that order! Haven't you done it *yet?* The party is next—" Noticing Will's presence, she modified her tone. "Oh, excuse me, I didn't know you had a guest."

"Never mind, missy, come inside and meet Mr. Kincaid. You know the Kincaid ranch up north of town? Will here just moved back to town after a stay back East."

Will hadn't mentioned the ranch, his stay in the East, or anything except for his interest in a certain piece of property. Evidently Maximillian McCutcheon had done his homework. The young woman entered, her bronze taffeta gown rustling audibly, and held out her slender hand. With no hint of the irritation he felt at the interruption, Will smiled, nodded and accepted the polite overture. He hadn't retained his bachelor status this long without learning to read the signs. McCutcheon was on the lookout for a man who could afford to take on the care and feeding of his daughter.

No, thank you. As much as I want a deed to your property, I don't want any strings attached.

McCutcheon was good at the game, but Will was easily his equal. Shortly before noon they came to terms, and after declining an invitation to luncheon, Will left with a signed agreement to pay three times what the property was presently worth. From there he went directly to office of the lawyer who had served his father. The faces behind the desks were new, but nothing else had changed, not even the ornate brass hat rack.

Leaving the office some forty-five minutes later, he felt like jumping up and clicking his heels together. A few years ago he might have done just that. Instead, he allowed himself a calm, mature glow of satisfaction. Once word got out that he'd paid top dollar for his bank lot, the land around it would appreciate in value. It would be a good idea to buy up as much as possible purely on speculation. Paper investments were good, but the right land in a new and growing state was even better.

All in all, he congratulated himself, he'd had a damned good day. He'd escaped McCutcheon's lair with the one thing he needed to get started on his bank, and managed to sidestep the lure of his daughter, as well. It occurred to him that the neighborhood he'd just left was probably the right area to start looking for a house of his own. He had assumed he'd start out living out at the ranch, with plenty of time to decide, but that was before he'd learned that Caleb had a new family of his own now. Too many things had changed over the years since he'd left home.

Instead of heading to the boardinghouse where he had arranged to take his meals, he veered in the opposite direction. What the devil, when a man had something to celebrate, he needed a drink, not a plate of beefsteak and eggs.

Lizzy was teetering across the floor with a carefully balanced tray when he walked in. Despite a pair of eyes as blue as the Montana sky, her looks had not magically improved overnight. She was still skinny as a bed slat. Her hair was a real mess, her face once more hidden under a layer of paint. She might try to dress the part with the black satin corselet and the red satin shoes, but as a lady of the evening, she was doomed to failure. This early in the day, there wasn't a man in the house drunk enough to make a pass at her. Even cross-eyed snoggered, Will doubted if they'd bother.

And yet...

Not your problem, Kincaid.

He remained at the bar for a few minutes, but then, realizing where his gaze kept straying, he left. His leaving had nothing to do with the woman, he assured himself, it was just that he had more important things to do. As long as luck was running his way, he might as well begin scouting out a suitable house. Nothing quite as ostentatious as the McCutcheons' place, but a man had to keep up appearances.

Harry Talbert, who knew everything that went on in town, filled him in on the dismal prospects. ''Folks aren't selling out, they're moving in. Ranchers wanting more grazing, young'uns growing up, moving out, wanting a place of their own—I don't hardly know what to tell you, son. I reckon you could hire a house built if you could find the right land, depending on what you're wanting. Carpenters are in high demand these days, what with half the businesses in town expanding, and those that aren't carping are hiring on as threshers.''

''What I want would probably take too long to build,'' Will replied morosely. ''I was counting on finding the right place, offering the right price and being able to move in right away.''

There, he'd planted the seed. If he knew Harry—and he did, from years past—before the sun set on another day the man would have a complete rundown on all suitable prospects, not to mention which builders would be available to start on his bank. The Kincaid name alone carried a lot of weight, but he'd be damned before he would trade on it for his own advantage. He had given up that right ten years ago.

Leaving the barbershop, he met a couple of men he used to carouse with, both graying now, paunchy, obviously settled in for the long haul. They reminisced, swapped a few stories—he heard the latest gossip, which he'd already heard from Harry, and when the men headed home for supper with their families, Will glanced up the street toward the hotel, and then down the street toward the Double Deuce.

What the devil, why should some scrawny little runt of a saloon girl keep him from enjoying a drink? It wasn't as if he were expected anywhere else.

Naturally, the first thing he saw was Lizzy. Too much to hope she'd be taking a break before the evening rush. Nor had a couple more hours on the floor brought about any miraculous changes, other than the fact that she looked tired. That wary look he'd come to associate with her was still there. More pronounced, if anything.

The place was gearing up for the evening. A few habitual gamblers were hard at it, oblivious to their surroundings as long as the cards kept turning, the chips kept piling up before them and the drinks kept coming. Lined up at the bar, half a dozen cowboys celebrated a night off. They were loud and obnoxious, but probably harmless. He knew the type. Hell, he'd worked with them half his life.

Finding a place at the end of the bar, he ordered a

straight Monongahela and forked over two bits. Cam slid his drink across the counter, cut his eyes over to where Lizzy was serving a table of well-lubricated card players, and grinned. One of the other girls sashayed across the room, rump swinging, breasts bouncing, and leaned against Will's shoulder as she slid her tray over the counter for a refill. "Evening, honey, don't you want me to show you to a table? You don't want to 'sociate with these bar bums."

Before Will could respond, Lizzy brought her tray back loaded with empty glasses. As if to avoid him, she headed for the far end of the bar. One of the drunks slung an arm around her shoulders and landed a sloppy kiss on the back of her neck, and Will froze. Moving quickly along the scarred mahogany surface, he placed himself between the men and Lizzy. "Excuse me, but I believe the young lady wants to get through," he said quietly.

The woman he'd just left called him something he wasn't. His parents had been married long before he came along. He muttered a belated "Excuse me," which didn't appear to help.

"Wha' th' hell d'you want, mister. Min' yer own—"

Lizzy turned red under her war paint. She was rubbing the back of her neck, as if to wipe away the unsolicited kiss. "Oh, please don't, please," she kept murmuring.

One of the other men struggled to wrest a six-shooter from his holster, but before metal could clear leather, Cam was there. "Take it outside, boys," the bear-sized bartender said quietly. "First gent that draws a gun in this here establishment is buzzard bait."

Lizzy eased through the mob that had suddenly collected and headed for the stairs. Cam called her back. "Come back here, you ain't off duty yet, girlie. You go up them stairs now, you take a payin' customer, is that clear?"

Someone made out a loud, ribald remark, and Will felt his whiskey threaten to return on him. Deliberately turning his back on the barkeeper, he glared at the room in general.

Most of the men dropped their glances, but a few were watching Lizzy, speculation in their bloodshot eyes. *What's she got hidden up under them skirts that a Kincaid is willing to pay for?*

Dammit, he knew that look, knew what it meant. And it wasn't going to happen, at least not tonight.

Turning back, he slid a wad of folding money across the bar. "Lizzy," he said quietly. "Send her upstairs, I'll be back later."

And then he left. He would not be back, but with a miserable sense of inevitability, he knew that before he could get on with his own affairs, he had to find some way to get her out of there. Find her a decent place to stay and a job in a respectable establishment, one where she wouldn't be expected to earn her living on her back. She was too young, too—

He didn't know what she was, but at least he knew she'd sleep safely for one more night.

Propped up in his own bed sometime later, holding a week-old copy of *The Chicago Daily News*, Will tried to figure out what there was about a clumsy waif with big blue eyes and a prickly attitude that could mess up his priorities so completely. He didn't have time to waste on her problems. He didn't owe her anything.

Fortunately, his nose had returned to its normal size, with only a faint red line across the bridge to show for his misadventure. His shirt had already been laundered, and his suit was being sponged, aired and pressed by the local tailor.

Yet he had paid the going rate for two successive nights for something he had no intention of claiming. Evidently, turning thirty had addled his brain. Or maybe traveling too many miles in too short a period was just now catching up with him, even though he had stopped twice to break the trip.

Or perhaps it was just one of the disadvantages of being a gentleman—the inability to walk away from a bad situation without trying to do something about it.

FIRST THING the next morning, Will started looking for a business that hired women. Respectable women. Because despite her present situation, he was increasingly convinced that Lizzy Price had, at least until recently, been just that. Amos Carlton's wife suggested the Mercantile, after telling him she had all the help she needed at the hotel.

Will wouldn't have wanted her working at the hotel, anyway. Half the men in town would have seen her at the Double Deuce. They might reasonably conclude she had simply transferred her place of business.

Tess Dillard was no more help. "You might want to talk to them that's building the new schoolhouse. I heard they sent off for a teacher, but he might not show up."

"Thanks, Tess, I'll keep it in mind." He hadn't exactly said who he was trying to find work for. A decent, well-spoken young lady, he'd told Millie Carlton.

At least he *thought* she was decent. Or had been until some lowlife had dropped her off at the DD in exchange for his IOUs. A real prince, Will thought, indignation stirring in his veins. Considering where he'd found her, Lizzy Price was surprisingly well-spoken, but a schoolteacher? For all he knew, she might not even be able to read.

Meanwhile, he had his own business to see to. With the deed for a lot in the center of town for his bank being drawn up by his lawyer, he spent another fruitless few hours looking at possible home sites. If no suitable houses were for sale, he would have to find a piece of land he liked and build his own.

On the other hand, if carpenters were in short supply, he might have to stay on at the hotel or lower his expectations, settle for a smaller house and let them get started on his bank. Which in no way explained why, acting on impulse, he found himself riding out to look over the old Tanner place a short while later. To see if it was still as awesomely awful as he remembered.

It was. Like a grand old lady, down on her luck. Shabby and obviously ailing, she still retained a certain elegance—a certain pride.

And once again, he thought of Lizzy. Not that she was ailing—at least, not so far as he knew. But both had obviously seen better days.

Back in town, he returned his rented mount to the livery. Discouraged at finding himself no closer to either of his goals—owning a bank, or owning his own home, he made up his mind to ride up to the ranch and talk to Caleb about that mare he'd mentioned. He needed his own horse, even if he had to keep her at the livery.

Actually, the day hadn't been entirely wasted. At least he had a deed for the land where one day soon, the First Whitehorn Bank and Trust would stand.

But he was no closer to finding a permanent place to live. Bank presidents rarely lived in hotels that lacked a presidential suite. Amos's establishment lacked a suite of any kind. Even the shared plumbing was barely adequate.

The idea that popped into his mind was not new. The first time the notion had occurred to him, he had promptly dismissed it, but like a cocklebur, it wasn't that easy to dislodge.

Lizzy and a house. A house and Lizzy. Like buzzards circling a lame cow, the half-formed thoughts refused to go away. He couldn't seem to forget the mixed message of hope and despair in her eyes that no amount of face paint could disguise.

Not your problem, Kincaid. It was getting to be a familiar refrain.

But it was his problem. He didn't know why, he only knew that his conscience wouldn't allow him to ignore her situation if there was a chance he could help her. Caleb had a wife and son, otherwise he might have considered taking her out to the ranch. Now, he felt as if he no longer had that right. Which left the boarding-house and the hotel. He did know that if she remained where she was, her fate was inevitable. She didn't have what it took to become a success at her chosen profession.

A sleepy-eyed janitor told him Mrs. Harroun's place was plumb full up to the rafters. Will thanked the man, handed him a coin and left. He happened to know the hotel had several empty rooms, but he couldn't bring himself to take her there.

Damned if it wasn't enough to make a man give up drink. Or at least find himself another saloon.

THE IDEA WAS THERE when he woke up the next morning, like a giant spiderweb waiting to capture the unwary. *Sooner or later you're going to need a housekeeper. Why not hire Lizzy for the job?*

Of course, there was the small matter of not owning a house. At the rate he was spending money, burying it under saloons and buying the favors of down-on-their-luck saloon girls so they could get a good night's sleep, he might well end up living in a room over his bank, which wouldn't do much for the image any successful investment banker needed to project.

But the kind of house he needed—the kind that would instill confidence in potential investors—couldn't be built in a day. And the banking business was built on confidence.

With that thought foremost in mind, Will set out to make three stops. The first stop was the barbershop, where Harry told him what he needed to know.

The second was the same lawyer who had handled the deal with McCutcheon. Acting on behalf of the Tanner estate, he said pompously, "You're a wise man, Mr. Kincaid. As representative of that unfortunate family, I can assure you—"

"Unfortunate?"

"Er, um—well, they're all dead but a great-nephew who lives in New York, y'know. However, I have his power of attorney, and I don't mind telling you that you'll be getting your money's worth, that you will, sir. The place is a real gem, built back when the territory was first beginning to open up. Mining interests, I'm told, but that was long before my time."

It was before Will's time, too, but he had no time to waste on a history lesson. The only surprise was that no one had snapped it up.

Standing on the corner of Main and Crossroad some forty-five minutes later, Will tried to sort it all out in his mind. When he'd first made plans to leave Chicago, common sense had pointed to New York, which was, after all, the banking capitol of the world.

However, his heart was in Montana. There came a time in a man's life when his roots and his family, no matter how alienated, came before all else. He'd been thinking in terms of Whitehorn as it had been ten years ago. It had changed. It came as something of a surprise to realize that he had changed, as well. As if he were caught somewhere between Montana and Illinois. Somewhere between the headstrong youngster he'd been in those days, and the pragmatic businessman he was today.

Before he could make up his mind what his next move was going to be—or rush back inside and call off the whole crazy business—Caleb emerged from the nearby barbershop.

Caleb had changed even more than the town. Maybe they had all grown up over the past ten years. "What the devil have you been up to, Will? Harry said—"

On the other hand, once a big brother, always a big brother. "Harry says too damned much. Always has."

"Then it's true?"

Too tired to inquire as to which of his recent actions

Harry had put on the town grapevine, he nodded. "Probably."

"You're crazy!" Caleb had never hesitated to voice an opinion. "God, man, I don't even want to hear about it. Yeah, I do, but first, what happened the night you got whacked by a tray and went upstairs smelling like a distillery with the same girl that tried to break your nose?"

Will was sorely tempted to walk away. He needed more time to come to terms with what he'd set into motion. But dammit, he was his own man now, fully responsible for his own mistakes. So he told him the whole story. The recital ended with the purchase of a worthless, elegant old ruin.

"Jehosaphat, you really *are* crazy!"

"That seems to be the consensus." Leaning against the sun-warmed board-and-batten, Will felt the last of his doubts drift away, replaced by a new sense of determination. This was the hand he'd drawn. He would stand pat and play it out.

"You know it's going to take a fortune to fix up that old ruin."

"Good thing I've got a fortune, then," Will replied with a wry smile. "What I don't have is time."

"What about your bank?"

"Like I said, I've bought the land. Good location, south end of Main. Now all that's left to do is hire a crew to clear the lot and build on it. I've already drawn up the plans."

"Oh, is that all?" Caleb interjected sarcastically. "You do know, don't you, that every carpenter between Butte and Billings will be too busy trying to shore up your mansion to build you a bank."

"My problem. I'm good at logistics."

"Yeah, well the woman's not your problem, little brother."

Some of his newfound determination ebbed away. "Dammit, Caleb, somebody's got to do something for her. You know what'll happen if she stays on there. She might be plain as a mud fence, but odds are she's a good girl who just happened to run into a streak of bad luck." Bad luck in the form of a sweet-talking, no-good, sonovabitch gambler who sold her to pay off his debts. "She's got no business in a place like that. All I intend to do is find someplace to stash her where she'll be safe until she's ready to move on."

"Uh-huh. So you went out and bought her a mansion."

"Stop grinning! I didn't buy *her* a mansion, I bought it for *me!* The girl's got nothing to do with it. I needed a house, and it would take too long to build what I want. And anyway, I've always kind of liked the old place. All it needs is a—"

"New roof, new windows, new porch, paint job inside and out and—"

"Don't you have something to do besides question my judgment?"

Caleb hooked his thumbs in the armholes of his vest, leaned against the sun-baked wall and shook his head. "It's your sanity I'm questioning, man, not your judgment."

"Yeah, well—while you're at it maybe you can give me the names of a few good carpenters, because I just signed the papers. From now on, the old Tanner place will be known as Kincaid's Folly."

Although, the reason he didn't bother to examine too closely, Will kept a room upstairs with Dixie.

Whatever lingered in the gentleman's corner flaming-brown eyes, under Butte's looming peace. Only you would have found it what somehow don't miss about being Dixie woman for the world. And when will burns out, delivers the thing indeed were her own way, by a day of rest.

CHAPTER FOUR

IT WAS AFTER DARK by the time Will got done with all that needed doing. So far, he'd been home three days and had yet to get a full night's sleep. At this rate he wouldn't have the energy to oversee the construction of his bank, much less the repairs on the old ruin he'd impulsively purchased. Making one small bedroom and the kitchen even marginally habitable had required the work of two handymen and one cleaning woman.

Will tried to recall the last time he had done anything quite so reckless. As luck would have it, most of his wilder gambles had paid off, but this time...

Kincaid's Folly was right. He might have bought the place for pennies on the dollar, but by the time he resurrected the old ruin, it would have cost him a healthy bundle.

Not surprisingly, Lizzy was serving drinks when he walked in. Will had a feeling he was going to end up paying for another night of her services. It occurred to him that the services of a skilled professional might help unravel some of the tension that had kept him tied in knots practically ever since he'd stepped off the train in Butte.

But not Lizzy. She admitted she was only a beginner, and while she wasn't quite as unappealing as he'd first thought, for reasons he didn't care to examine too closely, Will knew it would never work with Lizzy.

Whatever happened to the unwritten rule most gentlemen operated under? Unless a woman is the kind you would take home to meet your family, don't ask about hers. Don't get involved on a personal level. And with women of that type, all things mental were personal—only the physical was not.

Cam glanced up at Will, then across the room at Lizzy. Will felt the heat of embarrassment creeping up to stain his face. He swore under his breath. Maybe he should just walk away before he got in any deeper. If it had been a business proposition, he would have pulled out long before now.

Bracing himself to meet the bartender's knowing look, he ordered a straight whiskey, found himself an empty table in a far corner and tilted his chair back to survey the room. He could have carried his own drink, but these ladies counted on tips earned from toting an ounce or two of whiskey across the room.

Cam poured his drink and called on Lizzy to deliver it. Will wanted to believe he hadn't expected it, but he had. He studied the woman as she wobbled across the floor in her ridiculous shoes. Carefully, she lifted the glass from her tray and set it down before him, never once raising her eyes to meet his.

He placed a quarter-eagle on her tray and said, "Sit down, Lizzy."

"I'm busy."

"Sit," he commanded.

"I'm not supposed to sit unless—"

"Sit, dammit! I bought a drink. If I have to, I'll buy you one, too. That should keep Cam off your back for a few minutes.'' He signaled the bar for another of the same. This time, Cam brought it over, gave him a questioning look, then shrugged and walked away.

"He must think—'' Lizzy started to say when he cut her off. Will had a pretty good idea what the bartender was thinking. Obviously, he had already established a reputation as a man with lousy taste in women. Now he was about to establish his idiocy.

So be it. "I've found you a position and a place to stay.'' The "place to stay'' might be stretching it. Caleb hadn't pressed him, and he'd never come right out and said he was going to install Lizzy at the Folly. After assigning the task of readying two rooms, he had rented a wagon and ridden out to the ranch, where he had borrowed a bed and enough other furniture to get by on.

Caleb and Ruth had both insisted he keep the furniture. "It's yours,'' Caleb had told him. "Don't tell me you're planning to move in now. That old wreck will collapse the first time you slam a door.''

"It's not that bad,'' he'd replied, knowing it wasn't that far from the truth, either. He hadn't bothered to elaborate on his plans. Ruth would have insisted on taking Lizzy into her home, which might have caused trouble between her and Caleb.

"Thanks. Once I get things settled, I'll explain what's going on.''

"Yeah, you do that,'' Caleb said dryly as he hefted a three-drawer dresser and headed for the front door. He probably had a pretty good idea what was going on. "By the way, I've got a mare I haven't had time to finish off if you'd like to try her out. That is, if you can find the time." The last remark had been laced with sarcasm.

"Sure, why not? If she's any good, I'll buy her from you." They'd left it at that, because Will had been in a hurry.

And now, for some crazy reason, he had to assure himself that Lizzy would be safe until he could talk her into going along with his idea, which meant paying Cam in advance for another night. With every move he made, he was getting in deeper and deeper. The news had already spread about his buying the old Tanner Mansion. And while he'd like to think of it as an investment, if there was any investment potential in Lizzy Price, it was well hidden.

"I've bought a house," he said flatly. "I need a housekeeper. The job is yours if you'll take it."

"A housekeeper?" Under layers of bright blue mascara, her eyes narrowed in suspicion. "What kind of housekeeper?"

"Well, hell—how many kinds are there? I don't know how to take care of a house, and this one's going to need a lot more than a broom and dustpan." He started to explain, then thought of a better way. "Look, can you take off a couple of hours tomorrow morning?"

"Why?"

The woman would try the patience of a saint. Why did she have to be so suspicious of everything he said or did? He was damn well doing her a favor, wasn't he? What was that old saying about gift horses?

"So you can look over the house I bought and advise me on what it needs," he explained patiently, wondering why he had ever set off down this road. The only excuse he could come up with was that the woman affected him like a bad case of chiggers. She was an itch he was compelled to scratch.

Warily, she nodded. He named a time and told her to be ready. "And for God's sake, wear a decent pair of shoes. It's not like we've got sidewalks out there."

Wordlessly, she nodded again. "And wear something to cover your head. The sun's pretty powerful." Besides which, he'd as soon not have the whole town see her riding out of town with him.

"Cam might object," she whispered, reddening until the twin splotches of rouge no longer stood out on her cheeks.

He stood. "Don't worry about Cam. Just be ready when I come by for you in the morning."

He handed the proprietor a couple of bills, followed Lizzy upstairs, and let himself out the back way, just as he'd done before. It was getting to be a habit, traipsing upstairs with one of the girls. The runt of the litter, at that. So much for any pretense of moral rectitude; he couldn't even manage good taste.

After tomorrow, if all went well, he'd be out of this self-inflicted mess. A saloon, he told himself, oblivious to the flaw in his reasoning, was a fine place for men, but women had no business there.

THAT NIGHT before scrubbing her face and saying her prayers, Lizzy took one last glance in the mirror her father had given her for her sixteenth birthday. When thoughts of those happy days threatened to creep in, she quickly slammed the door on the past. She'd do well to keep her mind on present dangers until Cicero returned to bail her out of this awful place. He had promised to return in a week and pay back what he owed Cam, but the week had come and gone. Cam no longer felt compelled to keep his promise not to force her to work upstairs.

Housekeeper. Well, we'd see about that. She wasn't about to jump out of the frying pan into the fire.

"It's on the western edge of town," Will explained the next morning as they wheeled away from the saloon in the buckboard he had rented. As soon as he could spare the time, he needed to try out Caleb's mare. While he was at it, he'd have to see about fencing in a section of his newly purchased acreage.

"I'm still not quite sure what it is you want to show me." In the clean morning air, she looked surprisingly young and not too surprisingly, still wary. Her blue dimity frock had seen better days, but the quality was unmistakable.

Who are you, Lizzy Price? Will wondered, not for the first time.

Her face seemed unnaturally pale without the heavy cosmetics. Fortunately, most of her awful hair was hidden under a coal-scuttle bonnet that, while out of fashion, was obviously of first quality.

"This house I bought is going to need a lot of work." He was still figuring out his approach even as he explained. "It occurred to me that I'll need someone on the site to take charge while it's being brought up to standard."

Her eyes rounded at that. "Take charge of what?"

"Not the actual repairs. Naturally, I'll need an overseer keeping up with the building crew." At least he would if he could hire himself a team of first-rate carpenters. "But you see, it's a big house—" He refused to use the term *mansion,* not wanting to scare her off. "Like most houses, it needs a woman, not just to oversee the cleaning. I'm not sure how the rooms were laid out originally, but there'll be painting and curtains and things like that. I'm afraid I don't know much about what looks good."

Actually, he did. His likes and dislikes were firmly fixed after living in everything from the worst bunkhouses to the finest hotels these past ten years. "Now, personally, I prefer wood-paneled walls, but most of these walls are plastered. Which means they'll need paint or wallpaper, and I'm no hand when it comes to choosing patterns and colors."

"You want me to pick out what goes on your walls?" The question ended on a high squeak.

"Unfortunately," he said ruefully, mentally crossing his fingers, "I'm not married. My mother died when I was young. I haven't been back to Whitehorn in ten years, so I don't know any women I could ask to help me on this project beyond rough cleaning. If you turn me down I'll likely end up making a mess of everything. I've been told my taste in decorations is less than perfect." He'd been told no such thing, but what the devil.

"But—but why me? Because you like *my* taste?" Her brief laugher was openly skeptical. One more subtle hint that there was more to the woman than met the eye. If there was, he didn't want to know about it. He was half tempted to take her back where he'd found her and leave her there, with his blessings.

He turned to speak and was captured by the cameolike perfection of her profile as she gazed up at the mountains. You'd think she had never seen a mountain before.

You'd think he had never seen a woman's profile before.

The roads were rutted, the seats unforgiving. As they bumped along the rocky, sun-baked surface, Will tried to think of a tactful response to her question about why he was going to such lengths.

Because he liked her taste? Hardly. He had sense enough to know that what she'd been wearing at the saloon was probably not indicative of her personal tastes, but then, what she was wearing now could have come from a missionary barrel for all he knew.

If he allowed her a free hand she'd probably do the old place over in bordello fashion, in which case he'd have to hire someone else to undo it. Or live with it. That would really enhance his image as a successful banker.

Oh, what the devil, he'd just have to keep tabs on what she was doing as the job progressed.

"Now, about where you'll be staying," he said, clearing his throat and paying particular attention to the road ahead. "I considered the boardinghouse and the hotel, but it occurred to me you might not be comfortable staying in town—I mean a woman living alone, and all that."

"Because everyone knows where I've been these past two weeks," she said quietly.

"Now that you mention it, that could be a factor," he admitted, as though that thought had never occurred to him.

Fortunately, he was saved from having to explain further. "There it is, just up ahead. It doesn't look like much now, but with a little work…'' It looked like the very devil, and it would take more than a little work. He could probably have built two houses for what the repairs alone would cost, but he needed a house *now*.

"Oh, my," Lizzy murmured. "Oh, my mercy." It was a monstrous house, narrow, but a full three stories tall. It looked more pathetic than ever, stripped bare by the harsh light of a clear Montana morning.

Will looped the reins around the stump of a dead cottonwood and helped her down from the buckboard. "Watch the front steps—I'll see that they're on the list to be repaired. Well, what do you think?"

He shouldn't care what she thought of the old ruin, but oddly enough, he did. She was probably doubting the sanity of any man who would buy such a place.

So was he. "I, uh—I used to play here as a child," he admitted. "We all considered it haunted—you know the way kids are."

Seeing an odd look cross her face, almost as if she were in pain, he could have kicked himself. *Remember the rules, Kincaid—nothing personal!*

"Not that it was. Haunted, I mean. All old houses get a reputation, don't they?" He didn't want to put her off, but how could he explain buying such a monstrosity to a stranger when he couldn't even justify it to himself?

"I'm sure it's—that is, it must once have been… lovely."

She had a manner of speaking that struck him as odd, considering her circumstances. Despite himself he wondered how she had ended up in a place like the Double Deuce. He knew a man was involved—a man usually was in these cases. But it was none of his business, and he'd do well to keep that fact foremost in his mind.

A board creaked underfoot, and instinctively, he reached for her arm. "I'll have someone go over the floors first thing to be sure they're still sound."

She was frail as a bird. He released her almost immediately. Still feeling the warmth of her flesh, he planted his fists on his hips and looked around, struck all over again by his own recklessness.

And he'd thought he had outgrown it?

If he had half a grain of sense, he would take Lizzy back where he'd found her, turn his back on this old relic, head west to Butte and catch the next eastbound train back to Chicago. Or even New York. He had seen Caleb, met his new sister-in-law, his cousin and his nephew. Maybe somewhere along the way he could catch up with Brock.

Lizzy gestured toward the staircase. "The banister is lovely. Once the missing spokes are replaced, all it should need is a thorough scrubbing and then a good rubdown with beeswax."

"There, you see?" Will tried to infuse his voice with enthusiasm, but it wasn't easy when he was suffering under a ton of doubt. "It takes a woman to see these things. Me, I'd have probably slapped on a coat of barn paint and let it go at that."

Juliette Elizabeth Price-Hawthorne shot him a skeptical look. He was up to something. Until she discovered what it was, it would pay to walk carefully, and not just on account of the risky flooring.

The thought had barely formed in her mind when she stumbled over an uneven floorboard and would have fallen if he hadn't caught her arm and swung her around. Regaining her balance was easy. Regaining her composure was another matter, with his arms wrapped around her, mashing her face against his vest.

He smelled…male. Both her father and her brother had always smelled like cologne, tobacco and whiskey.

Will Kincaid smelled like clean linens, good woolens and sunshine. And while he might have the looks of a gentleman, the hands that gripped her arms had done more than leaf through the morning paper and help ladies into their carriages.

Stepping back, she drew in a shaky breath. "Thank you, I'm all right now."

She was *not* all right. What she was, was suspicious. If he had any intention of setting her up here as his paramour, this would be the time to set him straight.

And do what, Lizzy—go back to the Double Deuce? Oh, Cicero, how could you, she wailed inwardly.

"You're sure? Didn't turn your ankle or anything like that?"

She managed to laugh as she backed away and braced herself against a dusty wall. "I'm not wearing those awful red shoes today."

"Oh. Well, then, shall we continue the tour?"

And as if she weren't riddled with doubts—as if she were still every inch the lady she had once been, and he were every inch the gentleman he appeared, he took her arm and led her through the arched doorway.

"This is obviously the front parlor," she said, trying her best to ignore his size, his looks—his potent masculinity. He was a tall, strong man, and while his features weren't storybook handsome, the sum total was devastating.

And she'd do well to guard against being devastated.

"Facing north as it does," she said as if she were guiding a tour through one of the magnificent old homes along the Battery, "it might look best painted in a warm shade of yellow."

It really was a lovely old house. Even in its present deplorable condition, she could see the possibilities. The most remarkable thing of all was finding such a place out here on the wild frontier.

"Yellow," he said thoughtfully. "I do believe you're right."

"And through here—" She led the way, needing to put as much space between them as possible. "It could be either a study or a dining room."

"Nice fireplace," Will observed, trying to see his house through her eyes. It was a mess. The old place had obviously sheltered its share of drifters, grub-line riders. He'd need to have new locks put on and old doors replaced. No sensible man would leave an investment unprotected, he told himself as he took her arm again, this time to guide her past a patch of broken glass.

They toured the rest of the two bottom floors. Will refused to test the stairs to the attic, remembering the wretched condition they'd been in nearly twenty years ago. The kitchen had been cleaned that very morning, but it would need to be thoroughly modernized. He would order one of those new ranges for cooking and a table that didn't look as though it had gone through the wars. And some dishes and cutlery. And some chairs. The only chair in the house was the one in the small bedroom he'd had cleaned and furnished. Lizzy had peered through the door as they'd toured the second floor, but he hadn't explained who it was intended for and she hadn't asked.

"So," he said, back in the soon-to-be-yellow front parlor. "Will you take on the job?"

"I can't imagine why you would trust me to do it."

"Who else could I hire? Most of the women in town have homes of their own with families to take care of. As for the single ones..."

"They wouldn't consider it. It would be unseemly," she said in that surprisingly prim little voice that had seemed so at odds with her appearance the first time he'd laid eyes on her.

Unseemly. That was putting it mildly. God, that hair of hers was awful! Looked as if it had been dipped in a bucket of orange paint. She had removed her bonnet, using it to swat down cobwebs.

"I've never done anything like it before, you understand, but if you're willing to take a chance, I promise to do my very best to please you." She was staring down at the tips of her worn gray kid shoes, but he could see the color seeping into her cheeks. "What I meant was..."

She wanted to please him? Well, bless her heart, maybe she would have made a right fair saloon girl, after all, if he hadn't decided to rescue her. Will cleared his throat and said, "We haven't talked about your salary." He named a figure, and her head snapped up again.

"I'll hardly be here long enough to earn all that."

"You will if you see the job through. Once everything else is finished, I'll still need a hand in picking out furniture. This is the first house I've ever owned."

"Yes, well...I never actually furnished a house before, either."

"But you're a woman. Women know about things like that—curtains and those little ruffle-edged tables and all."

"Pie crust."

"Beg pardon?"

"They're called pie crust tables."

"There, you see?" He made the most of the minor confirmation.

Late afternoon sunlight slanted down through the filthy windows, capturing millions of dust motes. Will cleared his throat again and ran a finger under his collar. "Now, about your living quarters," he began.

"That's what that little bedroom is for, isn't it? I wondered about it. You have to understand, though, that if you're planning on moving in right away, I can't live here. My reputation would be ruined."

Will didn't have the heart to tell her that after working in a saloon it was already in tatters, even if she hadn't done all that much upstairs work. He himself had paid for a couple of nights, and he didn't figure Cam for the most discreet man in town. He had taken her up those stairs with half the men in the barroom cheering them on. To all intents and purposes, she was already a fallen woman.

"I'm staying at Amos's hotel in town. The room's yours if you'll take it. Otherwise I'd have to arrange for daily transportation, and—"

"Oh, please—there's no need for that. And I want you to know I intend to pay back every penny you've spent on me. I know you paid Cam for—well, for my time." Color flared in her cheeks again. He couldn't remember ever seeing a woman with thinner skin. It was a wonder she hadn't poisoned herself with all that junk she put on her face.

From something Cam had mentioned about a debt owed him by the man who had left her there, Will was probably going to have to pay a damned sight more for her freedom than the cost of a couple of nights. She didn't need to know about that, though. Even a saloon girl could have pride. It was a new concept, one he had never considered before, and didn't particularly want to consider now, but there it was. There was more to a woman than her profession.

"Thank you, Miss Lizzy," he said gravely. "Now, I've arranged for a woman from town to come out every day for the heavy cleaning. You're to tell her where to start. I'll send supplies out with her, and— oh, yeah—if you can find the time, I've had the kitchen cleaned up a bit, too. Once the new range is delivered, do you suppose you could see to feeding the workmen? Things will go a lot faster if they don't have to go home for dinner."

Another sop to her pride, the little minx. If she was determined to earn her keep, he might as well direct her energies. Otherwise there was no telling what she'd get up to.

So IT WAS SETTLED, Will mused on the way back to town. Lizzy, sitting as far away on the hard plank seat as possible, had been silent ever since they'd left the house. "I'll take you back to Cam's place and let you get your things. Then I believe I'll look into getting you a dog, just so you'll have some company. A guard dog. One that would scare the devil out of any would-be prowlers.''

Kincaid's Folly, he mused, just beginning to sense how deep a hole he had dug for himself.

CHAPTER FIVE

BY THE LIGHT of the oil lamp, Lizzy stared down at the orange water in the china basin and fought back tears. Crying wouldn't help matters. She had learned that lesson long ago. Scouring her head another ten times just might. At least her hair was now more the color of a persimmon instead of the bright shade of orange it had been when she'd started.

When the other girls had suggested dying her hair as a means of improving her looks, she'd still been in a condition of shock at finding herself held hostage for her brother's gambling debts. Ashamed, she had told no one, letting them believe she was there only because she needed a job and was not too particular.

A friendly group for the most part, the five other girls—women, actually, for all were older than she—had treated her as they might a doll, trying on first one outfit, then another, painting her face and teasing her hair until it stood up around her face like dandelion fluff. That and the dye, which they had sworn was not permanent, had made it impossible to comb ever since.

At the time Lizzy hadn't cared. The less familiar the face she confronted in her mirror, the easier it was to pretend it was someone else installed in the tiny room at the end of the hall in the rambling, noisy, smelly old saloon in a town that was new and raw and barely even civilized.

Except for a bit of backbiting when one of them was perceived as infringing on someone else's territory, the other girls were surprisingly good-natured. Back home in Charleston, such women were spoken of in whispers, if at all. At first Lizzy had been too stunned at finding herself in such a place to react when they had surrounded her like a flock of colorful birds, chattering and touching her face, her hair, criticizing her clothes, her figure, her way of speaking.

But she had learned many things since her parents had died and she'd been left in the tender care of an immature brother. One of the first lessons was that nothing would ever be the same again. No more paddling on the river. No more lawn tennis. No more parties, where she would allow herself to be talked into singing, and later, after the minister's wife had left, dance herself breathless to ragtime music played on a grand piano.

When her world had suddenly come to an end, she had learned to adapt, and thus to survive. She was still learning. She had done her best to be a good waitress, for that was what saloon girls did when they weren't occupied upstairs. Cicero had made Cam promise that she wouldn't be required to go upstairs. A week, he'd said. He would return in a week with the money he owed the proprietor, who had bought up his IOUs, and then they would move on to another town and start afresh.

So she'd served drinks and waited for Cicero to return, and counted her blessings when Cam hadn't forced her to work upstairs. Two weeks had passed, and no Cicero. Her luck had run out the night some drunken fool had pulled out his gun and started shooting and she'd dropped a tray and spilled whiskey all over a paying customer.

In a moment of weakness, with perhaps just a touch of self-pity, Lizzy allowed her thoughts to drift back to the past. If her entire world hadn't shattered back in Charleston nearly a year ago, Mr. and Mrs. Henry Cicero Price-Hawthorne, the third, would be preparing to officially launch their only daughter into society. She would be wearing white crepe, white slippers and her birthday pearls, with her pale, curly hair tamed into a fashionable pompadour.

With a swipe of her arm, Lizzy smeared the tears across her face and tackled her hair again. At least no one in Charleston would ever know how far she had fallen. Bad enough that everyone who was anyone in Charleston had known about her father's gambling. Everyone knew, although they were far too well-bred to mention it, that in one last desperate attempt to recoup, he had lost their home—the only thing he hadn't already gambled away—and then recklessly driven himself and his wife into the Ashley River. They had called it an accident—it had been pitch-black and raining hard, and the Price-Hawthornes had been on their way home from a party, where, as usual, her father would have had more to drink than was wise.

But Lizzy, who had been called Juliette then, had known in her heart that her father had taken the easy way out of his disgrace. Henry Cicero, the third, had been too deeply in debt ever to recover, thanks to a lifelong addiction to gambling.

And Henry Cicero, the fourth, had sworn on his father's grave that he would never again touch a deck of cards or a pair of dice. But as the spoiled only son of a prominent Charleston family, he'd been too weak to keep his promise.

They had left Charleston with little more than their shredded pride, their clothes and Cicero's gig, which had broken a wheel before they even reached the Tennessee border. Cicero had sold his horse, bought two tickets on a train headed west, and from there on, he had paid their way by gambling.

Lizzy had known what he was doing, of course, but as they had already sold everything of value they possessed, including the pearls her father had given her for her seventeenth birthday, she could see no other way. It wasn't as if either of them had been trained to earn a living.

After a run of hard luck in Kansas, during which they had both washed dishes in a restaurant for their meals, she'd suggested they stay there and work their way into the restaurant business. But Cicero, always a fan of Wild West shows, had had some idea of finding work on a ranch in the real Wild West and someday owning his own spread. "Not many people living out that far, not like home. Land'll be dirt cheap," he'd said, his boyish laughter inviting her to share his little joke, to share his dream.

So he had continued to gamble. It was only for seed money, he'd explained, because traveling with a lady was expensive. Once they arrived at their destination, he vowed never to touch another card. Instead, he would find work on a ranch and save every penny he earned. She could keep house for him, and one day they would return to Charleston for a visit. "We'll go home in style, Sissy, you just wait. But just for a visit, mind, because by then I'll have my own ranch to come back to.''

She should have known better. She *had* known better, but Cicero, even though he seemed younger, was actually eleven months older than she was. A gentleman born and bred, he had vowed to take care of her, and without skills herself, she'd had no choice but to let him try.

Well, she thought, examining her sore scalp in the tiny silver-backed mirror—she had managed to get herself out of the mess he'd landed her in without her brother's help. She loved him—she would always love him, but from now on she intended to stand on her own two feet.

And those feet, she thought with tired amusement, would be wearing her own shoes from now on. Cam must have been relieved to see the last of her, else he would have insisted she stay until Cicero repaid the money he owed.

With that thought Lizzy settled down for her first night's sleep in the huge, scary old mansion in the shadow of the Crazy Mountains.

THE CREATURE who met him at the door when he came to bring the dog was hardly recognizable as the woman he had brought out here only two days ago. Will tried not to laugh. He tried not to stare at her hair, which was no longer orange. If he had to name the color, he'd be at a dead loss. As for the style, it still stood out around her face, but great chunks of it had been whacked out, as if she'd been victim of a botched scalping. "Good morning, Miss Lizzy," he said solemnly.

She glared at him, her eyes looking larger than ever now that they were no longer weighted down by layers of shiny blue paint. "Stop staring at me that way, I had to cut out the tangles. If it offends you I can tie a rag around my head."

Recognizing her belligerence as embarrassment, Will tactfully changed the subject. "I've brought you a companion." He snapped his fingers and a black-tan-and-white dog sat up in the back of the buckboard, its ears pricked expectantly. "Her name is Ruby, and she's led a hard life. I believe she might have a touch of rheumatism, but if you'll give her a place in the sun and feed her now and then, she'll give fair warning whenever anyone comes within range of the house." He'd intended to buy a guard dog, something to protect his property against transients, but it occurred to him that Lizzy might not like being out here alone with a dog that was half wolf. "She's got a yip on her loud enough to start an avalanche."

Lizzy studied the dog. The dog studied Lizzy. "Then it's a good thing I'll be gone long before winter, isn't it?"

THE MASSIVE cast-iron range was delivered by freight wagon from Butte the next morning. Two men from the Kincaid ranch came to uncrate it, and Lizzy stared at it in horror. Surely she wasn't expected to cook on that thing...was she?

Mrs. Gibson, the cleaning woman, declared it the finest stove in all Whitehorn. "You'll be able to cook up a storm on that thing, Miss Lizzy. I reck'n Mr. Will's gonna get his money's worth there."

And that was another thing. The salary Will had promised her was far too much. Lizzy knew to the penny how much her parents had paid the household help. She was being paid too much for a job she wasn't at all sure she could do. She might have lost almost everything she had once held dear, but she still had too much pride to accept charity.

One of the more painful lessons Lizzy had had to learn, however, was pragmatism. Given the choice of working for Will Kincaid, working as a saloon girl—upstairs and down—or starving, she made the only sensible choice.

"I'll earn every penny of it, just you wait and see," she whispered fiercely after Will had driven off. Ruby lifted her head, flapped her tail and went back to sleep in a patch of sunlight falling through the newly replaced bay window.

WILL WAITED two days before riding out to the Folly again. It was only sensible, he told himself, to keep up with the progress. It was going to be his home, after all. Riding out every day or so to check on things had nothing to do with the woman he'd installed there.

He was met by the cheerful sound of hammers, good-natured swearing, and the sight of Lizzy on her hands and knees with a bucket and scrub brush, her shapely rear end swinging in counterpoint with her shoulders. With the door wide open to catch the draft, she was scrubbing the front hallway and singing softly in a voice as clear as a mountain lake.

He lingered to enjoy the sight and sound until it

occurred to him that he wasn't the only man enjoying the impromptu concert. Wheeling around, he circled the house, looking for something to criticize. The men went back to work, and the fact that he found nothing amiss didn't improve his temper.

She was still at it when he completed his tour of inspection, but the singing stopped the instant his boots hit the bottom step, "Where's Mrs. Gibson?" he demanded, crossing the front porch to step into the foyer. "I hired her to do the rough cleaning."

"She's upstairs scrubbing the walls." Applying a hand to the small of her back, Lizzy slowly got to her feet.

"Dammit, you're supposed to be overseeing the work, not doing it yourself!"

"Yes, it is a lovely morning, isn't it?" she said calmly. "Come and have a cup of tea and I'll show you what we've done so far, and then you can decide how you want to use the rooms."

If he'd been in danger of forgetting the citified manners he had learned back East, she quickly reminded him. Haughty as a duchess, she made tea in the kitchen, using a battered kettle and the rusted old cookstove, and served it in a pair of saucerless, mismatched mugs that had come from God knows where. The attic, for all he knew. Evidently the dishes he'd ordered hadn't arrived yet.

"I'm afraid I don't have anything to serve with it."

"Tea's just fine. I wasn't expecting refreshments." He managed a gritty smile. If she wanted to play lady, then he could damn well play gentleman. It probably wouldn't kill him.

So he settled into one of the kitchen chairs he had

ordered along with the table and range and watched her pour from a fat brown teapot with a chipped spout. He stared at her hands—the broken fingernails and the long, graceful fingers—and avoided looking at her hair, which was ugly beyond belief. Her face, innocent of paint except for a streak of grime across one cheek, was...

Well, it was hardly beautiful, but interesting. Surprisingly interesting. Miss Lizzy Price was a bundle of contradictions.

As soon as he could, he left—*fled* was too strong a word—making some excuse about an appointment.

THE NEXT DAY Will deliberately stayed away, using his time to round up a few more carpenters, all of them older, experienced men who wouldn't be so easily distracted. By offering them a bonus he extracted a promise that once they finished the Folly, they would go to work on the bank building he had designed, which was a smaller version of one he had particularly liked in Chicago.

Then, after an excellent midday meal at Mrs. Harroun's groaning table, he purchased a well-made buckboard and arranged for pasturage for Chili, the mare he'd bought from Caleb, who had refused payment until he'd caught sight of a warning glint in Will eyes. Next thing on the list would be to see to having a portion of his own acreage fenced.

By now, the new range should have been installed. Lizzy might even be cooking the midday meal. Despite first impressions, she was an earnest little creature who obviously wanted to feel as if she were earning her salary. He would rather have her puttering in the kitchen than on her knees scrubbing his floors and driving his carpenters to distraction.

By late afternoon, Will could restrain himself no longer. Collecting Chili from the livery stable, he headed out of town. The ride out, though only a couple of miles, had a soothing effect. By the time he pulled up before the Folly, he was in a far better frame of mind.

Control. There was a time when he'd railed at Caleb for having to control everything and everyone within range. Funny, the way, after all these years, he had uncovered the same trait in himself.

Bathed in the golden glow of a setting sun, the old house looked rather magnificent, even with two men on the roof and another working on the eaves. A portion of the roof sagged slightly. Much of the original gingerbread trim was still missing. New rafters could be had locally, but the millwork would have to be freighted in. The list of needed materials grew daily. He only hoped that once this job was finished he would have enough of his fortune intact to complete the grand structure he envisioned for his bank. One folly was enough for any man; he had already invested in two. The house, and Lizzy.

When Cam had explained that he had taken her in against money owed him and named an exorbitant sum, Will had been shocked. "The woman's a gambler?"

"Not her. Feller that left her here. Claimed she was his sister." Cam had waggled his bushy gray brows.

"So you took her in against her companion's marker?" If he'd heard the tale before, he hadn't paid much attention. At the time, her reasons for being here hadn't seemed all that important.

"I bought up the kid's IOUs when them gents he was playing with woulda taken it out of his hide. It come down to a draw as to which one could work it off quicker, him or her. She ain't much to look at, but he's worse'n useless. Weak chin, soft hands. I took her on, but maybe I'd'a done better with him."

So Will had anted up and Cam had handed over the IOUs, signed with an indecipherable squiggle. One thing he'd learned on the way to making his first fortune was that money spent was money put back into circulation. And as long as money was circulating, he would manage to snag his share. As a wealthy man he had more to spend, which would in turn benefit the town, which would only add to his own riches in the long run. What goes around, comes around. He'd heard it all his life, and in banking circles it was doubly true. And the Kincaids, after all, had a social responsibility.

Now his boots rang out on new wood as he strode across the wide front porch. A beaming Lizzy, her pink cheeks clashing wildly with her hair, met him at the front door. Wrapped in an apron that would fit a woman three times her girth, she invited him inside. "Come and see what we've done."

The first thing he noticed was the smell, a combination of harsh soap, new lumber and something else— something that reminded him of branding time back at the ranch.

"See the new windows? I thought first we'd paint the walls and then we'll finish the floors. After that, we can decide on rugs and draperies."

We.

He really should resent it, yet somehow, he didn't. He had invited her to take charge, and she had done it.

It was determination to earn her keep that put that proprietary note in her voice.

They toured the second floor, where Violet Gibson, widow of the man who had taught both Caleb and Will to hunt and trap, was attacking a filthy fireplace, her skirts tucked up between her ample thighs and pinned in front. "Lord, help us, Mr. Will, you liked to scared me to death!" She fumbled with the pins, and her skirts fell modestly over her boot tops. "You didn't say nothin' about me cookin' for your men, so I didn't. Left it to Miss Lizzy. But if you was to ask me, I reck'n I could manage both jobs."

"No, no, that's all right, Mrs. Gibson, you keep on with what you're doing." A vision of Lizzy in a similar situation, her skirts tucked up to her waist, caught him off guard, and he hurriedly led the way back downstairs.

"The freight wagon delivered some more things this morning," she said in that breathless little voice that was so at odds with the determination he'd glimpsed more than a few times. "I had them put in the room off the kitchen. You can look them over and tell me what needs doing."

It would be the plumbing. He had made up his mind when he left Chicago that when he built himself a house in Whitehorn, it would have indoor plumbing. As the Tanner place hadn't been equipped for such modern conveniences, it was going to require a bit more than the appliances, themselves.

Lizzy touched her hair self-consciously and then she squared her shoulders. "You're probably wondering what I've been doing all day."

"No, I'm not. What I'm wondering is, what the devil is that smell?"

"Oh. Well now, I never actually said I was a good cook, did I?"

His eyes narrowed. Ruby wandered into the front room and leaned against his thigh. As a guard dog, about all she could do was bark, but she'd outlived her usefulness on the ranch, and so Will had claimed her before the new manager could have her put down.

"We got the stove set up, with the stovepipe and all, this morning. It's a—a lovely stove, but you see—"

Yesterday Will had asked Tess Dillard to get up an order of basic supplies and send it out to the Folly. He wouldn't have had any idea what to include, other than coffee, tinned milk and sugar. Except for a few lean years when he'd had to hunt or fish for his supper and cook it on an open fire, he had dined in restaurants these past nine years. "Not what you're used to, huh?"

She beamed, looking almost relieved. "That's it! I'm not used to—to the oven. But I managed to scrape most of the black parts off the biscuits yesterday, and the meat—well, the men said it tasted all right, anyway. They're really quite nice."

There were degrees of "nice". By hiring older men and letting go a couple of the younger ones, he thought he'd handled any problem that might arise. He would have to talk to them again. Trouble was, there was no way he could do it without calling attention to what it was he was trying to obscure.

Standing in front of the fireplace that had been scoured with vinegar and washing soda, Will looked at the small woman he had once considered plain as a mud fence. There was nothing plain about her. Even her hair, which was her worst feature, could hardly be called plain.

He didn't know exactly what to call it, but nothing about the woman was plain, as in homely. As in ordinary.

Nothing at all.

CHAPTER SIX

THE CARPENTERS were good. The work was progressing far more rapidly than he'd expected. There was still a lot to do, but in spite of his eagerness to begin work on his bank, Will didn't want them to skimp on repairing his house. Lizzy was beside herself with excitement over the way the place was taking shape. As often as not when he rode out late in the afternoon for a brief check on the progress, she would be outside, shading her eyes against the setting sun to admire each new accomplishment.

Yesterday it had been the last section of porch railing. Today it was the ready-milled trim he'd ordered by telegraph, with a bonus for prompt delivery. At this rate, the job would be done within the month, he thought, nodding to the old carpenter he'd known slightly all his life. When Lizzy wandered over to join them, the old man's face split in a wide, yellow-toothed smile. "Now, don't you go trippin' over them tools, Miss Lizzy, I'll have Homer clear 'em off the porch directly he comes down off'n the ladder."

"Have you come to have dinner with us? I cooked sausage and beans."

Will opened his mouth to speak, but the foreman beat him to it. "Meant to tell you, m' wife's got this church social this evening, supper on the ground and all. She'll be needin' me to help her tote the basket."

"Oh. There certainly are a lot of church socials in town. Wasn't there another one just the other day?"

The man looked embarrassed and muttered something about raising money for the new school. It was the first Will had heard of such a project.

"Well, then, you'll have to stay, Will. I've cooked far too much, I'm afraid. I'm almost certain I measured a cup of beans for each person into the pot, but I must have miscounted. There's enough to feed an army. For dessert I cooked dried apples...." Her voice trailed off as a worried look replaced her eager smile.

"I reckon the other men'll be wantin' to leave early, too, ma'am. We all go to the same church. Never miss a social, nosiree. Wife wouldn't hear of it."

Lizzy looked so crestfallen, Will wondered how the man had the heart to disappoint her. Obviously she had labored over a special treat for their dinner.

Sausage and beans? Chuckwagon fare, at best. In fact, their old cook back in the days when Will had been a part of the ranch operation could cook circles around half the chefs in Chicago. You wouldn't find fancy garnishes on the tin plates he served when they rode up to bring the herd down for the winter, but his fried mountain oysters and sonovabitch stew, made from calf's brains and a variety of internal organs, were the best in the world.

Lizzy sighed. Against his better judgment, Will heard himself saying, "I'd be pleased to join you for supper, Miss Price." He stressed the formality in case any of the men got the wrong idea about their relationship. She was a temporary housekeeper, that was all. The sooner her brother came back to take her off his hands, the better.

If he really *was* a brother. More than likely, the man who had left her at the saloon had been her lover. What brother would leave his sister in a place like the Double Deuce?

What brother would rob his own brother's safe?

Wrenching his mind away from distracting thoughts, he said, "You and the men think about that barn I'm needing, Millard. If you could work it into your schedule, I'd be much obliged."

Meanwhile, the sooner he found his housekeeper another position, the sooner he could get his mind back on more important things. The trouble was, he wasn't having any luck finding her a suitable job, much less a safe place to stay. Not that he'd gone out of his way to look.

Will had just taken his seat at the table when Violet Gibson strode into the kitchen to remove her apron. She took one look at the small blackened links in the skillet, at the large covered pot on the stove, and shook her head. "I'll be leaving now, Miss Lizzy. First thing tomorrow I'll start on them back rooms upstairs."

"Are you sure you won't stay, Mrs. Gibson? I cooked plenty for everyone."

"Church social. Wouldn't want to miss that, now, would I? How-do, Mr. Will. Glad you come along to keep Miss Lizzy comp'ny."

Will cut a sideling glance at the covered pot and put on his diplomat's smile. "My lucky day, Mrs. Gibson. Sure you won't join us for supper?"

The minute the woman left the room, Lizzy, at her

most pugnacious, said, "You don't have to stay. Nobody invited you."

"Now, I could've sworn I heard you inviting me to join you not five minutes ago. Is there something wrong with my hearing?"

Lizzy blinked furiously and thrust out her surprisingly firm little chin. The tip of her nose grew red. "You don't need to spare my feelings. I'm not a very good cook, yet—actually, I'm a terrible cook, but I can't bear to waste all that food."

Before Will could assure her she was a wonderful cook, the best in the world, she took out a single plate and slapped it down on the table.

"Please. I'd rather stay, if you don't mind," he said quietly. "We need to talk."

Without a word, she took down another plate. There were no napkins. He'd ordered a set of plain dishes and flatware, enough to get by with until he was ready to move in. Over beans that were unsalted and undercooked, sausage that had been all but incinerated, and lumpy, unsweetened stewed apples with a dollop of cream, he told her they needed to make a list.

"Tasty," he said, forcing a smile as he poured more cream over the tart apples.

"Mrs. Gibson brought the cream. I would have used sugar, but it was full of ants, so I threw it out."

Gamely, he told her he would have done the same. "Never could abide ants in my food. They taste like spoiled pickles."

"Actually," she said, flashing a hint of a dimple, "they taste more like capers."

"Capers?"

"It's a sort of flower bud that's been cured in

brine...I think. Our old cook used to—'' She clapped a hand over her mouth.

Pushing his plate back, Will tipped his chair and crossed his arms over his chest. "Go on. Your old cook used to do what?"

"Nothing. I was just making conversation. If you're finished, we could have coffee in the parlor, only you don't have any furniture there yet. Is that what you wanted to talk to me about? Furniture styles, and how you'd like things arranged?"

She was talking too fast and looking so miserable, he gave in. She had her secrets—so did he. It was increasingly evident that she came from a respectable background, and that somehow, she and her rapscallion brother, or at least, the man she'd been traveling with, had managed to get into more trouble than they could handle.

He knew how that was. She was young—too damn young for him to be thinking the kind of thoughts he'd been thinking lately. He did remember how it was, though. When you were young and on your own, mistakes could pile up faster than they could be dealt with. He had managed to survive and even learn from most of his mistakes.

How would it be with a woman? What lessons had she been forced to learn before winding up at the Double Deuce?

The meal over, Will wandered into the room at the front of the house that had been designated the front parlor. Discouragingly bleak, the walls were a dingy shade of gray, the patched plaster making ugly white blemishes.

"Yellow," he said when Lizzy joined him in the

doorway. "I do believe you're right. Now, the first question is, should we paint the woodwork to match, or sand and varnish it?"

Ignoring the acrid smell emanating from the kitchen, he drew her out, asking her ideas on furnishing one room after another as they wandered through the house. At this point, what she did with his house didn't seem half as urgent as solving the puzzle that was Lizzy.

They talked about furniture. Horsehair and velvet and some guy named Louis. He promised to order whatever she thought he would need. And whatever it was, he would live with it. Live with it long after the funny little woman who called herself Lizzy Price was only a distant memory.

She talked with her hands. Graceful gestures that were no less effective because her hands were reddened and her fingernails were broken. There was a faint glow of perspiration on her upper lip.

And then she yawned, covering her mouth with the back of her hand. "I'm so sorry," she murmured. "The carpenters come early, and I try to have coffee made, at least."

He could picture her, scurrying to the kitchen in her nightgown to set the water to boiling, then racing back upstairs. What would she sleep in? Red satin? White flannel? The nights were growing cooler. He would have to see about installing a new furnace.

Flannel, he decided, because picturing her in a skimpy film of red silk was more than his imagination could handle. Wearing virginal white flannel, sleeping in his bed. The same bed he had slept in more than half his life, dreaming little-boy dreams of fishing for brown trout and hunting bison and grizzlies, wildfowl and lost gold mines.

Later on had come the adolescent dreams of girls and kissing, and what went on beyond kissing. Later still had been the kind of dreams a man dreamed when he *knew* what went on beyond kissing.

After he'd robbed his brother's safe and left home he had stopped dreaming. Not until several years had passed had he dared to dream again, and now, here he was, well on his way to making his biggest dream come true. If he hadn't taken on Lizzy's problems he'd have been even closer to his goal. But Lizzy, he reminded himself forcefully, was only a temporary setback. Sooner or later he'd be rid of her, and then there'd be no holding him back.

"You'll need a new mattress, and lots more linens," she stated, her pale eyebrows knitting in a slight frown.

"There you go. That's why I hired you—you know about these things." Was he spreading it on too thick? The woman obviously needed reassurance. Needed something, at least, and reassurance and a safe place to live was all he was prepared to offer. "I'll bring the buckboard tomorrow and we can ride into town and see what Tess Dillard can come up with. They've got a good stock of drygoods. What she doesn't have we can order from a catalog if you'll help me pick things out."

It would serve as a test, he rationalized, to see if it would be safe to set her up in town. To see if anyone would remember the skinny, orange-haired woman who had briefly worked at the Double Deuce. Mrs. Harroun would never have hired a saloon girl to work in her boardinghouse, but Lizzy no longer looked like a typical saloon girl. Never had, for that matter.

"All this is going to cost you a fortune, and we've hardly even begun." She looked so earnest, he felt something in the region of his heart that was likely only indigestion. The gullet and the heart weren't that far apart...were they?

And that was another thing. No matter how often he told himself she was simply an obligation he had assumed—a way of passing on a few favors that had been done for him during the lean times in his past—he was beginning to suspect that bringing her here had been a mistake. He should have given her enough money to leave town and let it go at that. She would have survived...more or less.

But he'd started down this road, and it was too late now to turn back.

Squaring his shoulders—and incidentally, his resolve—Will turned toward the front door. Lizzy followed him outside. It was one of those evenings when the last rays of the setting sun seemed to hang on forever, gilding the entire world for one magical moment.

Which was why, Will told himself later, he had done something irreversibly stupid.

Something *else* irreversibly stupid...

Turning back, he took her face in his hands. With a feeling of inevitability, he lowered his face to hers. Every sensory organ he possessed was acutely aware of the faint scent of lilacs that seemed to surround her, even when she was scrubbing his walls with the harshest lye soap.

He was going to have to kiss her. It was either that or lay awake another night while his imagination ran wild. Something about this particular woman acted on his senses like a lodestone.

A breath away from touching her lips with his, he paused, as if to give her time to pull away. Or to give himself time to come to his senses.

Neither thing happened. So he closed the infinitesimal distance and covered her lips with his. Hers were trembling.

God, maybe it was his!

She was unbelievably sweet—like a rosebud, a bundle of velvety petals pinched tightly together, guarding the sweetness hidden inside. How could anything so slight and bony feel so soft and feminine in his arms? He gathered her closer and deepened the kiss. She might have worked in a saloon, but he could almost have sworn she'd never been kissed by a man before. Maybe a chaste peck on the brow by a father or a brother...

A brother? Or the man who had left her at the Double Deuce? The man who, sooner or later, would return to reclaim her.

The fragment of thought disappeared as he became sharply aware of the warm hand on the back of his neck, the slender body crushed tightly against him. Despite a momentary stiffening, she wasn't struggling to escape.

Despite his own stiffening, neither was he. When her lips parted slightly, he pressed his advantage. With the tip of his tongue he began to explore the satiny interior, savoring the taste of her, the sweetness. His tongue touched hers and she made a kittenlike mewing sound, then tentatively joined in the play.

Easy, easy there, friend, this is not the kind of kiss you give a woman unless you're planning on taking things a lot further.

And he wasn't. He couldn't, not and keep his honor intact.

Reluctantly, he began to ease away, allowing his hands to move from her slender back, where he could practically count her ribs, to her shoulders. He withdrew his mouth, and then, acting on impulse, went back for a second serving, this time limiting himself to merely rubbing his closed mouth gently against hers.

Finally setting her away from him, he stared down at her small, dazed face, at her awful hair, and thought, *Man, you are losing your mind!*

"There now, that's a nice way for friends to part, don't you think so?"

His smile was painfully forced. If God smote him dead on the spot, it would serve him right. Without another word, he turned and strode across the weedy ground to where he'd left his mare. He managed to put a safe distance between them before he turned and waved, the sick smile frozen on his face.

She was still there. A small woman, she looked even smaller seen against the gaunt facade of his house. She didn't return his wave. She didn't return his smile. It was all he could do not to race back to reassure her that he'd meant no disrespect. That her being a saloon girl and his buying her freedom and then offering her a handsome salary didn't mean she was in any danger from him in *that* way.

Now all he had to do, he thought morosely as he headed into town, was to convince himself.

WITH THE PLUMBING being installed and the last of the walls ready to be painted or papered, Lizzy was busy from morning to night, with scarcely time to think. She had done all the thinking she could afford to do once she'd realized what had happened—that she had gone and fallen in love with a man who thought of her as—

She didn't know what he thought of her. As a saloon girl? A paid employee? A charity case?

She was all of the above to one degree or another.

She had to believe Cicero would come back for her any day now, she simply had to. He would go directly to the Double Deuce, and Cam would tell him where to find her, and then he would come and take her home.

Or at least, take her somewhere far, far away, so that they could start over again.

Violet Gibson was a godsend. Not only did she bring out a catalog for Lizzy to immerse herself in during the long, lonely nights with only Ruby for company, but she taught her things. Useful things, such as soaking the beans and leaving off the salt until the last hour of cooking. She taught her how to test the oven for biscuits by holding her hand in the open door until she felt her fingernails begin to draw. If it happened too quickly, the fire was too hot. Not quickly enough, and her round little blobs would be dry inside and as hard as chalk. Perhaps she could find work as a cook when Cicero returned for her and they moved on to another town.

"We could go ahead and order the curtain rods," she suggested as the two women worked side by side in the kitchen after the men had eaten and gone back to their various tasks.

"Might as well order the curtain material while we're at it. If I know Mr. Will, and I've knowed him

since he was a young scamp, he'll not want to mess
with picking out all the foofaraws.''

Foofaraws, Lizzy had come to realize, meant anything that involved style, color or pattern. Which included walls, rugs, furniture and draperies. ''Maybe we
should wait. If he decides to marry, then his wife will
want to choose, don't you think?''

Violet Gibson shot her an odd look and stacked the
plain white crockery plates back inside the cabinet. ''I
reckon,'' she allowed. ''Leastwise, we can get on with
washing the rest of the windows and waxing the woodwork.''

Which is what they did. Lizzy felt a restlessness that
lent her energy. The house was as clean as they could
make it until the floors and the walls were finished, and
still she needed to be doing something.

Caught up in her daydream, Lizzy didn't know when
Mrs. Gibson left to go home. She wasn't aware that
outside, the hammering had stopped while the men
waited for a lone rider to join them. The first hint she
had that someone had arrived was when Ruby lifted
her head, flapped her tail and looked expectantly toward the door.

Only then, with an inner sense all its own, did her
heart began to pound. It had been three days since Will
had waved goodbye and ridden off toward town. Three
days since he had kissed her. Three whole days, during
which she had turned the situation over and over in her
mind and concluded that the only way to deal with it
was to pretend it had never happened.

To pretend he had never kissed her, that he had never
held her in his arms, with her smelling of lye soap and
burned sausages, and him smelling of clean linens and

healthy male sweat, with a faint hint of some citrus-scented hair dressing.

To pretend she hadn't tumbled headlong, heartfirst in love with the man, never mind that he was a large, handsome banker, a member of a prominent Montana family, and she was a—

Well, for starters, she was homeless. A vagrant. An ex-saloon girl.

The last thing Will Kincaid needed to establish his reputation as a respectable businessman was someone with her qualifications. Even if it became known that she was a member of one of Charleston's best families, her father's reputation had been tarnished long before he had died, owing a king's ransom in gambling debts.

And now Cicero seemed fated to follow in his footsteps.

Schooling her features not to reveal the turmoil inside her, Lizzy dried her hands on her apron and hurried to the front door.

"Sissy?"

Cicero? "Cicero!" With a joyful cry, she caught her breath, then raced out to meet him. "Oh, Cicero—oh, look at you, you're all dressed up! Where have you—come inside and tell me everything!"

The handsome young man in the dandified three-piece suit lifted her off her feet and swung her around, laughing even as he took in the mess she had made of her hair, and the apron that enveloped her slight form.

"You little scamp, I had a heck of a time finding you. What are you doing way out here? No, don't tell me, let me tell you something, instead."

Lizzy wanted to hear it all, but as usual, Cicero took his own sweet time, drawing the tale out so as to place himself in the starring role. "See, I knew Cam would take good care of you, because he knew if I came back and found out you were unhappy, he'd never get his money."

"You paid him off?"

"Every last penny. And you know what? I've still got enough to make a down payment on that ranch of ours. It's down in Wyoming, more land than you've ever seen—grassland, the prettiest creeks and everything. There's a house and some barns, only we'll have to share it with Sam Douglass—he's the old geezer I'm buying out, on account of he doesn't have any family left, so you see, he needs us as much as I—that is, we—need a place of our own."

And she did see. Eventually. Cicero had found his cowboy dream. That her own dream would have to be sacrificed was hardly an issue. It had never stood a chance. "That's wonderful, Ro—I'm so glad for you. I've been working here as a housekeeper, and I'll have to—"

"Yeah, Cam told me. He said you were pretty much a liability serving drinks—said the breakage alone set him back more than you were worth."

"Did he tell you he—" Lizzy lowered her head, unable to meet her brother's eyes. It would kill him if he knew what had so nearly happened to her. He'd trusted Cam. A large part of the reason they could never get ahead was that he was too trusting, playing cards with hardened gamblers who made a career of pretending to be good-natured amateurs just so they could fleece young innocents of their money.

"Yeah, he said this fellow hired you away from him,

and he let you go before you cost him any more money in breakage.''

"I wasn't all *that* bad.''

"Remember that dishwashing job we had in Kansas City?''

"That wasn't my fault, that wicked old man pinched me!''

"Yeah, well, I told you if you'd only agreed to sing for our supper, we'd have been eating high on the hog.''

"And I told you—'' Lizzy began, but he cut her off.

"I know, I know—you hate performing in public, but back home in Charleston—''

"I sang for friends. My throat would close tight if I had to sing for strangers—for money.''

"Once we've bought into my friend's ranch, you won't have to worry about your throat closing up. You'll be the owner's sister. You can sing your heart out, and the hired help will have to answer to me if they so much as look at you crossways.''

His smooth face had held the same look of excitement so many times before. It was a little-boy-on-Christmas-morning look. In some ways, her brother hadn't changed since he was fifteen and had won his first game of draw poker against three older, far more experienced players.

"I'll have to give notice so that Wi—Mr. Kincaid can hire someone to take my place.''

"You can write to him from town. I'm not letting you stay here another night, Sissy. It's not seemly, living out here all alone with a strange man.''

Lizzy started to explain, but in the end, it was really better to leave now. Ruby would be all right outside until Mrs. Gibson arrived in the morning. She would leave her the ham, which was too hard to slice, anyway, and a bowl of water. "Just let me get my things together, then." She managed to smile, but her heart wasn't in it.

THERE WASN'T A single reason in all the world, she thought later that evening, why she should be unhappy. Here she was, in the town's finest—actually, the town's only—hotel. It wasn't very fancy, but at least the beds were clean and there was a bathroom at the end of the hall.

And somewhere under the same roof, Will Kincaid was sleeping.

She hadn't seen him yet. Cicero had insisted on having her supper sent up to the room, which was probably best in the long run. The last thing she needed was a scene between the two men. Cicero had a quick temper when he thought his pride was being attacked.

The meal that had been brought up by a maid was far better than anything she could cook, but it was a far cry from the quail and oyster pie, the shrimp gumbo and the Huguenot torte their old cook used to serve. And so she allowed herself a few tears because she was homesick and heartsick, and whatever awaited them in Wyoming probably wouldn't quite live up to Cicero's dreams, and he would grow restless and they would move on again, leaving her own dreams farther and farther behind.

At least he had repaid what he owed Cam. She was free to leave Whitehorn. However, if they were going to be here long enough, she would like to buy a small gift for Mrs. Gibson. A pretty handkerchief, perhaps, to tuck in her sleeve when she went to one of her church socials. The Mercantile was just down the street. There'd be time to find something in the morning, even if they left on the early stage.

The letter to Will was more difficult. She was half tempted to say simply, "I'm gone," and leave it at that, but she owed him more. He had rescued her from a potentially disastrous situation, one she hoped Cicero would never learn about. If he thought for one minute he'd left her with a man who had tried to barter away her virtue, he would never forgive himself.

"Dear Will," she began, and pondered even that much. Dear he was, but should she have called him Mr. Kincaid?

Dear Will,
As you will have discovered by now, I've left your employ. My brother returned for me, and we'll be leaving for Wyoming, where he was fortunate enough to have purchased a large, lovely ranch.

There, it was only a small white lie. Cicero had said he'd already made a down payment on a ranch...hadn't he?

Thank you again for your kindness. I left Ruby at the Folly because she's yours, after all, but I have enjoyed her company. I gave her ham and water and left a note asking Mrs. Gibson to look after her.

Could the woman read? If not, she'd have sense enough to take the note to someone who could.

Please tell Homer and Millard and all the other men goodbye for me. They were kind enough to eat my cooking, which I'm quite sure was dreadful, if not actually poisonous. Perhaps in Wyoming I'll learn to do better.

End on a light note, she told herself. And for heaven's sake, don't weep all over the paper and smear the ink!

Cicero came in just before ten that night. His cheeks were red, his eyes bright with excitement. "Here's two dollars. In the morning, you can walk down to the Mercantile and buy whatever you think you might need. We'll be leaving on the noon stage."

"Two dollars? Cicero, I'll need more than that." Tomorrow would have made two weeks, at which time she'd expected to be paid her salary. "I don't even have a decent hat after we sold practically every stitch of clothing we both owned to get out of—"

"Three, then. It'll have to do for now. Later on, I'll give you some more, but for the moment, my funds are tied up in, um—an investment."

She could only stare at him. "An investment," she repeated slowly. She knew all about her brother's investments. He was gambling again.

Oh, please, Lord—not now!

NOON CAME AND WENT. Lizzy had walked down to the Dillards's store as soon as Cicero had left, wanting to be back at the hotel when he came for her. The sooner they left town, the better. She'd bought the handkerchief and left it in care of Tess Dillard, to be given to Violet Gibson the first time she came to the store, and with the remainder she had purchased a plain straw hat that would shade her face if all they could afford were outside seats. Which might well be the case. Pride alone prevented her from collecting her salary.

By two o'clock, her stomach was making funny gurgling sounds. She cornered a maid with an armful of linens and asked if she might have a tray sent up from the kitchen. It would go on the hotel bill, and if Ro didn't have enough to pay, then they would end up washing dishes again. It wouldn't be the first time. At least it was better than trying to sneak out without paying.

It was just past three when Cicero barged into her room without knocking. Lizzy knew from the look on his face that something dreadful had happened.

"Dear Lord, Ro, what have you done?" she asked, her fingernails biting into her palms as she held on to her temper by a thread. "I thought we were supposed to be on the noon stage."

"Now, Sissy, it's not all that bad. I thought if we gave Mr. Douglass more time, he might come down on his price, is all."

"You did no such thing, you lost all your money again."

Deep breath. Don't throw the water pitcher at him, it won't solve anything and you'll have to pay for the breakage. "Tell me the truth. You tell me what you've done or I'm walking out of here and selling my services to the first man who'll pay me."

Cicero rushed across the room, his shamefaced look giving over to one of horror. "Don't talk like that! It's just a small setback, honest—a temporary—"

"Temporary? How temporary? Should I find Mr.

Kincaid and see if he'll have me back?'' She had left the letter with the desk clerk. By now, Will would have already read it and accepted her resignation.

''No, please—that is, I promised Cam—''

If her blood turned to ice water, she could not have felt any more chilled. ''You promised Cam *what?*''

CHAPTER SEVEN

WITH EXAGGERATED PATIENCE, Cicero described how he'd gone by the saloon for one last drink and just happened to notice a table of greenhorns playing draw poker. One of the men—scarcely more than a boy—shoved back his chair and left, and out of sheer idle curiosity, Cicero strolled over to the table to watch the play.

Lizzy's face said it all. "You simply cannot pass by a poker table without gambling, can you?"

"But my luck's been running so good, and besides, I didn't do it for me, Sissy, I only wanted to see you arrive in Wyoming in style. Wearing a pretty new dress and riding in our own buggy instead of the hired stage."

Feeling as if she'd aged fifty years in the past few minutes, she dropped onto the foot of the bed. "And just who is it in Wyoming you're hoping to impress? Your Mr. Douglass?"

He mumbled something about their status as one of Charleston's first families. Evidently he'd been bragging again. Lizzy cast a speculative eye toward the heavy china ewer, but only shook her head. "And Cam—where does he come into this pathetic tale of woe?"

Addressing his shiny boots, the young man said, "I,

um—lost some money. Cam said he'd take responsibility because it was his place, and I'm pretty sure the cards were marked." He shrugged his bony shoulders. "So Cam said you can work there again until I can get together enough money to—"

"I don't want to hear it."

"He said he'd made more money off you than all the other girls put together," Cicero said hopefully.

"And that's all right with you? For me to act the whore as long as it gets you off the hook?" There was an edge of hysteria in her voice. Glad of the words she had picked up in the saloon and from the carpenters, she cried, "Damn your sorry hide all to hell and back, Cicero Price-Hawthorne, if Mama hadn't died, you'd have sold her, too, wouldn't you? How much am I worth? Two dollars an hour? Five dollars a night? Let me warn you in case you didn't know it—Cam *lies!* He lied to you when he said I wouldn't have to work upstairs, and he lied to you when he said he'd made money on me. I broke enough glasses to fill the entire Yellowstone River! Once I even dropped a full bottle of whiskey and it spilled out and Cam turned around so fast he skidded and fell down and knocked over a jar of pickled eggs. And you know what else? I never even had a single upstairs customer!"

Actually, she had—Will had paid for two full nights, only he hadn't wanted her, either. "Everyone knows— at least everyone who's ever met that wretched old man—that Cam has ways of getting his hooks into anyone who comes into the place, either to drink or to gamble or—well, whatever. One way or another, he gets a cut of any money that comes through those doors."

By then Cicero was crying. Great, gulping sobs that made her want to hold him and comfort him, and then knock the starch out of him. "You'll never grow up, will you? The whole world revolves around little Cicero, same as it always has. You're just like Papa." Which was both the best and the worst thing she could think of to say.

WILL FORCED HIMSELF to stay away from her—to stay away from the Folly. The men knew what they were doing; the work would proceed without his supervision. As for him, he had about as much business falling in love at this stage of his life as a six-legged jackass had entering a waltzing contest.

And he'd been close. Too close for comfort.

So for three days he stayed out at the ranch, getting to know his young nephew, Zeke, and his new sister-in-law, Ruth, and getting reacquainted with Caleb who it seemed, was about to become a father again. Trouble was, their obvious contentment made marriage seem like an enviable condition.

At any other time Will might have been tempted to follow their example, find himself a suitable woman and settle down. But at this particular point in his life he had no business even thinking about marriage, especially as the only woman who interested him happened to be an ex-saloon girl. If he was hoping to put his past behind him—all the harebrained stunts he'd pulled as a young man—marrying Lizzy wouldn't help.

Marrying Lizzy?

Coming home from the bank each day to a radiant smile and a pair of open arms? After a warm, wet welcoming kiss she would serve him coffee and one of her delectable sugar buns, hot from the oven....

And later they would go upstairs together, and he would slowly undress her, and she would pull the end of his necktie, if he still happened to be wearing one, and then she would unbutton his shirt. Slowly. Her gaze never leaving his, even when her fingernails raked lightly across his nipples....

Yeah, well. It was only a dream, after all.

Oh, hell, this was embarrassing, especially in a man his age. Especially when the woman he was thinking about was at least a decade younger. Turning toward the fence, he hooked his boot heel on the bottom rung and pretended to study the herd, hoping Caleb wouldn't notice his uncomfortably aroused condition.

What he needed was space. The ranch was no longer big enough—too many people around. What he needed was solitude, just until he could get his mind back under control. He would like to think he'd learned to control his manly urges since the days when he used to sneak into the old DD to ogle ladies' bosoms. Evidently, there were some things a man never learned.

"You all right?" Caleb was giving him a curious look.

"Who, me? Oh, sure, I'm fine. Just thinking. Nice beeves. They'll finish off first-class."

"Yeah, I'm counting on it. By the way, I heard from Brock last week. Meant to tell you, but you're a hard man to catch up with these days."

"He's headed home, I hope. God, do you realize he wasn't even shaving last time I saw him?"

"Yeah, well, he might not be shaving now. Our baby brother's got a new bug up his arse—can't decide whether to study for the ministry in Arkansas or pan for gold in the North Carolina mountains.''

Will swore a solemn oath and then broke out laughing. "And you thought *I* was trouble."

"I *knew* you were trouble. Hell, man, you've always been wilder than a muley deer in heel fly season. Now you're even bigger than me. Hate to tell you, but even gussied up in your fancy city duds, you still look more like a wrangler than a banker. How's it coming along, by the way?''

"What, the bank?''

"Sure, the bank. What'd you think I was talking about?''

And so Will talked about his plans for the bank, and then he talked about the Folly and what a great investment it was, and he left the ranch a few hours later, knowing he had to go back. Hoping he could keep a cool head and not embarrass them both when he saw her again. On the ride back to town, where he intended to bathe and change into something that didn't smell of horses, he managed to convince himself that it wasn't need that drove him. He didn't actually *need* to see her. To hear her voice, to see the way her eyes lit up when she smiled—the way her nose wrinkled ever so slightly when she laughed aloud.

He didn't actually need water when he was thirsty, either, or food when he'd gone three days without.

Kincaid, you are in deep trouble.

CAM IS NOT *going to take me back,* Lizzy told herself hopefully as she waited just inside the swinging doors. If she could have stayed outside while Cicero came to terms with the saloon owner, she would have, but people had started to stare. Respectable women didn't hang around the saloons, not even in the middle of the day.

She had made her brother drive her out to Will's house, but the place was locked up and there was no one there. She had too much pride to go to his family's ranch.

"It's all settled," Cicero said smugly, striding toward her with a broad grin on his boyish face. "He says that upstairs stuff was just a misunderstanding. You're to serve drinks, wash dishes and sweep out in the mornings. I know it's no fun, Sissy, but it won't take long. Once I pay back what I lost last night—"

"You didn't lose it to Cam, you lost it to those sharpsters who lured you into gambling."

"Yeah, well—you see, Cam is sort of like a banker. They say it wasn't like that in the old days when another guy owned the place, but Cam—well, what he does is buy up a fellow's IOUs. But once I pay him back what I lost, plus interest, we're out of this town like—"

"Interest?"

"Well, sure. That's the way it's done. If I borrow money—"

"If you lose money, you mean."

"Same thing. I pay something for carrying costs— um, twenty percent figured weekly," he said quickly. "But it's not going to take me near that long to pay it back."

Lizzy closed her eyes. She couldn't afford to think about just how he intended to earn enough to pay Cam back. "That damned, dratted, awful pirate," she swore feelingly. "No wonder he could afford to double the size of this wretched place. How much?" Miserably aware of all the curious eyes turned their way, she pressed him unmercifully because she had to know. There was no question of her going through the up-stairs-downstairs routine again, because she simply wouldn't. But if she had to work off her brother's debts, she needed to know exactly where she stood. Maybe poor Ro couldn't help his weakness—he was his father's son, after all—but it was time someone in this family took charge and started acting like an adult.

The idea had been simmering as soon as she'd known Ro was going to try to get her to work in the saloon again, but she wasn't ready to confide in anyone yet. If Ro knew what she was planning, he'd insist on managing the whole show, and first thing she knew, he'd have gambled the rest of her life away. She loved him—he was all the family she had left, but she knew better than ever to trust him again.

"How much?" she whispered fiercely.

Cicero, his cheeks blazing with embarrassment, hung his head. "It's only ninety dollars this time. I lost everything I was saving up for the ranch, but all I owe Cam is the money I lost trying to win it back, so you see, we're not as bad off as it might seem."

WILL STOOD in the lobby of the hotel, reeking of sweat from helping Caleb's wranglers break the new stock, and stared down at the folded note. She was gone. The ungrateful little witch had walked out on him. According to the night clerk, she'd been staying at Amos's hotel right here in town with some wet-behind-the-ears dude in a fancy vest, the whole time he'd been out at the ranch.

Well, damn. If that was all the gratitude she could

scrape up, after everything he'd done for her, then good riddance.

Upstairs in his room, he went over the brief note again in an effort to read some deeper meaning into the polite words. *What* large, lovely ranch? *Where* in Wyoming? And what the hell was wrong with Montana, if a man wanted to buy a ranch?

Just who the devil was this joker, anyway? Was he really her brother, or was he her lover? No brother in his right mind would leave a sister in a place like the Double Deuce.

Her handwriting, he noted absently, was better than his own, but then, he'd known hardened prostitutes who wrote a beautiful hand, complete with more fancy flourishes than an ostrich parade.

She was gone, dammit. He ought to be dancing in the street—at least now he could get his mind back on track. Instead, he felt like he'd been bushwhacked. Battered, angry and disbelieving.

AT LIZZY'S INSISTENCE, the showdown took place in the privacy of Cam's new office in the newly completed addition, where the smell of new lumber was already tainted by the stench of cheap tobacco. Cam seated himself behind a scarred table, that and a straight chair being the room's only furniture, and lighted up another of his stinking cigars. Lizzy and Cicero were forced to stand. If Cam thought that gave him the upper hand, he was sadly mistaken. Lizzy had learned the art of social maneuvering from her mother. It wasn't easy holding your head up in Charleston's finest drawing rooms when you owed practically everyone who was anyone in town.

Ready to take the upper hand, she opened her mouth to speak when Cam blew out a stream of smoke and said gruffly, "All right now, missy, what's this about singing?"

Cicero said, "Singing? Did Sissy tell you about that? Why, back home in—"

Lizzy elbowed him aside and stepped forward. Her knees might be knocking, but nothing in her attitude even hinted that she had ever been dragged through the mud, either literally or figuratively. "Sir, we both know I'm rather inept as a serving girl. I'm certain my brother told you that I'm not going to work upstairs, either. So would you mind telling me why you agreed to take me back?"

"Now, Lizzy," Cicero placed a hand on her arm.

She shook it off. "And this time I'd like the truth, please. If we're going to arrive at an agreement, I need to know exactly what's at stake."

"You want plain speaking?" the older man grinned, revealing a full set of square, yellow teeth. "Truth is, little lady, I made more off'n you in two weeks than I made off the other gals in a month of Saturday nights."

"Now, see here, sir—!" Cicero stepped forth, lifting a pale, bony fist.

"Hush up, Cicero, I'm conducting this interview." She turned back to the saloon owner. "That's not possible. I only earned upstairs money two nights." She ignored Cicero's gasp. "The others ladies were up and down several times a night, every one of them."

Cam nodded and laced his stubby fingers together over his belly. "You could call it bonus money. Might even call it ransom money. Me, I call it smart business. If a man walks in and says he wants to pay off another man's debt, I ain't going to refuse his money. And if the gentleman that owes the debt comes along later and insists on paying me off, too, ain't no law says I gotta turn him down.'' He glanced at Cicero, who looked as if he might lose his breakfast at any moment. ''So now we're startin' out fresh, clean slate. Ninety dollars, plus interest. Clock started runnin' on it last night about midnight, give or take an hour, but seein's how you're wantin' to settle up, I reck'n I can afford to be generous.''

Bracing herself, Lizzy drew on every ounce of poise she possessed and began to lay out her plan.

WILL STOOD on the banks of the Yellowstone River and stared toward the southeast, as if he might catch a glimpse of a skinny, yellow-haired woman and a sharp-looking gambler hightailing it down the road toward Wyoming.

The air was clear, but it wasn't quite that clear. She could be a hundred miles away by now, or even five hundred. ''Good riddance,'' he muttered, not meaning it now any more than he'd meant it when he'd read her note nearly a week ago. His first impulse then was to go after her.

Fortunately, he'd come to his senses in time.

His second had been to head for the Double Deuce and get royally drunk, but then that would only remind him of Lizzy. Of where and how they'd met. Hell of a thing, when a man couldn't even drop by his favorite saloon for a couple of drinks without seeing ghosts.

Same thing with the Folly. He was half tempted to sell the place as it stood, if he could find a taker. He had ridden out there directly after he'd left the ranch, before he'd gotten the note she'd left at the hotel. Violet Gibson had been struggling to lift the dog into her wagon. "I don't know where Miss Lizzy went to—somewheres in town, I reckon, but she's gone, all right. Left me a note, said to look after Ruby, see that she had a good home. I'm fixin' to take her home with me, that is, less'n you want her back." Both her eyes and her voice had been laden with pity, which he'd pretended not to notice.

He didn't want pity, dammit, he wanted Lizzy.

There, he'd said it. Not aloud, but even admitting it to himself was the first step toward recovery. On the heels of that painful admission came the anger. If he hadn't gone into the DD with Caleb after burying the money—if he hadn't met Lizzy in the first place—if he hadn't been fool enough to buy that damned old ruin, his bank building would be almost finished by now, and he'd be too busy getting his business set up to be moping over a stubborn, irritating female with the haughty airs of a royal princess. She had no business being so damned irresistible. Hell, she didn't even have a bosom!

Caleb didn't need him, the ranch was working as smoothly as it ever had. Smoother, without the two of them constantly butting heads. He could stay in town and stew over the ungrateful little witch, or he could move out to the Folly and stew over her there. Or he could go somewhere where he wouldn't see reminders everywhere he looked.

He couldn't love her. How the hell could he love her? He'd only kissed her once!

So he'd packed his bedroll and fishing gear and headed out to the river to fish. To watch the clouds pile up over the mountains, to watch the grass turn brown. To get his mind back on track so he could get on with the rest of his life.

Only it wasn't working. With whopper trout practically leaping out of the river, all he could think about was the way she'd looked that first night at the saloon, her skinny little ankles wobbling as she tried to balance in a pair of shoes three sizes too large. So determined not to trip, not to spill anything—not to call down Cam's wrath on her skinny little shoulders. That orange hair, those big, earnest eyes—and him, reeking of the whiskey that dripped off his face, soaked through his shirt and his trousers while his nose bled and swelled up big as a bear paw. And Caleb, nearly busting a gut to keep from laughing.

As the light gradually faded after a spectacular sunset which he'd barely noticed, Will quickly cleaned a small trout and cooked it on a spit over his rekindled fire. Tomorrow, he promised himself, he would go back to town, check out of the hotel and move into the Folly. If he needed to lay a few ghosts to rest—and he did— then he might as well get started.

CHAPTER EIGHT

YOU CAN DO this, Lizzy told herself, just as she had every night for the past week and a half. The first few nights had been the worst. She'd been certain her throat would close up. No matter how many times she had sung in the past, it had always been for friends, never for strangers. For fun, not for money.

Dear Lord, she thought as she steeled herself to sweep open the makeshift curtains, I'm a stage performer. A professional entertainer!

Which, she thought wryly, was several cuts above being a saloon girl.

Inside the newly opened section of the Double Deuce Saloon, the rafters were throbbing to the wail of two fiddles and a banjo. Lizzy, wearing a long black skirt and a blue shirtwaist, with her flaxen curls subdued for the occasion, stood in a circle of lamplight and waited for the din to subside. This would be her third performance. She had planned five short songs and no more than two encores. Naturally, she would refuse all proposals—decent or otherwise.

"Sing 'Clementine' fer me, li'l angel!" shouted an inebriated patron.

"Do 'Camptown Races!'" cried another.

Lizzy waited until the stamping and whistling subsided. There were still no seats in the new addition.

Cam had had benches built and sent off for a billiard table. After her second performance, he had ordered an upright piano from Sears and Roebuck. Lizzy would like to think that by the time it was delivered she would have repaid her brother's debt, plus the exorbitant interest, and would be well on her way to earning the money to repay Will. She was still sick with shame to think he had actually *bought* her.

And on top of that, he had offered to pay her a salary.

Closing the door on those thoughts, she lifted her head and began to sing in a full, clear voice, "'We are tenting tonight, tenting tonight, tenting on the old campground....'"

The poignant words spoke of hearts that were lonely, of soldiers far from their home, but they echoed the sadness of her own heart. She had wept rivers over the loss of her parents, her home, her friends—all she had once held dear. That loss could be laid at her father's feet. She had cried nightly over the indignity of having to work as a saloon girl, and for that she blamed her brother, but her own weakness was equally at fault.

Now her life had taken an irreversible turn, and this time she had only herself to blame. No one had compelled her to promise Cam her services as an entertainer. She had set the rules, herself. She would perform five nights a week, the rest of the time being hers to do with as she pleased. And for that she would be paid a percentage of the business she brought in.

"Now, how d'ye figger that, little lady? I been doing a land-office business in this here place ever since I bought it off'n the man that built it. Got so successful I had to expand." He hadn't taken her seriously at first.

"You might have to expand again. Let me use the new room—you don't have your billiard table yet, anyway, so it won't cost you anything. The men can buy drinks up front, but once they come through that door, I get a percentage of what they spend."

Cam had brayed like a donkey, but Lizzy had stood her ground. "For every night there are more than ten patrons in the theatre—" she had already begun calling it that in her own mind "—I'll give you the recipe for a fancy drink. That way, you can draw on a more sophisticated clientele."

The grizzled proprietor had had a field day with that, mimicking her Carolina accent, which she had done her best to play down once she'd left Charleston.

"Good American whiskey, home brew and applejack for them that wants it. I got no call to serve fancy drinks."

"The ingredients don't cost that much more and you can charge several times as much. If the new drinks don't sell you can take the ingredients out of my pay."

So they had settled on the terms, and now Lizzy sang her heart out from Tuesday through Saturday, two hours each evening. And Cam learned how to mix a Floater, a Smasher and a Virginia Fancy and charge three times more than he did for a shot of straight whiskey. Once it was known that Lizzy was the source of the recipes, the men had fallen all over themselves to be the first to try one of what they called Angel's drinks. It was hard to keep a straight face, seeing the tough, rawhide types who frequented the Double Deuce, clutching a fancy cocktail in their horny hands.

Cicero was waiting to escort her to the boardinghouse when she finished her evening's work. Mrs. Harroun had agreed to allow them rooms if Cicero would take on the job of handyman until her regular help had recovered from a snakebite. He'd wanted to refuse, but one level look from Lizzy was all it had taken to remind him of just who was responsible for the fix they were in. Earning even a little was better than losing everything.

"Seventeen men were waiting by the time I walked into the room," Lizzy proudly announced as they shared a nightcap of cocoa and buttermilk pie on the porch of the boardinghouse. "By the time I finished my first number, several more came in, and—*and*," she stressed, "three of them were drinking my cocktails."

"Where'd you learn how to mix drinks?"

"Remember my maid, Sally Lee? Her father was the bartender at Papa's club. I let her borrow my Jane Austen and she lent me her father's recipe book."

Cicero snorted in disbelief and she said defensively, "Well, it was all the poor girl had to share. I couldn't very well hurt her pride, could I? I only glanced through it, so I could only remember a few of the recipes. I might have gotten a few things wrong, but nobody seemed to notice."

"I wish we could go back to the way things were," Cicero said wistfully.

"Well, we can't. And knowing how things really were, I wouldn't want to. Poor Mama..."

"Poor Papa. You don't know how it is, Sissy. One day you're playing cards with a bunch of friends, maybe losing your allowance, maybe winning someone else's. Next thing you know, you're in way over your head, and the only way you can reach shore is to keep trying and hope your luck will turn. That the next card, or the one after that, will get you out of the hole you're in, only somehow, it never turns out that way." He sighed, looking tired and scared and far younger than his nineteen and a half years.

There was no longer any doubt in Lizzy's mind as to who would be looking after whom. Rising from the porch rocker, she moved to stand behind his chair, resting her cheek on the top of his sandy hair, murmuring words that were meant to be comforting. "It's going to be all right, Ro. Once we get out of debt, we'll leave town and go to Wyoming, and maybe you can work for your rancher friend, and it'll be almost as good as owning your own ranch."

It wouldn't, but it was all she had to offer.

AFTER A FEW DAYS of roughing it on the river, Will had cleared his head enough to accept the truth. Lizzy was gone, and it was his fault. He should have told her how he felt, but for once he hadn't trusted his own judgment. That same judgment, based on knowledge, experience and intuition, had led him to some spectacular coups.

It had also led to a few spectacular failures.

And now, because of where he'd found her—because he was a selfish bastard who was too impressed by his own worth and too damned stupid to see beneath the surface to hers, he had thrown away the most valuable thing of all. The one thing that could have given meaning to his whole life.

What good was success if there was no one to share it with? Back when he'd first begun to make a few good deals—and then a few even better ones—he had celebrated with a night on the town, as often as not with a lovely companion whose name he would have forgotten before they parted company the next day. Shallow, meaningless pleasures.

Given a choice he would rather share one of Lizzy's culinary failures in his own kitchen than dine at Chicago's finest restaurant with the most expensive courtesan in the world.

He would rather have one of Lizzy's kisses than a week in the bed of Delilah DeLyte, with all her remarkable skills.

To think he might have had it all, he mused dismally as he rode into town and dismounted in front of Harry's barbershop, if only he hadn't been so blind. At first when he'd begun to suspect how he really felt about her, he hadn't believed it, then he hadn't known quite how to approach her. If she knew how much he had paid Cam for her freedom, her precious pride would have been shattered beyond repair.

Timing. It all came down to timing. Maybe he'd better give up on trying to open a bank and go back to work on the ranch.

LIZZY TOOK a deep breath before sweeping back the curtains that had been hung just yesterday over the back door of the new extension. Making an entrance was a part of her performance now. Small things mattered, she was discovering. Such as the rose she carried with her each night. Heaven help her when Mrs. Harroun's rosebush stopped blooming, because there wasn't a florist closer than Helena, so far as she knew.

But the important thing was that the woman who had learned to touch her cheeks and her lips sparingly with rouge and pile her hair into a seemingly artless arrangement that allowed curls to escape to brush her face, was Lizzy Price. Not Juliette Elizabeth Price-Hawthorne.

They called her the Golden Angel, which made Ro swell with pride. After only a week and a half, he was already talking about managing her career as a professional singer in big cities, maybe even as far west as San Francisco.

The stomping and whistling that invariably greeted her entrance ceased the moment the curtains fell shut behind her. Hushed reverence took its place. For the first time, a few of the town's more independent women were among the audience, not just the other girls who worked there, who always managed to sneak in for a few minutes each night. They were among her staunchest supporters. Even Cam had been known to stand in the door for a few minutes, a scowl on his weathered face.

She sang several Stephen Foster songs, and then an old ballad she only half remembered from her childhood. Melly used to sing it in the kitchen, with Sally Lee singing harmony. It came as close as anything had in ages to breaking her composure.

"Thank you, thank you so much," she murmured. Stepping forward, she prepared to toss her rose, now sadly wilted from being clutched in her hot hands, out into the audience.

That's when she saw him.

If a pit had opened up before her, she would have willingly stepped into it and disappeared. He was here. *Will* was here!

As quickly as she could, she eased back behind the curtains, escaped onto the balcony and made her way toward the back stairs. Ro would be waiting to escort her back to the boardinghouse.

"Lizzy!" She hadn't been fast enough. "Lizzy, dammit, you come back here!"

She flew down the remaining stairs, but he flew faster, his feet pounding on the new wooden steps.

"Here now," Cicero cried, moving to stand in front of her the instant she reached the bottom. "You're not to bother the angel, sir, she's done for the night. Come back tomorrow night and—"

"Angel, my sweet arse, she's a liar and a—"

Ro aimed a blow at his jaw. Lizzy groaned. Will swatted the fist away and growled, "Go inside and tell Cam to serve you a sasparilla, boy. The lady and I have some talking to do."

"No, we don't," Lizzy chimed in. "Ro, you stay right—"

Will glared her to silence. "Go away, son, this doesn't concern you."

Cicero Price-Hawthorne, of the Charleston Price-Hawthornes, manfully stood his ground. "Anything that concerns my sister concerns me, sir."

Lizzy moved to stand between them, hands on her hips. Dear Lord, Will looked awful! There were shadows around his eyes and he looked as if he had been ill. "Are you all right?" She had to ask. She'd been half expecting him to come storming after her all week. "Has something happened to the Folly? That lightning storm we had the other night..."

"What about your fancy ranch?" Even his voice sounded raw and painful.

"My fancy ranch? Oh—*that* ranch. Well, you see,

we decided—that is, I thought it might be better to—"

"What my sister is trying to say is that I lost the money we were going to use to buy it—at least, to start buying in."

"Your sister," Will repeated. Oh, God, yes. He was her brother, all right. The same delicate build, the same guileless blue eyes. With that choirboy face, he'd be an easy mark for every cardsharper in the state of Montana. He was beginning to see what had happened.

"Cicero, this is Mr. Kincaid. He was—that is, he's the man who hired me when I left Cam's place."

The kid bristled all over again, thrusting his jaw, fisting both hands. If he shaved more than a couple of times a week, Will thought, it would be a waste of shaving soap.

"Stop it, Ro. Mr. Kincaid has been—"

"Will."

"*Mr. Kincaid,*" she repeated, glaring at him until it was all he could do not to kiss her senseless. And he'd thought she was a victim? She was a Valkyrie. "Mr. Kincaid," she stressed again, "has been my friend as well as my employer. You owe him money, because he had to pay Cam what you owed him before Cam would let me go, so you can just apologize. Right now," she snapped when both men stood slack-jawed a moment too long.

To his credit, the young man managed to recover his aplomb. Good breeding in there somewhere, Will mused. The boy apologized with a mixture of reluctance and sincerity. Will accepted the apology with a nod, wondering not for the first time just who the hell this woman was. Where she'd come from. At least he was beginning to see how she had come to be working in a place that most respectable women would have shunned like the devil on horseback. Working, this time, on her own terms.

"Lizzy, we have some talking to do."

"You'll call her Miss Price-Hawthorne, sir, and anything you have to say to my sister you can say in front of me."

"Go to your room, Ro, I can handle this."

"But Sissy—" the young man protested. The look she gave him would have sent a lesser man scurrying for cover. "All right, but I'm going to wait up until you get in, and if you're not in your room in half an hour, I'm coming after you."

They waited silently until he turned the corner. "Protective little dickens, isn't he?" Will said, taking her arm and steering her away from the saloon. As it happened, they'd been standing not five feet away from where he and Caleb had recently buried a couple of trinkets and a small fortune in gold.

"You have to understand, I'm all he has left. We take care of each other."

Will bit back a remark about the quality of her brother's care. From now on, that wouldn't be a problem. "No other family?"

She shook her head. A few of the curls that had been temporarily tamed tumbled over her forehead. "I know how much you paid for me, Will, and I want you to know you'll get every penny of it back."

"Lizzy—Lizzy, don't. It wasn't you I paid for, it was—call it a termination settlement. You see, I needed you more than Cam did."

God, wasn't that the truth!

"Don't." She stopped and turned to face him, looking younger, more vulnerable than ever in the light from a full moon. "Will, I'm tired of living a lie. I'm tired of pretending, so if we're to maintain any sort of a—a friendship, don't say things that aren't true. Mrs. Gibson would have done a perfect job as housekeeper. You didn't need me, you were just being—kind, I suppose." Her shoulders drooped, but the light of battle still hadn't quite left her eyes. "I don't want your pity, I want—I want the truth."

"The truth," he repeated slowly. "Cards on the table, so to speak."

She sighed, and the hot coals of resentment he'd been fanning ever since he read her note burned out, leaving only the warm promise of hope.

"Harry Talbert—the barbershop just down the street? Harry was singing the praises of Cam's new entertainer. Woman called the Angel. Yellow curls, kind of choppy looking, but pretty—blue eyes, not much of a figure, but a voice that would make the devil lie down and weep."

She opened her mouth and then closed it again.

Oops. His diplomatic skills definitely needed polishing. "Or maybe what he said was that you, uh—you didn't take up much space."

She lifted her brows in open disbelief. Will thought—he couldn't be sure, but it looked as if the corners of her mouth twitched a bit. So he gathered his courage and waded in. "All right, then, here it is. The plain, unvarnished truth. First, I'm so crazy in love with you that I can't even eat—haven't been able to sleep more than a couple of hours at a time since I found out you were gone. Second, I've squandered so much money on that old ruin I'm going to have to cut back on the size of my bank—I guess it was pretty pretentious, anyway, for a town this size.'' He was ticking the items off on his fingers. ''Thirdly—'' he said, when she grabbed his hand and clasped it between her own.

''Wait,'' she said breathlessly. ''Go back to the first one.''

''The first what? Oh—you mean where I said I love you?'' Standing in the shadow of the old saloon, Will gazed down at the woman who had stolen his heart before he'd even realized it was endangered. ''It can't come as any surprise. For weeks now I've been acting like a jackass high on locoweed, and I'm generally conceded to be a fairly intelligent man.'' He tried to make light of it, as if his heart weren't lodged in his throat. ''Some might even say suave.''

''Mmm-hmm.'' Her eyes were dancing like moonlight on the water. Emboldened—at least she hadn't taken a swing at him—he started to reach out for her, then thought better of it. Anything he needed to say, he'd better get it said before he laid a finger on her, because once he touched her—once he kissed her again...

She went on staring up at him, her eyes big enough to swallow the moon. He said, ''What? What, Lizzy?''

''Open your arms.''

And when he did, she walked straight into his embrace. Just like that, the battle ended, the only shot fired being the one that had shattered a mirror and tumbled her into his lap.

They ended up out at the Folly. Will wasn't about to take her to the hotel. The boardinghouse was out of the question, as the last thing he needed was an interfering brother and a nosy landlady.

The old house had never looked so grand, nor the future more promising, as it did when he carried her inside. His footsteps rang hollowly on the bare floor as, laughing, they crossed the foyer that still smelled slightly of scorched beans, climbed the staircase that smelled of beeswax, and entered the small bedroom that smelled of lilacs and fresh linens and Lizzy.

"YOU UNDERSTAND, I'm talking marriage, kids—the whole kit and caboodle," he said sometime later. By now, he figured, her brother would have got up a search party. It wouldn't be long before they had company.

Holding her in his arms, he leaned back against the plain wooden headboard of the bed he had slept in for the first twenty years of his life. Someday their son would sleep there. A daughter would have one of those fancy poster beds with a ruffled canopy.

Things would change—the old house would ring with new life after decades of standing alone. His hair would grow thin, Lizzy's gold would slowly turn to silver. But for as long as he lived, he suspected that one thing would never change. One look and he would want her. One touch—a kiss, and he would be helpless against the spell she had woven around his heart.

They had to get married quickly. Yesterday wouldn't be any too soon. But before he did anything else, he had to put her mind at ease about her brother. The kid couldn't do much more damage on the ranch than he himself had done had at that age. It was worth a shot.

"Would you rather be married here, or in town?"

he asked after a long, sleepy kiss that threatened to reignite banked coals.

Her fingers idly twisting the hair around his nipple, she considered the question. "Do you think your brother would allow us to be married where you grew up? I'd like that—the family thing. Your family, I mean—and Ro."

They had got past the will you or won't you before they'd ever left town. She would. He would. The details they could work out later.

"They'd love it. They're going to love you, sweetheart. Wait'll you meet my little brother, Brock. He's not home now, but sooner or later, all the Kincaids wind up here."

It hadn't escaped him that Lizzy was closer to Brock's age than to his own. She'd told him a lot about herself. Not everything—he was pretty sure of that, but he could wait. Now that she was his, he could wait forever. Hell, one of these days he might even quit grinning!

THE BRIDE WORE an ivory gown that had belonged to Will's mother. With a little alteration, it fit like a glove. Will wore a yellow silk vest with his best black suit, his boots gleaming like patent leather, thanks to Harry's attention.

Harry was there. They were all there, practically the whole town. Amos and Millie, John and Tess from the Mercantile. Violet Gibson had started crying before she'd even climbed down from her wagon and hadn't stopped since. She had come early to help Ruth with the preparations.

Ruth was wonderful. Little Zeke passed around fry

bread and coconut macaroons with suspiciously sticky fingers while Cam handled the bar. The old Double Deuce had actually closed down for the occasion, so that all the girls could be present.

Will had opened his mouth to protest her choice of bridesmaids, but then backed down. What the hell— this was Whitehorn. This was Kincaid land. If Lizzy wanted to invite President Harrison and any of the James brothers that had made it out to the frontier, it was fine by him.

Above the heads of two saloon girls and the carpenters who had taken a day off from working on his bank, Will met his bride's eyes. She was glowing. Radiant. Little Zeke was hanging on to her satin skirt with sticky fists and she was ruffling his hair with her fingers.

Soon, he told her silently. She nodded and beamed.

Soon they would go home together. Caleb had sworn they wouldn't be subjected to a shivaree, but the ranch hands—including the newest hire, young Cicero Price-Hawthorne, of the South Carolina Price-Hawthornes, had their heads together.

Soon, Will promised with his eyes. Soon and forever.

The Gamble

Carolyn Davidson

PROLOGUE

August, 1896

"MAKE A SHERIFF outta James Kincaid?" John Dillard asked unbelievingly. "It'd take an act of God to keep him sober enough to pin on a badge."

"Anybody got a better idea?" Will Kincaid leaned back in his desk chair. His spanking new desk chair, in his brand-new bank.

"Hell, we all like James, and Lord knows we need a good man to wear the badge," John said. And then his gaze swept the room. "How we're gonna get him to quit drinking is the problem."

"Well, if he'd just cut back a little..." Harry Talbert said slowly. "Maybe, we could take a chance on him."

"You can't have a sheriff with a hangover every damn morning of his life, and I fear that unless someone gets hold of him and straightens him out..." Will looked helplessly around at the men in his office.

"You mean like Lizzy did with you?" Harry asked with a chuckle.

Will flushed, and then grinned. "A good woman can work magic, and I'm the first one to admit it." He sobered quickly and leaned forward, one hand uplifted. "James is my cousin. I care about him." He cleared his throat. "Now, we all know he's got a head on his shoulders. He'd make a fine sheriff. If we keep our eyes open, and the opportunity arises, do all of you agree with me on this?''

The men gathered together in the twilight hour glanced at each other, then as one, nodded their heads emphatically. All but one.

"I'll bet you a five dollar gold piece you'll never get him to consider it," Cam said. As the brand-new member of the group, the owner of the Double Deuce Saloon had a vested interest in the proceedings. James Kincaid, in the few short weeks Cam had owned the place, had become one of his best customers. And, if he'd ever seen a drinking, gambling man, James Kincaid was it.

Will's jaw hardened. "All we have to do is wait for something to come up, maybe arrange the right opportunity, then get him to consider the job, right?"

The men nodded in unison.

"All right, then." Will looked at Cam and his eyes glittered with controlled anger. "I'll take your bet, barkeep, and raise you another gold piece to boot," he said quietly.

"You're on," Cam told him, grinning widely. It would be the easiest money he'd ever made.

CHAPTER ONE

THE MAN BEHIND the bar poured a shot of whiskey into the glass, then spun it across the slick, wooden surface toward his customer. "It's still morning," he said, with a measuring look at the man who eyed the amber liquid.

"It's never too early in the day for some things." James lifted his drink, lips twisting in a sardonic grin. His gaze swept the interior of the dusty saloon, lingering for just a moment on a red-haired woman with a satin dress stretched over her voluptuous form. Not what he had in mind, he decided easily. His head tilted back as the whiskey slid easily down his throat, and he winced at the impact of it on his empty stomach.

"Hair of the dog, Kincaid?" the barkeep asked with sympathy and amusement. His bushy eyebrows lifted as James thumped the heavy glass on the bar.

"One more should do it," James said, his blue eyes narrowing as he focused on the four men who slouched around a table at the far side of the room. "That game been going on long?" he asked in an undertone.

"All night," the barkeep told him. "They just keep movin' those little piles of money back and forth between them. I've been waitin' for one or the other to go to sleep over there."

James lifted his glass and sniffed at its contents, then

replaced it on the bar. "Maybe I need to help them out, sorta relieve them of their dilemma." His voice slurred on the word, the only sign of inebriation he allowed to blur his image. The mirror behind the bar reflected his likeness and he cocked his hat at a jauntier angle, bending forward to peer into his own blue eyes. He brushed his index finger beneath his full moustache then straightened his string tie with a hand that barely trembled.

"Why don't you walk up them stairs and take a nap, Kincaid?" the barkeep asked mildly. "There's an empty room at the end of the hall. You look like you've had a long night."

James grinned, knowing that his smile was his best friend. He'd coaxed more than one woman into his arms with its seductive gleam, hoodwinked more poker players than he could count with an innocent flash of teeth and curving lips. "Naw, I'll just amble over and clear that table for the gents. Give them a chance to fold their cards in an honorable manner." He spoke concisely, each word slowly formed and enunciated.

Outside the door, a commotion took his attention as he turned from the bar and he looked askance at the swinging doors, then back at the poker game. Boots thumped the wide wooden walk and skirts swished as women hurried past. A shout from farther down the street warned of danger, and then the sound of jangling harness and shrieking horses penetrated his whiskey-soaked mind.

"Sounds like trouble," the barkeep said, pulling his gun from beneath the bar. He held it at his side, his gaze fastened on the swinging doors.

"I'd say so," James said flatly, his stance altered as

if by magic. The grin was gone, the eyes alert beneath the wide brim of his hat. He stalked to the entrance and looked over the top of the double doors, then eased one of them open. The sidewalk was clear, as if a giant broom had swept it clean of humanity. All except two men who stood hesitantly in front of the new bank across the street.

With red bandannas tied around their faces and saddlebags flung over their shoulders, they sure as hell looked like a couple of fools who'd robbed the damn place. Where their horses had disappeared to was any man's guess, and the pair of them were waving guns in the air and cursing up a blue streak.

The morning stage, which was still vibrating from its sudden stop in front of the hotel next to the bank, seemed to offer them the next best exit. Ignoring the rearing horses, who'd reacted badly to the gunfire, they leapt from the sidewalk, ran to the coach and shouted instructions to the hapless driver.

From within the vehicle, a woman's shrill voice called upon heaven to help her, and James felt a twitch at the corner of his mouth, even as his hand lifted the gun from his holster. Fool creature needed to learn that God helps those who have enough sense to run from danger, he thought wryly. Bending low, he left the dubious shelter of the swinging doors and crouched behind the even more uncertain refuge of a four-by-four post that held up the porch.

The two men glanced quickly at the stage driver who was making a hasty exit, leaping to the ground and then running full tilt toward the hotel doorway. One of the bank robbers climbed atop the stage, the other pulled open the door and dragged the shrieking female from its depths, casting her like a bit of rubbish to the ground.

"Now, that wasn't the least bit polite of you," James murmured, lifting his gun to take careful aim. The slight tremble in his hand was gone, the barrel shone dully in the morning sunlight and his aim was true. As the stagecoach rumbled into motion, the horses rearing and plunging forward at the command of the second robber, James pulled the trigger. The would-be driver fell to the ground, motionless in the dirt.

The second man turned toward his cohort, then looked frantically across the street, lifting his gun to level its barrel at James.

"Well, damn," James muttered, firing a second shot.

The bank robber's finger twitched on the trigger as his body jolted. The gun fell to the dusty road, and the man fell in a heap, holding his arm and cursing with a steady stream of cussing that made James shake his head in disbelief. The man had quite a vocabulary, limited though it was to words not fit for the ears of his listeners.

From the ground only feet away from the wounded man, a wail of protest erupted, and James looked again at the female who'd made such an inelegant exit from the stagecoach. Her eyes were scrunched up behind wire-rimmed glasses, and her mouth was pursed in a way that gave him pause. She looked about ready to shed a bucket of tears, and if there was anything in this world James could not endure, it was a crying female.

He left the shelter of the post, jamming his gun back where it belonged and strode across the street. She didn't look much better up close, he decided, all dusty and teary-eyed, her skirts hiked up above her knees.

Her knees. His glance swept the length of her legs and returned swiftly to those pink, rounded, dimpled knees. Beneath them, garters held plain, lisle stockings in place, and he allowed a swift appraisal to bathe his aching eyes with pleasure. Damn, she did have a fine pair of legs. Calves rounded and curvaceous, just right for a man's palm, he decided judiciously. And slim little ankles that barely showed above the tops of half boots.

But those knees. He shook his head. A man could examine those pretty little legs for half a night, and still find something to look at. He'd warrant they were as soft and smooth to the touch as they were appealing to his eye. He reached down with one hand and grasped her elbow, levering her to her feet. Her head bent, she gripped the valise against her chest and wobbled a bit. James released her as she nodded her thanks, gaining her balance readily.

"Kincaid!" A voice shouted behind him and he turned quickly, almost steady on his feet now. "You saved the day," the jowly storekeeper said, approaching with hands upraised. A wide smile wreathed his face, and he turned to the gathering crowd. "Did y'all see what happened?"

Heads nodded and voices vied for notice, with several townsfolk all too willing to give their version of the short gun battle. From the bank, a dark-haired man stepped to the sidewalk, and James stiffened. Will might not take kindly to having James as a champion, and yet, the banker made his way in a deliberate fashion across the dusty road. His black suit was unwrinkled, his shirt pristine and elegant, and black shoes gleamed with a fresh layer of polish. His mouth twisted in a smile.

"They tell me I have you to thank for rescuing the bank's money," he said diffidently, approaching James. "Many thanks, cousin."

"Told you I'd come in handy one of these days," James said with a sweeping bow that almost brought him to his knees.

"I'm glad you've proved to be good for something," Will Kincaid answered smoothly, shooting a glance at an approaching merchant.

He turned to watch as several men lifted the erstwhile robber to his feet and nudged him into movement toward the jailhouse. "Looks like you've left one of them alive anyway, James," Will said. "Too bad you didn't save us the trouble of hanging him."

"I didn't aim to kill the other one," James admitted, watching as the dead man was lifted from the dirt and carried past the jail to the undertaker's parlor.

"Sir?" The voice was soft, and the single word trembled with emotion. James turned and looked down at the woman who'd so recently been greeted with violence. Her hat was still tilted precariously over one side of her head, her glasses sliding to the end of her nose. Her shoulders sagged as she held tightly to the satchel that threatened to pull her arms from their sockets. It must hold all of her hard, cold cash, he decided, looking her over with aching eyes.

Her skirts hung almost to the ground, hiding all but the toes of her boots, and, sadly, all of her legs. "Ma'am?" he said respectfully, lifting his hat in a fluid movement, then placing it again upon his aching head.

"I want to thank you for rescuing me," she said

softly. Her eyes seemed about to fill with tears once more, and he grinned his best coaxing smile in her direction.

"No trouble at all," he said. "Just doing my best to keep law and order in our fine community." Fool woman hadn't been in any danger, he thought, once she'd been plopped in the road, but if she wanted to be grateful, he'd grin and bear it.

"Is that so?" Will said.

"Never say that I didn't uphold justice, Will," he warned, glancing back with a grin at the woman beside him.

"Too bad you're not looking for a job, James. The town hasn't had a sheriff in more than a month, ever since the last one got a chance at a marshal's job," Will suggested smoothly.

"That doesn't sound like such a bad idea," John Dillard said from behind them. The storekeeper tugged at his apron and eyed James approvingly. "You'd make a dandy sheriff, Kincaid. You sure can use that gun. And I'll bet you the new schoolmarm here will vote for you, won't you, ma'am?"

Schoolmarm? James had heard that a teacher was arriving, had watched as the new school was built. And this pitiful creature had been chosen to teach the handful of girls and clutch of young boys who would fill its walls. The young men, hovering on manhood, and with a determined disdain for book learning, might elect to attend school after all, just for the sport of it, James decided.

Amos Carlton, still in his shirtsleeves, with red garters holding them in place, joined the small group. "We're needing a new man to fill the sheriff's shoes and look after things. I'd say your cousin could handle the job, Will. What do you think?''

Will nodded ''He can shoot straight, that's for certain,'' he said deliberately. ''But we don't need a drunk in the jailhouse, at least not sitting in the sheriff's chair.''

''Maybe he'd be willing to go on the wagon,'' Amos said hopefully, glancing at James, whose head was pounding mercilessly as he attempted to keep up with the conversation.

''He'd never manage that for longer than a day, maybe two,'' Will said sadly. ''James has three things in life that interest him, two of them are booze and gambling.''

''What is the third?'' the young woman asked, her wide eyes moving from one to another of the men who discussed James as if he were not present in their midst.

James grinned then and allowed the power of his blue eyes to focus on the brown-clad creature. ''You don't want to know, ma'am.''

She blinked, then shriveled within her clothing, a retreat that jarred James from his cocky stance. Her eyes dulled and she glanced down at the dirt beneath her boots. Her hat slipped just a bit farther to one side and she slapped at it with her hand, losing her hold on the valise she clutched. It slid down her front, one arm not enough to hold its weight, and James reached for the leather handles.

His hand covered hers and she winced as he grasped it tightly. ''Let me take that,'' he said politely, willing her to look at him. She might be untidy and about as fetching as a poulter pigeon, but she was obviously a lady, and he'd managed to damage her dignity or hurt her feelings, one or the other.

"If you gentlemen will just direct me to the schoolhouse, I'll be on my way," she said primly, lifting her chin and giving her attention to Will. Her free hand shoved at James's fingers, attempting to take hold of her bag, and with a show of stubborn courtesy, he lifted it until the backs of his knuckles rested precariously close to her bosom.

"I'll be glad to escort you," he said firmly, his jaw tightening. All this yattering was about enough to urge him on his way, to put space between himself and the talk of filling the sheriff's chair with his unworthy behind. And this frumpish little piece of womanhood was the excuse he needed to walk away from the group that had managed to gather, with him plumb in the middle of the circle. Besides, his head was banging to beat the band, and all this talk of making him sheriff was enough to turn his headache into a full-blown wallbanger.

The woman released the bag, managing to slide her fingers from beneath his grip, and he jutted his chin forward. "You got more stuff on board the stage?"

She nodded, her eyes squinting as she looked up to where a large trunk was strapped atop the vehicle.

"We'll send it on over to the schoolhouse, ma'am," Harry Talbert said, his half smile befitting a man who knew most of the secrets in town. Being a barber made him privy to confidences that would have shocked many of the ladies whose husbands sat in his chair for their haircuts and an occasional shave. His gaze took James's measure. "Sure looks like sheriff material to me," he murmured, adding a nudge of his own.

James smiled swiftly. "And you oughta know, if anyone does, Harry. Reckon you've seen me at my best, and worst, too, come to think of it." Harry's back room held a bathtub big enough to soak away a man's troubles, and deep enough to bury a hangover.

Bag clasped in one fist, James took the young woman's elbow with his other hand and steered her from the circle of townsfolk. "So you're the new schoolmarm," he said staunchly, noting with pride that his feet trod a straight line.

Behind him Will grinned widely, waving at Cam who watched from the doorway of the Double Deuce Saloon. "Might's well get ready to pay up," he said smugly.

Cam shrugged. "We'll see."

The new schoolmarm trudged along beside James, then glanced up at him from beneath lowered brows. "It *is* you that smells like the bottom of a whiskey barrel, isn't it?" Her steps were short and mincing next to his long strides, and she inhaled sharply as his grip tightened. "I wondered which of those men had been imbibing so early in the day."

"Never too early for some things, ma'am," he murmured, repeating his dictum spoken in the saloon. And only fifteen minutes or so ago, he realized. So rapidly had events taken place, he'd barely scanned one woman and deemed her unappetizing in the daylight, when another had come under his scrutiny. Now, he reflected with a quick glance at the flowered hat that was the only scrap of color in her entire getup, this one might warrant a second look. Even the dowdy clothing could not conceal her trim lines.

He'd probably never get another gander at those legs

though, he decided glumly as they paced the length of Main Street, but he could savor the memory of those pink knees while he considered the idea.

She'd determined to be silent, it seemed, trotting along beside him, one hand lifting to anchor the hat, the other holding her skirt from the dust that spurted behind her every step. The schoolhouse was dead ahead, right on the edge of town.

"They tacked on a room behind for the new schoolteacher," James volunteered as he led her around to the back door. "They were looking for a man, I believe." His eyes cut swiftly in her direction. "I don't think you qualify."

"Indeed not," she said stiffly, stepping onto the small, square porch. "Is the door locked?"

"Doubt it," James answered. "Nobody locks their doors in town, except the business places."

"I'll need a lock put on," she said primly. "A woman alone can't be too careful."

His head was pounding double time as he ducked to enter the single room. They'd been expecting a short teacher it seemed, with the lintel only a few inches more than six feet from the floor. His hat would have brushed against the new wood, and he reached to lift it from his head. Her valise was deposited by the door and he shrugged his shoulder, relieved from the weight of her leather case.

"That thing weighs a ton," he said. "You carrying bricks in it?"

She shook her head. "No, just books."

"Books." He bent to peer at her more closely. "You mean schoolbooks for the children? I thought the town provided those."

"These are some from my own personal library," she told him, blinking at him above her glasses.

Her eyes were green, with little sunbursts surrounding the soft, lustrous color. A bit unfocused, he thought, perhaps because she tried so hard to meet his gaze, frowning at him intently. "I read a lot," she said. And then stepped back, as if she'd just realized that she was alone in a room with a strange man, and there was a narrow, unmade bed just six feet distant from her location.

"Do you read, sir?" she asked, her fingers knotting together at her waistline.

"Ever since I was six years old," James answered, wishing he could spread himself across that narrow cot and hold the thin pillow across his aching eyes.

"I imagined you *could* read, sir. I just wondered if you enjoy the habit."

The grin was automatic, and his skin felt stretched by it, sending throbbing tendrils of pain into his scalp. "There's other habits I enjoy more," he admitted. His eyes closed abruptly and he rubbed one hand over his forehead. A bed to hold his considerable length in a prone position seemed to be essential right now, and he turned to the door.

"I'll take my leave, ma'am," he said abruptly. "Someone will be along with your trunk." Maybe he'd take Cam up on his offer of a bed. Heading for the boardinghouse he graced with his presence on occasion wasn't a good bet. Old lady Harroun would likely peel a strip off his hide if he came in looking like he was nursing a hangover.

He stepped to the ground and trudged a return path toward the center of town.

"Sir?" Behind him a flustered voice beckoned, and he turned, patience vying with pain as he waited for her to speak.

"Your name?" she asked, standing on the square porch, her brow furrowed. "I need to know who you are."

"James Kincaid," he answered.

"I'm Kate Elliott," she offered. Then waited.

"Pleased to meet you," he said politely, turning away slowly so as not to lose his balance.

"Thank you, Mr. Kincaid," she said swiftly. "I appreciate your escort, and especially your quick action. Shooting—" Her pause was sudden and he looked back at her. "You killed a man, didn't you?"

"Yes, ma'am, I guess I did." She looked pale, downright pasty, in fact.

She crumpled, as if her bones dissolved beneath the dark dress, allowing her to settle in a pile of brown serge smack-dab in the middle of the porch. Her eyes were damp again and James stifled a groan.

"I just realized I've seen a shooting, and watched a man die, right before my eyes," she murmured. "I've only just arrived, and already I've seen the frontier at its worst."

"Ma'am, I'm sure sorry you were exposed to such a thing on your first day here," James said, walking slowly back to the porch. He squatted in front of her, balancing on his toes, wondering if he would be capable of rising again. "I didn't mean to kill the man," he reminded her. "I don't generally shoot to kill."

Her eyes were solemn. "Are you a gunfighter?"

He shook his head. "No, ma'am. I'm a gambler, a drinking man and pretty much the black sheep of my family. I just happen to have a talent for shooting a gun."

"Will you be the new sheriff?" He thought she looked hopeful, and he shook his head, deliberately dousing that idea.

"No, ma'am. There's no way in hell I'm about to do that."

CHAPTER TWO

KATE STRIPPED from her clothing, yearning for a long soak in the big bathtub that graced the second-floor bathroom in her girlhood home. She recalled stretching out in it, her toes pointing and still unable to reach the far end. Of course that had been years ago. Nowadays it would still hold her in a generous way, but no longer could she duck under the water and lie prone beneath its surface. She'd grown up, and wasn't that the truth.

Her laugh rang hollow in the room she occupied. And that's all it was, just a room. No curtains graced the two double-sash windows, no pictures hung on bare walls. A pair of her best towels covered the window glass, protecting her from the view of those who might pass by. And in that relative amount of privacy she undressed rapidly, washing as thoroughly as a small basin of warm water would allow, then dried her goose bumps with a rough towel.

The air was cool, and she hurried the process, slipping into her nightgown for warmth. Lace trimmed the sleeves and neckline, and, as she buttoned the row of tiny buttons, she peered in the oval mirror over her dry sink.

Dark hair surrounded her face, with waves falling to her waist. It wasn't an altogether homely face, she thought, her index finger rubbing the end of her nose, as though she might shorten it a bit if she applied enough pressure. And then there were her eyes. Why she couldn't have inherited her mother's soft brown orbs was something she'd never understood. Instead hers were strange, green, with streaks in them. She made a face at herself, then grinned at her foolishness.

Lifting her brush, she pulled it through the heavy length of her hair, and sighed with pleasure. It was a relief to free its weight from the tight bun she wore at her nape. Maybe someday, she thought, she might plait it in some sort of intricate way, and wrap it around her head, perhaps create an elegant style that would give her an illusion of height. As quickly as the thought intruded into her mind, she frowned, vanquishing it with a firm shake of her head.

Kate Elliott was far beyond the fancy fixings of a young girl. At twenty-three years of age, she was firmly on the shelf, and not likely to be snatched from her position any time soon. For tonight she would allow her hair the freedom to flow freely. Tomorrow was soon enough to twist and pin it into place.

She blew out her lamp, then crossed to the window where the pale glow of moonlight penetrated the towel hanging there. One hand pushed the cotton fabric aside and she watched, holding her breath as a star fell across the sky. An omen? Probably not. She'd long since given up on signs and portents. Wishing on a star, even a falling star, was childish. Her life was set into a mold she would be content with. Teaching held the promise of filling young minds with knowledge, gaining satisfaction for herself.

A man walked down the middle of Main Street and she bent closer to the windowpane, intent on the broad shoulders and long legs. Perhaps…no, probably not. If she knew anything at all about such things, James Kincaid was out like a light and sleeping off a massive hangover. The man had absolutely reeked of alcohol.

The towel fell into place and Kate turned toward the dark corner where her bed awaited her presence. She fumbled in the dark, seeking the thin mattress, and settled on it with a sigh. Drunk he may have been, but he did have the most beautiful eyes she'd ever seen on a man. His hair was black, wavy and inviting, and her fingers had ached to slide into its dark splendor. Black Irish. She'd lay money on it if she was a gambler.

And maybe she was. Leaving Ohio, traveling across the country by herself, taking a position in Montana was a gamble. *Life itself was a gamble.*

THE MORNING SKY was breathtaking. Kate stood on her tiny porch and surveyed the town, a decent-size community, yet diminutive beneath the Montana sky. Mountains in the west stretched in a dark chain across the horizon, and above them rose a blue eternity, cloudless and shimmering with promise. She resisted the temptation to join the parade of women moving down the sidewalk, and turned her head aside when a man glanced in her direction. And, as always, felt the separation that existed between housewives and a woman who found she must work to support herself in whatever way she could.

Those ladies who nodded and smiled at each other, carrying their parcels and shepherding their children from one place to the next had no concept of what Kate lived with every day of her life. An emotion she could only call *envy* washed through her as she thought of the joys inherent in cleaning, mending and cooking for a family. For her own family.

Instead she would teach those children, be looked upon as a threat by some of those women, with their watchful eyes ever on her, lest she cast her gaze on one of their husbands.

She turned away from the morning activities in town and trudged around the schoolhouse to the front door. It swung open at her touch and she stepped inside, keenly aware of the scent of unpainted pine. But here another aroma met her discerning nose; that of schoolbooks. Stacked neatly on her desk, they beckoned her and she moved quickly to the plain wooden table around which her life would revolve.

Here she would sit, listening to children read, hearing their spelling words, correcting their papers and noting their grades in a record book. She sat down in the chair and scooted it beneath the table. The books were varied, a stack of readers, a large atlas of maps and charts, and a pile of dog-eared arithmetic books.

She riffled through one of the new primers, inhaling the scent of paper and ink, reading familiar words that would initiate her pupils into the joy of stories come alive from these pages.

"Looks like you're all settled in, Miss Elliott." The voice was low, with a hint of gravel in its depths. James Kincaid stood in the doorway, one hand resting on the frame, the other tucked into his pocket. "I knocked on your door, and then figured I'd find you here." His gaze rested on her hair and she resisted the urge to smooth back the wispy strands that brushed her forehead.

"You figured right, sir," she said smoothly, removing her glasses for a moment, and watched as his mouth curled in a faint smile. He'd recovered, it seemed. Smoothly shaven and dressed in the garb of a dandy, he bore little likeness to the man who'd dragged her upright from the dusty road, then escorted her home.

"Just wanted to see if you were all right," he said genially, taking a quick survey of the room. "Looks like you only need a bunch of young'uns here and you'll be in business."

"Will they come of their own volition on Monday, do you think?" she asked. "Or must I somehow send out announcements that school will be in session?"

"How'd they do it where you taught last?" He pulled a small chair from against the back wall and sat down on it, his long legs awkwardly bent.

"I only taught for three years in Ohio, and it was a large school, with separate grades for the students. Everyone in town knew to send their children on the first day of school." She polished the lenses of her glasses on a fold of her dress, pleased to find something to occupy her hands.

"You taught one grade?" he asked, his eyebrow lifting in silent disbelief as if such a thing could not be.

"I had over twenty children in my second-grade class, Mr. Kincaid," she said sharply, sliding her glasses back in place. *And more books to work with than what she was expected to teach from here,* she wanted to say.

"You'd do well to go to church in the morning, get acquainted with folks. Some of the country families come in on Sunday. They'll pass the word along."

Kate watched him, noting the elegance of his gestures, the length of his fingers as he drew his hat from his head and held it against one knee. His eyes were penetrating, as if he looked beneath the plain dress she wore, seeking out her length and breadth, and she felt a moment's disquiet at his survey. *Surely he was not interested in...*

"Stand up, Kate," he said abruptly.

She jolted and rose quickly. "What's the problem?" Her gaze swept the room, and she turned to look behind her.

"Just walk over here," he murmured, tilting his head to one side.

She brushed ineffectively at her skirt, lifted a hand to her hair and patted the neat, tightly wound bun at her nape, then brushed back the loose strands curling at her temple as she stepped from behind the desk. "I'm not sure what you want me to do, Mr. Kincaid." She rested one palm against the tabletop and hesitated.

He grinned, transforming his face into a tempting vision of male beauty. She inhaled sharply, then covered the instinctive reaction with a cough. He was beyond handsome, she decided. Beyond well-favored. James Kincaid was likely the best-looking specimen of manhood she'd ever laid eyes on.

"I just want to see you walk," he told her softly, beckoning with one long index finger. His eyes glittered like sunlight on lake water, blue and brilliant between dark lashes. It wasn't fair, she decided, that he should be such a tempting rascal.

He should look downright foolish, all hunkered down on that small chair, his knees higher than his bottom. But somehow... Kate tilted her head, the better to focus on him. His grin widened, and white teeth showed between the edge of his moustache and his bottom lip. She stepped toward him, aware for the first time in her adult life of the manner in which she placed one foot ahead of the other.

And he watched her, his mouth twisting just a bit, his eyes narrowing a shade as she neared him. And then he stood, his hands holding the brim of his hat, his cheeks wearing a slash of ruddy color. He cleared his throat and allowed his scrutiny to include the plain lines of her serviceable brown dress.

"Ma'am," he murmured. "You're too well put together to be all wrapped up in clothes that look more like my maiden aunt should be wearing them."

She gawked, her mouth opening abruptly, her eyes widening, and her hands rising to cover the blush that crept up to cover her cheeks. "I'm sure my mode of dress has nothing to do with you," she said, despising the quaver in her voice. "I'm decent and presentable. That, sir, is all that is required of a lady schoolteacher."

He moved to the doorway, and she rued every nice thought she'd had about him. *Handsome is as handsome does,* her mother had said, more than once. And somehow, that particular saying seemed to be applicable to James Kincaid. He was rude and crude, no matter how well put together both face and form happened to be, and if she didn't need this job so badly, she'd spit those words in his face. Although, she decided, he probably didn't have an awful lot of influence with the folks who would be judging her performance.

"You're a good-looking woman," he repeated. "I'll bet you'll be married off in no time, once you fix yourself up a little."

"And who said I wanted to be married?" she asked.

Her cheeks felt hot, and her breath was short. "I'm a woman with a career, Mr. Kincaid. I don't have time to cater to a man."

Eyes like blue marbles raked over her again. "You need to be having children of your own, ma'am. If I was a marrying sort of man I'd be knocking at your door on a regular basis." His grin flashed and she swallowed a retort as he spent his charm in her direction.

"As it is, I'd do well to stay away from you, I suspect. I'm just the man who could ruin your reputation before you know it."

"*Why* are you here, Mr. Kincaid?" she asked stiffly, unsure whether or not she'd been insulted by his palavering.

He rocked back on his heels. "Just to see if you were in need of anything, ma'am. Thought I'd steer you in the right direction toward the Mercantile, maybe carry your parcels home for you." He shrugged those wide shoulders then. "'Course, I don't want you to feel obligated in any way. I'm only the man who saved your hide yesterday."

"Phooey!" she said in an inelegant burst of disgust. "You know very well I was already in the clear had those men managed to escape with the stagecoach."

He looked pained. "Now that wasn't what you said right out there in the street in front of half the town. You thanked me very kindly for coming to your rescue."

She had the grace to acknowledge his thrust. "So I did. But then I was understandably upset by the circumstances."

His mouth twitched and she caught a glint of humor in his eyes. "You won't think it's so funny when they pin that badge on your chest," she said, relishing the clenching of his jaw.

"Being the sheriff is not my plan."

"So you said. It might interfere with your career, I suppose," she offered softly, enjoying his defensive stance, hands on hips and jaw thrust forward.

His brow rose. "My career?"

"Why, yes," she told him casually. "Didn't you say you were very good at drinking and gambling? I assumed that you wouldn't give those up in favor of such a mundane job as sheriff." She looked at him thoughtfully. "Of course, there's always the possibility that staying out of the saloon might not be an option for you."

His jaw clenched tighter and was stained with a ruddy hue. "And what the hell is that supposed to mean?"

"I've had only limited experience with drunkards, sir, but from what I understand, once a man is addicted to that particular vice, there isn't much hope of staying clear of a whiskey bottle."

"I'm not *addicted* to anything," he boomed.

"So you say," she answered, doubt alive in her tone.

His eyes narrowed and he advanced one step. "There's only one thing I can't seem to stay away from, Miss Schoolmarm."

She scooted back, her legs pressing against a student desk. He'd turned from amiable to angry in one swift moment. Perhaps she'd pressed too hard, allowed her sharp tongue to touch him in a raw spot. "I'm sure you keep yourself under perfect control, sir," she whispered, her eyes fixed on his flaring nostrils and taut lips.

"Aren't you going to ask me what my downfall is?" he murmured.

She shook her head. "I don't think I want to know."

"Women," he growled. "I can't seem to stay away from women." His hands reached for her and she yelped, a shrill sound that creased his forehead with its velocity. "My head was aching before I got here, and you're making it worse with your noise. Don't know any other way to shut you up, I suppose. At least not one that works as well as this."

She felt her eyes widen as his head dipped in her direction. His hands clasped her upper arms and he drew her against his lean, hard length. Heat surrounded her, throbbing throughout her body, sending warmth to her every part as he lifted her from the floor. Heavy-lidded eyes swept her face, and his head tilted to one side. She caught a scent of soap as she inhaled, something fresh and cool in her nostrils. His mouth brushed hers, and she shivered, anticipating the harsh, punishing force of his lips.

It was not to be. Gently, carefully, he eased her lips apart just the least bit with the pressure of his mouth. She heard her moan of fear, knew when it turned to a whisper of amazement, and then, in an automatic gesture she lifted her hands to clutch at his shoulders. His grip eased and he lowered her to the floor, his moustache soft against her lips. She clenched her teeth, trembling in his grip, shivering as his tongue tasted the inside of her lower lip.

Her eyes opened wide and she stepped back, gasping a bit as he lifted his head.

"Kate." His mouth was twisted ruefully, his eyes were dark with an emotion she could not name, and he leaned forward to touch those warm lips against her forehead. "I offer my apologies. That was beyond good behavior. I don't usually insult a lady right off the bat."

She shook her head. "I was unkind, Mr. Kincaid, with my remarks about your drinking habits. I should not have judged you so quickly, although now you've given me even more valid reason to doubt your ability to behave yourself."

"So I have," he agreed amiably. "You wouldn't be the first good citizen to call me a ne'er-do-well," he said with a shrug. "But—" he paused and allowed a grin to curl his mouth "—if you're interested, I'm still available to walk you to the Mercantile."

Her heart stilled for a long moment and something within her sounded a warning. James Kincaid might do her more harm than good. He was a rascal, bone-deep and to the core. But he'd just given her the first taste of passion she'd ever known, and for the first time in her life, she saw and recognized Eve's apple, and felt a shaft of understanding for that hapless female.

THE MERCANTILE was busy, with what James recognized as the "Saturday crowd" in attendance. Farmers brought their wives along, and youngsters gazed with longing eyes at the display of candy, lined up in tall jars on the counter like so many tin soldiers.

John Dillard and his wife, Tess, scurried back and forth behind the long counter that ran along the back of the store. They lifted merchandise from the shelves for their customers' perusal, offered their opinions on a variety of subjects, and then when the final calculations were done, accepted money from the customers.

Several apparently bought on credit, Kate noticed, watching as Tess Dillard added a long column of figures on brown paper and then wrote the total on a page in her black account book.

John Dillard looked across the width of his store and nodded his head at Kate, then lifted his brow in a questioning gesture as he spotted James next to her. "You ready to wear that badge yet, James?" he called jovially. The man with him followed his lead and surveyed James silently, then with a slow shake of his head, turned away.

"Apparently Clovis Teal doesn't think I'm sheriff material," James said in an undertone, bending so that Kate could hear his comment.

She felt irritation clawing at her, and cast her own glance at the man in question. "What does he know about your qualifications?" she murmured. "He obviously didn't see you shoot those ruffians yesterday."

"A man who can shoot straight probably isn't all they're looking to find," James told her. "You said yourself that I wasn't much more than a drunken gambler."

"I didn't." The words were low, terse and loaded with as much denial as Kate could fuel them with. "You'd be good at..." She hesitated, unwilling to state an untruth. "You could probably—"

"Yeah, maybe I could," he interjected quickly, and she untangled her tongue. His long fingers picked up a piece of dress goods that was folded on the counter in front of him. "This'd look nice on you," he told her, holding it against her bodice, tilting his head to one side to consider the effect of blue-flowered dimity beneath her chin.

"You could what?" she persisted with a frown, her mind on his qualifications.

"What you said."

Her sigh was exasperated as he placed the fabric back on the counter and picked up another, with shades of deep-rose and pink on a white background. His mouth drew together and he shook his head. "Naw, the blue's better. You're too..."

"Too what?" she demanded, looking down at the discarded material. "I look good in pink."

"Maybe," he said easily. "Red would be better, more lively. Pink's kinda girlie."

"I am a girl," she reminded him, and drew his immediate scrutiny.

His eyes were sparkling, his mouth turned up in a grin that begged her response. "No, ma'am," he answered slowly and quietly. "You're a woman. There's no doubt about that." He watched as she felt a flush settle on her cheeks, warming her skin.

"Those pieces of fabric are already set aside for Millie Carlton," Tess Dillard said from across the counter. She scooped up the folded material and placed it next to the big, iron register. "She's pickin' out some findings to go with them."

"I already told Miss Elliott that the pink wasn't her color," James said cheerfully.

"What is her color?" Tess asked with a grin. Obviously James was on good terms with the storekeeper's wife, Kate thought. The woman turned to Kate and her eyes carried a hint of recognition. "I saw you yesterday, when you got dumped in the road," she said quickly. "Are you recovered from your fall?"

Kate nodded. "I'm fine, thank you. I just came by to pick up some supplies this morning."

"You looking for a piece of dress goods?" Tess asked. "I've got some pretty green fabric on sale, and some ready-made things, too. Maybe the green would look better than the pink, at that. Are you one to do your own sewing?"

Kate felt flustered as several other ladies turned her way, obviously waiting for her reply. "Not today, thanks," she answered quietly. "I just need a few things for meals."

"Some folks will invite you for supper a couple of times a week," Tess offered. "If they'd known there was a woman comin' instead of a man teacher, they'd have arranged for you to stay in the homes of those who send their young'uns to school. You know, a month here, then another there."

Kate subdued the shudder that held her in its grip. That she would be shuffled from one house to another over the school year was unthinkable. "I'm very happy with the room behind the school," she said quickly. "I can cook on the woodburner, so long as there's a pot there and a skillet."

"You'll need a coffeepot," Tess said. "They didn't outfit the place. I guess they thought they'd just wait till the teacher showed up."

Kate thought of the money she'd brought with her. Fitting out a kitchen had not been in her plans. But then, she'd been a bit short on plans of any sort when she left Ohio. Only anxious to see the last of small-town folks with long memories, eager to begin again where she was unknown.

"I'll take a small skillet and a two-quart kettle," she

said. "If you have a small teakettle, that would be fine. I can brew tea in a cup."

James stepped back, leaving the women to their planning and Kate felt lost for a moment. And then a small, golden-haired creature with eyes as blue as a summer sky stepped up beside her.

"I'm Lizzy," she confided. "Will told me about you."

"Will?" Kate's mind raced. *Will? The banker? James's cousin?*

Lizzy flushed becomingly. "He's my husband," she said, pride in every syllable. "He told me about the ruffians who pulled you out of the stagecoach." Her voice lowered as she bent close to whisper in Kate's ear. "I also heard that Will's cousin walked you over to the new schoolhouse." She stood erect and looked around the store, then whispered again. "Did you come in here with him?"

Kate nodded. "He offered to escort me, and carry my packages home for me."

"Will says that James is a *scoundrel*." Lizzy's cheeks were pink and her golden curls bounced as she nodded. "He likes him, you understand, but he says James may not be the best man for you to acknowledge as a friend."

"Will is probably right," Kate said agreeably. "But at the moment, James is also the only person besides yourself and the storekeeper's wife who's done much to welcome me to town."

"You got your stuff together, Kate?" James was behind her, his voice gruff, and Kate turned quickly, wondering just how much he'd overheard. He nodded to Lizzy, tipping his hat in a courtly manner, then looked

past Kate to where only the bare essentials she'd enu-
merated to Tess waited.

"I just have to get a few things," she said. "You
can go on if you need to, Mr. Kincaid. I can handle
this."

"I brought you here and I told you I'd carry your
stuff back home for you," he told her. "I'm above all
things a man who keeps his word. Take your time."

"Oh, my," Lizzy breathed in a wispy undertone.
"He is a handsome one, isn't he? No matter what Will
says," she added in a whisper and a quick glance at
Kate.

Kate watched the tall, broad-shouldered figure amble
across the store and her heart stuttered in her chest.
"My mama would think so," she admitted.

And so do I, her honest heart agreed.

CHAPTER THREE

THE MEN WHO GATHERED in the churchyard to meet with Kate after Sunday morning service looked familiar. She recognized the storekeeper, of course, and nodded, greeting him by name.

"Mr. Dillard." She smiled politely, forcing her lips into a steady line.

"You remember Amos Carlton, don't you, Miss Elliott? He owns the hotel, he and his wife." John Dillard presented another gentleman. "And this here is Harry Talbert, the fella that owns the barbershop." He looked behind himself and motioned at a familiar figure. "Come on over here, Will. We need to have a word with Miss Elliott."

Will Kincaid moved reluctantly into the circle and nodded at Kate. Behind him, Lizzy stood waiting, and she raised her hand, fingers wagging a greeting in Kate's direction.

"Miss Elliott." Will offered his hand and she placed hers on his palm. His grip was warm and solid and she met it with a firmness he could not mistake. A reluctant smile curved his mouth and she was struck with his resemblance to James. And why not? They were cousins, after all.

"We only received news that the state board had hired us a woman a day before you arrived," Amos

Carlton said. His tone was apologetic and Kate smiled reassuringly, urging him to continue. "We'd expected a man, and so built the new schoolhouse to accommodate a gentleman. If we'd known ahead of time that our first choice was not available—"

"I know," Kate interrupted cheerfully. "You'd have shunted me off to one student's home or another, rather than give me the privacy of a place of my own."

Will cleared his throat and Kate turned to him expectantly as he spoke. "Surely you understand the position this puts you in, Miss Elliott. The parents of your students might not approve of you, being an unmarried woman living alone on the edge of town." He looked as though his shirt collar was suddenly too tight, Kate thought.

"And may I ask why it should concern anyone as to where I live?" she asked. And then proceeded to state her case. "Gentlemen, we are very near to the twentieth century. Surely you are men of intelligence, and farsighted enough to realize that women are gradually going to come into their own. I thought, from what I had read in books and periodicals, that Montana was the most liberal state in the union, so far as the rights of women are concerned."

"Yes, ma'am," Mr. Carlton answered. "That's all true, but you have to understand that this is a small town and folks are pretty rigid in their standards of behavior."

Kate pushed her glasses up her nose and viewed the men surrounding her with a discerning eye. "As am I, gentlemen. I have the highest standards...." *Except that I've made it my business to become a friend of the town's bad boy.* She cleared her throat. "If you read my qualifications, I'm sure you will recognize that I am of good character and ably suited for the position of teacher to the children of this community."

"There's no question of your character, Miss Elliott," Will said staunchly. And yet his eyes held a modicum of doubt, Kate decided. Due no doubt to James's shenanigans in the Mercantile on Saturday morning.

Holding up yardgoods in front of her, as if he measured her for a dress, and then making a big fuss over the bundles of foodstuffs she'd purchased, staggering under the load he carried. She'd stalked out the door ahead of him, leaving him to find his own way back to the schoolhouse, her own hands filled with the assortment of dishes and cooking utensils she'd found it necessary to purchase.

And now she would pay the price for James and his foolishness.

Lizzy Kincaid stepped forward to stand beside her husband. "I think that Miss Elliott will make a fine teacher for the children. And I hope she'll still be here when I have young ones old enough to sit in her schoolroom." Her cheeks flushed as she spoke, and Will looked down at her.

"That may be several years in the future," he reminded Lizzy, and then, as if to soften his words, he reached out one long arm to place his hand atop her shoulder.

Lizzy's eyes filled with quick tears. "I just think it's mean for four men to gang up on a young lady. It's not her fault she isn't a man."

Kate felt a laugh bubble from her throat and she swallowed it. Levity was not going to help her case this morning. "What would you gentlemen suggest we do to rectify this situation?'' she asked politely, shooting an appreciative look in Lizzy's direction.

"Well…'' Mr. Talbert uttered the single word, then hesitated. "I think we oughta let things stand as they are for now,'' he suggested mildly. "I'd say Miss Elliott is pretty well able to take care of herself, and she's not gonna be living clear down the road. If she's in need of help, there's any number of folks who would be glad to lend a hand.''

John Dillard nodded reluctantly. "I don't suppose we have much choice for now. However, if a man qualified for the position becomes available, we may have to rethink our decision.''

Kate fumed. There was no other word for the churning maelstrom that set her insides to quivering. With an effort that included a set jaw and clenched fists, she stepped back from the circle of men. "Well, unless there is something else important you wanted to discuss with me, gentlemen, I'll be on my way. I'd suggest that you pass the word around town that school will be in session tomorrow morning.''

She turned from the small group, aware suddenly that a clutch of townsfolk stood within hearing distance, and were busily taking her measure. It was enough to make a body downright daring, she decided, and turned back to the gathering of influential gentleman who had so kindly decided she would be allowed to live in the stark, unadorned room they'd tacked on behind their schoolhouse.

"I'd like your permission to order some writing tablets and an assortment of pens and pencils for my students. Also a chalkboard to be hung on the wall and a supply of chalk and erasers. I'll expect each pupil to have his or her own slate and we'll make do with those until school supplies arrive.'' Even to her own ears her voice was imperious, and she gloried in the discovery that every eye was on her, the women looking downright approving, most of them nodding their agreement.

"There wasn't money put aside for such things, ma'am,'' Mr. Carlton said stiffly. "The students have always gotten along just fine with chalkboards. Paper tablets are expensive, and children are known to waste the paper frivolously.''

Kate's brow lifted as she faced the man. "Indeed? In the school I taught in back in Ohio, each child was furnished with a tablet, and I sent home their work for the parents' approval daily.'' She sniffed delicately and located her hankie, brushing it against the tip of her nose. "Of course, I understand that on the frontier, folks probably don't set such store by book learning.''

"I'd say our children deserve as good as the kids in Ohio have,'' said a woman close at hand.

Tess Dillard stepped forward. "I'd say so, too,'' she said with just the right degree of force to bring her husband's head swiveling in her direction.

"Now, Tess...'' he began, and then as his wife's eyes narrowed warningly, he subsided. "You may have a point there,'' he conceded. "I think we may need to allot a small amount for Miss Elliott to order what she needs. We can have it shipped by rail and sent from Butte on the stagecoach.''

"Thank you,'' Kate said. No longer willing to hold her temper in check, she stalked away, nodding and smiling with gritted teeth as she sailed past the parishioners filling the churchyard. *The nerve. The very nerve of those pompous idiots.* Her feet scuffed dust as she made her way down the middle of the road, her eyes set upon the unpainted schoolhouse at the far end of town.

THE EARLY-MORNING CHILL forced Kate to don a shawl over her dress as she left her room to walk around the building. Why those men couldn't have been foresighted enough to add a door between the schoolroom and the teacher's living quarters was another question she planned on asking.

Three children stood on the front stoop, two girls and a boy, obviously members of the same family, if she was any judge. With golden hair and the same rounded features, they looked like stairsteps, the girls with starched pinafores and the boy with a shirt that had come untucked and a hat he wore cocked to one side.

"Welcome to school," Kate said, opening the door and allowing the three to walk in ahead of her. She made her way to her desk and sat down, opening her record book, a new one she'd purchased just before leaving Sedgefield, Ohio. She looked at the trio and smiled. "Do you want to give me your names and ages, please? And tell me what grade you were in last year, will you?"

She repeated the same litany several times over the next thirty minutes. Apparently the townsfolk observed an eight-thirty school opening, for by a quarter to nine, she was faced with a roomful of students, three of whom sat on the floor against the wall.

"We don't have enough desks, I see," she told them. "For today, I'll ask you three—" she motioned to the boys who slouched in the back of the room "—

to go to my quarters and bring back the two chairs you'll find there, and also the small stool you'll find near the stove.''

The three boys looked at each other and then shrugged, rising to do as they were bidden. Kate opened a book on her desk and began.

An assortment of three-pound lard pails and homemade lunch sacks held food for the midday break. Kate dismissed her students at eleven-thirty, watching from her desk as they fled the room and, bursting with typical childlike enthusiasm, flooded the schoolyard. Her own noon meal awaited her and she followed the children out the door. She walked around the side of the building and opened the door to her room.

Inside, she lifted cold hands to her warm cheeks and leaned against the door. It had been an ordeal, one she'd faced before, but always dreaded. The first day of school drew the lines, and she could only hope that the order she'd been able to maintain would hold firm for the rest of the day. She opened a tin of crackers and sliced cheese from a half-round she'd purchased at the Mercantile. Wrapping them in a towel, she retraced her steps and found a seat on the front stoop of the schoolhouse.

One of the towheaded girls approached and watched as Kate lifted a cracker to her lips. ''Would you like to sit with me?'' she asked. What was the child's name? Beth? Or maybe Alice. ''Beth?'' she ventured, and was rewarded by a smile that revealed a missing tooth.

''When did you lose your tooth?'' Kate asked, biting into the cheese.

''Last week,'' Beth answered shyly.

"Have you eaten?" Kate asked, and the child nodded reluctantly. "Would you like to share my crackers and cheese?"

Beth eyed the offering with eagerness and Kate spread the towel over her knees. "I'm not very hungry anyway," she lied.

"Why don't I believe you?" From the side of the building, James's voice was low and amused. Kate's head turned quickly and he grinned at her. Leaning against the wall, he slouched just a bit, his hat cocked at an angle, his eyes glittering. And on his chest, pinned to the flap of his shirt pocket, was a shiny, silver star.

"Do I call you Sheriff Kincaid?" she asked, and watched disbelievingly as a flush crept up his cheeks.

"It wasn't in my plan," he said defensively.

"So you said." She was enjoying this immensely. He was due some sort of payment for making her look like an idiot on Saturday, with his monkeyshines in the Mercantile.

"I knew you'd rub it in," he told her. "How long are you going to smirk at me?"

"I never smirk, sir," she said primly. "I only enjoy a bit of revenge now and then."

"Miss Elliott." Beth tugged at Kate's sleeve. "Who's that man? Is he the black sheep? My papa said they was gonna make the black sheep into a sheriff." Beth scrutinized James with avid eyes. "He don't look like a sheep to me, even if his clothes is black."

"Out of the mouths of babes," he murmured, leveling himself from his indolent stance. His thumbs tucked into the gun belt he wore and he approached Kate with a swaggering pose. One she would warrant was assumed for her benefit. "Are things going well?"

he asked, his eyes weary as he looked beyond her to the children who raced back and forth and tossed a ball in some sort of game.

"You look tired," she said quietly, ignoring his query, and watched as he shrugged.

"Haven't slept much the past couple of nights," he said finally. He looked back at her. "I have this thirst, Miss Elliott." His words halted and he frowned. "Not that I expect you to understand."

"Ah, but I do. Not from my own personal experience, you understand, but I've been privy to..." She hesitated and then spread her hands in a gesture of helplessness, as if she groped for words to express herself. She bent low to Beth. "Would you like to go to the pump and get me a drink, sweetheart?" she asked. And as the child nodded and ran off to do her bidding, Kate called after her. "Rinse the cup real well, will you?"

Beth hastened away, her steps confident as she set off on a mission for her teacher. And Kate turned back to James. "Just know that I do understand, Sheriff. If I can help, I'll..." *I'll what?*

"Maybe you could sit with me on your porch this evening, after dark when folks won't be watching." A suggestion of pleading colored his tone and she nodded, uncaring of the position in which she might be put. Memories of another time, another place, filled her mind as James turned and walked back toward town. Memories of a man who begged on bended knee for his wife to forgive him, and all in vain. Kate closed her eyes, and the vision of her father was there.

James came after dark, and Kate watched him walk beneath the lone tree that graced the schoolyard. In its shadows he hesitated and she lifted her face, aware that he watched her. "You sure about this?" he asked quietly.

She nodded, then reinforced the small affirmation with an invitation. "Come sit by me," she said, moving to the edge of the stoop.

They were silent for a while, watching the flickering lights in houses scattered on the edges of town, then looking outward, to where stars sprang from the black velvet sky. Hovering in the background was music that rose and fell in intensity from the open doors of the saloon. She heard the rollicking piano and an occasional shout of laughter that carried in the still night air.

And then in a moment of total silence, James turned to look at her. "I'm surprised you allowed me to visit, Kate. Folks may talk, you know."

"I'm trying hard to like you, Sheriff." Her fingers folded upon themselves in her lap and he reached to touch the back of her hand.

"I'm trying to make that happen," he said simply. "I want you to like me."

And there would be little effort required on his part to make that happen, she realized. With his fingers warm against her skin, she spoke of the first day of school, relating small incidents that took her fancy. Her amusement brought a smile to his lips, and once, a chuckle that escaped. "I'll bet you were a pistol in your early years," she said after a moment's silence.

"Still am," he agreed. "And I reckon that's the about the most polite word for it. My family has a whole string of expressions they use to describe me."

He looked up at the stars and then grunted. "All but Will."

"I'd think the position of sheriff ought to elevate you a little in your family's opinion," she said. "Some folks must think you're a worthy person or they wouldn't have pinned that badge on your chest."

"To tell the truth," he drawled, "there isn't a whole lot of crime in Whitehorn. Probably just about enough to keep my gun well-oiled once in a while."

"You don't have bank robbers to contend with every day?" she asked with a smile. And then she watched as his mouth thinned beneath the dark moustache and he turned his head aside. "I didn't mean to remind you of that."

"That wasn't the first time I've shot a man," he growled. "Probably won't be the last."

"Still, it's not something to speak lightly of."

His fingers trailed warmth against her hand, and then he squeezed gently before he rose to stand before her. "I don't think it's something to take lightly," he returned. "Killing another human being is an act that stains a man's soul. Even when the job calls for it. In this case, it seemed like the thing to do, rather than have innocent folks at risk."

"Will didn't appear to cast any blame your way. Are there others who would hold such a thing against you? Or would find you less than honorable?" she asked, wondering how anyone could resist the man. She certainly hadn't had much success at it.

"Caleb, for one," he told her. "Owns a ranch, kinda northwest of town. His wife, Ruth, is a native. Cheyenne, I think."

"You're not on good terms with him, then?"

His shrug was eloquent. "You don't need to hear my sad tale." His smile was jaunty as he grinned at her. "Tell me about yourself, Kate."

So she did.

"WELL, HOW ARE YOU liking your new position?" Tess leaned both hands on the counter and bent toward Kate. "You've been rasslin' with those young'uns for two weeks, Miss Elliott. Are you ready to throw in the towel yet?"

Kate laughed aloud. "Of course not. Once I managed to get desks enough to go around, and learned everyone's name, things fell right into line."

"Are those big boys givin' you a hard time?" Tess asked. "They probably won't be there every day when the threshing machines come by. They'll need to be helpin' out at home. Most of them just like to pester the teacher anyway."

"They're not giving me any trouble," Kate said. "And I've wondered about that. I've heard tales of boys bigger than the teacher who cause problems."

Tess leaned closer. "I think the new sheriff gave them a talking to. I understand he nailed a couple of them who were all set to turn a sack full of mice loose in your room. Told them they'd answer to him if they pulled any pranks." She smiled archly at Kate. "I do believe our new sheriff is fond of you, Miss Elliott." Her eyes grew tender and Kate sensed once again the affection this woman shed on the town's black sheep.

"Contrary to what you may hear about him," Tess said firmly, "I think James Kincaid has the makings of a fine man. He just needs a little polishin' up, some gettin' his life in order."

Kate thought of the evenings she'd spoken with James, sitting in the dark, yet in plain view should anyone pass by. Perhaps he was, in truth, getting his life in order. There'd been no recurrence of his small foray on her, that second day she'd spent in this town, when he'd kissed her and teased her unmercifully. It seemed that the sheriff was more in need of companionship than the foolishness with which he'd first besieged her.

He came to her at eventide with perspiration on his brow, with circles under his eyes and with hands twitching as he sat next to her, or leaned against the tree next to her porch. Sitting, his long fingers gripped his knees at times as though he must hold the trembling at bay and she found herself talking endlessly as he listened with bowed head. Other times he paced, silent and impatient, as though demons drove him. And so they probably did, she thought.

And in those evenings he came to know her, as well as anyone ever had. She'd told him her whole life story, she realized, a quiet, prosaic, perhaps dull description of a young woman whose greatest adventure was this, this vigil she shared with a man seeking peace. Yet, as if drawn to the quiet words she spoke, the small tales she related, he returned, silent and aching with a pain she understood.

And then he would rise and walk from her, sometimes without warning, without a word of farewell. Other times he turned to her with a look she could not decipher, his eyes shadowed by the night, his words soft as he bid her good-night. And when she thought, after three evenings spent alone, that he might not come back, that he was over the worst of his struggle to remain sober, he returned.

Leaning against the tree that shaded the schoolhouse, just outside her door, he'd spoken slowly, haltingly, thanking her for her kindness. And then gone, walking away with a steady gait, his hands deep in his pockets, his hat level atop his head.

"Miss Elliott?" Tess called her name, and Kate was aware that it was not for the first time.

"I'm sorry. I was lost in thought," she said with a rueful smile. She looked down at the pile of articles she'd assembled on the counter. "I think this will be all for today," she told Tess. She looked longingly at the stack of new dresses Tess had folded and sorted by size. Maybe another time, when she was brave enough to don a gown of green or blue perhaps. But not pink. And her mouth twisted in a smile as she recalled James's words. *Pink's kinda girlie...you're a woman.*

"I'll just add this to your account," Tess said. "You can pay it when you get your wages at the end of the month."

"Thank you," Kate said, thankful for the tidy amount of cash she'd brought with her. Best that she hold on to it for now. A woman alone must always be prepared for any emergency.

She stepped from the door of the Mercantile, into a clear, sunny day. The sky stretched overhead and she was stunned by its beauty. The mountains held an appeal she could barely resist, and not for the first time she wished she could travel in that direction, see close up what those towering, majestic peaks offered to the eye.

But that would never do. A woman would not be allowed the freedom to take a trek such as that, not alone, not without proper escort.

Or improper escort, she thought, her mind turning again to the joy inherent in such an adventure. She looked again to the southwest, then up at the sky, where the sun cast its rays in these last days of summer. Beyond town, the wheat fields lay beneath the sunshine with golden heads drooping, awaiting harvest.

She felt a surge of joy. School was called off for two days so that the students could help with the threshing. She'd spent a pleasant hour with Lizzy, sitting on the front stoop of the school. Lizzy was happy with Will and Kate was drawn to the pretty, young bride.

Perhaps she would take her up on her impetuous invitation to visit at the bank owner's home. Pausing, Kate considered the idea, trying to recall the instructions Lizzy had given for finding the house that was outside of town. If she had her druthers, she'd head for the mountains, even if only to see them from closer range. Perhaps another time.

"You're looking a bit pensive, Miss Elliott." A voice she would have recognized in her sleep spoke with teasing words, and Kate spun on her heel. It was James and her heart skipped a beat as she greeted him.

"I'm just wishing I could get in a buggy and ride to the edge of the mountains." Her laugh was soft, and wistful. "I come from the flatlands of Ohio, you know. There's something about those heights that seems to compel me."

She took a step forward, her chin lifting as she searched the highest peaks in the distance. "Something there tugs at me," she whispered, and then blinked at sudden tears. "You'll think I'm foolish."

"On the contrary," he said. "I'd never think you

foolish. And if you want to go to the mountains, there isn't a reason in the world why you can't."

She cocked her head and peered up at him. "You're joshing me, aren't you? I'd just about decided to go visit Lizzy."

He shook his head solemnly. "No, ma'am, I'm not. If it'll make you happy to ride a bit in a buggy, I guess I can make it happen. I owe you, Kate Elliott."

"No, you don't," she said quickly. And then she took his measure. His eyes were clear, the circles smoothed out, only the fine lines at the corners remaining, and those a legacy of days spent in the sun. He stood tall, and straight, and the silver star shone with just a bit of pride, she thought.

"How is the sheriff business going?" she asked, smiling, enjoying the sunshine, the revelation of healing in his features.

"They've quit watching me, stopped holding their breaths every time I walk past the saloon," he said, and a touch of pain dulled the brilliance of his eyes. "I just may make it, Kate. I may turn out to be a decent member of the Kincaid family yet."

She opened her mouth to defend him, and he grinned widely, not the cocky, insouciant flash of teeth she'd seen on those first few days, but a genuine look of amusement, of pleasure. There was perhaps even a touch of admiration in his eyes as he took her measure.

"Why don't you trot on home with your things and I'll get a buggy and pick you up at the schoolhouse in half an hour. I'm sure the town will survive without either one of us for next little while."

She hesitated, and watched the joy begin to fade from his blue eyes. "Yes. All right," she said quickly. "I'll be ready."

CHAPTER FOUR

KATE PULLED her bonnet from her head once the town was safely behind. "We won't get all the way to the mountains, will we?" Her sigh spoke of resignation as her hat was settled beneath the seat.

James shook his head, and his grin flashed. "Probably not. But you'll be closer to them than you were this morning. Does that count?"

He was a consummate flirt, and she should probably be flattered that he practiced his wiles on her. Yet, flattery seemed to be beneath him, she decided. He was straightforward, charming and intent on pleasing her today. For that she would be grateful.

"Yes, it counts," she admitted, lifting her hand to shield her eyes from the bright sunlight. The mountains towered in the distance, closer than they were an hour earlier, to be sure, yet some distance away. She turned to look at him, and was caught up in the amusement that tilted his lips and sparkled from his blue eyes.

"I think I needed to be away from town for just a bit, needed the chance to take off my bonnet and roll up my sleeves and..." Her voice trailed off as his gaze touched the dark tresses she'd combed earlier, when it seemed she couldn't bear the constraint of pins against her head.

"I like your hair down over your shoulders," he

admitted easily. "But if you don't watch out, you're likely to get sunburn on those arms." One hand gripped the reins loosely and the other reached, long fingers stroking her forearm.

A chill traveled the length of her spine and goose bumps rose to meet his fingertips. "Doggone," he mused softly, "I'd have sworn your skin was warm, and you're all shivery instead." His hand enclosed hers and he brought it up to his mouth, his lips warm against her knuckles, his moustache a soft brush, teasing her skin.

She should pull from his grasp. She should ask him to return to town, and insist that he release her hand. If only her own fingers weren't so intent on clinging to his callused skin, she'd do that very thing. The edge of his moustache brushed the back of her hand again, and she wondered at its soft caress. It had felt the same the day he'd pressed those same lips against hers, and at that memory she shivered again.

"You want my coat?" he asked, his eyes narrowing, his hand drawing hers to rest against his chest.

Kate shook her head. "I think you need to release me, James." There, she'd said it, politely and softly, and her breath caught in her throat as he shook his head.

"Naw, I don't think so, ma'am." He drew the reins closer and the horse slowed, then halted, shaking her head, causing the harness to jingle. Birds flew across the meadow at their right, where wildflowers bloomed in a profusion of bright color. A rabbit bounded through the tall grass ahead of them, where the track they followed veered a bit to the left, and a scent like no other she'd inhaled rose from the man before her.

His jaw was set now, his eyes seeming darker, and his nostrils flared a bit, as though the air he breathed was scarce. "I believe I'm gonna kiss you, Kate," he whispered, and she watched as his head bent, and a flush ridged his cheekbones.

"Do I have a choice?" she asked, intent on the small scar next to his right eye, the dark, waving tress that fell over his forehead.

"No, ma'am. You don't." Almost apologetic, his words brushed against her mouth as his lips parted just a bit over hers. "You surely don't," he sighed. "And neither do I, I'm afraid."

It bore little resemblance to his first attempt, when he'd left a memory of that brief caress to burn against her mouth. He'd apologized that day, and if his movements now were anything to go by, she would not receive such polite regrets today. His mouth softened, enclosing hers as he suckled her bottom lip, touching it with the edges of his teeth. He tasted of spearmint and coffee and the sound in his throat spoke of satisfaction as he leaned against her, her back supported by the buggy seat.

She clung. Indeed, she could do little else, for his hands took possession, one at the back of her neck, the other at her waist, and she was pressed indecently against him. The width of his shoulders was measured by her palms and then she shifted her grip, sliding her hands to his nape, her fingers tunneling through dark hair. A whimper rose from her throat and he took it within his mouth, then breathed it against her cheek.

"Kate." He spoke her name softly, with a lilt she'd not heard before. "Is it Katherine?" he asked, and she recognized the touch of Irish some of his words contained.

"No, just Kate," she answered. And then wished in her deepest heart that her mother had had the forethought to name her with those soft syllables he breathed against her throat.

"Have you ever been seduced?" he asked, his words sounding whimsical as he brushed damp kisses across her skin. "Ah, no. Of course you haven't," he said, answering his own query. "You're a lady, through and through, Kate Elliott. And I'm a rascal. A scamp, my mother used to say."

She was speechless. For the first time in her life, she could think of no words to express the mixture of disbelief, tinged with pleasure that swamped her. Too honest to deny the pleasure of his touch, too candid to believe his motives were prompted by a rush of passion on his part. He was funning her, she decided, and that was something she could cope with.

"A scamp?" she managed to say, clearing her throat with effort. "I'd call you a tease, Mr. Kincaid. It's a good thing I'm immune to your brand of palavering."

He lifted his head, and she was intrigued by the heat of his gaze, puzzled by the whimsy of his smile. "I'm not teasing, Kate," he murmured. "The only thing keeping me from hauling you out of this buggy and down on that nice thick bed of meadow grass is the fact that you're a virgin—and I'm not a marrying man."

Her heartbeat increased. Fingers that had clutched for purchase against his nape flattened and slid from his shoulders to form fists against his chest. She pushed against him and he relented, tilting his head, as if he must observe her from a new angle. His lips were damp and shiny and she fought to keep her fingers from them.

"I have no desire to marry you, Mr. Kincaid," she said quietly. "I consider you my friend." Her gaze left his lips and she looked directly into his eyes, wanting her message to be clear. "I have no plans for taking a husband."

He lifted a brow. "Ever?"

Kate shook her head. "I prefer the privacy of living alone."

"You don't want a family? Children?"

"I deal with children every weekday," she said, gathering her composure, wondering if her mouth wore such a moist, swollen look as did his.

"They're not yours," he stated. "You'll have no one to follow on after you."

She laughed softly. "This is the man who, until just weeks ago, drank and gambled for a living? Now you're concerned about leaving a legacy?"

He sat erect, frowning. His hands slid from her, fingers leaving a trailing caress behind as he smoothed the folded cuffs of her dress. "I hadn't thought about it before, to tell the truth," he admitted. "Now, with Caleb and Ruth making a home place and William married to Lizzy...I guess I feel like it's time to begin taking stock."

"You're a Kincaid," she said matter-of-factly. "You're expected to carry on the name, I suppose." Her hand reached for him and his eyes followed its movement. "And that in itself makes you a marrying man, I think." A long index finger touched his silver star and she wiped off a minuscule speck of dust, her smile reflected in her voice. "And now you're even civilized...sort of."

He laughed, a rusty sound that made her stomach tremble. "Me? Civilized? I doubt anyone else would use that word when they speak of me, ma'am."

And that was the part of him that appealed to her, she realized. That faintly dangerous, dark and desperate element he kept hidden from those who rubbed elbows with him daily. Even as a man struggling with a hangover, he'd courted laughter. Only moments after he'd killed a man, she reminded herself. He had depths she had only begun to probe, secrets she wasn't sure she wanted to hear, and yet, he lured her with his seductive touches, his brash humor.

And she, who had determined never to be dominated by a man within the bonds of marriage, found that resolution wavering for the first time.

"Shall we drive closer to the mountains?" she asked. "Or have you changed your mind?"

He turned from her, lifting the reins, his glance amused. "I take it I haven't frightened you off, then?"

"I'm not afraid of you, James," she told him.

"You don't think I'll change my mind and seduce you after all?" His grin widened as she shook her head.

"I'm not the sort of woman men look at in that way. I'm too old for such shenanigans."

"I'd say you were just about the right age," he said easily. "Old enough to know your own mind, and beyond the age of wishing on the first star. And, just between you and me—" he leaned closer as if he would impart a mysterious secret "—you're never too old for such *shenanigans*."

THEY HALTED beneath a tree, and Kate wondered what bird had dropped a seed in this empty place, what rains had nourished the seedling and what winds had caused it to lean toward the east, even as its roots clung to the earth below. The road behind them was faint, disappearing over a slight rise, and to both north and south, the land stretched as far as her eye could see. A line of dark shadows lined the southern horizon, and ahead of them rose the majestic peaks she'd yearned to behold.

James stepped down from the buggy and lifted his hands to her. "Come on, Kate. We'll eat here. I strapped a basket on the back."

"Who cooked for you?" she asked, allowing his hands to grip her waist, feeling a moment of sheer panic when her feet left the buggy floor and she was airborne, only to slide against his hard, angular frame as he lowered her to the ground.

"Mrs. Harroun," he said, stepping to the back of the buggy where he undid the leather straps that held the basket in place. "She runs the boardinghouse."

Kate walked beneath the shelter of the tree, settling herself against the trunk. "Have you thought of finding a place of your own to live? Now that you're gainfully employed?"

"I've been *gainfully employed* for years, sweetheart," he told her, depositing the basket at her feet. "Being a gambler isn't the same as being poor as a church mouse. Not always, at least," he said as an afterthought. "Not if you're a very good gambler."

He sat on the ground next to her and lifted the basket lid. "I think there's fried chicken in here and a jar of fruit and a couple of forks to eat with." He leaned closer and withdrew a towel-wrapped object. "Looks like a loaf of bread, too." His brow quirked as he flashed her a look of inquiry. "You mind eating from a jar?"

Kate shook her head. "No. I don't believe it pays to be fussy on a picnic. Especially when someone else is in charge of the food." She took the proffered fork and waited as he opened the heavy glass canning jar, pulling the rubber ring to break the seal. The lid in one hand, he offered her the first bite, and she pierced a slice of golden peach with her fork, lifting it to her mouth.

His gaze followed the action and his mouth thinned as she felt a trickle of juice drip from her chin. She wiped at it with her index finger and he reached to snatch her finger, caught it within his grasp, then lifted it to his mouth. Capturing her fingertip between his lips, his tongue moved to suckle the pale liquid from her flesh.

It took her breath and he watched as her eyes darkened and then widened, meeting his with a look of pure astonishment. "Have you never felt desire, Kate?" he asked. The woman he'd brought to this place was indeed more innocent than he'd thought. The creature he'd once considered plain and bookish, whose only attributes appeared at first to be a pair of long, shapely legs, had somehow turned into an alluring female. Through her spectacles, her eyes seemed huge, their green depths holding feminine mysteries, secrets he yearned to discover.

She drew him as a stallion is drawn to a fine, long-legged mare, her scent luring him. Kate Elliott, for all her denial was *prime*. Tempting, yet forbidden.

For even at the depths of his gambling and carousing, he'd steered clear of innocence. Some small part of him had adhered to what was honorable as far as women were concerned. His mother, Penny, might not have been without fault, but she'd been a lady, and even in the years after she'd walked away from Thomas Kincaid, leaving him with a small boy to raise on his own, James had heard only kind words for the woman who had borne him.

Unwilling to open himself to the heartbreak his father had faced on that long-ago day, James had elected, on his downward path to ruin, only to socialize with women who would not be harmed by an evening's dalliance with a rogue such as himself.

Kate did not fall into that category. Not unless he planned to marry her. And wasn't that an idiotic idea?

His hand was steady as he handed her a piece of chicken, taken from an assortment on a pie tin, and her wide, dark eyes met his warily. "Eat, Kate."

Marriage. The thought had crossed his mind a few times, but never lingered there. Now it lodged there, and he considered the notion. He could do worse than Kate Elliott. It would certainly be no great sacrifice to bed the woman—far from it, in fact. And his sons and daughters would likely inherit her intelligence and stand a chance of being upright citizens, given her good sense and moral integrity.

Yet, she was grimly determined to evade the clutches of matrimony, and his natural sense of curiosity nudged him. "What frightens you, Kate? Do you see shadows in the dark? Are you haunted by old ghosts from the past?"

Her teeth were white against the breast meat she'd

only begun to devour, and he was tempted to laugh aloud as she halted abruptly, then withdrew it from her mouth. A dainty handkerchief was tugged from her pocket and used to wipe her mouth before she answered his impetuous questions. The hesitation was long, and she placed the scraps from her piece of chicken on one side of Mrs. Harroun's pie tin before she looked up to meet his expectant gaze.

"Did no one ever tell you that a cat died of your symptoms, James?"

"I'm a curious sort of fella, sweetheart," he said softly, leaning to brush a lingering crumb from her lower lip. He'd considered leaning to lift it with the tip of his tongue, then thought better of it. "You've told me about your upbringing and the years you've spent teaching, but I don't recall much being said about your folks. Their marriage, in particular. It makes me wonder."

"I don't have any old ghosts," she said tartly. "I've never been frightened of the dark, probably because I have enough sense to stay in the house at night." She smiled suddenly, a whimsical smile he thought, as if she remembered the score or so of evenings they'd shared over the past weeks.

"Very little frightens me, actually," she told him. "Deep water, maybe, since I can't swim. Thunderstorms, perhaps. I saw lightning strike a house once and burn it to the ground." She picked up a chicken wing and looked it over, as if it held the answers he sought. And then she regarded him soberly, and he caught a glimpse of pain reflected in the depths of green eyes.

"I heard my mother weep far into the night, more

than once, because she could not hold the love of the man she'd married. He drank, James, and he was not a harmless man when he emptied a bottle. My mother did not share his love of whiskey and so he found other women who were not so particular.''

''I'm surprised you allowed me to escort you that first day,'' he said quietly.

She nodded. ''I've wondered myself why I didn't walk away, once I realized the state you were in.''

''And did you come up with an answer?'' he asked.

''No.'' She lifted the crusty wing to her mouth and bit into it, tearing the meat from the bone, then chewing it with a steady movement of her jaws. She tore a strip of meat and held it between thumb and index finger, then raised it to his mouth.

Her fingers brushed his lower lip and he took the morsel from her, watching her intently. Another tidbit was captured by her, crusty and enticing, and she considered it, offering it for his approval. Leaning forward a few inches, he took it with care, then touched her thumb with the tip of his tongue, securing it between his lips to draw the traces of crisp coating from her skin.

She blinked and he suppressed a smile. ''You're flirting with me, Kate. You want to watch it. I might take you seriously.''

''I've never flirted in my life,'' she retorted, the spell broken as she snatched her hand away. And then her innate honesty won out and she bit at her bottom lip, worrying it for a moment before she made her admission of guilt. ''Until now. I wasn't sure I knew how.''

He inhaled, aware again of her scent, the floral fragrance she used so sparingly, the sweet woman aroma that rose to announce her body's response to him. Lifting his leg, he bent his knee to conceal the evidence of his own reaction to her warmth and feminine appeal. "You do well for a beginner," he allowed, reaching for another piece of chicken. "How about another wing?"

"I don't think so," she said. Then leaned closer to peer into the box. "Is the bread sliced?"

He handed her the towel-wrapped loaf. "I don't know. If not, just tear off a piece. I don't think Mrs. Harroun sent a knife along."

Kate frowned at the loaf, then followed his instructions. "My mother would have a fit," she murmured, gazing at the ragged specimen she held.

"She'll never know," James said with a chuckle, then bent forward to sink his teeth into the thick chunk. "This is what is known as breaking bread, I believe," he told her solemnly. "It's approved of in the good book, you know."

"What do you know of the Bible?" she asked, tearing off a bite carefully, then dipping it into the peach juice.

"I went to church, once in a while, growing up," he admitted. "My father looked in a bottle for answers after my mother left us, and when that didn't solve his problems, he started in going to hear the visiting ministers who included our town on their route."

"Where is he now?" she asked, offering him the loaf.

"Gone. He followed her back east once I was grown. Gave up the family ranch and walked away."

"Did he find her?"

James shook his head. "I don't know. Haven't heard from him in years."

"What a waste," Kate said briskly. "Life is too short to throw it away. I made up my mind I'd never shed tears over a man, or let anyone break my heart. I think your father would have profited from the same determination. There isn't a woman alive worth wasting a man's life over."

James took the peach jar from her and speared a slice of fruit. "You may be right. I sure wouldn't argue the fact." He sucked the slice into his mouth, savoring the smooth feel against his tongue. "Funny, both of us coming from families so much alike," he said after a moment. "Makes us two of a kind, don't you think?"

"I'll tell you what I think," she said abruptly, rising and shaking crumbs from her lap. "I think if we don't get into that buggy and move out, we'll be getting back to town after dark, and my name will be dragged in the dirt."

She was probably right, he thought. The jar lid was screwed into place and the box packed up within minutes. The sun was further to the west than he'd realized and he looked at it, where it touched the topmost peaks of the mountains as it prepared to slide beyond the white snowcaps. "Maybe we'll start out earlier another time. We're almost in the foothills now." Regret tinged his words and he heard Kate's sigh.

"The story of my life," she whispered. "Too late, again."

"I'll bring you back," he said impetuously. "I promise, Kate. We'll go to where the road for a buggy ends, and walk up aways. Or maybe we can ride horseback, and take some of the lower trails, where the trees meet the rocks and there are caves and ledges and places where you can see for miles.''

She smiled and shook her head. ''Probably not, James, but it's something to think about. I've gotten this close anyway.'' She turned to face the majestic peaks and her shoulders squared. ''They're beautiful, aren't they?''

He clasped her upper arms, drawing her against his chest. She leaned back against him, acquiescent, as if they shared some mystical union—here where the birds sang and the wind blew from the west and they stood alone in the wilderness, two infinitesimal creatures beneath the Montana sky.

He could not resist. She was, in that moment, representative of all the needs he'd ever acknowledged in his life—warm, alive and filled with the same yearning as he for this wide open country.

He turned her in his embrace, and she moved willingly, responding as he lowered his head to touch her lips with his. Her arms slid upward, clasping his shoulders. Her face tilted beneath his and her mouth welcomed the touch of lips and teeth and tongue against her own. She was eager, and unknowing, and he sensed the innocence of her response, careful to withhold the full force of desire that claimed his body. And yet he could not withhold the passion he felt for her, and his mouth sought and found the tender flesh of her throat and temple.

His lips visited the curve of her ear and the line of her jaw, until he had learned the width of her forehead and the gentle slope of her nose. Until he had tasted and tested each particle of skin available to him without loosening the buttons of her dress. And his good sense told him that she would not allow such a thing to take place.

"I've never been kissed by any other man," she whispered after she'd caught her breath and lifted her hands to smooth back the hair he'd managed to put into a state of disarray. "But I've wondered. I didn't know so much was involved," she said, finally meeting his gaze. "I mean, I thought you just rubbed your lips together, and smacked a little." Her smile was shy suddenly as she ran the tip of her tongue over her lips. "Does everyone kiss this way? Or is it only you?"

"I never kissed my mama this way, I'll tell you that, sweetheart." And then he set her from him. "Of course, that was a long time ago, now that I think about it. I've learned a few things since then."

"I think so." Kate pressed her palms against her cheeks. "I'm all flushed," she said, and her eyes reflected the desire he'd called forth from her depths.

James placed one hand on the side of her throat, feeling the pulse pounding beneath his fingers. "You haven't the least idea how hard it is to keep my hands from you," he told her. His gaze swept downward to where her breasts filled the front of her bodice. "I want to kiss you there," he said, recognizing the guttural harshness in his voice.

Kate looked down at herself, then swiftly crossed her arms across the swollen crests that pushed against her clothing, begging for his notice. Her breathing was harsh, her nostrils flaring as she inhaled sharply. "I've never…"

She paused and he nodded, feeling the flesh draw taut over his jaw as he smiled, torturing himself by vivid imaginings that would no doubt keep him awake long hours into the night.

"I know that, Kate. But you will. One day, you will."

CHAPTER FIVE

LIZZY'S CHEEKS were pink with indignation, her eyes wide as she glanced over her shoulder, lest her words be overheard. "I heard you spent most of yesterday with James. The man at the livery stable told Will that James left his horse there and took a buggy for the whole day." She bent closer to Kate and her whisper held doomsday in its depths. "If the men hear about it, you could lose your position, Kate."

And wouldn't that be a fine state of affairs, Kate thought glumly, and then squared her shoulders bravely. "They don't have anyone else to teach, Lizzy. I doubt they're going to kick me out of the schoolhouse." She shot a glance at a passing matron, then smiled cordially as the woman nodded her head. "Apparently the word hasn't spread yet. Besides, I didn't do anything wrong. I went for a buggy ride with the sheriff. And he would certainly be considered a respectable man."

Lizzy's mouth turned down at the corners. "Not to hear Will speak, he isn't. He's proud of James for truly staying sober, but everyone knows he has a reputation with women." Her forehead wrinkled as she whispered her fears. "I don't want you to be the subject of gossip, Kate. You're a fine person, and you've been so nice to me. You're actually the first lady in town to..." She bit at her lip.

"You're the wife of the banker, Lizzy. That automatically gives you a certain amount of prestige, I would think."

Lizzy looked uncomfortable and her lips trembled. "I just know that I don't want anything to go wrong for you, Kate. It's hard enough to be a woman on her own, without having folks point their fingers your way."

Kate shrugged. "I don't like the idea of people talking about me, either. Especially when I've done nothing wrong." She sighed, considering the problem. "I suppose the worst that could happen would be for the council to find a man to fill my position."

Lizzy gasped. "Do you think they would?"

"Maybe. But at the same time, they did send me a letter that says I've been hired for the school year."

"Men don't always keep their word, you know," Lizzy said quietly, and then her scowl disappeared and her lips curved into a determined smile. "Shall we go out to my place and sit on my porch? I've got hours until Will comes home for supper."

"Are you ladies in need of an escort?" James appeared in the doorway of the Mercantile, one hand tilting his hat rakishly over his forehead. "How do you do, Cousin?" he asked politely, flashing a grin at Lizzy.

She blushed predictably and cast wide eyes in Kate's direction. "We were just leaving to have a cup of tea," she told James. "Are you working, Sheriff?"

"Just let Cleve Brownlee out of jail," James said. "He's all sobered up and ready for another night at the saloon.'' His grin vanished as he spoke, and Kate thought a trace of pain dwelt in the depths of his blue eyes.

''Is that the extent of your work for today?'' she asked quietly. ''No fights to break up or cattle rustling to worry about?''

''I told you things are pretty quiet these days in Whitehorn, Kate. There's a fella out beyond Caleb's place I have to see. He's a new ranch hand and Cam, over at the bar, said the man's the spittin' image of a wanted poster in my office.''

Kate felt a quick thrust of fear as James spoke. ''Be careful.'' Her whisper was low and he nodded, his glance all encompassing as he smiled at her.

''If you're not in need of company, I'll be on my way,'' he said with a final flashing smile. ''You ladies keep things in order while I'm gone.''

It was impossible not to watch as he strode across the street, a certain arrogance in his bearing, one the Kincaid men seemed to have in common, if James and Will were anything to go by, Kate thought. They were a pair, with handsome features and an elegance that ran bone deep. A pair, yet so different. James with his devil-may-care grin and Will, whose smile lit with tenderness when Lizzy was its recipient.

''You're a lucky woman, Lizzy,'' Kate said impetuously. ''Will dotes on you, doesn't he?''

''He's a wonderful man, and yes, he loves me. I wonder sometimes that he became a banker, with so much fire and—'' She halted, one hand lifting to cover her mouth. ''I didn't mean to say that,'' she whispered through her fingers.

Kate bent closer. "I'm pleased that he has fire. Maybe he's more like James than you realize."

"James?" Lizzy's hand fell and her mouth pursed. "James is a rascal, Kate. The women in town all give him the eye, you know, even though they don't approve of him. There's just something about him..." Her gaze focused on Kate's cheeks, and the rosy glow Kate knew was well in place.

"Why, you're smitten with him, aren't you?" Lizzy asked softly. "And I'll just bet that your ride in the country was more than just an innocent afternoon of small talk."

Kate grasped Lizzy's elbow and hustled her down the sidewalk. "I don't know how I feel about James Kincaid," she muttered. "He's the only man I've ever allowed such liberties, and maybe if I had a little more experience with gentlemen I'd know better how to—"

"Liberties?" Lizzy squealed the word, and spun to face Kate. Her own cheeks were flushed as she peered into Kate's dark eyes. "He took *liberties?*"

Kate smiled at Amos Carlton who stood in the doorway of the hotel, nodding with a genteel gesture, then hustled Lizzy down the walk. "Hush. Don't let anyone hear you say that word. Besides, I'm not sure if that's what you call what he did."

Towing an amused Kate by the arm, Lizzy's stride lengthened as she led the way to Will's buggy. "He can wait till I come back to get him," she muttered as they set out for the big house outside of town. It didn't look like Lizzy, Kate decided as they climbed the steps to the big porch, but once inside she changed her mind.

"Come on into the kitchen," Lizzy instructed her.

"We need some tea and a lot of privacy for this conversation."

The tea was made, cups and saucers chosen and a tin of cookies opened as Kate looked around the tidy kitchen. "It's lovely," she said wistfully. "You have wonderful taste, Lizzy."

"I tried to make it look like the kitchen in our home when I was growing up," Lizzy said, pouring the steaming brew. "Will says it's comfortable." The tea cozy in place, Lizzy settled into her chair.

"Now tell me what James did to you."

Kate chose a cookie with care, uneasy with divulging the details of their moments of privacy. "He kissed me," she said finally. "And I didn't know that kissing was like that."

"Like what?" Lizzy's eyes were wide. "Like married kissing?"

"Is there a difference?"

Lizzy considered the thought for a moment. "It's almost like making love sometimes, I think. And before I made love with Will, I didn't know that kissing could make me feel so ready for his loving." She sobered and reached for Kate's hand. "He didn't do more than that, did he?"

"No, not really." *I want to kiss you there,* he'd said, and her breasts tingled as she recalled the scalding heat his gaze had evoked.

Lizzy sighed, relief alive in her features. "He's not the marrying kind, you know," she warned.

"He told me."

"You are." Lizzy's pronouncement was firm.

Kate nodded her agreement.

FOR THE SECOND TIME, Kate was invited to eat supper with the Teal family. Clovis Teal's three children escorted her proudly to the outskirts of town after school, Beth on one side, Alice the other, while their brother, Clovis Jr., ran on ahead.

"Clo says it's sissy stuff to walk home with the teacher," Beth said earnestly, peering up at Kate. "Me and Alice don't," she announced. "Our mama says it's a privilege to have you over for supper. She's fixin' something special, since Pa bought a side of pork."

The scent of sauerkraut announced the menu as Kate turned up the walk to the Teal home, and Marjorie Teal came out onto the porch to greet her. "We're so pleased to have you here. I hope you don't mind that we eat early. Clovis has a meeting tonight with some men in town, and he asked if we could get supper out of the way."

"I don't mind," Kate said easily. "I have papers to grade later on, and I'd like to walk home while it's still daylight anyway."

"Maybe there'll be someone around to escort you," Marjorie said archly.

Kate stared at her blankly, and then smiled. "Perhaps young Clovis will walk with me."

Marjorie laughed knowingly. "I'll warrant there's more chance of..." She grimaced, pressing her lips together. "Come on in," she invited, turning to open the door. "The girls can help set the table and we'll be ready to eat. Mr. Teal should be here right shortly."

Mr. Teal appeared before the food was dished up, and ate quickly, casting more than one long look in Kate's direction. Beth and Alice chattered about their day at school, Beth proud of having won the weekly spelling bee, and Alice pleased by her promotion to the next level of reading.

"Miss Elliott has lots of books on her shelf," Alice said. "And she promised I can read them all before long." Her head held high, she lorded it over her brother, who didn't share her love for the written word. "Clo will probably never get to read one of Miss Elliott's books. He's still working on his first primer."

"Well, maybe your next teacher will work a little harder to teach Clovis to read," her father said bluntly. "Miss Elliott seems to have a lot of spare time on her hands these days, gallivanting around the countryside."

Kate's heart clutched in her chest, and she cast a questioning look at the man. "The school was let out yesterday for threshing. I considered it a holiday," she said quietly.

"Seems to me the town students could have been in school anyway," he retorted.

"Our three went out to help at your brother's place," his wife reminded him gently. She smiled at Kate. "When threshing time comes, every man, woman and child is called into service. We all pitch in to help our families."

An undercurrent of disdain lined Clovis Teal's words as he stood abruptly. "I've got to get to the bank, Marjorie. We're to meet at six-thirty. Amos Carlton says there's a couple of new items we need to discuss."

"You didn't have any pie," Marjorie said anxiously.

"Later," he said dismissing her with a glance, then turning his attention to his children he issued plain and simple instructions. "You young'uns behave now."

"Yes, Pa," Beth and Alice chorused, and young Clovis nodded glumly.

"He's not usually so short-spoken," Marjorie apologized as the screened door slammed shut behind her husband. "Tell you what. I'll fix us all a piece of pie anyway." She rose and the girls turned to Kate, chattering incessantly as they vied for attention.

She answered their questions, viewed their treasures as they left the table and returned with boxes of small items they cherished, and ate Marjorie's pie with appropriate words of praise.

Yet, the niggling thoughts in the back of her head urged her to set off for the schoolhouse. Something was gone awry. Clovis Teal had been a man bent on skullduggery, if she was any judge. And something told her that her name would be spoken at the meeting he was attending.

EVEN A BOOK was not enough to hold her interest tonight, and Kate placed her copy of a familiar classic aside. Usually the words soothed her, comforted her aching loneliness. Tonight she was all at sixes and sevens. She couldn't think of a single thing that would cheer her heart or put a genuine smile on her lips. And wasn't that the biggest lie she'd ever told herself, she thought glumly.

James Kincaid was smack-dab in the forefront of her mind, and no amount of reading or grading papers was going to displace him. She rose from the table and walked to the open door, looking out upon the darkness that enveloped the schoolyard. Lights from houses in town glowed softly, the flickering lanterns outside the hotel and saloon calling attention to those places of business. A row of dark windows lined the sidewalk, and Kate saw no trace of a tall figure pacing the wooden boards.

James was probably at home at Mrs. Harroun's boardinghouse, all tucked up in his bed for the night. Either that or he'd found someone to spend the evening with. And that vision did nothing for Kate's peace of mind. That James might be in the company of another woman made her chest ache, bringing quick tears to her eyes. He'd paid her enough attention over the past weeks, that she was dead certain he enjoyed her companionship. He'd kissed her, for heaven's sake, and that alone was right next door to a commitment in any man's language.

Unless that man was a scalawag and a gambler. Not to mention being a reformed drunk, or at least a man well on his way to being permanently sober. Of course there was always his own statement of fact, that first day he'd come to the schoolhouse and ordered her to stand, then walk before him.

Aren't you going to ask me what my downfall is? he'd asked in that deceptively mild tone. And then he'd grinned and told her, while her face had reddened and her heart throbbed a mile a minute in her chest. *Women,* he'd announced with a narrowed gaze that seemed to penetrate the layers of her clothing. *I can't seem to stay away from women.*

And then he'd kissed her, a gentle, tender caress, and she'd been stunned by the enormous wealth of emotion his touch evoked.

"James." She whispered his name into the darkness, then jerked in alarm as his voice answered her murmured summons.

"I didn't know if you could see me in the dark,

Kate,'' he said quietly, stepping around the side of the building. ''I left my horse tied out back, in case any of the townsfolk are out and about.''

Kate's hand pressed against her chest and her eyes closed as sheer panic tested the limits of her heart rate. ''I didn't see you there,'' she said after a moment, each word gasped into being.

He stepped up to the door and peered at her through the screen. ''Then what made you call for me?'' He tugged the door open and slid past her, drawing the heavy inner door closed behind himself. His arms circled her waist and he pulled her against his long length. ''Are you all right, sweetheart? You're shaking like a leaf.''

She clung to him, all her anxious moments set aside as she basked in the warmth and comfort of his embrace. So quickly she'd come to love this man. And at that thought, her heart stuttered and climbed into her throat. James was not a marrying man, even Lizzy could see that. And it didn't pay to have deep feelings for a man who was so dead set against matrimony. Especially a man so obviously unsuited to be the sort of husband she'd settle for. A sober, dependable.. someone. Someone she could count on to come home at night without another woman's scent on him and an empty whiskey bottle in his pocket.

Someone *dull*. Not like the man who even now was breathing soft words against her throat.

Kate Elliott would have to take herself in hand. And she would. Just as soon as James took his long fingers off her waist and stopped the nuzzling he was doing beneath her ear.

''I was thinking of you,'' she said quickly. ''Your

name must have slipped past my lips." Her mind searched frantically. "I didn't know if you'd come home from seeing to that ranch hand. You know, the one that looks like a wanted poster in—"

"Whoa," he said quietly. "Just simmer down to a slow boil, Kate. I don't mind if you're thinking of me." His grin developed slowly, encompassing his eyes and bringing to light the small dimple in his cheek. "Matter of fact, I kinda like the idea of you having me on your mind. And yes, I just came back from talking to the rancher, Matt Darby. The fella I wanted to check on rode off when he saw me, and Darby and I went looking for him. I'm willing to wager he's the one with his picture on my wall."

"Wasn't that dangerous, out riding around looking for a hardened criminal?" Kate had the absurd need to touch his face, to caress the line of his jaw and ease the small lines beside his eyes.

"Naw, honey. He's not exactly Jesse James. Just a young kid who was in on a bank robbery down in Wyoming six months ago. We didn't find him anyway. He's probably long gone." James dropped a quick kiss on Kate's mouth, and then tilted his head back to watch her reaction.

"I'm pleased to know you were worrying over me, though."

"I wasn't worried. Not really," she countered. "I just wondered..."

"I'm safe and sound, Kate." He turned her easily, her feet moving in rhythm with his, and then her back was against the door and he was pressed against her. He scooped his hat from his head and placed it on a hook beside the door, leaving a black strand of hair to curl across his forehead. "How much persuading would it take for you to let me stay here for a couple of hours, Kate?"

"*What?*" Distracted by the curl, she blinked up at him and then watched as his mouth twisted in a grin. Her hands gripped his shirt, pushing at his chest. "You must be out of your mind, James Kincaid. The men in town had a meeting tonight, and according to what Clovis Teal insinuated, they're upset because I took a holiday yesterday and was off *gallivanting* around the countryside. They'd tar and feather me if I let you spend time in my room."

"We could just cuddle a little," he whispered, his mouth against her ear, his warm breath bringing shivers to every inch of her skin. His hands swept up her back, then slid to her ribs, holding her in a firm grip. He bent his head, his eyes half closed, his mouth half open, and his mind clearly bent on seduction.

Even with her limited knowledge of men, Kate knew enough to call a halt to the hands that seemed to relish her softness. "Stop it, James," she said sternly.

His mouth touched hers carefully and she heard a soft moan, felt its breath against her lips. "Kate?" He sought no answer, but only spoke her name, his lips nudging hers apart. "Sweetheart..." The single word was a sigh and his grip on her waist softened, his hands sliding up her ribs, drawing her against his chest. His arms circled her then, and one broad palm pressed against her nape, holding her captive for his kiss.

A married folk's kiss? Even as Lizzy's words resounded in Kate's head, James slid his tongue between her lips, teasing at the tender flesh inside her mouth, persuading her to allow him entrance between her teeth. *I didn't know that kissing could make me so ready for his loving.* Lizzy had it down pat, Kate decided, with what little sense she had left.

She'd said no. She'd told him to stop. And now she clung to him like a woman besotted, and she silently berated herself for the weakness in her knees. There was only one way to stop the man, and as difficult as the words were to speak, she'd better spit them out in a hurry, or he'd have her persuaded into that narrow little bed across the room.

"When are we getting married?" The words were barely a whisper, and for a moment Kate wondered if he'd heard them. His mouth blessed hers, suckling for long seconds on her lower lip. And then he lifted his head, his narrowed eyes searching hers as if he questioned his hearing.

"Married?"

"I won't give you a husband's privileges without a wedding ring, James," she said quietly, her breath catching in trembling little sobs. "And I've looked in the mirror enough to know that even if you were considering the idea, you'd find someone a whole lot more suitable than me to do it with."

"Damn, Kate. Damn." He repeated the curse word, shaking his head, then dropping it to rest against her shoulder. "Just a minute here."

"I think you need to leave," she said, sliding from between his long, hard body and the equally firm surface of the door. His hand lingered on her shoulder, then slid to her cheek. The callused palm was warm and welcome against her skin and she closed her eyes as though she would refute the pleasure of his touch.

"Please, James."

"Yeah." He sighed, bent to her and kissed her lips with a chaste, swift caress and then stood erect. "I'm just about as close to breaking my word as I've ever been." He grinned at her, but his eyes were weary. "You don't want to marry me, Kate. You were just trying to get my attention."

"It worked, didn't it?" She smoothed her hair, her eyes refusing to look too closely at the temptation he offered. "My mama married a drinking man, James. Being sober for a matter of weeks is no guarantee, as far as I can see."

"You don't have much faith in me, do you?" he asked, his smile vanquished by the pain she dealt with her harsh words.

She bent her head, focusing on the toes of his dusty boots. "Does it matter?"

"More than you know. I need someone to believe in me, Kate, and right now you're about the only candidate for the job."

"I think we're about at a standstill," she said carefully. "You want more from me than I can give you. I'm a virgin. You know that, and yet you would have persuaded me to throw my virtue away."

"Probably not," he told her. "I might have given you a little pleasure, honey, and snatched a look at those pretty legs of yours, but I'm not going to give folks anything to talk about."

"Just you being here is enough to…" She closed her mouth with a snap, exasperated at him. "And you're not going to get a look at my legs. They're just ordinary limbs, no different than any other woman walks around on."

"Ah, that's where you're wrong, sweetheart," he

crooned. He looked down at her, this small female who had wormed her way past his barriers and found a place in his life. "There's nothing ordinary about you." His fingers touched her lips, then traced the line of her cheek.

"I might have overlooked a lot of things at first, concentrating on your legs the way I did, but the first time I really looked into your eyes, I found out how beautiful they are. You've got skin smooth as cream and your hair is enough to set a man dreaming about hot nights and cool sheets."

A flush colored Kate's face and he grinned, his pleasure in her overcoming the keening sadness her lack of faith had delivered to his soul. "You've about made me rethink my decision about marriage, honey."

"Well, I haven't," she retorted. "And all your palavering isn't going to make a difference, James. I have a career here, and much as I enjoy your company, I'd like to keep my reputation above reproach in this town."

He might have taken her at her word if it weren't for the shimmering tears that balanced on her eyelids. He'd made her cry and that would never do.

"I'm leaving, honey," he said, snatching his hat from the hook by the door and planting it firmly on his head. Stepping to the table, he blew out the lamp, leaving the room in darkness. The better to hide her tears, he thought, reaching to open the door.

"No one will see me leave," he assured her. "You're reputation is safe, sweetheart."

She stood in the shadows and he filled his eyes with her image, like that of a dream he'd only begun to enjoy before awakening to reality.

CHAPTER SIX

"THIS TOWN hasn't had much need lately for a posse, has it?" James asked, then looked around at the four men who'd formed a loose semicircle in front of him. John Dillard tugged at his collar, slanting a glance at Amos Carlton. "I'm not asking any of you to ride with me," James said, quirking an eyebrow. "I'm just wondering if there's anybody available who might know how to shoot a gun."

Harry Talbert straightened his white barber's apron. "I'm not much for riding, to tell the truth. But I'm sure there's a plenty of young fellas who'd like some adventure."

"Any idea where I'd find them?" James asked, enjoying the discomfort he'd set into motion.

Amos nodded eagerly. "I think Joe over at the livery stable wouldn't mind ridin' with you. And then there's a couple of ranchers you might could call on. Matt Darby for one, since he's the guy that hired a wanted man and caused all this trouble. Then there's your cousin, Caleb." His eyes lit and he snapped his fingers. "Maybe Will would like to go along."

James grinned. "I can't see Will chasing a bank robber."

"I'd think he'd have a vested interest, so to speak, in such an undertaking," John said pompously. "Now,

I wouldn't be able to ride with you, what with a shipment coming in today, and Tess being alone in the store.''

"Ah, hell. I'll handle it myself," James told them. "I might have known this sheriff job was gonna be a lonely one."

"We'll stand behind you, James," Harry said quickly. "We've been thinking about giving you a raise in pay, you know."

John opened his mouth and seemed to think better of it. But Amos, understanding the way of such things, nodded promptly. "Yes, I'd think a good sheriff deserves a living wage. You'll be wanting to buy a house and settle down in your own place, I'd think."

James turned and grasped the reins of his gelding. "Well, if I come back alive, we'll talk about it, gentlemen." He slanted a look at Amos. "I'm thinking real hard about settling down. You're right on that score, Amos."

One hand on the saddle horn, James mounted easily, then looked down at the men. "Anybody seen Miss Elliott this morning? I thought she might be out and about, seeing as how it's Saturday and all the ladies are gathering."

Cam shot him a warning glare. "She's probably doin' some teacher stuff over at the schoolhouse. I imagine she's got some catchin' up to do, what with takin' a day off this past week."

"I told the lot of you we needed to wait till a man became available," Amos said hotly. "But you said, *'Oh no, we've gotta have a teacher, right now.'* And so we did, and look at the problem we've got." His tone mocked his cohort's anxious reasoning.

"What sort of problem?" James asked mildly.

"You should know, Sheriff," John Dillard said. "Not that we're blaming you, being a man and all. But a teacher must be beyond reproach."

"I think we'd better discuss this when I get back, gentlemen," James told them, irritation surging beneath the affable surface he strove to present for their benefit. His hand gripped the reins and his horse skittered, tossing his head. Without another word, and barely a look for the men who'd stirred his anger into being, he headed toward the livery stable.

THE MOMENT Kate set foot in the Mercantile, three women made it their business to tell her the details of James going off in search of the young bank robber. Tess took her by the arm, offering soothing words as she led Kate toward the latest selection of ladies' wear, delivered just today.

"James is a crack shot," she said softly. "John said so. He'd have gone along to help, but with all the business we have on Saturdays, he couldn't leave me here alone, you know."

"James went alone?" Kate asked. Her hand stroked the fine fabric she held, but her joy in choosing new clothing had disappeared with Tess's words.

"He'll probably find some ranchers to help," Tess said brightly. "After all, how much danger can there be in looking for a young man barely old enough to shave?"

"He'll be carrying a gun," Kate muttered. "And when you put a gun in a young man's hands, especially when that young man has a price on his head, you'd better be prepared for trouble."

Tess gnawed at her lip, holding a dark-green gown against her apron. "Well, in the meantime," she said, "I think you'll find some real nice stuff in this shipment of dresses, Kate. Plain green or blue will work well for teaching, since I know you want to look the part, but there's always after hours. And a nice flowered print or striped dimity would look wonderful on you."

"I've about decided to give up the black things I brought with me," Kate told her. "I was in mourning for my father when I left Ohio, but I've worn my share of dowdy clothes. I'm ready for something pretty."

"I didn't know your daddy died recently," Tess said, sympathy alive in her voice. "I'm surprised you had the courage to leave your family at such a time. Especially coming all the way to Montana, all by yourself."

"I haven't mourned greatly for him," Kate admitted. "He wasn't much of a husband, and less of a father. It just seemed the thing to do, buying black gowns and looking like I was in the depths of despair all the time." She lifted her chin and met Tess's gaze. "I've decided it's time to look like a woman, a young, available woman."

"Well," Tess said, "you surely won't have any trouble finding a good man to marry around here. We've got more available men than we know what to do with."

"That's what I'm counting on," Kate said firmly. "I've been told that I've got nice eyes and good skin, and I look pretty decent when I get cleaned up." Those weren't the exact words James had used, but there was no way in this life she was about to quote him verbatim.

"I think there's already one man who's taken more than a liking to you, Kate. Everyone in town is talking about James hauling you off in a buggy the other day. I'm surprised you didn't come back with a marriage proposal."

"He's on my shortlist," Kate said nonchalantly, picking up a striped taffeta dress. "This would look beautiful for Sunday church, wouldn't it?" And with a month's wages in her pocket, she was shopping in earnest, she decided. Looking frumpish was a thing of the past. If James Kincaid—with his beautiful eyes and elegant bearing—thought she was decent looking, she'd better give him something to really take a gander at.

FOUR HORSEMEN paraded past the schoolhouse just before dark. One of their number rode awkwardly, hands tied behind him, his horse being led by a tall rancher. Third in line was James, astride his mount, but slumped in the saddle. And bringing up the end of the line was a man who bore all the earmarks of being a Kincaid. Tall and built like a mountain, he rode his horse in an easy manner, his gaze fixed on James. Riding at a slow trot, they passed the schoolhouse, and Kate inhaled sharply as James lifted his head, his dark eyes sweeping over her for a moment.

She stood perching on the stoop and watched as they traveled to the jailhouse, where two of them dragged the youth from his saddle and shuffled him into the sheriff's office. James slid from his saddle, leaning against the side of his horse, as if he sought strength enough to make it across the sidewalk.

From the barbershop, Harry Talbert hustled across the street, hand uplifted. "I'm coming, James," he called, his voice carrying in the still twilight. Lending a shoulder, he slid his arm around James's waist and together they stepped into the jailhouse, leaving the door open behind them.

Within minutes, a woman followed Harry across the street, carrying a teakettle and a small satchel. Close at her heels, Will crossed the street, apparently having worked late at the bank. Still dressed in his suit, he presented an incongruous picture, hastening with long strides, one hand tearing at his string tie, then shedding his coat as he neared the jailhouse.

Kate watched, her hands clenching at her sides. Did she have the right to go there? Or would James not thank her for making a spectacle of herself on his behalf? From all appearances, he was being tended already, but the thought that he was wounded pierced Kate's heart with a pain she could not describe.

She set out slowly, then her footsteps quickened as she neared the sidewalk and stepped up, pacing its length to where the door of James's office stood open. A lamp was lit within, and she halted in the doorway, barely able to swallow a gasp as she caught sight of the bloody wound he bore in his upper arm.

Will squatted before James, his gaze fastened on the wound now being tended. Mrs. Talbert, for surely it was the barber's wife, Kate decided, was washing blood from the gaping hole, and James sat with head bowed and teeth clenched as the woman muttered words of sympathy.

"There now, we're almost done, Sheriff Kincaid," she said, "and it's not nearly so bad as some I've seen. Why, in a few days you'll be as good as new." She turned him a bit and Kate saw a smaller, neater hole in the back of his arm. At least the shot had gone right through, and there wouldn't be any digging into his flesh to find a bullet.

Mrs. Talbert glanced up and smiled at her. "Here's your friend, Miss Elliott, come to see you, Sheriff," she said brightly. "I'll just warrant she won't be the only one wanting to offer thanks for you chasing down that bank robber."

As if Kate gave two cents for the whereabouts of a criminal. The urge to catch James's head against her breast was almost overwhelming. And then she watched as Will opened the desk drawer and pulled forth a bottle of whiskey.

"Here," he offered gruffly, "have a swallow, James. You need it. It'll take the bite out of the pain."

Kate felt her face grow pale; as surely as if someone had pulled the plug on a tub of bath water, she felt the blood leave her head. Of all the stupid things to do, offering a man whiskey, when he'd been so obviously steering clear of the stuff for weeks on end. And yet, she could not deny the look of hunger James focused on the dark bottle. Not any more than she could contain the joy when his words denied the offer.

"I've been looking at that bottle for weeks, Will, and closing the drawer on it every time. I'm not about to use a little gunshot wound to excuse getting drunk." He waved his free hand at his cousin. "Take it home with you if you like. I've seen all I want to see of it."

"James?" His name, softly uttered, sounded wistful

and uncertain and Kate cleared her throat. His head swiveled toward her and his gaze swept over her, from the top of her head to the tips of her shoes, taking in the new dress she wore, admiring the waves she'd coaxed into place as she'd piled her hair in a sweeping arrangement before her mirror. And all for the benefit of the man who watched her with hope alive in his eyes.

"I'm fine, Kate," he said shortly. "Like Mrs. Talbert said, I'll be good as new in a day or two."

"Well, I just wanted to know if there was anything I could do," she said, backing toward the door. It would not do to get any closer to the man, with her hands itching to touch him, her mouth aching to kiss his forehead, her arms yearning to hold that solid frame against herself.

"We'll take him on home to Mrs. Harroun's place," Will said kindly. "The boy's locked up tight in a cell, and tomorrow we'll wire the marshal to come pick him up."

"This is Miss Elliott?" The tall, tanned rancher stepped forward. "I'm Caleb, James's cousin," he said. "My boy, Zeke, is one of your students." His dark-blond hair hung almost to his collar, and sharp eyes that matched those of James and Will took her measure. "I've heard about you, ma'am."

Kate nodded distractedly. "I've enjoyed teaching your boy, Mr. Kincaid." Her skin felt taut, and a trembling had begun in her limbs. Leaving here seemed her best option and she backed to the doorway, aware of Will's scrutiny.

"Do you want me to walk you home, Miss Elliott?" he asked quietly. "I'm sure Lizzy would feel better if you have an escort. She's liable to skin me if she finds out I let you find your own way.''

"I'm fine," Kate told him. "You just take care of the sheriff." The doorjamb at her back, she cast one last look at James, watched as he opened his mouth to speak, and winced as Mrs. Talbert tightened the bandage she'd applied with deft touches. James frowned and his face paled.

"There now, that's good and snug. It won't bleed through, Sheriff. I'll take another look at it in the morning."

"We need a doctor in town," Will said, his own eyes fastened on James. "Since Doc Leland died we've been doing without."

"That's a good job for the council to take on, I'd say," Caleb stated firmly. "Maybe they'd do better to fill the empty doctor's office rather than stir up trouble in other areas."

"That's been all taken care of," Harry said quickly. "We've got word from Kansas City, and things are well in hand."

"A new doctor?" Caleb asked, and then his lips thinned as Harry shook his head with a quick glance at Kate.

And what all that was about was enough to set her walking at a fast clip as she headed for the schoolhouse. An eerie feeling had come over her at Harry's words, and his warning glance. Whatever the word from Kansas City had been, she was dead certain that it involved her.

"I'M GETTING a raise in pay," James said, blurting the words as if they were the sole reason for his visit. He'd knocked on her door in broad daylight, right after school was let out for the day on Tuesday. Three days since he'd been wounded, and already he was riding his horse and wearing a jaunty grin. That his arm was held at a stiff angle, and his shirtsleeve was stretched tautly over the bandage beneath it was a minor thing, Kate decided.

"You look wonderful," she breathed, stepping aside to allow his entry. "I've been worried about you." Her head tilted to one side as she fixed her gaze upon his face, then allowed her eyes to travel his considerable length. "I can't see any lasting effects, other than the bandage."

"I'm fine," he said with a touch of arrogance. "That's not the first time I've been shot, and it probably won't be the last. It goes with the territory, honey."

She winced inwardly at his words. He probably knew what he was talking about, but it wasn't a subject she wanted to discuss right now. "You're getting a raise in salary?" she prompted, closing the door as he took a seat at her table.

"Yeah, the town council came to me this morning and told me they want to pay me enough so I can buy a place of my own." He lifted a brow as he leaned across the table toward her. "Good ol' Will didn't let the cat out of the bag, and he's the only one who knows I've got more money in the bank than any of the rest of them. Hell, if they want to pay me more money, I'll take it. The job's worth a bundle, and since they've had a time getting someone to play the part, they might as well pay through the nose to get a good sheriff."

"I'm pleased that they appreciate you," she said. "I

think Will was quite taken back when you turned down the whiskey Saturday night.'' She hesitated and then reached to clasp his hand. "I was proud of you, James.''

"Were you? I didn't do it for your benefit, Kate. I didn't know you were there when he dug out my old bottle and offered it. I heard Mrs. Talbert speak your name, but I was in a fog, and I wasn't trying to impress you with my turning down a drink. God knows I could have used it. But I figured it would defeat the purpose of all those nights you spent helping me dry out if I snatched at the first good reason I had to take a swig.''

"I know.'' And she did know. She'd thought it over long and hard for three days, and if she knew anything in this world, it was that James Kincaid was done with his drinking days.

"Kate, I came here to ask you something. I know we talked about this, round and round in fact. You've told me you don't want to be married, and I've told you I'm not a marrying man, but I keep thinking, what we really need is each other.'' He held up his good hand to forestall her protests.

"I don't know what went on in your life to make you so determined about this whole idea of marriage, but I'm willing to try to change your mind, if you'll let me.''

Kate's hand tightened on his fingers and she closed her eyes. "I have memories of whiskey bottles lining our cupboard shelves when I was a child, James. My father was a man who believed in offering a social drink to company, who took care of his family and provided well for us. Until a business reversal almost put us in the poorhouse.''

She released her grip on him, and rose, unable to sit still while the memories rolled through her mind. "He began to empty those whiskey bottles, and then when my mother protested, he went to the saloon in town and drank there. We struggled to survive, and I was the lucky one. I'd already paid my tuition at school and was in my second year of normal college when everything fell apart.

"He came home, night after night, smelling like cheap perfume and stale booze, and my mother wept for all the things she'd lost. When the sheriff came to tell us we were being evicted from our home, my father put a gun in his mouth and pulled the trigger."

"Ah, damn!" James rose and came to her, his arms encircling her, his movements careful. "I can't even hug you properly, Kate. And if ever a woman needed a good hug, you do, sweetheart."

She leaned against him and the hot, bitter tears stained his shirtfront as she poured out her anguish on his broad chest. He held her, silent now, as if he recognized that no words he could speak would heal the wounds she'd carried with her. And then she lifted her head, her fingers digging into her pocket for the handkerchief she kept there. She wiped her eyes, blew her nose and yet he held her, loosening his embrace, giving her freedom to tend to her ministrations, yet obviously unwilling to release her from his hold.

"I'm sorry, James. I don't usually carry on so." She looked at him through teary eyes, and managed a small smile. "As you can see, I've decided to stop mourning the man. I took all my black and brown dresses, except for one, and burned them in the yard. I decided I'd been foolish to pretend mourning for a man I couldn't respect.''

"Where's your mother now?" he asked.

"She moved in with her sister, and she's happy there. My brother is out of school and working at the newspaper in town, and Mother takes in sewing to help pay her way.''

"Does she need money?" he asked quietly, and Kate looked up quickly, shaking her head.

"No, she's fine. And you needn't feel in any way responsible, James.''

"Ah, but I do, sweet Kate. She's going to be my mother-in-law, and I'll never let her want for anything.'' He made a face, an embarrassed look bringing high color to his cheeks. "I've really got rather a lot of cash, honey. You won't have to teach school anymore if you don't want to, once we're married.''

Married. The word rang in her head, and she spoke it aloud. "Married? You're planning marriage, just like that?''

"I told you we needed each other, Kate, and I meant it. Marriage seems the thing to do, seeing as how I can't keep my hands off you, and the next time I have you alone in the dark, I'm planning on ending up in a bed.''

"Do I have a choice?" Not that she really wanted one, but it would be nice, she thought, to have a more formal proposal offered.

Apparently James agreed, for he led her to the table, pulling her chair around to seat her properly. And then he knelt before her, his wounded arm held gingerly across her lap. He picked up her hand, turned it to kiss the palm, and then spoke words that fed her hungry heart as no others ever had.

"I love you, Kate Elliott. I want to turn your name to Kate Kincaid, and I want to do it just as soon as I can talk to the preacher. I want to take care of you, and all you have to do is say yes. Can you do that sweetheart?" He lifted pleading eyes to her and she melted, her arms sliding around his neck, her face pressed to his, her tears of joy puddling against his damp shirt.

"I love you, too," she whispered. "I think I've loved you ever since you came in the schoolroom and sat on that ridiculous little chair and made me walk back and forth in front of you and told me I was a good-looking woman."

"I was wrong," he said softly. "You're a beautiful woman. Every bit of you is as soft and feminine and warm as a female could be. I'm gonna take a good long time taking off your clothes and rolling your stockings down, ma'am. You have got the best lookin' legs I've ever seen on a woman, with the prettiest rosy knees, and—"

"Stop it!" Her command cut into his softly drawled words and he looked pained.

"I was only letting you know how it's going to be, honey."

She felt the heat rise from her breasts to cover her face, and she closed her eyes. "I think there are some things I'd rather find out later on, if you don't mind. You're marrying a virtuous woman, James. I hope you won't be disappointed."

He rose, drawing her with him to stand in the circle of his embrace. "I'm not planning on being the least bit dissatisfied with you. I've had a little taste of you, don't forget, and I'll warrant there's more passion in that slim little body than you have any notion of.''

''I don't want anyone to know right off,'' she said. ''If the town council knows we're married they can break my teaching contract. It states very plainly that I'm supposed to be a virtuous, single woman. Maybe if they don't find out right off, I can bargain with them at the next town meeting.''

''You really want to keep teaching, don't you?''

She nodded. ''It's all I've ever wanted to do with my life. Later on, when we have a family, I'll probably be content to stay at home, but for now, I think the children need me.''

''All right,'' he said agreeably. ''We'll wait for a couple of weeks before we spill the beans. And in the meantime I'll ask around and find us a place to live, and if there isn't a house on the market nearby, I'll have one built. It'll only take a month maybe, once I get a crew of men to work on it.'' He looked down at her and his mouth was unsmiling, his brow furrowed. ''But I'm not waiting for you for a month, Kate. We're getting married right away. We can keep it a secret for a while if you really want to, but I'm not waiting past the end of the week for you to be mine.''

CHAPTER SEVEN

"Lizzy? Will you stand as my witness?" Kate breathed the query softly and was rewarded by a squeal of delight from her friend. Eyes turned their way as they hugged each other tightly, and the other customers in the Mercantile smiled at the sight.

Lizzy popped her hand over her mouth, backing away. Then, eyes sparkling, she grasped Kate's hand in hers and dragged her to the open door, stepping out onto the sidewalk. "You're getting married?" she said, the words spoken on a gasp of air as if she could barely catch her breath.

Kate nodded, looking around lest the passersby hear her words. "Tomorrow afternoon, at the parsonage. James is making the arrangements, but we don't want folks to know yet."

"Why?" Lizzy was openmouthed. "I'd think he'd want to shout it from the housetops. Imagine that! James Kincaid getting married, and to a perfectly respectable woman. Will wonders never cease."

"He's respectable, too," Kate interjected quickly.

"But only lately," Lizzy reminded her. "And it's all your doing, Kate. You've been the best thing in the world that ever happened to James. Will says so."

Her eyes closed and then opened wide. "Can I tell

Will? I don't know how I'll keep it to myself unless I can let him in on the secret.''

"James is going to ask him to stand up with him," Kate told her. "I'm afraid the town council won't let me keep teaching after I'm married. If they break my contract, it'll leave those children in the lurch until a new teacher can be found. Besides, we don't have anywhere to live for now, and James wants to have a house built, so we'll just keep it quiet until the house is finished and we can move in together.''

Lizzy's brow furrowed. "Why not wait till then to get married?''

Kate felt the flush rise to cover her cheeks. "James won't wait,'' she whispered.

Lizzy shot her an arch glance. "I guess I understand that all right. Men have a hard time—'' Her hand rose to cover her mouth and she gulped. "I didn't mean that the way it sounded," she said, her blush matching Kate's.

Kate grinned, although she wasn't too sure what had set Lizzy off. "I don't want to wait, either," she said. "So after school tomorrow we'll go to the parsonage, and if you and Will meet us there about five o'clock—''

"And then you can come to our house for supper," Lizzy said, her mind in forward motion now.

"Well, we'll see," Kate said. "James wants to take a long drive in a buggy on Saturday. We'll probably leave early in the morning.''

"Where will you stay? Overnight, I mean?''

"In my place behind the schoolhouse, I think.''

"That's an awfully narrow bed, if I remember right," Lizzy said dubiously.

Kate smiled. "We'll manage.''

THE WEDDING was small, quiet and perfect. Lizzy and Will were dignified, yet obviously happy, and Will's exuberant hug brought a wide smile to James's face after the ceremony. Lizzy wiped tears of joy and whispered final instructions in Kate's ear.

"Just enjoy yourself," she said. "James will know what to do, and if he's anything like Will, he'll do it well."

Kate nodded, her thoughts echoing Lizzy's words. *I'm counting on that.* A trace of apprehension slowed her footsteps as she stepped from the house onto Will and Lizzy's wide, sweeping porch. "Thanks so much for the meal. It was wonderful," she told Lizzy, studiously avoiding Will's gaze. He, in turn, was shaking James's hand, once more congratulating his cousin.

"I'm going to sound out the rest of the council members about Kate teaching after you're married. It looks kinda iffy, though." He looked over at Kate and Lizzy and lowered his voice. "When will they start your house?"

"Next week," James said. "I bought a lot on High Street, next to the mill owner's place. A double lot, in fact. Tommy Blair, the new fellow at the mill, said he'd get a crew together and get started Monday for sure."

"Shouldn't be too hard, now that the threshing is done with, to find men looking for a few weeks work," Will said.

"I'm working on that," James told him, stepping down from the porch and drawing Kate to his side. "We'll see you in church on Sunday."

The buggy was halfway to the schoolhouse before Kate spoke. "You're going to church with me?"

"Don't you want me to?" he asked, bending to peer down beneath the brim of her bonnet.

"Oh, yes. I do." She slid her hand through his arm. "Do you think folks will guess? I mean, will we look married?"

James mouth twitched. "I'm not sure how I'm gonna look on Sunday, but right now I'll bet I look like a happy man."

"Will folks see us driving into town?" she asked cautiously.

"I'll drop you off and take the buggy to the livery stable," he said. "Don't be anxious, Kate. Things are going to work out. It's going to be dark by the time I get there."

"Anxious? You think I'm anxious?" She bit at her lip. "Whatever for?" She was far from anxious for the sun to go down, if the truth be told. And it was almost at the horizon now. With darkness would come the moment of truth, and she had no idea what James would expect of her. She'd caught on pretty well to the kissing game, but beyond that her education was sadly lacking.

"I don't know much about this, James," she said suddenly, blurting the words in a rush.

"I don't expect you to," he said quietly. "And I don't want you to worry about it, Kate. I'm a grown man, twenty-eight years old, and I'm aware that you're a virgin. I won't push you, honey. We'll do this nice and easy."

This. The single word entailed the whole marriage act, the unveiling of male and female, and the ultimate coming together of husband and wife. So casually

James was able to speak of such a thing. And so heavily Kate's own inadequacies loomed over her head.

"Well, at least you've seen my legs already," she said, "and you liked them. Maybe the rest of me will please you, too." She drew her skirts about her as the buggy approached the door of the schoolhouse, ready to alight.

James lifted her down, then climbed the single step to her porch and looked down at her. "I'm already pleased with you, honey. You don't need to worry on that score. Go on in. I'll be back in a few minutes."

He was true to his word, and in less than ten minutes he returned. His hand turned the knob, and he swung the door wide. "Come here, Mrs. Kincaid. I'm going to carry you over the threshold. This may not be our home, but it's where we're starting this marriage, and we'll do this right."

Her feet barely touched the stoop when he scooped her into his arms. She clung to his neck, ducking with him as they entered the room, and then she felt herself slide to the floor, James's arms circling her waist and drawing her tightly against him. He turned, taking her with him, one foot rising to push the door shut, and then she was immersed in his kiss.

She heard the latch fall to lock the door against intruders, was aware of his hands untying her bonnet, then felt the release of her hair tumbling down her back as he loosened the pins binding its length. They scattered to the floor, each small sound magnified in the silence, and still he kissed her. His mouth was warm, his lips avid, as though he could not taste deeply

enough of her essence. And she gave what he demanded.

The genteel man who had paced by her side vanished. Gone was the dapper groom, with starched shirt
and black string tie. And the supper guest at Will's
table was transformed into a man who it seemed had
lost all intention of "taking it nice and easy."

"James?" Kate came up for breath, aware of the
trembling hands that cupped her face, looking up to
meet the gaze of blue eyes that blazed like a hot summer sky. "It's not dark out yet," she whispered, and
was immediately aware that the coming of nightfall
was not a necessary thing so far as James was concerned.

"I can see you better in the twilight," he murmured.
"And I'm going to slow down, in just a minute, honey.
I just need to taste you a little, and then we'll work on
getting you out of those clothes."

Even as he spoke, his hands were working at the
buttons she'd taken so long to match with their corre-
sponding bound buttonholes. They marched up the
back of her dress and while she'd admired the way the
dress looked on her, and the becoming ruffle that
served as a collar, buttoning it had taken an inordinate
amount of time. Now, it seemed, James was having no
such problem.

He slid it from her shoulders and his mouth followed
its path, his lips touching her skin with reverent ca-
resses, across the width of her shoulder, then over the
curve to her arm. It was a slow journey and he nibbled
and tasted the skin, causing shivers to travel the length
of her spine. His laugh was low, sounding of triumph
and satisfaction, and Kate felt a smile curl her lips.

Her petticoat was untied and allowed to fall, and then he stood before her, his eyes shedding their warmth on the upper curves of her breasts. Beneath her camisole, she felt them tighten, and squared her shoulders, resisting the urge to cover their fullness. James had said he wanted to kiss her there, and as much as she felt the discomfort of being undressed by James's hands, she felt a moment's pride, knowing for the first time the feminine joy in being the object of a man's desire.

The movement of fingers that trembled told her he was eager; the narrowed gaze he dealt her and the ruddy slashes of color on his high cheekbones sent a message of bridled passion even an ignorant bride could not mistake.

Her chemise was undone, stripped from her and James touched her bare skin with long, callused fingers. Tenderly, as if her flesh were fragile, easily marred by his big hands, he held her breasts in his palms, and she caught her breath, a sense of exquisite yearning rising within her being, bringing tears to her eyes.

He bent his head, and his mouth touched her, there where the rosy peaks ached for the caress of his mouth and tongue. "I warned you I'd do this, honey," he reminded her, and she nodded, too caught up in the heated, yet delicate movements of his mouth to murmur a sound. Deep inside, there where she'd known a child would one day form and grow, she felt a tightening, a warmth and then a sense of emptiness, as though that part of her ached for James's attention.

She moved restlessly, her hips swaying, her bottom tightening, and James laughed again and shifted one hand to press against her, moving in a slow circle on the seat of her drawers. Inflexibly, he pulled her closer, and then she was pressed tightly against his lower body, where a blunt ridge nudged her female parts. Her breasts were damp from his tongue, cooled by the absence of his mouth, and she shivered in his arms.

His shirt was harsh against the tender flesh, yet she rubbed against the fabric, easing the ache that would not be stilled. Again he chuckled, and his head dipped to capture her mouth, whispering words she could not decipher, phrases uttered in a dark, passionate voice. "Sweetheart…" It seemed to be his favorite name for her, and she reveled in its sound. "Honey…let me…" His hands slid to the front of her drawers and he untied them with deft touches and she felt them slide down her legs to pool around her feet, joining the petticoat and dress. But for the stockings she'd fastened with a new pair of garters, blue ones with lacy edging, she was buck naked. And now it seemed his attention was to be bestowed on the silken stockings themselves.

He knelt in front of her, his hands unrolling the pale, cobwebbed hosiery, fingers behind her knees, only to spread wide as he caressed the rounding length of her calves, circled her ankles, then lifted her feet from the confines of her shoes. The stockings were poked into the shoes, and his fingers rubbed her feet, paying special attention to her high arches. She wiggled, inhaling sharply.

That such a simple touch should send shards of heat to that already swollen, molten place between her thighs was not to be believed. But it was so, and she shifted, her hips beginning the slow movement she could not seem to control.

Rising, James lifted her, carrying her to the narrow

bed in the corner, and, bending, he placed her atop the quilt. "I don't know if this is going to work, Kate. What would you say to putting the quilt on the floor?" He grimaced, and his smile was faint. "I'd rather have you on a nice, big bed, but I'm afraid this will have to do for tonight."

She nodded, gathering the quilt around her as she rose, then stood looking at him. Should she drop it to the floor, or lower herself and wait for him to join her there? There had to be some sort of etiquette about this whole procedure, but Lizzy certainly hadn't mentioned it.

Standing before her, James unbuttoned his shirt, then undoing his belt, he opened the front of his trousers. "I've slept on a floor before," he said wryly, "but I'll warrant you haven't, have you?"

She shook her head, too entranced by his actions to speak. He apparently was planning of divesting himself of all his clothing, right in front of her. And what else could she expect? He'd managed to strip her with hardly a murmur on her part. His shirt dropped to the floor and Kate sat down abruptly, unable to look aside as he lowered his trousers and stepped out of them. Somehow he'd shed his boots and now he slid his stockings off and tossed them aside.

"Kate? Shall I leave my drawers on? I don't want to upset you." For the first time he looked somber, unsure of himself and she responded quickly.

"No. I don't care, James."

His brow quirked. "Now just what did that mean?" he asked.

She inhaled deeply and pushed the quilt aside, watching his eyes widen at her action. Without another word, he shoved his drawers to the floor and kicked them off. With a swift move, he was beside her, spreading the quilt around her like the tablecloth at a picnic meal. And for some reason she felt akin to the main course. He knelt before her and pressed her shoulders to the quilt, reaching up to the cot for her pillow. Sliding it beneath her head, he arranged her hair, spreading it across the white surface.

His eyes glittered fiercely as his fingers tangled in the waves and curls, and then he gripped a handful, allowing it to slide between his fingers. "You look exactly as I'd imagined," he murmured, touching her collarbones and tracing their length. His gaze roamed to her breasts and she felt the taut drawing sensation there, knowing that he watched as it happened.

His tongue touched the inside of his upper lip and his words were slurred as he whispered her praise. "That's nice, very nice," he said softly. Bending, he tested the puckered crests with his tongue and her bottom rose from the floor, her head tilting back in an involuntary movement. "Ah, Katie girl, you like that, don't you?"

She could not speak, for even as his mouth made magic against the softness of her breasts, his hand moved to capture that part of her that ached for his touch. Opening to his urging, she allowed his fingers the freedom to explore as he would, feeling the tingling that radiated through her moist tissues, knowing a moment's pause when he sought and found the source of her need.

And then groaned aloud as he claimed the narrow passage with a gently probing finger. Her hips rose again to meet the tender invasion and James eased his way a bit farther.

"You're not going to make this easy for me, sweetheart," he whispered. "You're as tight as a miser's pursestrings, and I'm afraid I'll hurt you before this night is half begun."

"I don't care," she whimpered, aching to clench that errant finger and hold it fast. If only... She could not begin to understand what it was she wanted but surely James knew. Surely in all his years of wandering he'd found the answer to her need, and would do whatever it took to ease the craving that possessed her. "Please, James," she begged.

His hand left her, his head rose from its place against her breast and she reached for him, blindly, eyes tightly closed. "James?" It was a plaintive wail and he responded in an instant.

"I'm here, sweetheart," he murmured against her ear, kneeling between her thighs, making room for himself, and hoping in his heart of hearts that he would not leave her wanting. She was soft, small and innocent, and those were qualities he'd never encountered before in a woman.

Especially the innocent part. Now, when he wanted the most to please, he felt the most incapable of that very thing. She was vulnerable before him, and he shrank from the piercing of her maidenhead, certain it would bring her pain.

And yet, there was no way out. In order to bring pleasure, pain must occur. Or at least that was what he'd been told, back in those days when it seemed unlikely he would ever know the purity of a virgin in his bed. She trembled beneath his touch, and yet when her eyes opened and looked into his, he saw no fear, only the heat of desire.

One hand beneath her bottom, he lifted her, easing his way past the opening of her tight passage. And then he lowered himself over her, pressing against the barrier that blocked his way.

"Hold tight, sweetheart." The words were forced through gritted teeth, sounding guttural as he whispered them against her ear. She clenched around him, and with a measured thrust, he surged within, wincing as she uttered one small, sharp cry. He held himself still, waiting for the acceptance of her body to enclose him, determined to linger, unmoving, until the taut muscles relaxed, lest he cause more pain and tearing to her fragile flesh.

"Are you all right?" he asked, praying she would nod, or smile or in some way tell him he had not totally botched this whole thing.

"Oh, James!" It was a sigh of repletion if he was any judge of such things. And he lifted to look into her eyes. "I feel so full, so complete, as if I were made for this." Tears ran from her eyes to be caught by the soft hair at her temples, and he bent to touch them with the tip of his tongue.

"I know I hurt you, sweetheart, but it couldn't be helped."

"It's all right. I'm fine," she assured him, and then as he moved, withdrawing, then pushing deeper into her body, her eyes widened and she whimpered, a sound he knew with certainty was not associated with pain. Her legs lifted to wrap around his hips, and she tilted her bottom upward, the better to contain his length.

"All right now?" he asked, the words gasping from his throat as he eased into a steady rhythm. She nodded, her eyes closing, her forehead creasing as if she must concentrate on the sensations that brought her hips into a movement to match his. And she was more than "all right" he discovered, her breath shuddering in her throat, her small, keening cries delivering a message of desire met and fulfilled.

His body betrayed him then, her rapture catapulting him into a shattering release he could only endure, teeth clenched, head thrown back, and the sound of her name echoing from the low ceiling of the room.

"Ah, Katie," he whispered. "I'm hoping you're not too sore, sweetheart." He rolled to his side, carrying Kate with him, drawing the quilt to cover her as he tucked her against his heart. Her legs tangling with his and her arm clutching his neck, Kate hung on like the moss on the north side of a tree.

She clung to him, and he held her closely, one hand sweeping from nape to the rounded curves of her bottom, as if he must assure himself that he had not damaged her, or in any way left her wanting with his primitive possession of her body. The noble thing to do, he thought, would be to let her heal for a day or so, and he set his mind to the decision. Only to have it put aside by her next words.

"No, I'm not hurting," she said thoughtfully. "And what little pain there was I forgot as soon as…" She giggled. His Kate actually giggled and he hugged her closer. "Lizzy was right," she murmured against his throat. "She told me that if you were anything like Will, you'd know what to do, and you'd do it well."

He laughed, reason returning with her matter-of-fact

statement. "She did, did she? And when did you have this conversation?"

"On the porch, when we left their house." She yawned widely and stretched. "I was all worried for nothing, wasn't I?"

"Were you?" he asked. "Worried, I mean? Were you afraid of me, Kate? Afraid to take a gamble on a man like me?"

"Afraid?" She seemed to consider the idea for a moment. "No, never that. Just a little wary, maybe. Actually, you were the one who took the gamble, marrying an old maid. I didn't want you to be disappointed in me, James. And I didn't know anything about this part of it. Still don't know much, for that matter."

"Once I teach you a few things, you'll be just fine, honey," he said complacently, teasing her gently; then waited for her outburst.

"Don't sound so cocky," she warned him, shoving him to his back and rising over him to prop her arms against his chest. "I may not know much about this yet, but I'm a fast learner, Mr. Kincaid, and I have a good imagination."

So much for nobility, he decided. "Well, Mrs. Kincaid," he drawled, "let's just see what you can come up with."

HE LEFT BEFORE DAWN, and Kate burrowed into the thin mattress of her cot, her body aching in numerous places. But it was a pleasant ache, she decided, one she would no doubt become accustomed to over the next fifty years or so. James had left reluctantly, but with her hand firmly pressed into his back, nudging him out the door. He'd run at a lope around the outskirts of town, so that his final approach to Mrs. Harroun's boardinghouse would be from the opposite direction.

But first he'd kissed her, a longing kiss that told her without words that he hated to leave, and she relished the evidence of his ardor. Her breasts were reddened from his beard, for even though he'd been freshly shaven in the parsonage, by morning's first light, his jaw wore a dark shadow. She yawned again and closed her eyes. Surely he would sleep for hours before he came to claim her with a buggy from the livery stable.

"KATE!" The door rattled, and knuckles rapped sharply. "Kate, open the door."

She rolled to the floor, staggering as the quilt tripped her up, then lurched across the room to slide the latch open. "What?" She rubbed her eyes and blinked at the man who stood in full sunlight. "How come you're so early?" she asked.

"It's almost ten o'clock," he said, his gaze roaming her length, most of which was covered by the quilt she grasped. All but one rounded breast, and it was to that spot he was drawn. His long index finger rose and brushed against the puckered crest, and then he laughed boyishly as she shivered and frowned at him.

"Get in here before someone sees you," she scolded.

"I thought you'd be up and rarin' to go," he teased. "And here you are inviting me back to bed instead." At her snort of denial, he laughed aloud, then pulled a chair from the table and straddled it, leaning his arms on its back. "I'll just watch while you get dressed, honey."

"Hmm, I don't think that's a good idea," she told

him. "I've got to wash up first, James." Turning her
back, she drew clean clothing from a shelf against the
wall, spreading it on the bed. A teakettle on the stove
held water and she poured her basin half-full.
"James?" She turned to face him and watched as understanding painted his features.

"Tell you what," he began, rising and approaching
her. "I'll leave you to it, if you'll kiss me first, and let
me nuzzle just a little bit." His grin was warm and
admiring and she bent to his whim, lifting her arms to
encircle his neck, giggling as his moustache brushed
against her mouth, bringing goose bumps to her flesh.

It was several minutes before he closed the door behind him and Kate was left with a reminder that he
would wait ten minutes, no longer, and then he'd be
back.

She was ready in eight, leaving her hair to be
brushed in the buggy, James having made it clear that
he would not abide the notion of pins and braids today.
A familiar-looking basket was tucked beneath the seat,
and with a crack of the reins, they headed in the direction of the mountains.

It was as he had promised, that other day when he'd
taken her as far as the lateness of the afternoon would
allow. Today there was no such restriction on them,
and he took her up a slope to where a ledge provided
a resting place. There he spread the quilt and opened
the basket of food. They looked out on the rolling hills,
back toward the town of Whitehorn, eating and pausing
to share some small tidbit of food, their voices rising
in laughter, then falling into whispers of intimate con-
fessions.

"Do you truly love me, James?" she asked, and as

if he knew what the query cost her, he was quick to respond.

"More than life, my sweet Kate. I'm not eloquent. I haven't spoken those words to another woman, and so I lack practice. But I know I owe you a debt I'll never be able to repay. No matter that I doubted it for a while, I recognize now that you had faith in me, when there wasn't much left of James Kincaid to recommend him either as a man or a husband."

"I didn't think I'd ever find someone like you, James. I had decided I would settle, and find a man I could respect, whether love entered into it or not."

She curled close and his arm enclosed her. "I spent a lot of time wandering, Kate. I drank and gambled my way through a bunch of saloons, and found out in the process that I have a lucky streak a mile wide. After a while, it didn't matter anymore, so I came back to Whitehorn. After Will opened his bank, I put my gold in it, and then settled into old Cam's place. It was sort of my home away from home, I guess. There didn't seem to be anything worth getting sober for, so I just gambled enough to buy liquor and left my gold in the bank to draw interest."

"Didn't you ever want to have a ranch like Caleb? Or be a merchant or banker like Will?"

He shook his head. "About the only thing I was really good at was shooting a gun, and I'd done enough of that to know that I was a force to be reckoned with. Maybe that's why I never had to tangle with anybody. I think men that knew me well, knew that I could handle a weapon and they steered clear of me."

"Well, you managed to get hired as sheriff because

of it," she said smugly. "So that sort of talent can't be all bad."

"Do you know?" He paused and drew up his knee, turning Kate to lie across his lap. "I don't mind being sheriff. I feel like I'm doing something for the town I live in, and I feel good when I walk down the street and folks nod and smile at me. My cousin Will used to be the only one who really liked me."

"Caleb seemed to respect you the night you brought in the young man."

"I hope so, and that's something I never thought I'd admit, that I want the respect of my family."

CHAPTER EIGHT

"I THOUGHT YOU were going to keep this a secret. And I certainly hoped you'd be circumspect in your behavior. I can't respect a man who holds his woman up to ridicule." Will's voice was tight with restrained violence as he sounded his anger in the middle of the sheriff's office.

"And who asked for your respect?" James tossed the query at William with a glare, aware only of the pain the words dealt him. "I'd never hold Kate up to ridicule. I'd think you'd know that."

"Well, what do you call the fact that you kept her away from town till long after dark, and then spent the night with her?" Will stalked to the window, glaring at the street. "You got my wife in a tizzy, what with the women talking about Kate in the Mercantile this morning."

"We're married," James said stubbornly, even as he rued the thought of Kate being spoken of in disparaging terms.

"You know that and I know that, but no one else is supposed to be privy to the information, James. It was your idea to marry her right away, so eager to crawl into her bed you couldn't wait until you had the house built. And now she's paying for your indiscretion."

"I'll take care of it," James said stubbornly, still

flinching from the scorn Will had heaped upon his head.

"Well, the council got word from Kansas City last week that a man teacher is available, and they're about set to buy Kate a ticket back to Ohio. This is just the sort of thing they needed to break her contract."

"They can't do that to her." Setting his jaw, James headed for the door. "I'll go talk to them."

"Talk away, cousin," Will told him. "Not that it's going to do you any good. They were looking for a man when they hired her, but one wasn't available. They've already sent for the fella. He'll be here Thursday."

"And in the meantime, they can just figure out a way to send him back," James said. Snatching his hat from the chair, he settled it on his head. "I'm going over to the vacant lot and see how the men are coming with my house. They may have to hurry things along. I'm not going to wait for a month to move in."

He'd barely crossed the street when Amos approached, flagging him down, a belligerent frown pleating his brow. "Say there, Sheriff. I think we need to talk for a minute." He swung in alongside James, half stepping to keep up with the angry man. "I hear your house is all laid out. The men got it staked and measured this morning. Now they're haulin' lumber from the mill yard. Right handy building it so close."

"Yeah." James tugged at his hat brim and stepped up his pace, his long legs outpacing Amos.

"Hold on, Sheriff," Amos said loudly. "We need to talk about an important matter, and you're not listening to me."

"I'm madder than hell, Amos. You don't want to be raggin' at me today."

Amos puffed up, and James thought he resembled nothing less than a banty rooster, all ruffled and cocky. "Well, what I got to say is important. The council is ready to fire your lady friend, and we thought you might be interested. Maybe you could tell her for us and sorta soften the blow, so to speak."

"If there's anybody getting fired it'll probably be me, once I clean the floor up with the whole damn council." James came to a stop in front of the Mercantile and glared at the hapless hotel owner.

"You're talking about putting my wife out of a job, and I'm not about to make it easy for you. She's a fine woman and the fact that she took a buggy ride with me yesterday is no reason for the town to throw her to the wolves. We haven't had a decent teacher in town for two years, and now that you've got one, you're going to replace her with some dude from Kansas City." He leaned closer to Amos, his teeth gritted, his face ruddy. "I don't think that had better happen, Amos."

"What are you talkin' about, James?" John Dillard stood in the doorway of his store, broom in hand, leaning forward a bit, his eyes narrowed and focused on the men before him. "Did you marry Miss Elliott? Nobody knows anything about it." He stepped onto the sidewalk and then down onto the road, taking his place beside Amos. "Or are you just feeding us a line, tryin' to save her neck?"

"Her neck doesn't need saving," James said, his voice low and controlled. "She's my wife, and if you're planning on making something of it, you just go ahead and try. We'll be moving into my house as soon as it's finished, and until then, if I want to haul her around in a buggy, or go visit her at the schoolhouse, I can't see that it's anyone's business but ours.''

"Married?" John rocked back on his heels. "Well, you don't say." He chuckled, tilting his head to one side. "Married, huh?" He looked over his shoulder toward the open door of his establishment. "Tess!" His voice was beyond loud, James thought, attracting attention from half the town, as he waited for Tess Dillard to exit the store.

She stood in the doorway, exasperation written on her features. "I don't have time for foolishness, John Dillard," she said sharply. "You may not have work to do, but I have three customers waiting for me to help them."

"Step out here," her husband ordered, "and listen to this." He waved her impatiently toward himself, and as she crossed the sidewalk, he grinned. "Wait till you hear this, Tess. It'll give you something to talk about all afternoon. James, here, and the new teacher are married. Their buggy ride was all aboveboard."

"Well, land sakes alive," Tess said, a smile lighting her face. "I surely hated to think badly about Kate. She's a fine woman. To tell the truth, Sheriff," she said, with a trace of anger in her tone, "I was ready to hang you out to dry, taking advantage of a lady."

"I didn't," James said, his wrath cooling somewhat. "And she still is. A lady, I mean."

"Well, I swan," Tess said wonderingly. "Where you folks going to live till your house is done? There sure isn't room in that little bitty space behind the school. And Kate staying at Mrs. Harroun's place is out of the question. It's full of men.''

"Harry.'' John shouted a greeting to the barber, who'd come from his shop, apparently curious about the fussing and fuming going on in the middle of the road. "Come on out here, Harry,'' John said, waving the man forward. "We got things to discuss.''

James stood to one side while the three men put their heads together, feeling more and more like an outcast in his own town. If they thought for one minute he was about to hang up his mad and turn sweet as pie, now that they'd decided not to tar and feather Kate, they were mighty mistaken. The first thing he needed to do was get to the schoolhouse. Kate was probably knee-deep in young'uns, with the whole bunch of them doing sums or studying the books she'd brought with her. Maybe reading to them herself.

And this town had better think again if they wanted to bring in an upstart from Kansas City to fill her shoes. His fuse began to burn short again as he considered Kate's embarrassment should the men have castigated her for bad behavior.

"Now look here,'' he began, one hand on Amos's shoulder, the other pushing John to one side. "I won't have any of you saying anything to Kate about losing her job. If you want some dude to teach school here, you'd better build him another place to do it in. That schoolhouse is Kate's.''

Tess laughed aloud at his words. "She won't care about that, once you move her into a new house. She'll have her hands full takin' care of it and you and thinkin' about a family of her own.''

"You don't know Kate,'' James said gloomily.

"She's a teacher, and a good one at that. She's not about to pull up stakes and walk away."

Harry Talbert turned to James. "Let's deal with first things first here, Sheriff. We've decided something, and I think it'll work. We're gonna call a town holiday starting tomorrow morning, and every able-bodied man is going to pitch in and get your house up just as soon as we can."

"You're gonna *what?*" James turned to John. "What about your store?" And then to Amos. "Who's gonna run the hotel?"

"We've both got wives," Amos said. "Hell, maybe we'll just close things up for a couple of days and everybody can pitch in. We'll even haul Will out of the bank and hand him a hammer. We'll pass the word around to the men close to town and get some of them to help."

Voices rose and fell as the townsfolk gathered and the word was passed. James found himself the recipient of congratulations and pats on the back, and his arm began to ache within ten minutes from all the hand shaking going on.

"Somebody needs to tell Miss Elliott," Tess said, "and it's not gonna be me. I've left my customers long enough. I'll pass the word around to my customers for the rest of the day." Her cheeks were rosy as she picked up her skirts and hurried back inside.

"I'll tell Kate," James said firmly. "And in the meantime, y'all better figure out what you're gonna do with that Fancy Dan you got coming from Kansas City. If my wife doesn't teach in the new schoolhouse, then I'll be giving you back your badge."

KATE STEPPED from the school doorway, her gaze taking stock of the students who ran across the school yard. Several sat beneath a tree, eating the food they'd brought from home, four boys played keep-away with a fifth youngster's hat, and Beth waited patiently on the stoop. "Have you eaten?" Kate asked the child.

"Yes, ma'am. I just thought I'd keep you company while you have your dinner."

"Maybe you'd let me talk to Miss Kate for a few minutes instead," James said, riding his big horse around the side of the building.

"Yes, sir," Beth answered, eyes wide as she watched the approach of the big animal.

"One of these days I'll give you a ride on my horse," James said with a grin. "Would you like that?"

"Oh, yes, sir, Mister Sheriff," the girl answered quickly. And then ran to where her sister sat with several friends.

"Today, I'm taking Miss Kate for a ride," James said softly. "Step up here, ma'am."

She shook her head. "We're supposed to be prudent, James, and you're breaking all the rules. I can't go off and leave my pupils."

"Want to bet?" he asked with a raffish grin. He lifted fingers to his mouth and a shrill whistle rang out, drawing the attention of every child in the yard. "Now just listen to me," he shouted. "Miss Kate and I have a couple of things to talk about and I don't want a one of you to misbehave while we're gone. Any questions?"

One of the oldest boys trotted closer. "No, sir, Sheriff. We'll make sure everything is just the way it oughta be. Me and Jake Darcy will take charge.''

"Fine," James said. "We'll be back in ten minutes." He bent low to scoop Kate up by the waist, lifting her with seemingly little effort to sit across his lap. She clung for dear life, certain she would fall beneath the hooves of the giant beast he rode, and gulped for air once he settled her against himself.

"Hang on, sweetheart," he murmured in her ear. "We aren't going far." His horse set off at an easy lope and James circled the main street, riding quickly behind the houses and the sawmill that made up the southern edge of the town. In moments, he'd pulled his horse to a stop and Kate sat up straight, her head swiveling from one busy group of citizens to another.

Several men were hauling lumber from a big wagon, three others were laying out tools on a buckboard, and most of the men in town were making it their business to pace off the boundaries set for the house James had ordered to be built.

"What's going on?" Kate asked. "James, you're going to let the cat out of the bag. You'll be advertising that we have some sort of an arrangement, what with you hauling me here on your horse in front of God and everybody."

"Everybody knows by now, sweetheart. The fat's in the fire, sure enough, and those men are gonna do their best to see to it we have a bedroom ready by the end of the week."

"You don't mean it," she sputtered. "What happened?"

"I'll tell you all the particulars later, honey. For now, I want to introduce you to the gentlemen who are going to build our house.'' He raised his voice and all activity ceased as he shouted several names. Those men looked up at him, grinning, then the rest turned their way and Kate felt a flood of color wash over her face.

"This is my wife, folks. We got married the other day, and we'd sure be grateful for a place to hang my hat. I never expected to have the house finished so quickly, but I'm thinking Mrs. Kincaid will appreciate all your hard work."

"We'll see to the hat rack in jig time," Amos shouted. "Startin' tomorrow morning the walls will be going up."

"Why wait till tomorrow?" Will called, striding down the street toward them, rolling up his white shirtsleeves as he came. "Let's have at it, gentlemen."

It was too much. Kate burst into tears, burying her face against James's shirtfront. "I can't believe this," she sobbed, her hand poking in her pocket in search of a hankie.

"Here, take mine, honey," James said with a laugh. "It's bigger." He offered his red bandanna and she snatched it gratefully.

"I'm taking the lady back to school, folks," James said cheerfully. "I'll be back."

"It just doesn't seem possible, James." Kate sat on the stoop, looking toward the scene of activity. The sun was setting, yet the men still crawled over the bare lumber that outlined the form of a house.

"Their wives took food over to the lot for them. They're having a picnic."

Kate bit at her lip and voiced her greatest concern.

"I heard that a man is coming to take over the school-room later this week."

"Don't worry about it," James told her. "They can just ship him back to Kansas City for all I care. That schoolroom belongs to you. Now, let's take a walk and look at our new house."

ON THURSDAY MORNING, James watched from the doorway of the jailhouse as the stage rolled up in front of the hotel, and his cousin, Will approached it. The gentleman in question was definitely on board, and if the amount of luggage he carried with him was anything to go by, he'd come prepared for permanence.

"Mr. Powell?" Will asked, and then offered his hand as the tall, slender gentleman climbed down from the vehicle. "I'm William Kincaid, the local banker. Welcome to Whitehorn." The driver tossed down two large cases made of leather and they hit the road, a cloud of dust rising to coat their already travel-worn surfaces.

The young man eagerly shook Will's hand, then turned to lift his valise from inside the stage. "I'm anxious to begin work. I taught three grades in my last school, and I know this will be a challenge, but I'm sure you'll be satisfied with my references."

"Yes, I'm sure you'd be more than satisfactory, no matter what your position," Will said, looking to where the rest of the town council waited on the side-walk. James stood to one side, thankful that he wasn't wearing his cousin's shoes today. What Will was going to do with the young teacher was a problem all right, but if James had anything to say about the whole thing, the schoolhouse was Kate's domain.

"We've already read your references," Will said awkwardly, "and you're more than qualified. But a small problem has arisen, and we need to have you meet with these gentlemen."

Cam stood in the doorway of the saloon, and held the swinging, louvered door open for the five men to troop inside. Will looked back at James and lowered his brows. "Get yourself in here, Cousin."

James shrugged and followed the group, willing to listen in, so long as Kate was not displaced from her position. The five men sat around a table and James leaned on the bar. "I'd offer you a drink, James," Cam said in a low voice, "but I wouldn't want your wife after me."

"I wouldn't take it, even without my wife to keep me on the straight and narrow," James told him with a grin. "You've lost one of your best customers, Cam." The barkeep shrugged, pulled a pair of five dollar gold pieces from his pocket and palmed them, grinning as Will began to speak.

"Sir," Will began, "I told you there was a slight problem, but I think we've resolved it to everyone's benefit. It seems your studies included a great deal of mathematics, and that brought to light another offer you might consider." He took a deep breath and offered a brilliant smile. "Have you ever thought about working in a bank?"

KATE AND JAMES walked through the house, Kate admiring the wallpaper that graced the parlor walls. "I can't believe they decided so readily to allow me to continue teaching, James. And then to put this house together so quickly,'' she murmured, twirling in a circle in the middle of the floor.

"There's still the stove to put in place in the kitchen and a wood burner in the parlor,'' James said. "They should be here in a couple of days.'' He rubbed his fingers over the wainscoting beneath the floral wallpaper. "I'm glad Mr. Blair had a good supply of oak for the woodwork.''

He took her arm and led her through the wide doorway into the hall. "Come on, honey. I want to show you the rest of the house.''

"I've seen it, James,'' she said, glancing up at him. "I've been here every day after school all week long. I helped hang all the wallpaper in the bedrooms and the dining room.''

"I moved my stuff into the bedroom early this morning, Kate,'' he said quietly. "I'm going to sleep here tonight.''

"There's no bed yet.'' They stood in the doorway of the room they would share, where their children would be born, and where Kate anticipated numerous nights of pleasure in her husband's arms. "When will our furniture arrive?''

"Holt Garrison is almost done with the bed. We'll have to use boxes for our clothes till he gets the dresser done. He's giving us a good price though, and I think it's worth waiting for. I checked out the Sears and Roebuck catalogue and showed him a picture of a nice one. Would have cost us fifteen dollars plus shipping if I'd ordered it, but he's giving it to us for just twelve-fifty.''

"Is the rest of the furniture coming next week?'' Kate asked.

James nodded. "Might be closer to two weeks, but

no longer than that. Can we just pretend we're camping out, Kate? Make do for a while? I hate to ask you to live here without decent chairs to sit on and a bed to sleep in, but even the bed's going to take another day or two.''

She grinned and turned to him. ''For a man who spent his wedding night on the floor, I'd say you're getting pretty picky.''

His arms circled her waist and he drew her tightly against his needy frame. ''I'm tired of leaving bruises on you, sweetheart. That floor is a miserable place to sleep, and if you're half as lame as I am every morning, you'll be more than glad to have a bed.''

''I'll stay here tonight with you, if you like, James,'' she offered. ''It wouldn't take long to bring my things over from the school.''

''The sun's about to go down, honey. We'll have to hurry,'' he told her, dragging her behind him as he headed into the hallway, long strides taking him to the front door in moments. ''Will's new bank teller will be pleased as punch to move into your room behind the school. Providing him with a place to live was the best end of the deal as far as Will's concerned. He just made it part of the salary.''

''How did Will persuade the council to let me keep my contract?'' Although she was pleased at the outcome, it seemed strange that the council had not fussed over her breach of contract.

James cleared his throat hesitantly. ''Well, I figured if they really wanted me for their sheriff, they needed to make some concessions. I told them they could take back the tin star unless they let you stay on as teacher.''

"James! You might have lost your job over this. There was no guarantee they'd do as you asked."

His grin was wide now as he reached for her. "They really want me, honey. And I let them know you were more important to me than any job in the world. Now, let's get your things out of the way so Will's new employee can move in."

"They'll have to move him out one of these days, when the school begins to overflow," Kate told him. "I'm almost filled to capacity now. In another year or so, we'll need more room, and I'll be after the council to take down the wall, or put a door in it, so we can have two rooms for classes."

"It'll all work out," James assured her, lifting her into the wagon he'd hired.

"You knew before you brought me here tonight, didn't you?" Kate said accusingly, watching him as he circled the horses and climbed up onto the seat.

"Knew what?" he asked innocently, snapping the reins over the mares' backs.

"You knew I'd want to move in with you, furniture or not, didn't you? And you hired the wagon so you could bring my things over tonight."

"I might have had it in mind," he conceded, urging the animals into a faster pace. "How long do you think it will take to get your stuff together?"

Her look was measuring. "Why? Are you impatient?"

AS IT TURNED OUT, he was the soul of patience, arranging quilts on the bedroom floor, spreading a clean sheet and fluffing pillows. Kate placed a lamp on her trunk, arranged her brush and mirror beside it and viewed the uncovered windows with an eye to privacy.

"How about if I tack my old towels up, like I did at the schoolhouse?" she asked.

"It's dark out, honey," James pointed out. "Once we blow out the lamp, there's not a soul can see in."

"What about in the morning, when I need privacy to get dressed?" This was becoming complicated, she decided, rising to search out the towels that already bore holes from the nails she'd pounded through the hems. "I know they're here somewhere," she murmured, fretting as she sorted through a box of her belongings.

"You just dumped everything in here," she wailed, casting a fulminating glance at James.

He sat on their lone chair, one he'd snatched from Will's kitchen, with the promise to return it as soon as his own arrived. One foot crossed over the other knee, he tugged at his boot. "You know, you could pull my boots off for me, Kate," he said mildly. "A good wife would help her husband get undressed."

"Don't you dare take off another thing, James Kincaid," she muttered. "The lamp is still on, and if anyone sees in here, they'll know we're going to bed."

His grin widened. "Don't you suppose they'll know that anyway? That's what folks do at night." The boot slipped to the floor and he worked at its mate, then rose and took her by the hand. "Look here now. We're married, and you've been sleeping with me for over a week already. No one has looked at you and snickered, have they?"

Kate shook her head. "No." Tears formed in her eyes and she blinked rapidly, holding them in abeyance. "I just…" She looked around the room, her gaze drawn to the pallet James had formed for them. "I don't know what's wrong with me, James. Maybe I'm just tired."

"I know how to fix that up, honey," he promised. "A good night's sleep will do wonders."

"Sleep? If all you want to do is sleep, I could have stayed in my old place," she wailed.

"Let me show you something," he said, coaxing her across to the window. Bending, he blew out the lamp, then placing her in front of himself, he pointed his index finger at the scene beyond the glass panes, to where the lights of scattered houses made up the town of Whitehorn. "Those are our neighbors," he said. "They're the people who'll make up our circle of friends in all the years to come, Kate. I'll warrant you'll find women out there who will be as close to you as sisters, through thick and thin. And you'll teach their children and carry food to them when they're sick, and sit in church with them on Sunday mornings."

His big hands were taking liberties even as he spoke, unbuttoning the front of her dress, then delving beneath to lift her camisole, his fingers deft as he stroked the firm flesh he discovered there.

"Can anyone see in?" she whispered, not willing to call a halt to his wandering hands, yet edgy as she considered being on display for the neighbors' benefit.

"Naw. Not a soul," he assured her, stepping back a pace from the sparkling windowpanes. His fingers lifted her glasses and placed them on the windowsill. "But, just in case, why don't you turn around here and we'll get you out of these clothes, and you can crawl under the quilt."

"You told me I could undress you," she reminded him, her own fingers busy with buttons and belt. His shirt slid from his arms, and his trousers fell to the floor.

Eager hands divested her of every stitch of underwear in no time flat, and Kate found herself beneath not only the quilt, but under the muscular frame of a man who did not seem intent on sleeping. At least not for a while.

He loved her carefully, tenderly, his hands and mouth assuring her of his need, his words hot and sensual as he explored the curves and hollows of her body. Her legs, as always, were examined and caressed, and James curled long fingers around her knees, parting them to make room for himself.

"I knew the minute I saw these knees, I'd have to have you, Kate. It took me a while to get another look, but I hadn't forgotten one inch of your pretty, long legs." He lifted them to his mouth, his lips suckling at the flesh, his moustache brushing against her skin.

He made his way up her body, and his plea was one she could not resist. "Help me, honey." He breathed the words against her forehead. "I need you, sweetheart. Take me inside."

Her hands trembled, her desire for this handsome, devil-may-care man well nurtured by his tender regard. "I never thought a man like you would look twice at an old maid schoolteacher," she whispered, reaching to grasp his male member in her hands. She shivered, knowing what was to come, her eyes filling with tears of joy as she looked up at the dark curls he could not tame.

His hair was ruffled from her fingers and his jaw

was shadowed, his shoulders wide and muscular, and she caught a glimpse of something primitive in his veiled gaze. In the moonlight, he seemed almost savage, his lips drawn back, his teeth bared, and she gloried in the sight. He was her man, her chosen mate. Strong and hard-edged he might seem to the rest of the world, she knew him as no other would, had felt him tremble as she held that part of him that would forge their bodies into one.

She guided him, lifted her hips to accept his entry, and found that indeed the magic was there between them. The surging desire, the passion that drove them to completion, the love that enclosed them in a world of their own. He held her, whispered words that pleased her, finally rolling to his side to hold her against his heart. And then he slept, and she curled even closer, wrapped in his arms as his lips touched her forehead, and his voice murmured soft words, as if he would hold back the night.

"Shh," she whispered. "Go to sleep, James." And he nodded, his breathing even and deep.

That she could hold such power over this man was a wonder, and yet it was so. He loved her, and though he might tease her about her legs, she knew without a shadow of a doubt that his devotion went far deeper than admiration of her physical being.

They were mates, meant to forge a measure of this great country into a heritage of their own. She sensed it, as if by their joining, some great destiny had been sealed. He was a part of the Kincaid clan, an important part, and the unity of the family would be the foundation upon which a dynasty would be built.

But for now, there was only man and woman, the coming together of two people who had found love, and had earned the right to share their lives beneath the Montana sky.

Be sure to watch for Brock's story,

THE GUNSLINGER'S BRIDE

by Cheryl St.John,
on sale in September 2001!
Please turn the page
for an exciting preview....

CHAPTER ONE

January, 1897

Brock Kincaid squinted at the slate-gray clouds that had been shifting down from the Crazy Mountains since he'd broken camp that morning, and pulled his sheepskin collar around his neck against the bitter wind. Born and raised in Montana, seven years away hadn't dimmed his ability to smell a blizzard coming from the North. He built a fire and melted snow for the horses. There were two: one he rode, the other carried his bedroll and supplies, as well as gifts carefully chosen for the brothers he hadn't seen since he'd left the Kincaid ranch behind.

Caleb, the oldest, would be there, running the ranch, but Will had been gone when Brock left, having headed out after repeated disagreements with Caleb. Brock had no idea where he was now, just as they hadn't a clue where he'd been or what he'd been doing. For their protection, he'd been careful to hide his identity...and his whereabouts.

Cooling the water with a handful of snow and holding the dented pail for his mount to drink, Brock scratched the animal's bony forehead and yawned. Imagining his brother's reaction to his return had kept him awake most of the night, and he'd started out after only a couple hours' sleep.

After the horses were finished, he stowed the pail, then bent and scooped snow to scrub across his tired face. A few more hours and he'd reach Whitehorn, where he could board the animals and get a night's rest before heading to the ranch. He wanted to be alert and prepared before facing Caleb.

With a creak of cold leather, Brock mounted and let the gray pick his way around overgrown scrub and drifted snow. The packhorse whinnied and shook its head, and Brock paused to gather the slack from the lead rope until it calmed. Wolf tracks and bright-red blood spattered on the pristine snow several yards to his right told him he didn't want to be around after dark. He drew his .44 Winchester from the scabbard on his saddle and rested it across his thighs. Damn, but a warm bed would feel good tonight. It had been a long time since he'd been comfortable.

A minute later, the crust of snow on the ground crunched beneath the horses' hooves as he nudged his mount forward.

A few parents near the building waited with wagons or horses. Brock let his gaze scan the students.

Was his nephew Zeke among the children? He did a quick calculation and figured the boy would be eight by now. Brock's heart chugged nervously. Was someone from the Kincaid ranch down there to meet the child? He studied those waiting, but none struck him as familiar. From this distance he couldn't make out brands on the horses.

None of those departing headed for the Kincaid ranch, but several children ran toward town.

Brock observed the willowy, dark-haired woman who locked the schoolhouse door and trudged through the snow toward the main street.

Once the area was clear, he rode out of his secluded spot and followed. Whitehorn looked much the same as it had the last time he'd seen it, false-fronted buildings with signs proclaiming the businesses: the telegraph office, a dressmaking shop, the No Bull Meat Market, the Double Deuce Saloon, *Whitehorn News*, Watson Hardware. Big Mike's Music Hall and Opera House was new, as was a structure that looked to be made of oil can bearing a sign advertising Fish for Sale.

He passed Old Lady Harroun's boardinghouse and the Centennial Saloon before stopping at the livery. Lionel Briggs, a long-faced fellow, emerged from the warmth of the forge and greeted him. "How long you stayin', mister?"

"I'm not sure," he said, keeping his hat pulled low. "I'll pay for tonight. They need feed and rest." He pulled his glove from his numb fingers and reached inside his coat for silver coins.

"I'll treat 'em good. Check their feet?"

Brock nodded and paid him.

The man stared suspiciously, a frown and then recognition registering on his face. "Brock Kincaid! I'll be damned! Thought I recognized that voice."

"I'd be obliged if you didn't mention that you'd seen me," Brock said. "I'd like to get some rest before I visit the ghosts."

"Where ya been all this time?" the man asked.

"Some said you was workin' with Bill Cody. Others claimed you'd settled down in New Mexico."

"I saw some of New Mexico," he replied noncommittally, pulling down his rifle and unstrapping his gear. "Can I leave my bedroll in a stall?"

"Certain you can."

"Still get a decent meal and room at the Carlton?"

Lionel nodded. "Amos still runs a good place. That hasn't changed. Wife's sickly now, though."

Brock threw his saddlebags over his shoulder and thanked the livery man.

His boots clomped across the boardwalk as he headed for the hotel. He'd reached the wide dock that fronted the hardware store when a couple of laughing boys wrapped in heavy coats, wool caps and scarves shot out the door and ran into his legs, knocking him sideways. Groping for balance, he dropped his gear and grabbed a wooden post.

"Jonathon! Zeke! Apologize to the gentleman. You weren't even looking where you were going."

A slender russet-haired young woman without a coat appeared in the doorway, a white apron covering her plain dress and calling attention to her curvy figure.

"Thorry, mither," the shorter of the two said with an endearing lisp. "We wathn't lookin' where we wath goin'."

The other boy struggled to pick up Brock's cumbersome saddlebags and hand them back to him. "Didn't mean no harm," he said. The wool cap he'd worn tumbled off his head and he turned to grab it, knocking into the smaller boy. Both of them landed on their butts on the icy loading dock.

Chuckling, Brock bent over and plucked both of them up and steadied them on their feet. The youngest one gazed up, dark-blue eyes wary of the stranger. A wisp of wavy blond hair escaped his cap. Was this a Kincaid nephew? He glanced at the other boy, also fair-haired and blue-eyed.

Then he turned and saw the young woman for the first time.

She was staring at him, her complexion gone pale, a sprinkling of freckles standing out against the pink rising in her cheeks. "Abby?" he asked uncertainly.

A combination of things had driven him away from this town. The constant discord in the Kincaid house was surely part of it. The other part—the bigger part— was the fact that he'd killed this woman's young brother.

She stared at him still, as though not believing what her eyes were telling her. Once his identity registered, her expression quickly changed to one of cool hostility. "Come inside boys," she said curtly.

"But we didn't get licorith yet," the younger one complained.

"We didn't mean to knock the man down," the other added.

"No harm done," Brock said kindly, stooping to pick up his leather bags. He couldn't help casting an-other hungry look at the boys who reminded him so much of him and his brothers at that age.

"One of you Zeke Kincaid?" he asked.

The taller boy's eyes widened. "How'd you know that?"

"Come inside *now*, boys!" Abby told them sharply.

"Are you Zeke?"

The lad nodded, then gave Abby a quick look. Caleb's son. Brock's nephew. Brock looked him over hungrily, all the years away from here seeming so wasted and lonely. Caleb'd had another child and he'd missed his birth. Abby must be watching them for Marie.

"Come in *immediately*," Abby ordered.

"Aw, Ma," the younger boy said unhappily.

Ma? The address hung in the air like the report of a bullet. Brock's gaze shot to Abby's face. Shuttered and distant, her expression revealed only her disdain. "*Your* son?" he managed past a dry throat.

"That's right. Jonathon is *my* son. Now excuse us." She nearly pushed the boys inside the store and slammed the door so hard the glass panes rattled and the bell inside clanged.

Her son? But that child was unquestionably a Kincaid. Had Marie died and Caleb married Abby? Had Will come back and married Abby?

Snow had begun falling in earnest, blowing up across the dock and dusting his boots. He wasn't sure how long he stood there in confusion, contemplating the shocking information and the possibilities. Of course, life here had gone on without him; why had he imagined everything would still be the same?

Through the square panes of window glass, he could see that the hardware store held a few customers. What Abby Franklin was doing in there, he had no idea, but he didn't want the entire town to know he was here before he'd had a chance to see Caleb, and the stove at the hardware store was the social gathering place on winter afternoons such as this.

Tamping down his questions and his eagerness to see his nephews, he adjusted the heavy bags over his shoulder and hurried through the snow to the hotel.

WHITEFEATHER'S WOMAN

by award-winning author

DEBORAH HALE

Discover the origins of Montana's
most popular family in the
MONTANA MAVERICKS
HISTORICAL SERIES

Kincaid Ranch foreman John Whitefeather breaks
all the rules when the Native American dares to
fall in love with nanny Jane Harris.

MONTANA MAVERICKS

RETURN TO WHITEHORN—
WHERE LEGENDS ARE BEGUN AND LOVE LASTS
FOREVER BENEATH THE BIG SKY...

HARLEQUIN®
Makes any time special ®

MONTANA MAVERICKS

THE GUNSLINGER'S BRIDE

by *USA Today* bestselling author

CHERYL ST.JOHN

Discover the origins of Montana's
most popular family in the
MONTANA MAVERICKS
HISTORICAL SERIES

Outlaw Brock Kincaid returns home to make peace
with his brothers and finds love in the arms of an
old flame with a secret.

MONTANA MAVERICKS

RETURN TO WHITEHORN—
WHERE LEGENDS ARE BEGUN AND LOVE LASTS
FOREVER BENEATH THE BIG SKY...

HARLEQUIN®
Makes any time special ®